About the Author

Maisey Yates is the *New York Times* bestselling author of over 100 romance novels. An avid knitter with a dangerous yarn addiction and an aversion to housework, Maisey lives with her husband and three kids in rural Oregon. She believes the trek she makes to her coffee maker each morning is a true example of her pioneer spirit. Find out more about Maisey's books at maiseyyates.com or find her on Facebook, Instagram or TikTok by searching her name.

Charlene Sands is a *USA Today* bestselling author of thirty-five contemporary and historical romances. She's been honoured with The National Readers' Choice Award, Booksellers Best Award and Cataromance Reviewer's Choice Award. She loves babies, chocolate and thrilling love stories. You can reach her on Facebook.

USA Today bestselling author **Kat Cantrell** read her first Mills & Boon novel in third grade and has been scribbling in notebooks since she learned to spell. She's a So You Think You Can Write winner and a Romance Writers of America Golden Heart Award finalist. Kat, her husband, and their two boys live in North Texas.

Second Chance

June 2025
His Unexpected Heir

July 2025
Their Renewed Vows

August 2025
A Cowboy's Return

September 2025
The Prince's Desire

December 2025
A Love Rekindled

January 2025
Their Enemy Sparks

Second Chance:
A Cowboy's Return

MAISEY YATES
CHARLENE SANDS
KAT CANTRELL

MILLS & BOON

All rights reserved including the right of reproduction in whole or in part in any form. This edition is published by arrangement with Harlequin Enterprises ULC.

This is a work of fiction. Names, characters, places, locations and incidents are purely fictional and bear no relationship to any real life individuals, living or dead, or to any actual places, business establishments, locations, events or incidents. Any resemblance is entirely coincidental.

Without limiting the author's and publisher's exclusive rights, any unauthorised use of this publication to train generative artificial intelligence (AI) technologies is expressly prohibited. HarperCollins also exercise their rights under Article 4(3) of the Digital Single Market Directive 2019/790 and expressly reserve this publication from the text and data mining exception.

® and ™ are trademarks owned and used by the trademark owner and/or its licensee. Trademarks marked with ® are registered with the United Kingdom Patent Office and/or the Office for Harmonisation in the Internal Market and in other countries.

First Published in Great Britain 2025
by Mills & Boon, an imprint of HarperCollins*Publishers* Ltd
1 London Bridge Street, London, SE1 9GF

www.harpercollins.co.uk

HarperCollins*Publishers*
Macken House, 39/40 Mayor Street Upper,
Dublin 1, D01 C9W8, Ireland

Second Chance: A Cowboy's Return © 2025 Harlequin Enterprises ULC.

Rancher's Return © 2024 Maisey Yates
Vegas Vows, Texas Nights © 2020 Charlene Swink
The SEAL's Secret Heirs © 2016 Harlequin Books S.A

Special thanks and acknowledgement are given to Kat Cantrell for her contribution to the *Texas Cattleman's Club: Lies and Lullabies* series.

ISBN: 978-0-263-41754-8

This book contains FSC™ certified paper and other controlled sources to ensure responsible forest management.

For more information visit: www.harpercollins.co.uk/green

Printed and Bound in the UK using 100% Renewable Electricity
at CPI Group (UK) Ltd, Croydon, CR0 4YY

RANCHER'S RETURN

MAISEY YATES

To my wonderful children, who are the greatest teenagers ever. There is no greater job than watching you become yourselves.

Chapter One

Welcome to Lone Rock...

He hadn't seen that sign in years. He wasn't sure if he felt nostalgic or just plain pissed off.

He supposed it didn't matter. Because he was here.

For the first time in twenty years, Buck Carson was home.

And he aimed to make it a homecoming to remember.

"You look like you want to punch somebody in the face."

"You look like you got in a fight with your own depression and lost."

"You look like someone who hasn't learned to successfully process his emotions and traumas."

Buck scowled, and glared at his three sons, who were only just recently *legally* his. "I'm good," he said, as his truck continued to barrel down the main drag of Lone Rock, Oregon, heading straight to his parents' ranch, where he hadn't been since he'd first left two decades ago.

"Are you?" Reggie asked, looking at him with snarky, faux teen concern.

"Yes, Reg, and I wouldn't tell you if I wasn't, because I'm the parent."

"I don't think that's healthy," Marcus said.

"I think that somebody should've taught you not to use therapy speak as a weapon," Buck said to his middle son.

"You're in luck," said Colton, his oldest, "because I don't use therapy speak at all. Not even in therapy."

"Yeah, the therapy hasn't taken with you," Marcus said.

"Hey," Reggie said. "Leave him alone. He's traumatized. By having to go through life with that face of his."

"*All right*," Buck said.

It wasn't like he hadn't known what he was getting into when he'd decided to adopt these boys. But becoming an instant father to fifteen-, sixteen- and seventeen-year-old kids was a little more intense than he had anticipated.

When he'd left Lone Rock he'd been completely and totally hopeless. He'd been convinced he was to blame for the death of his friends, and hell, the whole town had been too.

After everything his family had already been through, he hadn't wanted to bring that kind of shame to their door. So he'd left.

And spent the first few years away proving everything everyone had ever said about him right. He had been drunk or fucked-up for most of that time. And one day, he had woken up in the bed of a woman whose name he didn't know and realized he wasn't living.

His three best friends had died in a car accident on graduation night, driving drunk from a bonfire party back to their campsite. He had also been drunk, but driving behind them in his own car. He had made the same mistake they had, and yet for some reason, they had paid for it and he hadn't.

They'd only been at the party because of him. All upstanding kids with bright futures, while Buck had by far been the screwup of the group. Their futures had been cut short, and for some reason, he had gone ahead and made his own future a mess.

That day, he woke up feeling shitty, but alive.

And when he had the realization that he still drew breath, and that he wasn't doing anyone any favors by wasting the life he still had, he had gotten his ass out of bed and gone into a rehab program.

But in truth, he had never been tempted to take another drink after that morning, never been tempted to touch another illicit substance. Because he had decided then and there he was going to live differently.

Because he'd found a new purpose.

After completing the rehab program, he had limped onto New Hope Ranch asking for a job. The place was a facility for troubled youth, where they worked the land, worked with animals and in general turned their lives around through the simple act of being part of the community.

Buck had been working there for sixteen years. Those kids had become his heart and soul; that work had become his reason why. And five months ago, when he had been offered the position of director, he had realized he was at a new crossroads.

There were three kids currently in the program who

didn't have homes to go back to. And he had connected with them. It had been yet another turning point.

But that's when he had seen himself clearly. He had a trust fund he hadn't touched since he left Lone Rock. He had been living on the ranch, taking the barest of bare minimum pay. He had no possessions. He was like a monk with a vow of poverty, supported by the church. Though the ranch was hardly a church.

He used his paycheck for one week off a year, where he usually went to some touristy ski town, stayed in reasonable accommodations, found a female companion whose name he *did* know and spent a nice weekend.

But otherwise... He didn't have much of anything.

And he could.

He considered taking all his money and donating it to the ranch, but it was well funded by many organizations and rich people who wanted to feel like they were doing good in the world while getting a write-off on their taxes.

And then he remembered he had a unique resource.

His family.

He could give Reggie, Marcus and Colton a family. A real family.

Yeah, he was an imperfect father figure, but he had found that made it easier to connect with the kids at the ranch. Additionally, he had a mother and a father, six brothers and a sister. And they were all married with children of their own. He could give these boys a real, lasting sense of community.

And that was when he had decided to adopt those boys, buy a ranch in Lone Rock and reconnect with his parents. They had met on neutral ground, at various rodeo events over the summer.

His dad had been angry at first; his mom never had been. But he had explained what he had been through, what he had been doing and why he had been absent for so long, and ultimately, they had forgiven him. And welcomed him to come back home. He also knew they had done some work priming his brothers and sister to accept his presence. Or at least, the presence of the boys.

But…

He also had the sense all was not forgiven and forgotten when it came to his siblings.

Even so, he was looking forward to today's reunion.

At least he was pretty sure the sick feeling in his stomach was anticipation. And maybe some of the anger that still lived inside of him. At this town, at himself.

Well. Hell.

He supposed he didn't have a full accounting of all his emotions.

There was nothing simple about the loss this place had experienced all those years ago. His friends should be thirty-eight years old. Just like him. But they were forever eighteen.

He looked at his sons, sitting on the bench seat of the truck, with Marcus in the back.

It wasn't a coincidence that he had adopted three of them, he supposed. A more obvious mea culpa didn't exist. But then, he had never pretended he wasn't making as firm a bid for redemption as he possibly could.

Yeah. Well.

It was what it was.

"So we're meeting your whole family today?" Marcus asked.

"Yeah. For better or worse."

"You haven't seen them in twenty years," Colton said.

"No."

"God, you are so old," Colton said.

"Yeah. Really ancient," Buck said. "And feeling older by the minute around you three assholes."

"I do think you have more gray hair since you adopted us," Reggie said.

"I'll probably just pick up more girls with it," Buck said.

That earned him a chorus of retching gags, and genuinely, he found that was his absolute favorite part of this parenting thing.

Driving the kids nuts.

It was mutual, he had a feeling.

But he took it as a good sign that they felt secure enough to mess with him. They all definitely had their own trauma. Marcus didn't mess around using therapy speak by pulling it out of nowhere. He'd spent a hell of a lot of time sitting on a therapist's couch, that was for damn sure.

He turned onto the long driveway that was so familiar. But he knew everything else had changed. His parents had built a new house in the years since he had left. His siblings had been kids when he'd gone.

They were entitled to their anger, his siblings. They had already lost their youngest sister when they lost him too. And life had proven to be even crueler after that. So maybe his running off had been part of the cruelty, rather than the solution. Sobriety and maturity made that feel more likely.

But at the time, he had simply thought everybody would be better off without him. Hell, at the time that had probably been true. That was the thing. He had self-destructed for a good long while. He was pretty sure he would've done that even if he hadn't left.

So whether his family wanted to believe it or not, he really did believe that in the state he'd been in then, it had been better that he wasn't around. And then he had been afraid to go back. For a long time.

But his dad hadn't cut him off. His trust fund had still come available to him when he turned thirty. He supposed that should have been a sign to him. That he was always welcome back home.

But he'd left it untouched. Maybe that was the real reason he hadn't used it till now. He had felt on some level that he would have to reconnect with his family if he took any family money.

And it was the boys who had given him a strong enough reason to do that.

He followed the directions his mother had given him to the new house. It was beautiful and modern. With big tall windows designed to make the most of the high desert views around them.

"I didn't realize this place was a desert," Marcus said. "I thought it rained all the time in Oregon."

"In Portland maybe," he said.

"There's nothing here," Reggie added.

"There's plenty to do."

"Doesn't look like there's plenty to do," Colton said.

"You'll be fine."

"How come there aren't any cactuses?" Marcus asked.

He gritted his teeth. "Not that kind of desert."

"Are there at least armadillos?" Marcus, again.

"Still not that kind of desert," he said.

"What a rip-off," Marcus replied.

"I don't think you want armadillos, from the sounds of things. They're nuisances. Dig lots of holes in the yard."

Then, talk of armadillos died in the back of his throat. Because he was right up against the side of the house. He got out of the truck slowly, and the kids piled out quickly. And it only took a moment for the front door to open.

His parents were the first out. His mother rushing toward him to give him a hug. She had been physically demonstrative from the first time they had seen each other again.

"Buck," she said. "I'm so glad you're here."

"Me too."

"Hey," his old man said, extending his hand and shaking Buck's.

"You must be Reggie, Marcus and Colton," his mom said, going right over to the boys and forcing them into a hug as well. "You can call me Nana."

He could sense the boys' discomfort, but this was what he was here for. For the boys to have grandparents. To have family.

"You can call me Abe," his dad said.

And that made the boys chuckle.

He heard a commotion at the door and looked up. There were all his brothers, filing out of the house: Boone, Jace, Chance, Kit and Flint. Buck was about to say something, when a fist connected with his jaw, and he found himself hurtling toward the ground as pain burst behind his eyelids.

"Boone!" He heard a woman's shocked voice, though he couldn't see her from where he was lying sprawled out on the ground.

"Oh *shit*!" That, he knew was Reggie.

"Fair call," Buck said, sitting up and raising his hand in a "hold on" gesture. "Fair call, Boone."

"Violence isn't the answer, Boone," came a lecturing teenage voice.

"Sometimes it is," returned an equally lecturing different teenage voice. "Sometimes a person deserves to get punched in the face."

"Maybe not right now," the angry female voice said.

Buck stood up. And looked his brother square in the face.

"Good to see you again, Boone," he said.

"Don't think I won't hit you again," Boone said.

"Hey," said his brother Jace, moving over to Boone and putting his hand on Boone's shoulder. "Why don't you guys punch it out on your own time."

"I don't have anyone to punch," Buck said. "And I'll take one. Maybe two. But no more than that."

Chance and Kit exchanged glances, like they were considering getting in a punch of their own. For his part, Flint looked neutral.

For the first time, Buck got a look at the woman who had defended him.

"I'm Wendy," she said. "I'm Boone's wife."

And he had a feeling the two lecturing teenage girls

were Boone's stepchildren. His mother had filled him in on everybody's situation, more or less.

Right then, another woman came out of the house with a baby on her hip.

Callie.

His baby sister. Who had been maybe five years old when he'd left. He knew it was her. She was a mother herself. He had missed her whole damn life.

He was sad for himself, not for her.

There hadn't been a damn thing he could've taught her. He hadn't been worth anything at the point when he'd left. But he sure as hell felt sorry for himself. For missing out.

"Buck," she said. Her eyes were soft, no anger in them whatsoever.

"Yeah," he said, "it's me."

And he realized this whole reunion was going to be both more rewarding and more difficult than he had imagined.

Because his family wasn't a vague, cloudy shape in the rearview mirror of his past anymore. His family was made up of a whole lot of people. People with thoughts and feelings about this situation. About him.

Hell. He had spent a little bit of time with the therapist himself.

"Why don't we go inside?" his mother said. "But no more hitting."

"Yes, ma'am," Boone said, looking ashamed for the first time.

This didn't have to be easy.

Buck was used to things being hard.

But he was home.
For better or for worse.
He was home.

Chapter Two

The first week of school was always a little dramatic, but Marigold Rivers didn't mind.

She loved that her daughter told her everything. That she gave her the rundown on all the drama. Hers, her friends', everyone's. Marigold had not told her mom anything. Because she had been a sullen and withdrawn teen still recovering from her brother's death and had kept all of her feelings and bad behaviors to herself.

She was thankful Lily didn't do that. Lily told her about all her classes, about all her crushes, about everything.

This week, though, had been light on the drama. Senior year was starting off relaxed.

Marigold was almost grateful for that.

Even as the idea of her daughter graduating in nine months made her want to curl into a ball and howl.

In some ways, she supposed she was lucky to be thirty-three with her daughter very nearly out of the house.

All the dating and everything she had mostly missed out on as a young mom could commence. She could travel. Could engage in wild one-night stands with hot mysterious Greek guys, just like the women in her favorite books.

Of course, in those books, the woman was usually virginal—lord, that ship had sailed—and usually ended up pregnant. Marigold had seen that film before. The guy didn't stick around.

Or, maybe it wasn't fair to compare the actions of a nineteen-year-old boy to the actions of thirty-year-old men who were billionaires. And fictional. There was that.

Whatever.

In a few short months, Lily would be off to college. And yes, there was anxiety associated with that. With applying for schools, financial aid, all of it. And, of course, worrying about whether or not Lily was acclimating to her new life, new friends, new environment. Marigold would be missing her so much that she would probably wish she was dead, but at least there would be freedom. Probably.

Mostly, she felt sad that this stage of her life was over already.

Being a teen mom had been hard. But nothing was harder than this—preparing to say goodbye.

She schlepped half the load of groceries inside and called up the stairs. "Lily, I'm home."

Lily drove herself to school now, and that had been a big adjustment too. Her daughter having freedom. Her own car. She had gotten her license a little late, because of course Marigold was paranoid about teen driving. And teen drinking. And teen sex.

Her family was a deeply unfortunate after-school special.

Her brother had decided to drink and get into a car with another boy who had been drinking. So many kids made that mistake. Her brother had paid for it with his life.

She'd had unprotected sex. She'd gotten pregnant.

And while she didn't think of Lily as a *consequence*—at least not these days—she certainly didn't want the same thing for her daughter.

As a result, while she did her best to be the kind of mom who fostered open communication, she was also… well, she had been very honest with her daughter about life's dangers.

She had tried to do it in a way that wasn't just about making rules, but that also explained her experience. She'd done a lot of work on herself since she was seventeen. After her brother died, she'd lost herself. She'd been angry. Looking for someone to blame—and she'd found him.

She'd never forget the day she'd confronted him in the middle of town, screaming at him, blaming him for her brother's choices. Something she realized now hadn't been fair. Her brother had been a ticking time bomb back then.

She'd been looking for something—anything—to make herself feel better. Older guys had made her feel validated. The attention she'd gotten from them had been a temporary bandage. And then she'd gotten pregnant.

She'd realized she needed her parents. She'd realized she needed to actually heal some things inside herself instead of simply trying to make herself feel better for a moment. She'd gotten good therapy. She'd started to live intentionally, instead of in a reactionary way.

Thankfully, she and Lily had a really open line of communication.

Their life had been a good one. It's just that it was changing.

Today's grocery haul was intense, as it always was. Her meal prep business had grown exponentially in the last couple of years. She had started making food as a means of supporting herself and Lily when Lily had been small, and now she was doing weekly meals for so many families in town she could hardly keep up.

But it was great. She got to do something she was good at, at home, in her modest house's certified kitchen, and make a decent living at it.

"Lily!" She said her daughter's name again.

There was still no answer.

She set the grocery bags on the counter and started up the stairs. She texted Lily on her way up, to see if she could get her attention that way. Odds were, she was sitting in her room with her earbuds on, but she most definitely had her phone, and she had her read receipts on, so Marigold always knew when Lily had seen a text from her.

No reading.

She frowned. She knocked twice on her daughter's bedroom door, and then pushed it open without waiting for a response. She was greeted by a flurry of movement. By Lily practically doing a dive roll off the bed, and a boy Marigold had never seen before in her life standing up quickly and pulling his shirt into place.

"What the… What the hell is going on?" she said.

And somewhere in the back of her mind was a calm, rational, *healed* voice that said she needed to react calmly so Lily would talk to her. That she needed to be rational, so her daughter wouldn't be shamed. So she would know Marigold wasn't angry, *just concerned.*

That voice was far in the distance, and Marigold was somewhere else entirely.

That calm, still voice had no hope in hell of winning.

In general, Marigold fancied herself somewhere between crystals and Jesus. A little bit woo woo, a little bit traditional. But right now, she was straight into fire and brimstone, do not pass the rose quartz, do not collect spiritual enlightenment.

"Who is this?"

"It's not what it looks like," Lily said, in the grand tradition of every teenager who had ever been caught doing stupid shit. But Marigold knew, she *knew*, that it was always what it looked like.

She'd had the positive pregnancy test at sixteen to prove it.

"Oh please, don't treat me like I'm an idiot," she said, and found that was what actually bothered her the most.

"I'm not. It's just it's not like… We were just…"

The boy was looking at Marigold with the appropriate amount of fear, so there was that at least. He was a boy she had never seen before, tall and exactly the kind of handsome tailor-made to get nice girls like Lillian into trouble.

"Who are you?"

"My name is Colton," he said.

Colton. Of course his name would be Colton.

Colton sounded exactly like the kind of boy who would get you pregnant and disappear off to college, leaving you to deal with the consequences.

Her own Colton was actually named Christopher. Same dude, different font.

"Well, Colton, we are going to go have a talk with your parents."

"Mom!" Lily looked horrified.

She rounded on her daughter. "We're going to have a talk later. Have I taught you nothing? Have I taught you nothing about *safe sex*?"

"We weren't having sex," Lily said, looking filled with horror.

"Oh come on," Marigold said. "Do you think that's where he was going to stop?"

"Hey," Colt said. "I am very serious about consent."

Lily looked up at him. "So you mean that *is* what you wanted?"

Colton suddenly looked trapped. Good.

"It's what they all want," Marigold said.

"Mom," Lily said. "Can you please leave your teen trauma in the past?"

"No," Marigold said. "I can't. Because the result of my teen trauma is standing in front of me making more trauma. Let's go, Colton. I'm taking you home. Since I can see that your car is not here."

"Mom…"

"You're certainly not driving him home." And suddenly, she had a horrifying image of her daughter doing something drastic, running away or worse, if she were left unattended. "You're coming with us."

"Mom, I…"

"First of all, Lily Rivers, if you are going to mess around with a boy, you better do it when your mother isn't about to come home. Keep track of the time."

"Are you lecturing me now for not being sneaky enough?"

"I don't know. *Maybe*." Marigold had never been caught with a boy once.

"It's not like I thought you would care that much," Lily said. "I thought you would understand."

"Just come with me."

She led the two sullen, silent teens down to her car. They both sat in the back seat, and she didn't argue, even though part of her wanted to. "Give me directions to your house."

"I don't know the number yet. We just moved here."

"Are your parents home?"

"My dad is," he said. "I mean… I only have a dad."

"Okay," she said, doing her best not to feel sympathy for him. He was a sexual predator. Well. He wasn't a sexual predator. But she still felt wary of him.

"I can give you directions," he said.

"Good. Please."

She was filled with adrenaline. And anger. And she hadn't really thought through what she was going to say to Colton's dad when she showed up. Something along the lines of… *Keep your kid away from my daughter or I'll castrate him?* No. There had to be something less psychotic than that. Maybe.

She followed his directions out of town and off toward the mountains. Then she turned onto a dirt driveway, her car jumping around in the potholes. "You really live out here?" Maybe he was trying to get them lost.

"Yeah," he said. "I know, it sucks. There's not anything to do."

She heard him cut his sentence off just before the last word was out of his mouth, which was the only thing keeping her from leaping into the back seat.

She had spent all of Lily's life being both mother and father to her daughter. So it seemed completely right in that moment that she had felt very Liam Neeson. A particular set of skills, etc. But because she was a mother, her ultimate response had been less violent. Still, it included shaming him.

This felt like action, anyway, because when she was done with him, she was going to have to deal with Lily and having a very real talk about contraception and safety and all kinds of things she had sort of thought she had already done. Now she worried it hadn't been enough.

Finally, they pulled up to a very nice-looking, newly constructed ranch house backed by the mountains and pine trees.

"Well," she said.

And that was it. Because she didn't want to compliment the kid.

There was a gorgeous, brand-new truck sitting in the driveway too. So he was a rich kid. Likely why he thought he was entitled to whatever he wanted.

She felt no small amount of irritation regarding that.

She and Colton got out of the car, leaving Lily in the

back seat, and Marigold walked up to the front door, Colton slowly trailing behind her.

"You can go ahead and knock," she said to him.

He did, looking at her out of the corner of his eye. She felt right then like her mom powers must be functioning at a really high level, because truly, this kid hadn't had to do a single thing she said, and he didn't especially look like he wanted to, and yet he was obeying.

She appreciated that she incited this level of fear.

She heard heavy footsteps on the other side of the door, and then it jerked open.

And her heart tumbled down all the way into her toes. Because she knew this man. This man standing in front of her with a tight black T-shirt, a cowboy hat and an expression too grim to be real. He was still outrageously handsome, but he had settled into his looks. No longer a smooth-faced, cocky teenage boy, he was weathered now. He was…

He was gorgeous.

He was also the man who had nearly torn her family apart. The man who had been the source of her unfettered teenage hatred.

Buck Carson.

The man who had killed her brother.

Chapter Three

Well it wasn't every day that a man ran into a living, breathing, potential *mea culpa*. But he supposed it was more common when one had committed sins on the level that he had, and when one had returned home, back to the scene of those sins, after twenty years.

It almost felt like poetry to see Marigold Rivers standing on his doorstep. What he didn't understand was why she looked shocked to see him, and why she was standing beside Colton.

"Can I help you with something?"

She was sputtering, like a fish that had been hauled out of the river by an angler's hook and flipped up onto the banks.

"I… I didn't expect to see you."

"I didn't expect to see you either, Marigold."

Her cheeks turned a very particular shade of crimson. The last time he had seen her cheeks lit up in red, she had been shouting at him. Full-throated, on the street. The angriest teenage girl he had ever seen, yelling at him about how he was responsible for her brother's death. It had felt good in a way. Because she had said what he felt was the truth when everybody else was dancing around it. She had finally taken the knife and twisted it, and he had exulted in the pain. Because it had been exactly what he needed. A good scouring, a flagellation much harder than the one he had been giving himself.

It had been the catalyst to him deciding to leave. Because his poor mother had also been standing by his side, because she had been through enough, and he knew she felt like the family she had worked so hard to rebuild after the death of her daughter was fracturing.

And it was his fault.

He hated himself for it. And so, after that scene, he had hauled his ass right out of town.

In many ways, he had found a certain kind of salvation thanks to Marigold.

He doubted she would want to hear that.

"I didn't know you were back in town."

"Really?" He frowned. "I've been back about a month. I would have thought the rumor mill would've been going pretty strong."

"Maybe people were just careful. Around me."

"Well. Perhaps. Though, then they open you up to a moment like this. Where you were bound to run into me without a moment's notice. I see you have my son."

Her eyes went round. "He's your son."

"Yes he is. Has he been causing trouble?"

"I… I don't even know how to… I…"

"What have you been up to, you termite?" Buck asked Colton. He figured he might get more of a direct answer from the young man himself than the decidedly flustered Marigold.

"It wasn't what it looked like," Colton said.

"Shoot, kid. That is the wrong thing to say to the likes of me. Because I'll be the first to tell you, whatever it is, it is always what it looks like."

That seemed to jolt Marigold out of whatever trance she was in. "When I came home from grocery shopping today, I went upstairs to check on my daughter. And found your son in her room."

And right in that moment, it didn't matter so much that the woman standing on his doorstep was Marigold Rivers. What mattered was the very clear and sudden realization that he had been thrown into the deep end of parenting, and this was something he had no idea how to navigate.

"You did what?"

"I have concerns," Marigold said. "And believe me, my daughter has agency, and I'm going to talk to her about it—"

But he wasn't listening. Not anymore. "Listen here," he said to Colton. "And you listen real good. This is a small town, and people talk. You go messing around with a girl, and she is going to get a reputation you're not going to get. Do you understand? The responsibility that she's going to bear will be so much bigger than yours. You have to be careful. Not just in terms of safe sex, but all these other things. Because no son of mine is going to walk around thinking he's exempt from consequences."

"Yes, sir," Colton mumbled.

"Get your ass in the house. I'm going to talk to Marigold for a second."

"All right," he said.

Marigold simply looked stunned.

"I didn't know... I was about to say that I didn't know you had a son, but I didn't know you were back here. I haven't known a thing about you for twenty years."

"Well, I only recently have a son."

"What?"

"I just adopted three teenagers. And I'm realizing right now that I'm maybe in over my head. I spent the last sixteen years or so working at a camp for troubled boys. And the thing about working at a camp for troubled boys is that there are no girls there. So there's a little less of this kind of thing. Not none, mind you, but at least nobody can get pregnant."

She looked stricken by that.

"Not saying that anybody here is going to get pregnant."

"She can't. She's going to college. She's going to get out of here, and she's going to do better than me."

"I'm going to talk to him."

"I... I can't believe this. I can't believe that this is the first boy she sneaks into her room."

"Listen, I know you have plenty of reason to hate me."

She looked away, and then back up at him. "I don't hate you. I recognize now that my reactions back then were... I was young. I was angry. But do the math on how old I was when you left and how old I am now. And the fact that I have a kid the same age as yours."

"You were still in high school when you had her," he said, not needing to do the figures to understand what she was getting at.

"I was. I got my life back on track. The pregnancy forced me to get things together, and it forced me to let go of the things that were no longer serving me. I'm grateful for her. I wouldn't change my life. But I don't want this for her. I want better."

"You know that if we try to keep them apart it's only going to be worse."

She bit the inside of her cheek and looked up at him with wide, amber-colored eyes. "Of course. Of course it will. Because then they'll think they're Romeo and Juliet."

"Yeah. And I didn't pay a lot of attention in school, but I know enough to know that ended badly."

"Just a bit."

"I'm sorry," he said. "But let's… Let's talk to them. About ground rules. And maybe… There is a beginning of the school year carnival happening down in town. Maybe they can have a date, and we can supervise."

"They're seventeen," she said. "Not seven."

"Sure. But they're on probation, right?"

"I guess so."

He let out a long, slow breath. "I suppose it's kind of big of you to not say you are extra suspicious of him because he's my kid."

"Like I said. I did my best to get over the past."

"Sure. But you were awfully angry the last time we saw each other."

"I also had a poster of Orlando Bloom as Legolas on my wall. So, things change."

"Have they?"

"Yeah. I'm an Aragorn girl now."

"I only vaguely know what that means."

"It's okay, you don't need to get the reference. But yes,

things change. I have a teenager now. She's just a year younger than you were. A year younger than… Unfortunately, all of you were too young to take the blame. If it wasn't Jason's fault, then it's not yours."

He wasn't sure he had been looking for absolution. He didn't think he wanted it. Because holding the guilt close had accomplished a certain something in his life. And he didn't really mind that, when all was said and done.

"I actually don't need you to forgive me."

"Well, too late. I do."

That was irritating. He wasn't sure why. "I came back here to raise the boys. I mean, they're already mostly raised. But I wanted them to be around my family."

"That's a really nice thing for them."

"Thanks. I'll talk to Colton. You can talk to your daughter. And this weekend, they can meet up for the carnival."

"All right. That sounds like a plan."

"I guess I'll see you there."

"Yeah. I guess."

She turned and walked away from the door, and he was going to have to deal with Colton. But for just one moment, he reflected on the strangeness of this meeting. She might say that she forgave him, but that wasn't what he was after. Her walking up to his doorstep, walking into his life, must be a sign of some kind. That was the problem with going off on your own for twenty years. It didn't cure you of mystical thinking. If anything, that shit only got more profound. He had gone away looking for answers. Then he had found them. He had found purpose with the school, which had only deepened his certainty that there were times when a person stood at a crossroads and had to ask questions of the deepest part of their soul.

Hell, it was essential. And right now, he had a feeling this was meant to be. This was some essential part of his journey, and he had to pay attention.

He had a feeling that when they met this weekend, everything would become clear.

She got back into the car, her hands shaking. She was breathing hard. The events of the past hour didn't seem real, and it had all culminated with running into Buck Carson.

She *did* blame him for Jason's death. She just did. And as she sat there, trying to catch her breath, she became more and more certain of that truth. That no matter how much she had tried to get herself into a place that wasn't angry—into a place filled with forgiveness, filled with understanding and acceptance that some people were meant to have a short life, and sadly, her brother had been one of them—it was all only theoretical.

Because the person who had drawn the most fury and fire from her over the accident had left town, and she hadn't seen him for twenty years.

"Mom?" Lily's voice was tremulous in the back seat.

"I didn't kill him," she said.

"I didn't think you would."

"Sorry. I need a second."

This was one of those moments where she had to decide how up-front and honest she was going to be with her daughter. But if she wanted Lily to share with her, she supposed she had to share in kind. She tried to walk a fine line between being her kid's friend and her parent. They had grown up together, so their relationship was different from that of a lot of other moms and daughters. Sharing and talking had always been the method by which they understood each other.

"Colton's father is... I know him."

"What?" Lily leaned forward in the car seat. "How?"

"Well his dad was from here originally."

"He was?"

"He was...involved in your uncle Jason's accident."

"How?" Lily asked.

"Buck Carson, Colton's dad, was with Uncle Jason. Buck was driving in a car behind the one with all the boys in it. It's... I've been angry at him for a really long time. I blamed him. Because there was definitely... He was wild. He always was. He had a reputation for drinking. And yet I liked it when he was around. He was fun. Charming. Handsome."

"You were thirteen!" her daughter said.

So scandalized by an age gap. After being caught with a boy in her room. Kids today were a trip.

"Yeah. He didn't look at *me*, but I definitely looked at him. I think that's what made it worse. I idolized him. I thought he seemed like the fun kind of dangerous. But he wasn't. He was the dangerous kind of dangerous."

"Mom..."

"I'm not going to refuse to let you see Colton." Marigold started the engine. "I just wanted you to know what the situation was." She started to back out of the parking place, orienting the car so she could drive back toward the highway.

"I hear a *but* in that sentence."

"Yes. There are going to be ground rules and curfews. You are going to college," she said.

"I know. As soon as I can, I'm going to submit applications, and apply for FAFSA…"

"I want you to stay focused."

"Mom, I wouldn't… I listened when you talked about safe sex."

"I know. But no contraception is one-hundred percent and… And there's no point getting attached to him. Not when you're going to leave."

"I guess not."

"That being said, I'm not telling you not to date him."

Lily screwed up her face. "You're not? Because it sounds an awful lot like you are."

"I guess I just… I want you to think about all these things. That's all."

"Why can't I just date? That seems normal."

"Of course it is. Of course. But you have never dated. So you have to admit, it's not completely out of left field that when I came home and suddenly there was a boy in your room, it felt out of character, and I want to make sure that you're not…going off the rails."

"Just because you did doesn't mean I will."

"I know."

She had tried to be the kind of mom her daughter could talk to, because she hadn't known how to talk to her own mother. That wasn't a failure for her or her mom. They'd both been grieving. Her own mom had lost her oldest child. And Marigold hadn't wanted to talk. She had wanted to get into trouble. She hadn't been levelheaded like Lily. She hadn't planned for her future. She had thrown herself into trying to forget her pain. She hadn't thought to plan even one step ahead, not like Lily.

The truth was, nothing scared her more than her teenage self. And when it felt like there was any chance that sort of behavior could pop up for Lily, it made Marigold feel unhinged.

She was her own bogeyman. Knowing exactly what she had gotten away with at sixteen years old, seventeen years old—that was sort of the ultimate consequence. A comeuppance she could never have imagined back then.

Maybe this was also a comeuppance of sorts.

"I just really like him," Lily said. "He's not like the boys around here. He's…"

"More experienced," Marigold said, knowing she sounded dry and suspicious.

"I guess. Maybe."

"But also exciting, I guess, because he's a stranger."

"Again, I don't know. I just know that I like him."

Well, it was a little bit galling that her seventeen-year-old was having the kind of fantasy love affair Marigold had built up for herself in her mind over the years, that Greek island fling. Meeting a stranger who made you feel something.

Yeah. She was a little too familiar with why that was compelling.

"We're going to take you to the carnival this weekend."

"What?"

"Buck and I agreed that it might be a good way for you to have a chaperoned date."

"A *chaperoned date*? I am not a toddler."

"No. But we need to set some rules and expectations. I don't... I don't want you getting too involved with one boy. I want you to date. Actually talk to him. Get to know him."

"Mom."

"Well. I want you to be safe and well protected."

"I'm going to college soon. You can't keep me from living."

"I don't want to keep you from living. I don't want you to shut down and not tell me things. But I know you. I know you really well, and today was out of character."

"Maybe he makes me feel out of character."

This was really testing her 'being an open-minded mother' determination.

But... It felt so important that she get this right. She didn't want to lose her connection to Lily, but she didn't want Lily to lose a connection to her future. Lily was going off to school; she was going to build a future for herself. And that would allow Marigold to build her business, her future, in the way she wanted to. Greek vacations optional.

"You can see him again this weekend. And then we'll talk more. I just want you to tell me things. I felt blindsided by the fact that you hadn't even mentioned his name."

"I'm sorry," Lily said.

"It's all right. We'll figure it out."

She would. She would figure all this out. Because

the truth was, she had been through much harder things than this.

Marigold Rivers was nothing if not tough and determined. And this would be no exception.

No matter that there was a Buck Carson-sized complication in the middle of it all.

Chapter Four

This was the most wholesome thing he had ever done in his life. Sure, he might have spent the past twenty years trying to find balance. He might have even tried his hand at being one of the good guys. But wholesome? That wasn't really in his wheelhouse. Which made him a good father figure for misguided teenage boys, he thought. Because after all the life experiences they'd had, wholesome was out of their reach too. At least, he had thought it might be.

But here they all were, dressed in their Sunday best, about ready to go to a school carnival of all things.

"You will make sure to get the dirt out from under your nails?" he asked, looking at the boys.

"I'm not an animal," Colton said.

"At least not an armadillo. Since there are no armadillos here," Marcus said.

"Shut up," Colton said.

"Yeah, you all look like you pass muster to me," Buck said. It wasn't like he made a habit of scrubbing his own nails or anything like that.

He thought about Marigold and ignored the tension stretching across his shoulders.

It had taken him a couple of hours after she left to realize how pretty she was. And to start to wonder about her. Really wonder. Not in terms of her being an emblem of potential salvation, but as a human being. Who had a seventeen-year-old daughter. His friend's little sister had always been a small, sunny presence, and she had been annoying. Chipper and buzzing around like a fly. He hadn't given her much thought. He had been nice, because you couldn't be mean to somebody else's brother or sister, that was just a rule. But she had been young, and primarily inconsequential to him. But she was a grown woman now. And it was strange on a few levels.

The first being that he hadn't seen Jason's family in all the years since the accident. Well, not since Marigold had yelled at him in the street. And the second being that because of the accident, Jason and his family had sort of frozen in place in Buck's mind. Because Jason was dead, so he hadn't gotten to grow or change or age. He was eighteen forever. Buck often found it strange that his friends were frozen forever in that place, graduation night, with a lifetime of possibilities ahead of them, while he was...getting old.

He had lines on his face. Calluses on his hands. New scars, in and out, that had torn through his flesh or his soul in all the years since his friends had been gone.

And Marigold was no different. She had grown, and she had changed. She wasn't the same person she had been all that time ago. She wasn't a child anymore. She was a mother herself.

It was a wrenching sort of joyous realization. Because at least Jason's parents had her, had a granddaughter.

And Buck's son was working on defiling her, apparently.

He'd had a pretty stern talk with Colton about possible consequences. Yet he had felt like an imposter, because he had practiced few of those things he was ranting against when he was a seventeen-year-old boy. Sex had been a game. It was a small town; there wasn't shit else to do. He had been part of the wilder group of kids.

The truth was, there was a narrative that he had somehow led those more upstanding boys into that wild space, but they had done a good job taking themselves there.

It wasn't that part of it that left him feeling guilty. It was being involved at all.

It was being the one who survived.

Because what he did wonder was if any of his friends would've done more than he did. For the world. For themselves.

If they were supposed to fall in love and get married and have children.

If they were supposed to cure cancer or climb the tallest mountain. Or maybe they wouldn't have done shit.

It was impossible to say. But it was the not knowing that got to him. It was the not knowing, and never being able to know. That was what kept him awake at night.

It was just a damned hard pill to swallow.

And then... there was the fact that she was pretty.

She was damned pretty. And he had done his best to ignore that. Because there was pretty, the kind you could appreciate, and then there was *pretty*. The kind that hooked its way deep in your gut, made you feel something down beneath your skin. Something that was more than just aesthetic appreciation. Attraction.

That was the dumbest thing he had ever thought. But it was rattling around inside himself.

He could not be attracted to Marigold Rivers.

"All right," he said. "Let's head out."

The boys loaded into the truck, and they started toward town.

The carnival was right off the main street with booths lining the sidewalk and string lights woven overhead. There were balloons and streamers and all manner of jaunty decor strung up about the place. It was a Fall Festival, early September so not Halloween as much as apples, gingham and myriad other things he'd never much associated with.

It was... It was like a small-town TV show. Or a Hallmark movie.

The Historic Main Street was looking brighter and more vibrant since he'd left twenty years before, with many of the buildings restored, including an old bed-and-breakfast at the very end of the street that belonged to his brother and his new wife. His sister-in-law also owned the saloon in town. The whole main street was practically a Carson parade.

He parked his truck up against the curb, and they all got out. He took out his wallet, and some cash, and handed it to the boys. "You can go meet school friends. And this is your money to spend."

"Gee thanks, Dad," said Reggie.

"You're welcome," he said.

It didn't bother him that they only called him dad when they were being sarcastic.

"Colton, you're on notice."

"What did he do?" Marcus asked.

Buck hadn't made a big song and dance about what Colton had gotten caught doing, because he didn't want to expose Lily to any kind of gossip, and on top of that, he hadn't wanted them to think Colton was cool.

"None of your business," he said, planting his hand flat on top of Reggie's head and giving it a scrub. "Just go about your business."

"Are you going to babysit me?" Colton asked, once his younger siblings had cantered off.

"I don't intend to. But I imagine I ought to be there when we meet up with Lily and her mother. Since you made a very bad first impression."

"So you realistically think teenagers are just not going to have sex?"

"It's not about what I think or don't think," he said. "But what I expect is that you will treat this place we've moved to with some kind of respect. That you'll consider Lily, her feelings, her future. Because you know what? I was the kind of ass who didn't. When you make consequences for somebody else, Colton, that's not something a good person can just walk away from. And you're a good person."

"You really think so?" Colton was looking at him with skepticism.

"Yes. I do. And you know…about my past. You know about the damage I caused here."

"Yeah. But it's not really the same thing."

"Maybe not. But you know what it's about, it's about prioritizing having fun in the moment over thinking about what that fun could cost. And I want you to be better than that. I want you to be different than that. I know you can be. I want you to be better than me. Because when I was your age, I did sleep around, and I didn't care if girls got their feelings hurt. I didn't care that my dad was busy. He was traveling around with the rodeo. My mom was…dealing with things. She had lost one of her kids. And then had another baby kind of late… It just… Nobody was really paying attention to what I was doing. There were too many kids and too many other things going on… At the very least, I want you to put her mom at ease. Show some damned respect."

"Yes, sir," Colton said, mumbling. But Buck counted that as a win.

They started walking toward the festivities, and he saw Marigold and Lily standing right there.

"Hi there," he said. "Good to see you again."

Marigold looked…beautiful, her red curly hair spilling down her shoulders in loose waves, her amber eyes glistening. She didn't exactly look thrilled to see him. But she had shown up. She had done that for her daughter, he was confident.

Her daughter looked a lot like her. Red hair, freckles. She reminded Buck a lot of her mother when she had been young. She reminded Buck a lot of the Marigold who had stood in front of him yelling and hollering and basically telling him he was a murderer.

A stark contrast to the woman who stood in front of him now.

"Go have a wholesome date," Marigold said.

"All right," Lily said, taking Colton's hand and leading him into the carnival.

"They seem unhappy with us," Buck said.

"Well. Too bad for her. I guess I'm not totally used to being in opposition to my daughter, but there's a first time for everything."

"Yeah. I guess I haven't been in opposition to the boys much. But that's a real thing with foster kids… They either test you and try to drive you away, or you end up in a honeymoon phase where they're trying to be good so they don't lose you. I would say the boys have been much more on the honeymoon track. So I guess this is kind of my trial by fire. At least, I hope it is."

He felt silly, and a bit naive, saying that. Because he knew full well that all three of those boys had been in much bigger trouble than being caught in a girl's bedroom.

"They've been through a lot," he said. "Colton… Listen, Colton's story is his to tell. He's a good kid. If I thought he was going to be a danger to your daughter in any way…"

"It's weird," Marigold said, taking a step back from him. "I have a hard time looking at you and seeing who you were. But if I think too hard about the Buck Carson I used to know, all of this feels like pretty strange things for you to say."

"I know. I get that. I don't exactly know why you would trust me. But I'm not lying to you. He's a good kid. Twenty years is a long time."

"Yes it is. It's a very long time. A lifetime. It's more

years than my brother lived. We might as well address that. Because it is the elephant in the room, whether we want it to be or not."

"I have no problem hearing you out. If there's something you need to say." He hadn't exactly anticipated having this conversation standing at the edge of this carnival, but whatever needed to happen, he was just going to let it happen.

"I'm not angry at you. At least, I didn't think I was. But… I guess theoretical forgiveness is a lot easier when the person isn't around. But here you are. My brother is gone and you've had twenty more years on this earth." She shook her head. "So have I. And… I can't say that I feel entirely neutral about you. But I have a better appreciation now for how young you were. When I was thirteen you seemed like a grown man. But now my daughter is seventeen, and I know that eighteen is not grown. And I don't think you should have to suffer for something that happened all those years ago."

"But Jason did," Buck replied. "Jason, Ryan and Joey did. That's what it comes down to. We made a mistake. A youthful mistake. And because of that mistake they died, and I got a second chance. It was all a matter of being in a different car. Choosing to drive myself because I didn't want to sit in the back seat. Or whatever the reason was, I don't really remember. But I do know that what happened was not fair. You are right about that. There is nothing at all fair about the fact that a mistake for them was final, while for me it wasn't."

"You really have changed."

"I have. Because in the aftermath of their deaths,

when you came and yelled at me in the street, it confirmed what I already thought about myself. And if I was the bad guy, then it meant I got to go off and continue to be the bad guy. I got to go off and continue to serve myself. Which was what I did. For a number of years, Marigold, I'm not going to lie about that. But one night I picked myself up, and I decided to change the way I was doing things. I decided to make living matter. I needed living to matter. I needed their lives to matter. I needed their deaths to matter. That's why I'm here now. That's why I have the boys."

"Three boys."

He nodded. "That's why."

"It feels so complicated."

"It is. But I came back because I thought it was all right for me to be back here now."

"What do you mean by that?"

"When I left, it was because I thought staying meant visiting hardship on my family that I didn't want them to go through. At least that's the story I tell myself to try and make it seem like I'm not totally selfish. But the truth is, there was an element of selfishness to it. Of course there was. I wanted to lick my wounds. And leaving allowed me to do it in a place where there was no accountability. I didn't want to come back until I knew I wasn't using my family simply as accountability. If that makes sense."

"It does," she said.

There. He had gone and vented his guts out after having been back for five seconds. "None of that is your responsibility," he said. "You don't have to forgive me, no matter what you said before."

"All right. I'll remember that. But I think we might have to be cordial because it seems our children like each other an awful lot."

"Yeah. They do. Colton was pretty mad at me for lecturing him. My one concern, and I am going to be really honest with you, is that Colton is not a small-town kid. He was not as well protected as I assume your daughter is."

She nodded slowly. Not for the first time, he looked down at her left hand. She didn't have a ring. He looked back up, and she was studying him.

"I'm not married," she said.

His mouth quirked upward. "You must be used to men looking at your left hand."

"I am. At least, enough that I know to recognize the question when it's being nonverbally asked. Her dad has never been in the picture."

"I see."

"Sometimes I wonder if I should work harder at reaching out to him again. Because he went off to college. Or rather, he went back to college. I did let him know, but of course at the time…he didn't want to be a dad. It just seemed easier to let it go. So, from that standpoint, I understand what you're saying. Sometimes it does seem easier to just let go completely."

"Yeah. That's it exactly." He paused. "I don't have the whole world to offer those boys. I do have a trust fund from my father and a whole mess of extended family, and that seemed like something. Seemed like a good offering.

A real offering. So I decided to come back. I'm not sure that I'm loving all the connections, though."

She laughed. "I imagine not."

"We can agree that this is not a comfortable situation."

"No it's not." She had a feeling they were talking about more than Colton and Lily, so she deliberately turned the subject back to their kids. "With Colton, what you're basically telling me is that you're worried he's more experienced than Lily?"

"Yes."

"He probably is. Lily has never dated anyone before. She has a mother who got pregnant at sixteen. The paranoia runs a little high in our household."

"If you don't want them dating, I can tell him…"

"No. I think what we discussed earlier stands. If we turn them into Romeo and Juliet, it's only going to get worse. I'm just going to have to try to keep talking to Lily. Keep her communicating with me. It's the best I can do."

"You have every right to yell at me, you know," he said.

"Would that make you more comfortable?"

"Yeah. Now that you ask."

"Then I'm definitely not going to yell at you."

His lips twitched. They regarded each other for a moment.

"So. Want to…walk around the carnival?"

"I don't know," she said.

"What else are we going to do? Anyway, then we can keep an eye on the kids."

That was true, but really he wanted to keep talking

to her. She was right; he almost would've been more comfortable if she had yelled at him again. If she'd have picked up right where she left off years ago. Mainly because there was some part of him that still wanted to feel that guilt. That still wanted to feel that culpability for the accident. Because that guilt was his comfort zone. For a long time, he had acted out of a self-destructive place with that guilt. But he had stopped, and he had learned to use it as fuel. So maybe part of him was looking for more. Along with that extra bit of absolution. She felt linked to all that. He didn't want to lose touch with her.

"All right," she said.

The booths were set up on the sidewalks, in front of businesses. There were games and snacks and other things designed to appeal to teens, and all the proceeds went to fundraising for the school. There were caramel apples and balloon dart games. The kind of thing he never the hell would've gone to when he was in high school. He wondered if the boys were secretly enjoying this carnival, or if it felt really cheesy to them. But then, wasn't having something light and cheesy in your life a privilege?

Twenty years ago, he had been reeling from the death of his little sister. He had let it take the joy away from him. It was that loss that had put him on the road when his friends died.

So he had learned that the pain a person carried could hurt other people. No one was an island.

He had also learned that the ability to be happy was a gift.

"Candy apple?" he asked now.

"Oh sure," she said. "Why not?" She paused. "We're not on a date."

"No," he said. "We are not."

"Good. Just making sure."

"I don't think you can accidentally go on a date," he said.

"Well, I hope not. I'd hate to break my seventeen-year dateless streak."

"Seventeen years?"

"I have a kid. And yes, you can date when you have kids. But I decided that I didn't want to take the risk. Of having her get attached to somebody, and then having it not work out between us. It just always felt too volatile. I admire the people who do it. Who try to make that work. I just couldn't... I'd already had too many losses. And I didn't want to visit any on my daughter. At least none that I could help."

"Right." He felt sad for a second, because he knew the weight of those losses. He knew exactly what she was talking about. He had been part of that.

"Platonic candy apple," he said.

"That is allowed."

He bought the sticky, bright red apple for her, plus one for himself, and it was like being in an out-of-body experience. This strange kind of small-town moment he had never really experienced before. By the time his family had moved full-time to Lone Rock, he'd already been destroyed by the loss of his sister. So he had never really...done anything like this. Had never walked down the street with a pretty girl eating a candy apple.

He shouldn't be thinking of it that way now.

"So, what are your plans once Lily leaves home?"

"If you expect me to say *get a date*... Well. Maybe. It's not off the table. But the other big thing would be that I want to open a storefront for my business."

"What do you do?"

"Meal prep. I would really like to open a facility where people could come in and use it to do their own meal prep. I make the plan, they do the preparation. And I'd have a place to store more prepared meals so people could buy them for the week rather than being on my regular rotation. Which is what I do now—there are a certain number of families in the area who have me make their dinners for the week. I deliver them at a set time, and they don't have to worry about it. They just have to cook."

"That's pretty clever. I'll tell you, when I lived on the ranch for troubled kids, there was a cook. Three square meals a day, and I didn't have to think about buying the food, preparing the food, or what the food was going to be. That has been one of the harshest realities of adopting these kids and taking them away from the institution. I have to figure out what to cook for them."

"A lot of people hate it. I love it. I like figuring out how to work on a budget, how to make it as cost-effective and affordable as possible."

"That's great. So you're looking for a building?"

"Yes. I... I mean, that's what I *want* to do. Because I need to do something with my time once Lily is away. But it's going to take... I don't know. A pretty substantial loan, and that scares me. When Lily was younger, I never wanted to get into anything like that because it would mean putting our house at risk. I would never do that, not when she was little. But I feel like I can maybe branch out now. Take more risks."

"You have a place in mind?"

She shrugged. "There's a building, just up the street. It's been empty for a while. I would have it completely gutted and renovated, and it would be so expensive—"

"You need an investor."

"Okaaay..."

"Yeah. Somebody to assume the risk up-front, and help you get this going."

"That sounds like a great idea. I have no idea how I would go about finding one."

"I could be one."

She blinked. "What?"

"Yeah. Why don't you let me be your investor?"

Chapter Five

Marigold was astonished. And thirteen-year-old Marigold was *appalled*.

She could not take this man's blood money. His guilt money. Under no circumstances. Her principled younger self was outraged. Her older self was trying to figure out if it was the therapy, if it was coming to believe that things were more complicated than she'd previously believed, or if the real issue was that she just really wanted to say yes. Because if he would invest, then she could do what she needed to do with the business. Without risking her house or any of the other things she had built. She wouldn't have to worry so much about Lily's scholarships covering absolutely everything. It was just…a miraculously good offer at a moment when she needed it most.

But he was Buck Carson.

You're eating candy apples with him.

She was. And if she was totally honest, when she had asked him if it was a date, it had felt a little bit like flirting.

He was *very* handsome.

Which felt like a psychotic thing to think—given everything. But she'd always thought he was hot, and also, the man standing in front of her didn't bear a resemblance to the boy she'd vented her grief on all those years ago. Not that he physically looked entirely different, but he was different inside. She knew it. She could feel it.

He had kids now. Recently adopted kids. He'd said *yes* to taking on all the trauma they might have. He was trying to actively parent Colton in this situation with Lily and…

It was far too easy to simply detach this older Buck Colton from the Buck she'd known back them.

Maybe because she was so different too.

The Marigold of twenty years ago had been fascinated by his wild streak. He'd been a bad boy. He'd seemed dangerous, and she'd liked that. In the years after, she'd burned herself out on bad boys. She'd learned her lesson, and well. She wasn't the same person she'd been.

It stood to reason he wasn't either.

She didn't know if she was being desperately naive in saying yes to anything. In even talking to him.

In doing anything other than punching him in the stomach and running away.

But… On the other hand, didn't he owe her *something*?

Not like that. But if Jason had been here, he would've been the best uncle. He would've been another positive male role model in Lily's life, and he would've offered so much in terms of support. He had been such a great older brother.

"Don't overthink it. I want to help. I have money. I have a trust fund. And I want to invest in your business."

"But…"

"Yes. Because I feel guilty. Okay? It's because I feel like I owe you. I do. There's nothing wrong with that, is there?"

"I don't know."

She really didn't. Maybe because even inside it felt mixed-up.

"What happened back then was bad. It was a tragedy. There's no way to shift it into something it's not. It was awful. It *is* awful. We can't change it. We can't fix it. But I have dedicated my whole life to figuring out how to make something grow out of the charred earth the accident left behind. To try and make it mean something. When you showed up on my doorstep yesterday I thought…"

She stopped walking and turned to face him. "You thought what?"

"I thought it was my chance to fix it."

He meant it. He wasn't lying. He absolutely felt that way. It was clear he thought this was a chance for him to make amends.

Did she want him to be absolved?

She didn't feel the way that she once had about him. She thought she had forgiven him, and she had put all her complicated feelings off to one side. She had a daughter to raise. She had a life to get on with.

When her grief surfaced, she didn't let it have teeth.

She didn't allow anger at somebody else to mix with the moment, because she wanted the moment to honor Jason.

It was different with Buck there, though.

It was very, very different.

"Yes," she said, before she could think about it anymore. Before she could overthink it. Because there was no right answer here.

She could be angry at Buck forever, and maybe part of her would be. But it wouldn't bring Jason back. It wouldn't bring back Ryan and it wouldn't bring back Joey.

He was trying. He had lived on a ranch for troubled youths. He had adopted three boys who needed somebody.

It still didn't bring them back.

So whether she hated him forever or scorned his money and his help, that didn't make a difference.

Her refusal wouldn't fix anything either. Maybe it would make her feel morally superior, but it wouldn't actually solve any of the problems she had.

She would have to make sure her parents didn't find out, though.

She didn't know how they felt about Buck. They had never talked about it.

She had gone off the rails, and then she had gotten pregnant, and everybody had rallied around her. Since then, her parents had devoted themselves to being the best grandparents on earth. But that didn't leave a lot of space to talk about grief.

That was all right. Because in some ways it was easier. She didn't have to carry their grief along with her own. Maybe that wasn't fair, but it was the truth.

"I can't commit myself to working too much before Lily leaves…"

"But we can get construction started. We can make

a business plan, get permits—all that stuff takes time. It would be good if we could start as soon as possible."

"You're just now back in town. You have your family, other commitments. Why do you want to throw all in with me?"

"I already told you."

"You feel that guilty."

He let out a long, slow breath. "More complicated than that. I think this was what was meant to be. I… I don't ignore gut feelings. Okay? I really try to sit with them. I try to listen to myself. I try to see what God or the universe or whatever the fuck is out there is telling me. And it was telling me something when you came to my house yesterday."

"It wasn't just telling you that our teenagers have wildly racing hormones?"

"All right. It was definitely telling us that. But I think there's a point to be made here—this was meant to be in some way."

"You can still believe in fate?"

She had trouble with that one. Because she had a hard time believing her brother was meant to be gone. She had a hard time with people saying things like: it was his time. Because how could it be an eighteen-year-old boy's time? How? There was nothing just about that. There was nothing fair about it. She had a very hard time believing anything that even hinted it was meant to be.

And she would've thought he could understand that.

"Maybe not fate. What I do think is that sometimes we get pulled up. By the scruff of our neck. By the divine, I guess, and it's up to us whether we listen or not. I try to listen now."

She couldn't argue with that. Because she related to that experience. When she had found out she was pregnant, it had been like a divine hand reaching down to redirect her. It had been like a total shift in the way she saw things. But she could have chosen a different way. She hadn't had to keep Lily. She hadn't had to change. But she had heeded the feeling. Maybe that was what she felt now. A tug. Telling her she had to take his offer. This opportunity. Because it mattered. Because it was going to mean something.

Or at the very least it was going to make her life easier, and surely that wasn't a bad thing.

"Well, it's good for me. Though I suppose we need to come up with all kinds of official terms and conditions."

"Of course. I'll send them over to my lawyer. I just did an adoption, so I'm more familiar with the legal system than I'd like to be at this point."

"They aren't brothers, are they? I mean biologically." She felt clumsy asking the question, concerned she'd done it in a way that didn't respect the bond they all shared. But she was more curious about his life, about how everything had come together to create that family, than she wanted to admit.

"No. They were all three at the ranch for a while, and none of them were going to a home. Reggie..." His expression suddenly went remote. She saw his throat work. "His mom got killed by her boyfriend. Along with his younger sister. It happened while he was at the camp.

If he had been home, he would've been gone too. That poor kid."

Sympathy tightened her stomach. "Oh. Wow. That poor boy."

"When you meet him, though, don't be soft on him just because he's been through shit. He doesn't like that. He doesn't want pity."

She understood. It was hard when everyone knew something bad had happened to you. They were so careful. Sometimes so careful they decided not to speak to you at all. Reggie had a fresh start here. In some ways, that must feel good.

Buck knew too. And Buck had to find ways to help his son with his grief.

"That must be… That must be so hard," she said.

"It is. The kids come with a lot of baggage, but so do I."

She had to admit that it really did seem like he was trying to do the best he could with what he had. That he was trying to take a tragedy he had experienced and turn it into something good.

"Why don't you walk me up to your building?"

"It's not *my* building yet."

"We can put an offer in tomorrow if you want."

"Really?"

"I can pay with cash."

"It's expensive."

"Do you not realize that my dad's rich, right? My siblings and I all have huge trust funds."

She did sort of know that, but Buck had been gone and she'd assumed he'd been cut out of the cash flow.

"He still gave you money?"

"Yeah. I guess he always hoped I would come home. But I hadn't spent a penny of it. Not until I bought the ranch here."

"You already bought the ranch, and you *still* have money left over?"

"Yes. And I don't intend to live a life of excess. I intend to send these boys to college. I intend to get my ranch up and running. But I'm investing in your business. I'm not just dumping money into something."

"I don't know that it's going to earn much back."

"It will."

They walked down the street until they arrived at the vacant building. It was large and empty, once housing a department store when this street was a thriving thoroughfare during the gold rush. In recent years, the economy had picked up because more and more people were moving to Bend and pushing tourism out into Eastern Oregon, an area which had been desolate all the years before. And the town of Lone Rock itself was growing. Bend was so trendy it had become expensive, so moving to an outlying area that wasn't terribly faraway was seen as a great compromise by a lot of people. That meant the odds of her growing her business were good, and the real estate market was still competitive without being overinflated.

The building was still a mint green color with gold trim, and she loved how cheerful and old-fashioned it was all at once. It was easy for her to imagine different workstations where people could prepare their food. And a big commercial kitchen for her.

"This is it," she said.

"It's great," he said. "Really great. I love it."

"You do?"

"Yeah. I think you could really sell people on the community aspect of coming in and preparing meals together. Instead of it being drudgery, it would be a fun night out with your friends."

She loved that. She hadn't even really thought of that direction. She could furnish drinks, cocktails, coffee. She really liked the idea because for so much of her adult life she had been isolated. She'd had a daughter at a much younger age than anybody else she knew, and she was consistently a baby next to the other parents at Lily's school. And while she was relatively friendly with a few of the moms, most of the mothers of graduating seniors were ten to fifteen years older than her. The idea of community really appealed to her.

Maybe because it had been elusive for so long.

Maybe because she'd felt outside of it even before she'd had Lily.

Back when she'd been the sad girl whose brother was dead. And then the slut who would go with any guy that asked.

"Listen, if you want to, I wouldn't mind if you added me to your meal prep rotation," he said. "I'm dying trying to cook for these kids."

For some reason that made her stomach get tight. Made her heart throb. "I...yes. I'd like for that to be one of your investment perks."

"You don't have to do that."

"Maybe not, but it'll be a while before this is making

enough money to cover what you're proposing to put into it. So let me at least make food for you."

"Fine. But I'm paying for the groceries."

"Okay. I want to do this. I mean I really do. I said yes because I didn't want you to change your mind, and not really so much because I felt totally on board. But now I do. I mean I really do."

"Good," he said. "I'm glad. I'm glad that you're on board for this."

"My parents...."

"Right. Shit. You want me to talk to them?"

"Not right now." She wished she was brave enough to talk to them. About Jason. About Buck. About Lily dating Buck's son.

But it was like the words froze in her throat whenever she tried.

Before her brother's death, her house had always been loud and fun, filled with Jason and his friends and their mom making food for everyone.

When he'd died, it had been so deathly quiet, and she hadn't dared speak above a whisper. When she was home, she tried not to speak or feel anything. She went out and she partied and she made up for all that quiet then. And came home with her parents none the wiser.

Until she'd gotten pregnant, of course.

Then they'd all figured out how to speak again.

But it was about new life, not about death. About Lily and what was best for her and what Marigold could do to be a good mom, not about losing Jason.

They didn't talk about their loss.

Marigold didn't know how to, not with them.

"All right," Buck said. "It's an awfully small town, though."

"I know. I will talk to them. I will. I just... I need to figure all this out."

"Seems fair. And you have yourself an investor, Marigold Rivers."

He stuck his hand out, and she really had to think about that. But then she took a breath and clasped his hand in hers. It was rough. Hotter than she had imagined it would be. And for some reason, it made her tremble. And maybe now wasn't the best time to reflect on the fact that it had been nearly eighteen years since a man had had his hands on her body.

"You have a deal," she said, breaking the handshake as quickly as possible.

They were already going into business together. She wasn't going to muddy the waters by feeling attracted to Buck Carson.

There were lines. And this was one she was never going to cross.

Chapter Six

After the boys went to school the next morning, he contacted Marigold. "You ready to go down and make an offer?"

"Yes. I called a buyer's agent this morning."

"Perfect. We'll go take a tour, and then we can put in a formal offer."

"All right. I'll meet you down there."

"Sounds good."

He felt a bit like he was having an out-of-body experience when he got into his truck and started driving toward Lone Rock. He had been here a month, and it was starting to feel okay that he was home. Starting to feel familiar. Starting to feel like home, but it was still complicated. Sometimes it was like being in a time warp. Other times it was like he had never been here before in his life. Like he was a stranger.

But he was very firmly rooted in the here and now when he pulled up and saw Marigold and the real estate agent already standing in front of the building.

Her hair was so bright, like radiant copper. He hadn't realized just how guarded she'd been when she was talking to him, because there was an easy pleasantness on her face that he had not seen before as she looked at the other woman on the sidewalk.

He parked his truck against the curb across the street and got out. Instantly he saw the tension rise in her body, saw her shoulders go tight. The corners of her lips pulled taut.

"Hi."

"Hello, I'm Louisa Ramirez."

"Buck Carson." He remembered what they had discussed, her desire that he be more of a silent partner. He looked at Marigold, but she didn't seem bothered that he had introduced himself.

"I'm excited to show you that—" The phone rang, and Louisa looked down at her phone. "Just one second."

"Sorry," he said out of the corner of his mouth while Louisa took the call, turning away from them. "I know you wanted me to keep this on the down-low."

"You don't need an alias. I just don't want it spreading around before I figure out how to approach it with my parents. Louisa is new to town, though. Your name won't mean anything to her."

That was a novelty. Not being notorious to somebody in this small town.

Being back the past month hadn't been as rocky as he'd thought it might be, but it had still been a *thing*. Some of his brothers were easier on him than others. Boone was still pretty angry and stood by the punch he'd thrown when Buck had first arrived.

Some people in town recognized him right away. Some didn't. Some genuinely just thought he was one of his brothers from a distance and waved like they knew him. He always waved back.

The principal of the high school was a guy he'd graduated with, which had made him feel desperately old. But the man had been friendly enough to Buck when they'd talked about the boys and their individual situations.

This small town was a mixed bag. And he didn't hold it against the people who didn't quite know what to do with him.

"All right."

"Sorry," Louisa said, turning back to them. "Childcare. I had to make sure everything was okay. You know, the day care calls and your heart stops."

"I do know," said Marigold. "Even though it's been a while."

"Of course you do. Anyway. I'm going to go ahead and give you a tour of the inside. It's in great shape—it has been completely gutted, with new flooring, new walls, new electrical and new plumbing. It's a complete blank slate."

"Perfect," he said. She looked over at him in censure. "What? I mean, it's up to you, but it seems perfect."

"But it's up to me," she said.

"Of course," he said. "It's up to you." Gradually, over the course of their inspection, he realized Louisa was treating them like a couple. But why wouldn't she think that? And, since Marigold didn't want him to make a big deal out of their business partnership, he thought it was probably for the best that he not go making pronouncements. He didn't know if Marigold was noticing the subtle tone of everything. He supposed it didn't matter.

They finished the walk-through without incident, but he kept his eyes pinned closely to Marigold's face.

"We'd like to make an offer," he said.

She looked at him, and he thought she might want to scold him again for making the decision, but he knew she wanted it. That he could see plain as day.

"Yes," she said slowly. "We would."

He didn't see the point in offering under the asking price, so when they got the paperwork to make the official offer, he went ahead and put it in as it was.

"I'll take this to the seller," the agent said.

"Thanks," he replied.

They walked out of the building, and that left him and Marigold standing on the sidewalk.

"Thank you for that," she said.

"Not a problem. Do you know of any good contractors around here?"

"Yeah. I do. There's a couple that seem to have a really good construction business, ones that I've only heard good things about."

"Excellent. Then once the offer is accepted, we'll line that up."

"We have to, like, get permits and stuff?"

"That too, but we're going to need a concrete plan, and the contractor will pull those permits for us."

She squinted. "So you've done this before."

"I helped with some renovations at the ranch years ago, so I'm familiar with the logistics, yeah."

"I guess I needed a partner more than I realized." She looked at him for a moment, and it felt like their eyes locked together, for just a moment. His gut went tight. She looked away quickly. "Okay. I guess we're doing this."

"Yeah."

"So…" She squinted. "Lily wants to have Colton over to study. And she swears that they're actually going to study."

"Oh. Well. Sounds believable."

She snorted. "I told her they have to leave the door open in the room where they're studying the whole time. Also, I was wondering if you wanted to come over and work on the plans for this."

"Better idea. Why don't you guys all come out to my place, and we can do the planning there? There's more room, and the kids can sprawl out in public areas, but still have some quiet for studying."

"Oh. That's great. If we do that, let me do dinner. I'm very efficient at dinner."

"I'm not going to say no to that."

"Okay. It sounds good."

"Yeah. Still not a date," he said.

"No," she said. "Still not a date."

Lily was a little bit irritated with Marigold at co-opting the study night, but her daughter seemed pleased to go to Colton's house. Like it would give her a window into this boy she liked, and it would probably be enjoyable.

"I mean, I haven't gotten to go inside," she said.

"No, and now you will. But not into his bedroom."

"*Mom*," said Lily.

"Well. His dad and I both thought this plan would be a good idea."

"Right."

Marigold needed to explain to Lily everything that was going on. She had mentioned that Buck had offered to invest in her business, and for all that she had been uninterested in the topic, Lily had seemed happy for her.

"To be clear," Marigold said, "I am not dating his dad."

Lily's face contorted in horror. "Why would I have ever thought you were?"

A good question. As Marigold had schooled herself into a sexless paragon. She had fashioned herself into a puritanical version of a mother. Not a woman. A mother. She had never gone on a date, not in Lily's whole life, so why would Lily assume that of her now?

Marigold had mentioned dates several times in regards to Buck Carson, and she couldn't pretend that she didn't know why.

She was attracted to him. He made her heart beat just a little faster, but the problem was that with every heartbeat there was a little pain as well.

He was inextricably linked to her brother's death. That was an old wound, but one that had not been tested in quite this way in a very long time. Well. Ever, really.

She had distance and perspective. She had age and wisdom. But that was about it.

She also had very large gaps in experience, and a whole lot of peaks and valleys in her personal development. She was a mother. She had started a business. She had raised a child to this point. She had bought a house and made a budget.

All her experiences with men and sex were the experiences of a teenage girl. And maybe that was why she felt slightly teenage now. Attaching herself to the most ridiculous man she could have possibly attached herself to.

Or maybe the problem was that old attraction simply died hard.

She had always felt an attraction to him. Even when it had been a young and innocent fascination. Back then, he had been the boy who had the power to ignite her fantasies. Now he had evolved into the man who could apparently stoke a flame that had grown cold after so many years of neglect.

So maybe she was projecting when she continually mentioned dates. She was going to have to stop that.

"Well, it isn't, I just wanted to make it clear."

"It's worse than a date," Lily said. "You're supervising me."

"You made yourself worthy of supervision, Lily."

Lily scowled.

"All right. Let's just get there and see how it goes. Anyway, his house is bigger, and you were excited about seeing the house."

"Yes, yes."

Teenagers really were so mercurial. But normally, Marigold wasn't the subject of Lily's changing moods, so she couldn't say that she'd noticed so much. Or been bothered by it.

That felt significantly different right at the moment.

"It is a really nice house," she said as they pulled up to the large, modern dwelling.

"What does he do?" Lily asked.

"You didn't ask Colton?"

"I did. He said his dad used to work at a camp for troubled kids. Which is how he ended up adopting Colton. But that doesn't make any sense. Because I know everything is more expensive than you could possibly believe, and that you don't get paid good money for being a decent human being. This house is billionaire money. This is scamming other people's money. And yeah, you don't get that kind of money helping kids."

"Colton's grandfather is the commissioner for the rodeo."

"Really?"

"Yes. You don't really know the Carsons, but they were a big factor when I was growing up. They moved to town right before I started middle school. And they brought a lot of money with them. They had a lot of kids too, and they infiltrated every single school around. You couldn't ignore them."

"I don't know the lore," Lily said.

"Well. That's the lore. Abe Carson is the bigwig of the largest rodeo organization in the country. They travel all over the place putting on events, he has made a massive organization and he has tons of money. And what Buck said was that they had trust funds. All the kids."

"Wow. Must be nice."

"Right?"

"So that's what he used to buy this?"

"Yes."

"I guess at least a good person got the money."

It was interesting that Lily saw him simply as a good person. But then, why should she see him any differently? Jason's accident was theoretical to her. He had been gone long before she was born. And all Marigold could really say about Buck's connection to the accident was that he had been there. Everything else had been innuendo.

About the way he might've influenced the evening. It wasn't actually fair. Not if she stepped back from it.

It didn't make the wound less tender.

But that was all it was. Tender.

Such an old pain now. Dull and aching.

They got out of the car.

They walked up to the door together this time, rather than Marigold going alone, being on a warpath, and Marigold rang the doorbell.

Colton was the one who answered. "Come on in. My dad said you were making dinner?"

"He is correct. I'm offering dinner in exchange for the use of the house for studying. Since we decided not to do it over at our place. But I hear tell that you have a lot more room."

"Yeah. That is true."

They walked into the house, and Lily and Colton went off into a sitting room to the left. She heard noise coming from the kitchen and popped her head inside. "I just have a couple of bags to bring in," she said.

Buck was facing away from her, standing at the sink. His shoulders broad, his waist tapered. He was... He was gorgeous. It was problematic.

She realized right then that maybe she wasn't a paragon when it came to not dating so much as no one had ever been interesting enough for her to upset the delicate balance she had with her daughter. She had never met a man who tempted her to risk anything.

She had thought she was just super responsible and

enlightened. She had been a little bit self-righteous about it, truth be told. Yeah, on the surface, she'd tried to pretend she was okay with how everybody else lived their own lives, but actually, she had let herself get very up her own rear about the whole thing, and she could see now in that moment just how ridiculous it was. Because Buck Carson was bad on every level.

Getting involved with him would be wrong.

And she was tempted.

Because he was compelling. Beautiful.

He turned to face her, and the hard, stark lines of his expression took her breath away.

Those blue eyes, chiseled cheekbones and square jaw. It was like he was carved out of granite.

And suddenly, her fingertips itched to trace the lines there.

She was so screwed.

She couldn't pretend it was just a lack of male interaction. Because she was around men all the time. She lived in the world. There were plenty of single dads at the school. And they didn't make her feel like this.

She did wonder if there was some kind of sickness in all this. If she had some thwarted feelings from the past where he was concerned, and that was informing everything now.

"Yeah," he said, grabbing a dishrag and drying his hands. "Sure."

He did not look domesticated, and yet the vision of him in the kitchen doing the dishes like this was domestic. There was something about the contrast that was... Too much. Way too much.

"Just a second."

She scurried outside and grabbed her bag of groceries, bringing it back in. "I thought I would make us stew. I have a loaf of bread that I made this morning."

"Sounds great," he said.

"Yeah. It will be. I am a great cook."

"Glad to hear that."

"Especially since you're going to benefit from that cooking."

"Also, it's related to the investment that I'm making."

"True."

Silence fell between them, and she covered it up with movement, briskly making her way across the kitchen and beginning to unload the grocery bag. "I'm going to need a knife and a cutting board."

"Pretty sure I know where that is."

"If I find it faster than you, I'm going to shame you."

"The good thing about having a sister-in-law who owns a bar is that a lot of times I just pick up hamburgers from there."

"Oh, I mean, the burgers at Karen's place are good, but come on, not if you have them *that* often," Marigold replied.

"Do you actually go to the bar?" he asked. "There's not an embargo on my whole family?"

"No. Nobody…"

"Nobody wanted to punish the whole family because of me?"

"Basically," she said, feeling regretful. "Listen… I don't want to make you feel bad."

"Oh. I get something out of feeling bad. Or have you not noticed that yet?"

"You're awfully self-aware."

"It's one of my better qualities. But then, that's also a side effect of having been on my own for a long time. Nothing to do but think about myself. A form of narcissistic healing."

She snorted out a laugh. "I'm actually kinda familiar with that."

"Right. Single parenting?"

"Specifically, when I was pregnant."

"Tell me about that," he said, getting his cutting board down and putting it on the counter.

"Why?"

"Because I'm interested, Marigold. And I want to know. Because...we're doing this thing together. Also, I like you. I'm trying to get to know you."

She squinted. "Why?"

"Misplaced guilt, probably. But if it doesn't bother you, it doesn't bother me."

"Doesn't bother me." She took a breath and took her butcher paper–wrapped steak out of the bag and began to carefully take the paper off. "After Jason died, I didn't know what to do with myself. I wanted to disappear and I wanted attention. I wanted to explode, and I wanted to hide. I loved him. My parents were really going through it. Of course they were. They lost their son. I started rebelling in small ways. But really, the way I was able to get all those needs met was men."

"Boys, you mean."

She laughed. "I wish. No. I liked them slightly older. I didn't really want to sleep with somebody at my school."

"When you were fourteen?"

"Usually they were nineteen or so. A lot of times I wasn't honest about my age. Okay, anytime. Granted, it didn't come up. I don't think they cared. It was just the way I found this false feeling of control and power. And then it really came home to roost. Because I got pregnant. And he was headed off to college. He didn't want a baby. I realized I needed the baby. Which is maybe a terrible reason to have a baby, but I wasn't making the best decisions at the time, as we have established."

"And you had a bunch of assholes ready to take advantage of you being so lonely."

"That's the world, Buck. We make weird, bad decisions when we're in pain, and someone is always willing to take advantage of those reactions and traumas. I own my part in that. But you know, it's not any different from what we all did to you. We were angry. Collectively, as a community, and you were the survivor, so you became the scapegoat. Because nobody could yell at the three boys who had made the same decision you did. To get behind the wheel drunk, to get in a car with somebody drunk. To spend graduation night wasting their potential. The truth is… I was probably angry at Jason. But he was dead. So yelling at you was a replacement."

"Maybe." He looked sad. Thoughtful. That he still carried the grief of it all made her feel… Not better. That sounded mean. But she felt a kinship to him she had never imagined she might feel. "That whole period of time was a dark one for me too."

"So you mentioned."

"I had to hit rock bottom before I changed. I mean, I really had to."

"I think I would have too. If not for Lily. I think I narrowly escaped rock bottom. Some people would consider getting pregnant at sixteen rock bottom, I'm sure. But for me, it was the hand up that I needed. It was the only thing that was ever going to reach me."

"And now she's headed off to college. That means you did something right."

"I hope so. That's all you can do with kids, Buck. Hope. Hope you did the right thing. Hope your best intentions matter. Because sometimes they do and sometimes they don't. You hope the good you do outweighs the bad. The mistakes."

"Thanks," he said. He was silent for a long moment. "It's heavy. The way having kids makes you see things differently. The way being close to kids, even if they aren't yours, changes the way you look at your own life. Even when I was just working at the ranch, looking at those kids made me feel, for the first time, an appreciation for how young we were back then. But especially now. Looking at my boys. I feel old. And they feel so, so young."

"It's difficult," she said. "Because being a teenager should be a time when you're allowed to be stupid. But you and I both know that, depending on the stupidity…" She swallowed hard. "You just can't take some things back."

"No," he said, his voice rough. "And I'm trying to figure out how to impress that upon them while…"

"Not crushing them?"

"Yeah."

"I relate to that."

Again, she realized she had more in common with him than not.

It was such a strange realization.

Because she had thought he was an enemy. When in fact he was an ally.

"We just have to do our best."

She was chopping vegetables when he spoke again.

"You know. I lost my sister."

She stopped. She had vaguely known that. That the Carsons had lost a child before they moved to Lone Rock. But there were so many of them, and the loss had been abstract, so she had never really considered their grief. That it meant she and Buck had both experienced the loss of a sibling.

"You did," she said. "I'm sorry. I never really thought about that. I was… I'm really sorry that I blamed you."

"I'm not telling you that to make you feel sorry for me," he said. "I don't need or deserve pity of any kind."

"Yes. You do. Because you have really been through hell with all of this. And you had been through hell before all this too."

"I had a therapist diagnose me with survivor's guilt," he said. "And I thought that was the dumbest thing. Because why should you be in pain because you survived? I just don't get it."

"I think everything is just hard. And maybe part of the problem is trying to decide who's allowed to feel bad about what when… Life has a way of breaking us all down."

"Right. Cheery conversation," he said.

"Well. We don't exactly have a cheery shared history."

"True."

Suddenly, giggles erupted from the other room. He grinned. And it made her stomach go tight.

"I guess we're building a different shared history right now," she said.

"I guess so."

Chapter Seven

She put the stew on to simmer, and the scent that filled the kitchen was heavenly. He was damned glad he had enlisted her to help make meals. Because this was making his house feel like a home in a way it hadn't before. But there was also this…pull toward her. A pull that was not at all homey or in keeping with the conversation they'd had earlier.

He was actually pretty astonished to discover everything they had in common.

He hadn't expected that.

But even deeper, harder, was the attraction he felt toward her.

She was beautiful. He wanted to know more about her. He wanted to know everything about her.

And that was… That was the dumbest thing in the world. He had just adopted three boys. She had her daughter, ready to go off to school. Their kids were dating, and there was no guidebook.

For any of this.

When he called the boys for dinner, they definitely made a big song and dance about the food being better quality than they were used to getting from him. That was fine. He couldn't dispute that.

Marigold looked amused.

"Are you animals actually going to introduce yourselves?"

"Oh," said Reggie between mouthfuls of bread. "I'm Reggie."

"Marcus," said Marcus, not looking up from his stew.

Colton treated Marigold to a smile that was a little bit too smart-assed to be called polite. "We've met."

"Yes. We have. I'm Marigold. Lily's mom."

"We don't have to call you Mrs.?"

"No," she said. "First of all because I'm not a Mrs. and second of all because I like my first name just fine."

"Fair enough," said Marcus.

Lily looked marginally uncomfortable, but then, he couldn't blame her. He could think of few things that would've horrified him more as a teenager than having to sit down at a table with the family of a girl he was making out with, and he imagined that unease transferred across gender lines pretty equally. Colton, for his part, didn't seem to be having a problem at all, but Colton had an outsized amount of confidence for a boy of seventeen.

Likely, that was what attracted Lily to him. It was also what made Colton a potentially devastating heartbreaker. Buck also knew that from experience.

He had been a little bit *too* good at getting girls to fall in love with him. Not so good at getting anyone to *stay* in love with him, because he couldn't back up that charm with actual substance. Not back then.

Not that he had any evidence he could do it now.

Not that he had ever tried.

The odd one-night stand didn't exactly foster emotional maturity when it came to things like that. He liked to believe he had garnered maturity in other ways. But as far as romantic relationships went...

He looked up, his eyes connecting with Marigold's. Yeah. He didn't need to be looking at her when he thought about things like that.

"How are you settling into Lone Rock so far?" she asked brightly, looking around the table at all the boys.

"It sucks," said Reggie, chewing loudly.

"Boring," said Marcus, giving it a thumbs-down.

"I don't mind it," said Colton.

"Why do you think it's boring?" she asked, looking directly at Marcus.

"Because it is," Marcus said. "Respectfully."

"Is there a respectful way to call something boring?" Marigold asked.

He shrugged. "I figured I would give it a try."

"What kinds of things did you like to do back where you came from?"

Marcus squinted. "At the ranch? Or at home?"

He felt a small, strange kick in his stomach hearing Marcus refer to where he'd been before as home. But he supposed Marcus would feel that way. Because he had grown up in Cleveland, which was different from the ranch for troubled youth and different from Lone Rock, and Cleveland was what he thought of when he thought of home. Even if it had been inhospitable in a lot of ways. Even if he had spent years bouncing from house to house.

"Either place," Marigold said.

"There were always kids to run around with at home," Marcus said. "You could go out on the street and find whole group of them. Go play basketball."

"You can do that here," she pointed out.

"I guess. But I don't know any of the kids here. And I don't have a basketball."

"I can get you one," Buck said. "I didn't know you wanted to play."

He shrugged. "I didn't play at the ranch."

"Why not?" Marigold asked.

"I don't know," he said, looking down.

Buck had a feeling he did know. But he wasn't going to push.

He realized then that while he had experience with loss and with pain, even with leaving home, he didn't fully understand what it was like to be uprooted without your consent. To feel like everything was out of control. But these boys did.

Reggie's mom was dead. He didn't know his dad, and that made going home impossible. Maybe Reggie could get back to the house he had grown up in, but he would never be able to get back to the people. That was tragic. But Buck hadn't really given a lot of thought to the fact that home, in the traditional sense, still existed for Marcus and Colton. Their parents were alive. The system had separated them. And yes, the addictions and flaws of their parents had separated them. But the grief it must have created inside them to have *home* out there somewhere, and yet still out of reach...

"Do you like baseball?" Marigold asked.

"I do," said Reggie. "My mom used to take us to Fenway sometimes. When I was little."

"My brother played baseball. He loved it."

"Does he still play?" Reggie asked.

Buck's stomach dropped. But Marigold didn't look upset. She didn't look at Buck either.

"No," she said. "My brother died. But baseball is still a good memory."

"Oh. My mom and sister died," said Reggie. "But I think baseball is still a good memory for me too."

"I'm sorry, Reggie," Marigold said. "I know how hard it is to lose a sibling."

Buck knew some people might feel like they were witnessing a sad moment, but the truth was, everybody at this table had experience with loss. That was why the boys had a solid sense of dark humor, and it was why Buck never scolded them for it. Because they had seen the real ugly things in the world, and there was no need to protect them from that. Not when they had lived it. With that in mind, he knew this was a profound moment. One that meant something.

Because Marigold was identifying with Reggie, not pitying him.

Because Reggie didn't have to be afraid to talk about loss. It wasn't bringing down the room. It was something they all understood.

Buck had talked to Reggie about how he had lost his sister when he was little. To have both adults in the room truly understand him on that level was probably a unique experience.

"Maybe we can play some baseball," Buck said. "I'm bad at it. But there is a pretty good baseball team at the high school. The basketball team is terrible. But maybe they could use somebody who knows how to play."

Marcus looked thoughtful. "I dunno. Maybe I could learn how to play baseball."

Well. If you wanted a fresh start, that was fair enough.

"I don't want to play sports," Colton said. "There's already too much homework. Anyway, I'm a senior. I'm not going to be here that long."

"Do you have plans to go to college?"

"Buck says I have to go," Colton said.

Buck couldn't readily read the tone there. If Colton was happy about it or still annoyed. Colton had certainly never planned on going to college, not when he had been a kid in the system. But Buck was determined to give him the opportunity. If he didn't like it, if he failed out, that was fine. Buck just wanted him to have the chance.

It was amazing just how much this felt like a family dinner, when that was… Ridiculous.

They finished up, and she thanked him for the invitation. He thanked her for dinner. They said goodbye like they hadn't spent the last couple of hours having a deep conversation. Like they had just been adults interacting while their kids were studying.

"I'm meeting with a contractor tomorrow to discuss plans for the building," she said. She looked down. "I wouldn't feel comfortable doing that without you. Considering you need to approve that…"

"Sure," he said. "Sounds good."

Now he was going to see her tomorrow.

But that was good. He was listening. To his intuition, which said there was something here. Something he needed to accomplish through his reconnection with Marigold.

And so he was bound and determined to do it.

Chapter Eight

The next day, Buck put on his cowboy hat, a button-up shirt and a pair of blue jeans and went down to the local diner, where Marigold had said they were meeting the contractor over coffee and pancakes.

The boys were at school, and that meant Buck could focus on this project. He was also working toward getting the ranch prepared for cattle. But there was some time now between planning and when it would actually execute, so he didn't need to worry about it today.

When he walked into the diner, he saw Marigold, sitting at a table with her red hair pulled up into a ponytail and a deeply contemplative expression on her face. She had a legal pad in front of her, which he thought was cute and old-fashioned. She was holding a pen.

He gestured toward the hostess, who had been about to seat him. "I'm with her."

And then he went over and positioned himself across the table from her.

"Guess we're early," he said.

"Yeah. You want a coffee?"

"Sure. I'd never say no to that."

The waitress came by, and he ordered coffee, waiting on food until the contractor showed up.

"So basically, you need a kitchen," he said, a way to get her talking.

She nodded, and then started to explain the layout of the space. Buck really did think it was a great business idea.

"How did you get involved in this, anyway?" he asked.

"Well, I was cooking anyway. I wanted to be able to work from home so I could be with Lily, and I knew I was going to have to get creative because I didn't even graduate high school."

"You didn't?"

"No."

He knew a moment of anguish. Because her brother had died the night of his graduation. Because Buck had let his own life get derailed right after that. And it had carried back to Marigold. Who hadn't even had a graduation. The ripple effect of tragedy was an alarming thing.

Especially when he knew he could trace his own behavior back to losing Sophia, his youngest sister.

He swallowed hard and looked down at his coffee. And just a moment later, a man approached the table carrying a large binder. "Marigold," he said. "And you are?"

Buck stood. "Buck Carson."

The contractor reacted to his name. And Buck evaluated the guy as about his age. He wondered if they had gone to school together.

"I'm Jackson. Delaney."

Oh right. They had. They hadn't really been friends, because Jackson had been a jock and Buck had been a fuckup. So. One of those had been required to maintain a certain grade point average. The other had not.

"Didn't know you were back in town," he said.

"Yeah. I am. I moved back a month or so ago."

"Definitely didn't expect to see you with Marigold."

"Oh. Well. Jackson," she said, reaching across the table and putting her hand over the top of his. Buck felt his hackles rise. And he couldn't even quite say why.

Oh bullshit. You know why. You like her, and you don't want her touching anyone else.

Sure. But that was nonsense. What did it matter?

"I really would appreciate if you kept this to yourself for now. Buck and I ended up meeting because of our kids. His boys are at the school now. And Lily and Colton are… They're dating. So, we… reconnected." She repeated that part. Probably because it was difficult to distill all of this. Probably because it still made her feel uncomfortable. And fair enough.

"I told Buck about my business idea, and he offered to invest. But I am not ready for that to be public information."

"Oh yeah. Of course, but you're sitting here in the diner with him."

"I know. It's not cloak-and-dagger. I just… I don't want my parents to know yet that I am doing this with him. I'm going to talk to them."

"Listen, I'm not going to spread around what's happening. For a second thereabouts I thought maybe you were dating."

Marigold laughed. Too loud and too long, and her cheeks went red. "No. Absolutely not. But you know…

You know how kids are. And ours like each other. So what can you do?"

Jackson snorted. "Nothing. I mean, I know that well enough. If I was in charge of who Elizabeth dated, her roster would look a lot different."

Buck felt the need to defend Colton, but he knew it wasn't the time. Or the point. So they got to work discussing everything. And by the time it was done, he felt certainty in his gut.

When Jackson left, he turned to Marigold. "I'd like to talk to your parents."

"What?"

"I'd like to talk to them about this. And I'd like to extend… I don't know if an apology is the right word. Because being sorry about what happened is never going to change it. But I don't want to create a situation where you have to hide, and… I need to build these bridges with everybody. I accepted that when I came home."

"I don't know that that's totally fair," she said.

"Listen, I don't actually need absolution on the level you seem to think I do." He took a breath. "I've lived in a state of self-pity for a long time. You don't get anything accomplished. But I find that guilt, and the driving need to make up for the fact that I'm alive while they are gone, has turned me into a better person. I know that's a double-edged sword. Because it almost doesn't seem fair to have the chance to improve myself when they don't. When they don't get to grow and change."

"The truth is, you didn't cause that accident. The truth is, if you had been riding in the car, you would also be dead. The truth is, you didn't make anybody drink."

"Yeah. That is the truth. But the truth doesn't serve anybody. Not half as well as a villain does. It doesn't even serve me as well."

"So you just… You're just happy to be the scapegoat because it does something for you?"

"It makes me worth a hell of a lot more. And I can't deny that it matters."

"Let me… Let me call them."

She got up from the table and went outside. He watched, as she wrapped one arm around herself and put the phone up to her ear. She bit her thumbnail as she waited, and he couldn't take his eyes off her. She said hello, chewed her bottom lip. Beyond that he couldn't quite tell what she was saying.

She looked upset. And then resolved. Grim. She nodded her head. Then she hung up her phone and walked back inside.

"Okay. We'll go over there."

"All right."

The thought didn't scare him. Because the worst-case scenario was that her dad would shoot him. And if that happened, he would be upset for his boys, but his family would take care of them. Support in any scenario was one reason it had been important that he give them this whole network. He didn't want his boys' happiness, their security, hinging only on him.

So really, even the worst case didn't much worry him.

He felt like he had been living on borrowed time for the past twenty years. Also, he didn't sincerely think her dad would kill him.

"Should we go together?"

"Sure," she said.

"I'll drive my truck."

He remembered their house. A small, modest place right in town that had always felt quintessentially warm and familial to him. There was something about the smallness of it. It gave off a sense of togetherness. They were a nice family. They always had been.

"I don't know… My parents and I have never really talked about any of this. They didn't want to upset me. You know my mom was there when I confronted you…"

"Yeah. Don't worry about it. I don't need you to protect me from whatever they feel. They're allowed to feel it."

She nodded. "I actually want to protect them."

"I get that too."

They got out of the car, and walked up to the house together. He let her knock. When the door opened, both her parents were standing there. Jim and Nancy. They'd been the nicest people. Always welcomed the whole group of them into their house. Fed them, laughed with them.

It felt appropriate to say nothing. He didn't know why. When he looked at them, it was with all the awe and reverence he felt when he walked into an old church. A hushed quietness and a sense of something he couldn't quite define.

This really was staring down the past. Nancy was looking at him like she wasn't sure what to make of him. And then she took a step forward and reached her hand out. Her fingertips connected with his face, softly. She traced a line on the side of his mouth. And her eyes filled with tears. "He would be your age now."

He felt that, like a punch to the gut. A real, profound connection to that grief. As if it was fresh and new.

He nodded. "It's been a while."

"He would probably have some gray hair," she said.

"Maybe so." He could hardly speak around the lump in his throat.

And then she did something he didn't expect. She stepped forward and wrapped her arms around him. "Just let me hug you," she said. "For a second."

Buck had been through a lot. He'd cried about the loss of his friends. He'd cried when he got drunk and fucked-up on dark nights after that. But he'd not cried since he'd gotten sober. He had stopped indulging in self-pity. But this time, when he felt tears sting the backs of his eyes, it wasn't self-pity. It was the bittersweet ache of knowing he was giving her a chance, just a moment, to feel like she was hugging her son. It was realizing he was an emblem of the past in this moment in a different way. One he never had been before.

When she released her hold on him, he looked over at Jim. The man didn't say anything. But he nodded twice.

"Come on in," Nancy said.

They walked into the house and took a seat on a blue faded couch that he was fairly certain was the same couch that had been here twenty years before.

"What is it you have to say, Buck Carson?" she asked.

"I moved back to town about a month ago," he said. "I thought it was time. Time to stop running. Time to reconnect with my family. I adopted three boys, and they're teenagers."

"Lily is dating the oldest," Marigold said.

He waited for them to get upset about that. But they didn't react. Then he explained the business partnership. And how it had come up.

"But mostly, I wanted to say what I couldn't say back then. I'm very sorry. For what happened."

Nancy shook her head. "Nobody should bear the blame for that, Buck. Nobody. You were all too young to know how your actions could hurt you. It was a terrible thing. It still is. I grieved all the things my son could've had. But those eighteen years, that was his life. And I have also worked very hard to look back on that life as a wonderful, joyful thing. He had friends he cared for very much, and you were one of them. You were part of why his life was good. You weren't just a part of the end of it."

Buck sat there, completely astonished. This wasn't just forgiveness. It was something else. It turned him into someone with the capacity to heal and not just hurt. It changed all the memories. Everything he had ever thought about that relationship.

It changed everything.

"Just one minute," she said.

She got up off the couch and walked out of the room. And no one said anything in her absence. When she came back, she was holding a baseball glove. He recognized it right away. Jason had played for the school. He had loved it.

"Lily doesn't play baseball. But you said you have three sons. Do any of them play?"

"They haven't really had the chance yet. They... They all had it pretty tough."

"Do any of them want to learn?" Jim asked.

"You know, they might." It hurt to speak.

"Because I miss…" Jim cleared his throat. "I miss that. Throwing the ball around."

"Well, I'm no good at it," Buck said. "So if you want to…"

"Yes," Nancy said. "That would be wonderful. Take this glove and tell them they can use it."

She handed it to him, a precious, sacred object. And when he touched it, his throat went tight. "Thank you. I will take very good care of this. So will the boys."

"Well, they don't have to be too careful with it. They're kids. And a baseball glove is meant to be played with."

He saw that with clarity all of a sudden.

That they were kids. No matter that they were teenagers. They were so, so young.

He'd been young at eighteen too.

"Thank you."

When they walked back out of the house, he didn't know what to say. It was as if a weight had been lifted off him. One he had been clinging to for a long, damned time.

Marigold didn't speak at all, and when they got into the truck, he noticed there were tears sliding down her cheeks.

He looked over at her. "I didn't expect that," he said.

"Neither did I," she said. The tears fell fast. He had to fight the urge to reach out and wipe them off her face, because he shouldn't be that familiar with her.

"You thought they were angry with me."

She nodded. "Because I was. Because so many people

in the town were. But... She's right. You were a good part of Jason's life. And you haven't gotten to see yourself that way, and that's not fair. He was more than one tragic accident, one bad choice. And if he's more than that, then why can't you be?"

He felt something calcified inside of him crack, fall away.

"You're a good dad to those boys. I could see that last night when we had dinner. I could see how much they love you. You know, my brother had a great family. A wonderful life. Too short, but wonderful. I don't let myself feel happy for that often enough. When you told me about poor Reggie... He's a kid who hasn't known enough happiness. I'm glad he's knowing it now."

"Yeah," he said. "I have to tell you, I didn't expect this when I came back here."

"Did you want people to condemn you?"

"A little. My brother punched me in the face. I thought that might set the tone."

"He did?"

"Yeah. It's... It's getting better. He carried a lot of very specific resentment about being left to be the oldest. To carry all the responsibility."

"Well, we all fall victim to that, don't we? Making other people the bad guys in our story." She laughed. "Sometimes I wonder if Lily's father was never as much of a villain to me because I already had one."

"How can that guy not be a villain?"

"I think because he didn't matter. Anyway, my parents are... They're wonderful. And they're great grandparents. My dad has been a fantastic father figure to her.

She didn't need the loser that I had sex with one time. And I didn't need to be tied to him for the rest of my life. I'm grateful, in some ways, that he and I had a clean cut. Yes, some things were harder. But being with someone you don't care about, that's not going to make it easier."

"I don't know. The more I sit with that the more I just think maybe your family has a supernatural capacity to bend around a person's limitations and create as kind a story as possible."

She smiled. "That is an interesting way to put it. I appreciate it. And now there are no secrets. I have to remember that I shouldn't try to protect them. We didn't talk about you all this time because I was trying to protect them and they were trying to protect me. I think it would've been better if we had just been honest." She let out a long breath. "Holding on to anger is exhausting. It's a relief to let it go."

He wasn't so sure about letting go of guilt. Because it had been such a key, driving force for him.

Guilt was a comfort, really. It had been the thing that had ultimately pulled him out of the pit. Maybe that was a messed-up truth, but he had often felt that there were certain things some sorts of people had to be extra careful of. There was a reason he didn't drink now. Not even in moderation. It was, in his opinion, a crutch he was prone to leaning on far too much.

Not everybody was so careful.

Maybe guilt was a crutch too. But he wasn't going to wake up face down in a ditch because he had overindulged in guilt. So there was that.

But what had just happened in Marigold's parents'

house was one of the more profound things he had ever experienced. So maybe there was value in being changed by it. In moving forward differently than he had been. Maybe.

Right now, they were starting something new. Something fresh.

For the first time, it really did feel like something good was growing from all that charred earth. And he had Marigold to thank for that.

Chapter Nine

She had been delivering meals to Buck once a week for the past two weeks. Every time she saw him, it got less jarring in one sense and more complicated in another. Because he was gorgeous. And it wasn't a simple impersonal observation. It was something she felt. Every time she passed the bags of food from her hands to his, every time she was near him. He was becoming more and more himself to her.

Buck as he was now, and not the version of him she had yelled at in the streets, or even the version she had philosophically forgiven in his absence all those years earlier.

They also had conversations that filled in the gaps of the last twenty years.

Tonight, she was intent on dropping the food and leaving. Quickly.

But as soon as she showed up, so did her daughter's car, which was carrying not only her and Colton, but Marcus and Reggie as well.

Marcus and Reggie tumbled out of the back seat while Lily rolled the window down.

"Can we go to the movies?" Reggie asked.

"All of you?" Buck asked.

"Yes. Colton and Lily said we could come."

"Are they buying you a ticket for an R-rated movie?"

"Buck," Reggie said. "My life is an R-rated movie, man."

"That didn't answer my question."

"They're going to a cartoon," Colton shouted.

"We are not," said Marcus.

"Whatever," said Buck. "Fine. You can go to the movies."

"Send me money on my phone," Colton said.

"Fine."

"We need popcorn and stuff," he said.

"So, you need a hundred dollars, that's what you're telling me," said Buck.

"I wouldn't say no," Colton said.

Lily, for her part, looked appropriately chagrined.

"You can buy your own ticket," Marigold said.

"She doesn't have to," said Colton.

"Apparently my son is being chivalrous with my money." Buck smiled. "Get out of here, you heathens."

And that left the two of them standing there, by themselves.

"You want to come in?" he asked.

Did she want to come into the house where it would just be the two of them by themselves? She found that she did, perversely. But she also felt like she probably shouldn't. Of course, her feelings could be entirely one-sided. That was most likely. Also, they were adults. They were not hormonal teenagers who needed supervision to be alone in a room together. That was Colton and Lily.

Another potent reminder of why nothing was ever going to happen between the two of them.

There was ruining your kid's life, and then there was ruining your kid's life by having the hots for her boyfriend's father.

Wow. What a horror show.

"Sure," she said. She stepped inside, almost to prove that she could. Almost just to prove that there was no real bogeyman here. There was no lack of control she needed to be worried about, no attraction that was beyond the both of them.

It was just silly to think in those terms.

"You want to stay for dinner? You and Lily, when she gets back. I have a feeling they're all going to be overfull from what they're eating at the theater."

"Sure."

"I have these great preprepared meals," he said.

She laughed. She laid the bag on the counter. "I mean, there's a little bit of work yet to do."

"I can help."

"There's not much to it. We just need to put the chicken in the oven, along with the roast vegetables. Since there's time yet before they'll return."

"Sounds good."

She started getting the ingredients out. And compulsively, she began to put away the other preprepared meals she had brought, because she was here, so she might as well.

She could feel him looking at her.

"Sorry," she said. "I probably overstepped."

"No," he said. "You haven't overstepped with anything."

"The permits got submitted," she said, taking a deep

breath and wondering if the subject change seemed too weird. But there was something so warm, so lovely about being in here with him, and she was pushing against that reflexively. Against the feeling of contentment that had begun to bloom in her chest.

Maybe that was silly. Because over the last couple of weeks Buck really had become a friend. He had brought the boys to her parents' house to throw the ball around with her dad. Now the boys were considering trying out for the baseball team at school. Buck was part of her life. It might be unexpected in a lot of ways, but it was definitely reality. So maybe she just needed to stop being awkward.

"Glad to hear it," he said.

"Oh yeah. I am especially glad. I can't believe it, though. I can't believe that everything is progressing. I just… A month ago, I wouldn't have thought I would be here."

He looked around. "Specifically in my kitchen?"

"Well. That too." She paused for a moment. "It's a good thing. Because Lily is going to college."

"I know." He grimaced. "I do worry. About Lily and Colton. And the logistics of that relationship."

"I know," she said. "So do I." She took a breath and tried to ease the knot of tension in her chest. "He's a really good kid, Buck. Apart from being in my daughter's room that first day I met him, I mean."

"Yeah. Well. He is a good kid. A little bit feral, but he's trying."

"I know. I don't want either of them to hold each other back."

"Neither do I. But they don't seem to have an angsty,

over-the-top teen romance thing happening. I mean, they're going to the movies with Colton's younger brothers."

"Yeah," she said, smiling.

It really was the most wholesome, lovely thing. The way Buck and the boys had formed a family. The way Colton took care of Marcus and Reggie.

"I don't mean... Just to be very clear, it isn't that I don't think Colton is wonderful. I do."

"No, I know. Lily is a great girl. You've done an amazing job with her. I can only hope that I do half as well with the little bit of time I have... That is the only thing. I wish I had more time to parent Colton."

"I know you don't know this," she said softly. "Because you left home at eighteen and didn't really have contact with anybody, but parenting doesn't end at eighteen. Colton is going to need you a lot when he's off to college. And he's going to need this place to come back to. Your continued support when he's not technically a kid anymore, that's going to mean the world to him."

The corner of his mouth tipped upward into a smile. "I hadn't thought of it that way."

"I mean, it's a great way to continue to show that when you took him in, it was forever. I imagine he hasn't had a lot in the way of stability."

Buck shook his head. "No. Colton was put in foster care when he was three. He got bounced around all over the place for years before his mom lost parental rights. And then... He was running away from foster homes all the time. He got caught with drugs he was selling. And that was how he ended up at Hope Ranch."

Sympathy made her chest tight. "That poor kid."

"Yeah. He was fifteen when he came to the ranch. Alone in the world. Angry. He's had two years of stability. Compared to all those years without it."

"It's amazing what a difference it makes."

"I just wish… You know, it's one of those things. I just really wish I could've found them earlier. But in order to do that I would've had to find myself earlier. And I wasn't there yet."

"But you were at the ranch for sixteen years."

He chuckled. "Yeah. And for a while, that was just triage. Me trying to stop the bleeding so I could stay standing."

"I need a cutting board," she said.

"Right here," he said. He moved toward her, and then reached up into the cabinet above her head, bringing his chest right up against her, and when he looked down, the breath exited her lungs in a gust. He was so close. She could smell him.

He smelled like cedar, dust and hay.

She wondered about the plans he had for this ranch. He had mentioned a little about them a couple of times in passing when they were planning different things for her business. But she found she wanted to know more about him. And at the same time, she realized she also wanted to draw closer to him. She felt dizzy with it.

He seemed frozen there. He wasn't grabbing a cutting board. He was just standing there. His hand pressed against the cabinet above her, and her eyes drifted to his forearm, well muscled and glorious. To his mouth again, down to his broad chest. His lean waist. Highlighted perfectly in the maroon Henley shirt he was wearing.

"Buck," she said.

A warning, an invitation—she wasn't exactly sure.

But his name tasted like moonshine that neither of them allowed themselves to drink anymore. Intoxicating. Forbidden.

Then suddenly, he grabbed the cutting board and took a step back. "Here," he said.

"Oh," she said, taking it from his hand.

Their fingers didn't brush. He was very careful to make sure they didn't.

He cleared his throat. "Anything I can do to help? I thought all the prep was done."

"I decided I wanted to add a little bit more garlic. That's all. It's in the suggestions in the recipe, but since I'm doing it..."

"You shouldn't do it. You already did all the work."

"I don't mind. It's my job. And cooking is easy for me. Probably a lot easier than watching you stumble through the motions."

"Well, I have stumbled through the motions when you're not here."

"Yes," she said. "But crucially, I don't have to see it."

"Harsh," he said.

Their gazes connected, lingered for just a little bit too long.

She didn't know what to do in a situation like this. She hadn't wanted to kiss a man in a very long time. And the truth was, she wanted to kiss Buck Carson.

But it was inconvenient, and it was foolish.

"Stop looking at me like that," he said.

Well. He was going to make hiding it pointless.

"Sorry. I'm trying to figure out exactly what to do about it."

"About what exactly, Marigold?"

"Don't make it weird," she said.

"I'm not making it weird. But I am asking you. Honestly."

"No you aren't. Because you know exactly what I was thinking."

"Tell me."

He was daring her. The sensual challenge in his voice ignited something in her stomach.

How was that possible? Only a few moments ago, their kids had all been in a car in the driveway, and they had been bantering with them. It had all been so parental. And for her, being a parent had meant separating herself entirely from sexuality.

Or maybe that separation had been about protection. Not just protecting Lily, but herself.

Because she had only known how to use sex in a really unhealthy way. It hadn't been about pleasure; it had been about oblivion. Attention. It had never been about love; it had been about loss. About the emptiness inside of her. And she just hadn't wanted to work any of that out with her daughter around watching it.

He made her want to try. Because right now, they felt cocooned. Right now, this felt like a lovely, secret moment.

She wanted to take his dare. She wanted to find the part of herself she had put away so long ago and take it back out. Look at it. Examine it. See if it still shone as brightly as it had then. Because that was the thing. She could have regrets about the why of all the things she had done, but there was something wonderful about being young. And a little bit wild.

Both she and Buck had put away their wildness so effectively. And maybe that's what she was seeing when she looked at him. When their eyes caught and held. Maybe she was seeing the remnants of that wildness, a little spark.

It made her want to test it. To try it.

"Well, I was thinking about kissing you."

He made a sound, adjacent to a growl, and it left her feeling thrilled. Excited.

"That would be a very bad idea," he said.

"I know. That's why I didn't do it."

"But you mentioned it."

"After intensive questioning," she said.

"Because you were being so obvious."

They stared at each other for a long moment. She tried to take a breath, but she found the air in her lungs was frozen. And in a voice she barely recognized as her own, she heard: "Just once."

Maybe this was a gift to the girl she had once been. The girl who had idolized him. Who had thought the sun and moon hung on his smile. The girl who had been so devastated and damaged after that accident that she had lost pieces of herself. Maybe it was a moment to give that girl a small fantasy.

Because hadn't she been endlessly responsible? She had. She had made nothing but the best decisions every day of her life since Lily was born. And they had this small window. This couple of hours where nobody was here, where no one was watching them, and she just wanted to make one choice that was self-indulgent. Some might call it bad.

But they'd been so good. How could it be bad?

That was how she found herself taking a step toward him. And he didn't move away.

She put her hand on his chest and startled. He was so hot, so solid. She could feel his heart raging beneath her palm.

It had been so long since she had touched somebody else like this, and the last time she had, it hadn't been the same. It hadn't been slow. It hadn't been deliberate. She had wanted to be carried away from the moment. Right now, she wanted to linger in it.

She didn't want to forget who she was. She remembered. Every year, every mistake. Every version of herself that she had ever been. She allowed all of those Marigolds to enjoy the moment. Because in that moment, she was flooded by a rush of forgiveness. Not just for him, but for herself.

For the foolish things, the hopeful things, the wild things, the self-sacrificing things and the indulgent things.

Because she was all the decisions she had ever made, good and bad. And one didn't take away from the other, and none of it defined her either.

She moved her hand slowly down his chest, to the firm, flat ridges of his stomach. She stopped at the waistband of his jeans, her breath catching hard.

Then she reached her hand out to his face, tracing a line along his square jaw, relishing the sensation of his whiskers beneath her fingertips.

"You... You're so..."

"Shut up and kiss me," he said.

She didn't have time to respond, because he wrapped his large hand around the back of her head and pulled her in close, his mouth firm and hard against hers as he claimed her with an intensity that was unlike anything she had ever experienced before.

His body was so hard, his hold so tight, so perfect. She wrapped her arms around his neck and gave herself over to the kiss. Learning how to do it all over again. She followed his rhythm, parted her lips, and when his tongue touched hers, she gasped. Then sighed as he went deep, luxuriating in the slick friction of it.

He moved his hands down her back to cup her rear, and she arched forward instinctively, reveling in his touch.

She didn't know if this counted as one kiss, because eventually he was kissing her neck and back to her mouth again, then down to the curve of her breast.

She gasped.

He lifted her up off the ground and placed her on the counter, stepping into the space between her legs and deepening the kiss.

She wrapped her legs around him, realizing she was pushing this further, faster than she had meant to. But it was instinct. It was needed. So many years of not being held, not being touched.

She wondered then if she had been acting out of any

sort of great restraint, or if she had been punishing herself. She had decided she didn't deserve this. This magical alchemy of human connection. The glory of a man's hands on her body.

Suddenly now she wanted it more than she could remember wanting anything.

More than she could remember wanting to breathe.

Nothing was simple about this. He was Buck Carson. Their son and daughter were dating. Their connection was loaded. Like a stick of dynamite. But then, so was this. This need.

She gave back everything he was giving. He growled, and when his hands moved to cup her breasts, a sudden rush of reality crowded in.

"Wait," she said.

"What?" he asked, his voice deep, his words slurred.

"We can't. Colton and Lily are dating. We are business partners, there is so much… There is so much stuff."

He took a step away, letting out a deep breath. Then he looked up at the ceiling.

"What are you doing?"

"Trying to recite the alphabet backward."

Her eyes dropped to the front of his jeans. "Oh," she said.

He winced. "Yeah."

"I… I'm sorry. I haven't been with anybody in a long time."

"It's been a fair amount of time for me too."

"Seventeen years?"

He had to laugh. "No. But still. A while." He let out a slow breath. "And even if it had been yesterday, it wouldn't matter. Because you're you. And I have been attracted to you since the day you showed up practically towing Colton by the ear. It's you. It's not the celibacy or the fact that it's forbidden or anything like that. It's just you."

She'd had no idea how much she needed to hear something like that until he'd said it.

To not just feel desired, but special.

It had been a long time since she had felt anything like that, too. Maybe she never had.

"This is a really bad idea," she said. "I mean, not the one kiss. That was wonderful. But anything else…"

He looked at her, and there was fire in his eyes.

"Don't look at me like that," she said.

"I believe I just said that to you, and look at where we ended up."

"Definitely not preparing dinner." She took a deep breath. "Do you know why I've been celibate since before I had Lily?"

"I could take a few wild guesses."

"It felt easy in some ways, to not have her dad around. I felt like I was blessed with a lack of complication. That meant she was my daughter and I got to raise her on my terms. The idea of bringing random men into the life I so carefully made for her, for me, I couldn't bear it." She decided not to mention any of her errant thoughts about the possibility of it being a punishment. Like she had cut herself off for being overindulgent. "And she's leaving in just a few months."

"I understand that. But you aren't with her all the time."

"Aren't you listening? I don't like complicated. Maybe

because I had my fill of complicated a long time ago. You have to understand that."

He nodded slowly. "I guess maybe I should. But I was never trying to make my life simple. I think I don't know anything *but* complicated. I mean, I just adopted three teenage boys, so obviously simple is not my wheelhouse."

She laughed. "I get that. But…"

"Yeah. There's a lot of people who could get hurt."

She nodded. "Yes. There is."

"The thing is, nobody will get hurt if nobody knows."

She hadn't even considered that. "What would that even look like? Do you mean… If we just…"

"It's entirely possible to keep things only physical."

"Well, that's the thing. Our lives are kind of enmeshed. And that makes it difficult to be only physical."

"Friends with benefits. I hear that works."

Wow. That was an incredibly tempting offer. But she had to wonder…much like when she was on the cusp of that same feeling she'd had when he had first offered to help her with her business.

Wondering if she was just doing moral gymnastics because really, she wanted to take him up on the offer.

Everything felt too high stakes.

That was the bottom line. She couldn't go playing around with her daughter's first relationship. With her last few months of her daughter being at home.

Are you still making excuses?

She didn't think so. But when she looked at him, her heart beat faster, and that reminded her of scarier times.

More exciting times.

But scary, all the same.

"The kids will be back soon." She let out a long, slow breath. "Thank you for… That was actually the first time I've done anything like that for a long time. As you know. And it was really, really nice."

"And the sky didn't cave in," he said.

"No."

She had so many questions. About how he had conducted his life for these past two decades.

Not the stuff she knew—where he had lived, the work he had done. She wanted to know about his sex life. About his relationships. Because she was standing on the edge of those things, and she wished she could understand what made him think he could just be her friend with benefits. She also knew that talking about it was dangerous. That they needed to get back on less precarious footing.

So she didn't ask him. She just decided to finish cooking the chicken. And by the time the kids got home, she could only hope they didn't look like they had been caught with their hands in the cookie jar. She sort of felt like she had been, even though time had lapsed since they'd given in to that kiss.

Their eyes met across the table, and she decided, within herself, that whatever happened, they were going to be friends. And that was it. That was going to be the solid foundation by which they built everything. Their business… And everything.

After they'd driven home, she looked over at Lily. "Did you have a good time?"

"Yeah. I had a great time. Colton's brothers are really cute."

"They're not that much younger than you."

"No, but they seem like it. I don't know. They're nice kids."

It was funny to hear Lily talk about a fifteen-year-old and a sixteen-year-old that way. She supposed it reflected how mature her daughter felt at this point in time. How ready she was to be seen as an adult. Yes. Her life really was changing.

And Marigold thought about that kiss…

No. She was resolved.

And yet, friends with benefits…

She ached. She really did. Because what if they could do that? What if they could have a relationship nobody knew about but them? One that didn't complicate things. One that just eased both of their needs a little bit.

You would never let yourself have something that nice.

That very disturbing thought echoed in her head for the whole rest of the evening.

Chapter Ten

Buck's head was still reeling from that kiss. Hell, his whole body was on high alert. He hadn't slept a wink. He had ended up taking a cold shower at one in the morning to try and spite his overactive hormones. It really was a hell of a thing. And he was supposed to see her today on a matter of business.

Yet nothing inside of him felt ready to discuss business. What he wanted to do was take her in his arms again. Kiss her senseless.

How had that happened?

But he hadn't been lying when he had told her it was about her. About how much she made him feel.

About how much he wanted her.

It had been like that from the moment she had first appeared on his doorstep. And maybe that was the real reason he had kept her close. Maybe he was full of shit. Maybe it had never been about trying to follow his gut instinct. Maybe it had always been about wanting her. Maybe atonement was just an excuse.

That made him feel guilty.

And he would be lying if he said he didn't like the guilt. It was his comfort zone.

Right about now, he felt like Marigold's lips were his comfort zone. Where everything was that he had ever wanted.

He wanted to kiss her again, strip her bare—

"You passed the school driveway, Buck," Reggie said.

"Dammit," he said.

Colton laughed.

"Well, you're going to get your driver's license, and then they're going to be your responsibility," he said.

"I never said I didn't want my license," Colton said. "I think you don't want me to get it."

Well. Colton wasn't entirely far off. Driving was a fact of life. It wasn't like he had a long-standing hang-up. And he had been fine yesterday when Lily was driving the boys. Alcohol had played a factor in the accident that had taken his friends' lives. That aspect wasn't something that could be ignored. But…

As much as Colton was responsible—and he had become responsible in these last couple of years with a little bit of guidance, and having the chance to not live in chaos—Buck knew how stupid teenage boys could be. In a pretty damned haunting way.

"I do want you to get your license. It'll make my life easier. But there are going to be so many ground rules."

"I know, I know."

Buck turned around in an auto parts parking lot and headed back toward the school. He summarily booted the boys out of the truck and then headed on down the road toward Marigold's place.

He hadn't been to her house yet.

He thought it was strange that he was looking forward

to it. To seeing what sort of life she had built for herself and Lily. He knew it would be warm. Inviting. Well ordered. Because Marigold herself was all those things.

When he pulled up to the house, this theory was proven to be true. It was small, but well ordered, with a neat garden area in the front, and a porch with a rocking chair and a wreath on the door.

When she had said that she'd set out to make an entirely complete life for herself and Lily without Lily's father, he hadn't entirely known what that meant. But he got it now.

She was self-contained. Entirely happy without a man. Well. Almost.

He thought again about that kiss. It had been absolutely incendiary.

Maybe they could…

Maybe.

Because he'd never had a sexual entanglement that got emotional. And she clearly didn't need anything emotional from him. That was the perfect arrangement as far as he was concerned. A woman who didn't need anything from him but physical pleasure. Because he could do that. He could give that.

As part of being a marked man, a man who had to go through life atoning, he had made it his business to be the absolute best lover possible. He needed the women he had sex with to come twice before he got close to the peak of pleasure. It was part of putting more out in the world than he took away.

He wanted to make Marigold come even more times than that.

He gritted his teeth and got out of his truck, made his way toward that cute, neat front door.

School carnivals, a passel of teenagers, meeting her parents, this adorable house. All of it stood in stark contrast to the riotous, sexual thoughts making their way through his head.

It was like the deepest, darkest part of himself was rising to the surface and making waves that didn't belong in a beautiful, placid lake.

Wholesome.

That described so many of the interactions they'd had since he'd come back to town.

And then he'd kissed her.

Which had been anything but wholesome.

And what he wanted now was anything but wholesome.

He was about to knock when the door opened. There she was, her red hair wild about her face. Her eyes wide.

"Dammit," he said.

She stepped back, and he stepped in, closed the door firmly behind her and pulled her into his arms. He was kissing her before she could say anything. And she melted against him, kissing him back with a ferocity that didn't even surprise him, because the wild look in her eye when he had approached her, said everything he needed to know.

He could read her. It was so goddamned annoying. It would be better if he hadn't known. If he didn't see the sensual need in her eyes when he looked at her. But he did. Because it was the same need that echoed inside of him.

Because, for some reason, they felt that for each other

on the same level. Because for some reason they felt... inevitable.

Was this it?

That day she had come to his door with Colton—was it all leading to this?

Well, his dick would like to think so. But that seemed... Well, it didn't really seem like atonement. Because it felt a hell of a lot like pleasing himself.

He would put her needs first. He would put *her* first.

She wrapped her arms around his neck, her fingers pushing up through his hair, cradling the back of his head, moving down his back, and he did the same to her, feeling those wild curls, her petite frame, moving his hands all the way down to the delicious curve of her ass.

She was so gorgeous.

She was unlike any woman he had ever wanted before. Simply because she was her. Maybe because he knew her.

Maybe because he cared.

It wasn't about a generic desire to score points with the universe, but about wanting to see her experience pleasure at his hands.

This was an entirely different experience to any he'd ever known.

Friends with benefits?

Yeah. That was what it would have to be. Because they were business partners. Because of the kids. Because no one could ever know that this had happened, least of all Colton and Lily.

Shit. That would make him the worst dad in the entire world. Scamming on his son's girlfriend's mother.

The absolute worst. And Colton would have every right to disown him. Or punch him.

So no one would ever know.

No one would ever have to know.

That fueled him now. Made this feel darker, more glorious. Surrounded by her adorable house with gorgeous knickknacks. She had a shelf full of birds wearing scarves. And he wanted to strip her clothes off and see every inch of her bare skin. Right in front of those birds.

Maybe that was the whole point of it. That they had thrown themselves into this other reality. One where they tried to be acceptable. One where they tried to be neat. One where they tried to be better than they were. Better than their darkest, wildest impulses—but neither of them were. Because maybe no person was. And maybe they weren't two different things, or two different kinds of people. Maybe everyone had this inside of them.

They had suppressed it. They both had. She sure as hell had. But it was still there.

And it was pretty damned glorious.

"I want you," he growled against her mouth.

"Yes," she breathed.

"God help me," he said.

He lifted her up off the ground, her legs wrapped around his waist as he started to carry her up the stairs.

"You know where my bedroom is," she said.

"I'll figure it out."

He was resourceful that way.

"I don't have condoms," she said.

Everything stopped for a moment.

"I have one," he said.

Just one. One he always carried in his wallet for emergencies, even though it wasn't like one-night stands broke out without careful planning on his part. And there hadn't been one since he had adopted the boys. But he made sure to religiously replace that one condom, so it never went past its expiration date and didn't spend too long being exposed to the elements or anything like that.

He was safe.

"Oh," she said.

"It's a safety measure," he said. "I wasn't planning this. It's just…"

"Right," she said.

"Are you judging me?"

"No. I'm glad."

"Good," he said.

He claimed her mouth again, marveling at the fact that he could be thirty-eight years old and this on edge. That he could be this intent on having her.

That he could want her so very much.

He felt like a teenager. They were even having discussions about condoms.

He wanted her so much.

He brought her into the bedroom. He was certain it was hers. And because she didn't protest, he knew he was right. It was neat as a pin, like everything else in the house, her bedspread an adorable gingham. He was going to strip her naked on that gingham and do unspeakable things to her.

He set her down at the center of the mattress and stepped away from her, stripping his shirt up over his head.

Her eyes went wide. "Damn," she said.

"Thank you. That's awfully kind."

"It's hardly kind. A simple damn doesn't do justice to those muscles. I feel spoiled."

"Not as spoiled as I feel. Believe me. Because you are… I don't have any gentlemanly words for it, Marigold. I just know that I want you. More than anything. I can't explain it. Because it's something that goes beyond words."

"I don't need words. You can just show me."

So he did. He stripped off his jeans, his boots and socks, everything, and let her see how hard he was for her. How much he wanted her. Her eyes kept getting rounder and rounder.

"It's been a really long time," she said.

"I'll be careful," he said.

"Thank you," she responded.

He moved over the top of her, kissed her neck, slowly, very slowly, stripped the sweater from her body and unclipped her bra. She was as beautiful as he had imagined she would be. Even more so. Because he hadn't been able to imagine the exact ripe colors, the perfect softness and roundness.

And now he did. He cupped her breast, slid his thumb over her nipple. Watched her arch against his touch. Watched as her face contorted with pleasure. She was so beautiful.

So beautiful.

He growled, kissing her neck, kissing down to the plump curve of her breasts, taking one nipple into his mouth and sucking hard.

Then he moved down the rest of her body, gripping

the waistband of her skirt and tugging it down her thighs, taking her underwear with it.

She arched against him, and he held her down against the mattress, parting her legs for him so he could taste all that glory between them.

She was wet for him, and she tasted like heaven.

He gripped her so tight, she couldn't pull away from him. She was whimpering, crying out, and he could feel her whole body draw tight like a bow as she got closer and closer to the peak.

"Yes," he growled against her. "Come for me."

He felt her shatter against his mouth, and he kept on going, pushing two fingers inside of her as he did, as she unraveled completely. There on that sweet little bedspread.

And she was still the responsible, well-ordered mother of a teenager, but her hair was spread out on the pillow like a ring of fire, and her lips were swollen, her cheeks pink with desire.

He was still a man on a mission to be redeemed, a man with a black mark in his past so profound he didn't think he could ever erase it. A man trying to do right by three teenage boys, a man whose head was filled with plans for a new ranch and plans for the future of the kids he had just taken on.

But he was also wholly here with her. And she was with him.

They were all the things, all at once.

His chest burned with it all.

He moved up her body, kissing a trail along her soft skin, before kissing her mouth, putting his hand between her legs and wringing another climax out of her.

Then, only then, did he reach for his wallet.

"Are you ready?"

"Yes," she whispered.

"Good," he growled.

He tore open the condom and rolled it over his length, before positioning himself at the entrance to her body. Then he tested her readiness.

"I'm good," she said.

She gasped as he filled her, and it was tight. But she seemed to want it. Seemed to glory in it. Just as he did. She wrapped her legs around his waist and clung to his shoulders as he began to move.

It was like a baptism. By fire, by grace, by Marigold, and he couldn't get enough.

Because it was everything, and so was she.

He held on to his own climax as long as he could, gritting his teeth, biting the inside of his cheek to create enough pain that he wouldn't lose it completely.

And then finally, finally, she shuddered out another climax, and he embraced his own.

He growled out her name as he let the pleasure take him, and then everything was still. Quiet.

She let out a long, heavy sigh.

"Oh, I feel so much better," she said.

And then she laughed.

He withdrew from her, lying on his side. "Me too. But I'm glad that it's mutual."

"Was that really stupid?"

"I don't feel stupid. I feel fucking amazing."

"Me too," she said. "I don't want to… This doesn't have to be dramatic. I just… I haven't been with anybody in a long time, and I don't want to get married. I don't even want to have a boyfriend. I don't want to share my house with a man."

"Great," he said. And he couldn't quite pinpoint why an element of what she said made him feel a little dissatisfied.

"I just want… I want this. This that just happened. I like you. I know you came here to work with me. And we can do that. Now. We can talk about business. And then we can get dressed and go to our respective houses. Maybe we can even have dinner with the kids again. But they don't need to know."

She echoed every thought he had about this. It seemed perfect, and it seemed completely logical.

He loved it.

What wasn't to love?

"Friends with benefits," he said.

"Yes," she said. "Friends with benefits. I think it's a great idea."

"Fantastic," he said.

"Yes," she agreed.

"All right. So let's go over what we need to go over about the business."

"I'll go get my binder."

He chuckled, and lay back in the bed. Wholesome. Almost.

Everything was going to work out fine. They both knew what they wanted, and what they wanted was essentially the same thing. There was absolutely nothing that could go wrong here.

Absolutely nothing.

* * *

Marigold was trying to chop celery, but she kept spacing out.

And when Lily came home, Marigold startled at the sound of the slamming door, like she hadn't been expecting it. Because she had forgotten where she was. She might have forgotten who she was. The afternoon felt like a complete and total fever dream.

He'd come to her house, they'd had sex, and then they had lain in bed and pored over her planner like they weren't naked, and then they had ended up making out, and he had to run to the store to buy a box of condoms. Which they had made good use of.

They had made love and worked on their plans off and on for the whole day, until it was time for him to go and get his kids from school.

And she felt… Changed. Which wasn't how friends with benefits was supposed to go, she was sure. But she didn't know if there was a woman alive who could keep her head on straight when she was being thoroughly… rustled by Buck Carson.

She paused for a long moment.

Buck Carson. He was the object of so many complex emotions in her life.

This friends-with-benefits situation felt like acting out against the past. Against the pain she had once felt, against things that had been taken away from her.

And maybe it was acting out.

Yet, he had proven he was safe.

They wanted the same things. He was investing in her business. They had a connection that transcended sex, but sex was an equally strong connection. And neither of them wanted it to be romantic. Today hadn't been romantic.

She paused again.

"Mom?"

She snapped back to reality for the second time in just a few moments. She had forgotten that her first jolt was the door closing, which meant Lily was home.

"I'm in here," she said.

"I wanted to go to Colton's house for dinner tonight?"

"Sure," she said.

"You don't have to come," Lily said.

And that made Marigold feel sort of hurt. Also, she wanted to see Buck. Which was silly.

She tried to smile. "Okay. I won't. That's fine."

"Are you okay?" Lily asked as she made her way over to the fridge, opened it and took out a sparkling water. She popped the top on the can and stared at Marigold suspiciously.

"I'm very okay," she said.

"Good. Glad to hear it."

"Well. I hope you enjoy dinner at Colton's. Did you talk to Buck about it?"

"I don't know. Colton did."

As if on cue, Marigold's phone rang. Buck's name appeared on the screen, and her heart tried to race up her esophagus and out of her mouth.

"Hi," she said, answering the phone almost immediately. Lily was staring at her.

"Hey," he said, his voice soft as velvet, like hands against her skin. She shivered. She looked at Lily out of the side of her eye and then studied the celery she was chopping. "Lily tells me she wants to come to your place for dinner?"

"Yeah. I know I have those great prepared meals but I was thinking of grabbing a pizza for the kids to throw in the oven, and maybe you and I could go have dinner somewhere else so we aren't overrun by teenagers."

"Yeah. That sounds good."

"I'll come get you after Lily arrives at my place."

"Okay. See you then."

"What was that?" Lily asked.

"Oh, Buck just thought maybe it would be more fun if you guys were at the house by yourselves. I mean, with Reggie and Marcus, obviously. We aren't leaving you in the house alone."

"Oh," Lily said.

"He and I are going to go have dinner somewhere else. It's not a date."

She felt her face getting pink.

"Mom," Lily said. "You're blushing."

"I don't think I am," she said.

"You are literally bright red."

"I am not. Because there's nothing… I am just going to dinner with him so you can have some time with Colton."

"I don't know. I think you're weird about him."

"Yeah, I'm a little weird about him, because we have a strange…connection. Okay? We have a strange connection, and I don't really know what to do about it. I'm still figuring it out. Grandma and Grandpa were wonderful when they met him, and when I explained that you were dating Colton, and that he was helping with my business, but there's just a lot of history there."

"Did you ever date him?"

"No. I was thirteen, remember? I did not date him."

"Did you like him?"

"I told you that I thought he was handsome. But that's not the same thing as having a crush."

"Do you like him now?"

"I'm thirty-three years old," Marigold said. "I don't have crushes."

"You would be allowed to have crushes," Lily said. "I wouldn't care if you did date. I mean, not Colton's dad, but I wouldn't mind if you dated."

"I never wanted to do that," Marigold said. "Because I like our life the way that it is."

"But I'm leaving soon," said Lily.

"Yes. You are."

Lily frowned. "I mean… I like Colton. A lot. And he makes me feel things…" It was Lily's turn to turn pink. "It's really bad timing, isn't it?"

Marigold thought about the afternoon she had spent in bed with Buck. "I don't know. Maybe. Lily, I was worried about you getting hurt. I still am. And of course I'm worried about safety and responsibility and pregnancy and all that kind of stuff, but the truth of the matter is, Colton seems like a really good kid. And if he's good to you, it doesn't matter if it's forever or not. Maybe what he's teaching you is what a good boyfriend looks like. So that when you're lonely and away at college, and you like somebody, you don't accept less than what you feel right now."

Lily looked sad. "Maybe."

Marigold wondered if it was the same for herself. The sex that she and Buck had today had been transformative. Better than any she'd ever had, but of course that was the difference between having sex with teenage boys and having sex with a thirty-eight-year-old man who knew what the hell he was doing.

There had been such a gap in her experience—this was a teachable moment. Because Lily was right. Things were changing, and she was leaving. So that meant... It meant that Marigold should figure out what her future could look like. Maybe someday she would want a relationship. Maybe someday she would want to fall in love and get married. That would be... Well, it wasn't something on the horizon just yet.

She couldn't see past Buck being in her bed.

But maybe today was a learning experience. She would never settle for less than what she had felt in his arms. Because after knowing that existed, why would she?

She would never settle less for less than the insanity that had gripped them both when he had come to the door.

Why would she?

"Well, have fun at your dinner," Lily said.

"You too," she said.

And she felt just a little, tiny bit guilty that she wasn't being totally honest with her daughter, but there was no point to that sort of honesty. Lily didn't need to know that Marigold was having a sexual revolution.

If she was relieved that Lily left in time for Marigold

to get dressed up for said dinner, well, that was just the way of it.

By the time Buck got there, she was wearing a skin-tight dress and more makeup than she normally bothered with.

"Wow," he said. "You look beautiful."

He moved in and kissed her, and she didn't stop him. There was nobody here.

But as he deepened the kiss, she did press on his chest. "I'm hungry," she said.

"Me too," he growled, kissing her neck. She shivered.

"For pasta, not your penis."

He stepped back and barked a laugh. "Well, you have a way of putting a man in his place."

"I'm not trying to," she said. "I'd like to have dinner. Also, I'm too nervous to go having sex when the kids could just appear at any moment. Or at least, my kid could. When she's in school, great. But otherwise... We have to be careful."

"Yeah. I hear you."

"All right. Pasta."

"Just tell me where the best place is, and I'll take you there."

She picked her favorite restaurant, because she could, and the two of them got sparkling water, slightly to the chagrin of the waiter, she could see.

"You can have wine in front of me," Buck said. "I don't care."

"It's fine. I don't really drink much. It reminds me of... bad times. So, it's not really a relaxing escape for me."

"Fair enough."

"I wanted to thank you. For earlier today."

"No. The fact that it left you craving fettuccine instead of more of me doesn't exactly feel like a standing ovation."

She looked at him, feeling a shiver go down her spine. "I am craving you. But I'm also trying to be reasonable and rational."

"I think I might be incapable of that."

They ordered their entrée, and her stomach went tight. She really did wish this dinner would end with a kiss at her door. And her inviting him in.

She really did want him again.

"This is not a date," she said, looking resolutely at her menu.

"Of course not," he said.

They got their entrées and bread, and talked more about business, rather than steering the conversation back into the personal.

She looked down at his hand, the way it gripped the fork, and thought of the way he had touched her.

"So, you do have to tell me."

"I have to tell you something?"

"Yes. How has your…love life worked, exactly, for the last twenty years?"

"Oh, now you have questions."

"Yes. Because you are very, very good."

"Well. Thank you for the compliment. I… The honest truth is that when I was kind of off the rails there for a few years, it was a lot of sex. Mostly anonymous. I… I didn't care, about anything. I didn't want connections. I wanted oblivion."

"I relate to that."

"But after I started working at the camp, it wasn't that simple. Everything I did had to be a lot more...deliberate. I had leave every year, and every year I would take myself off somewhere faraway, to a tourist spot, find a woman and spend the week with her."

"Really?" She hated that woman. Whoever she was. Whoever she had been for all those years.

"Yeah. I mean, not for the last couple of years. I was deciding what to do as far as adopting the boys. I was realizing I needed to make some changes. Sex was more of an itch to scratch, I guess. Kind of like leisure time. It felt good and relaxing. I made it my mission to make it as good as possible for every woman I was with. And that made me enjoy it too."

"I see." Was that what she was? A sex vacation?

"No," he said, like he had read her mind. "It's not the same as you. You're different. Before, I never cared who the woman was. Blonde, brunette, slim, curvy. Didn't matter. Just somebody to be with for a little bit. It was the companionship, the touch—that was what mattered. With this, it's you. Because I haven't felt the need to go out and find anybody since I adopted the boys. And I didn't go out and find you. You found me."

"Right."

She held his gaze, and she felt something in her chest expand.

She didn't need to have feelings for him. She really didn't. It would be a mess. An absolute mess. And so would she.

"There's a big barbecue happening at my parents' house this weekend. Colton wants Lily to come."

Marigold closed her eyes. "I really do worry about them."

"Yeah. We all have to go through some heartbreak, don't we? And hey, maybe they won't. Maybe they'll go off to college, and it'll feel natural for them to let go of each other. Or maybe they won't. Maybe they'll find their way back to each other."

"Maybe." It felt so loaded, him saying that.

Was that what *they* were doing? Finding their way back to each other?

Don't romanticize it. Just friends with benefits.

"Anyway. I thought it would be nice if you could come. I could introduce you to my parents."

Her heart slammed against her breastbone. "Why?"

"Because," he said. "We're doing business together. Also, your daughter is dating my son."

"Yeah. Okay."

She wanted to go. That was the thing. And maybe it felt like a bit of a letdown that he didn't want to introduce her to his parents because she was special, or whatever else it could've been.

But, it also didn't feel like a letdown. It didn't.

Because she just wanted to spend time with him. And the reason didn't much matter.

They finished up their dinner and walked alongside each other back to the truck. It felt hideously awkward to not hold his hand. They had never held hands before, so she couldn't fully explain why it would feel awkward, but it did.

She let out a long, slow breath, as she settled into the passenger seat and let him drive her back to her house.

He walked her up to the front door, and she felt a tense pause inside of her. Her breath hitched; her heart lifted. Right then, she heard the sound of tires on the driveway. Lily pulled up alongside Buck's truck, and Marigold froze.

"I guess that's good night," she said.

"Guess it is," he said.

He waved, like they hadn't just been about to kiss. "See you this weekend, at least."

"Yeah. See you then."

He started to walk back to the truck and greeted Lily as she headed toward Marigold.

"Great timing," Marigold said, smiling.

"Yeah."

"Did you have fun?"

"I had a great time. He invited me to come out to his grandparents' house this weekend."

"Well, I hope you don't think it's weird, but I got an invitation also."

"It's not weird."

"Great. That sounds just great."

Chapter Eleven

Buck kept scanning the pandemonium of the yard, waiting to see if she was going to arrive. It was an unseasonably warm September, and they had set up tables outside for their barbecue dinner. His brothers were talking and laughing, and occasionally, even Boone almost smiled at him.

There were kids. So many kids. Toddlers and teenagers scampering around the place.

But he was waiting for Marigold to get there. And suddenly, her car rounded the corner, and both him and Colton stood up. Wow. He was acting like a teenager. Because he looked just like his son.

"Lily's here," he said.

"Yeah," Buck said, rubbing his chest. He had missed Marigold so much over the last few days. All he had wanted was to go to her house, get in bed with her. Take them both to the places they'd gone when they'd made love that afternoon.

He needed her again. So badly, it made his jaw ache.

But there just hadn't been a chance. Yeah, the kids were in school all day, but they both had inconvenient things like jobs.

He was getting the logistics worked out for the ranch. And the build for her new facility. And she was continuing to do the job she had already been doing.

When Marigold got out of the car, he couldn't say it was only his body that was affected by the sight of her. It was everything. She made his heart beat faster; she made everything in him feel like it was on red alert. That woman. Good God, that woman.

Colton was halfway to them before they finished getting out of the car entirely. He didn't have any of the self-possession that Buck did. Buck knew how to play it cool. Buck...was walking toward them too, and he hadn't even fully realized it.

"Can I help carry anything?" Buck asked, as Marigold got out and opened up the back of the car, taking out a basket.

"If you really want to," she said.

"I live to serve."

Her cheeks turned pink, and he knew exactly what she was thinking of.

"You know I do," he said.

She elbowed him in the stomach. And he laughed.

Then realized that Colton and Lily were watching them.

"You know, she *is* my best friend's younger sister," he said. Like that explained the familiarity. And not that he'd hooked up with her.

It felt good to say it like that. Like she was still Jason's sister, instead of it just being in the past. And Jason was still his friend. Like he had never lost the right to call him that.

They walked back over to where his family was, and he made introductions: Lily as Colton's friend, and Marigold as Lily's mother and his business partner. He had already told his family all about them, and about the fact that he was investing in the business.

Obviously, he had not told them that she was his friend with benefits. Because that was just between them.

Marigold had brought a basket filled with rolls and a couple of different cakes to put on the table for dessert. They paired beautifully with the barbecued brisket, hamburgers and sausages that his father had grilled up.

And even though Buck had been back now for a little while and had experienced family gatherings like this before, this felt different. Significant. Complete in a way that nothing else had.

He looked to his right, at Marigold, and wondered how much of it had to do with her.

Then he looked back at his food.

His sisters-in-law took to Marigold immediately and spent the whole dinner talking her ear off, while Lily was easily chatting to Boone's stepdaughters, who he intuited she already knew from school.

He stood up to go get another helping of food and just about ran into Boone at the serving table.

"Hey," he said.

"Hey."

He nearly got a smile out of his brother.

"Marigold is nice," Boone commented.

"Yeah," Buck said, frowning. "She is."

"You seem to like her quite a bit."

"What's not to like? Anyway, she's my business partner, and of course Colton is dating Lily." How many times had he said this exact thing to different people over the course of them working together, even in conversations with her? An easy, well tread justification for why they spent time together. For why he liked her.

It was the damnedest thing.

"Seems like you've been settling in pretty well," Boone said.

"Yeah. I guess. And the bruise on my face is healing."

"Sorry about that," Boone said, clearing his throat. "My wife informed me that it wasn't an appropriate way to greet my brother."

"I don't know about that. You had your feelings. You were entitled to them. I'm not going to pretend that my behavior in the past was…honorable."

He had talked to all his brothers quite a bit since he had come back. But Boone least of all. And they hadn't addressed the way they had greeted each other. And he wasn't sure—was that what was happening now? Maybe there was just enough distance between that moment and this one. Or maybe somehow the difference had to do with Marigold. He couldn't quite figure out how, but he felt different because she was here.

And maybe Boone could sense that.

"I felt like you left everything to me," Boone said. "All the grief, all the responsibility. Everything. And I… Believe me when I tell you, a certain part of me gets off on that shit. I'm a champion martyr, Buck. I was in love with my best friend's wife for over a decade." He looked across the space, at Wendy, who was currently talking to Marigold. "I wanted her, and I couldn't have her. And everything in my life felt like a struggle. I think I wanted it to feel like one. But you were my bad object. The person I blamed all of it on. Well, not Wendy being married to somebody else, but all the other stuff. I've dealt with a lot of things over the last few years. I have Wendy now. But apparently, I was still carrying around a little resentment toward you."

This felt comfortable. Being resented. Buck kind of wanted to thank his brother for it.

"Hey. I don't blame you. What I did back then was selfish. And at the time, I really did believe you were all better off without me here. It's that kind of depressive thought that sends you down really dark roads. And I went down a pretty dark road. But when the fog finally cleared, I realized how selfish it had been. At that point, I'd been gone so long I didn't know how to come back. That was selfish too. But part of me really was afraid I was going to disrupt whatever you all had put back together in my absence. I didn't want to do that. I threw myself into my work, but it was when I adopted those boys that I really understood… Family is important. It makes a huge difference to these boys and…"

"You can say it makes a difference to you," Boone said.

"Of course it does."

"Are you glad you're back?"

He felt like he was being jabbed in the stomach with a red-hot poker. "Yes. Of course I am. I missed you."

Emotion tightened his throat. He really didn't like how close to the surface all his feelings were now that he was home. Now that he had kids. Now that he was…

trying to be healed. Whatever all of it was...it was creating a damned difficult way to be.

Maybe that was part of why he had avoided coming home for so many years. Maybe that was why he had stayed away. Because somehow he had known that, if he came back here, he was going to feel things. Everything. And yes, he had done a lot of work on himself, but he had also spent a lot of time living a life that allowed him to control what people knew about him, what he talked about and when and what he allowed as far as emotional closeness.

Everything was more volatile here. Everything had been more volatile since he had adopted Reggie, Marcus and Colton. Because there was no control when it came to caring for kids.

They were mean to you, they were wonderful to you, and you loved them all the same. They jerked you around, endlessly. They made you feel like you would cut off a limb to be there for them. To do whatever they needed.

The experience had left him raw and vulnerable, frankly, and coming home had only made it worse.

He'd missed his family.

And he grieved the loss of those years. That was perhaps the hardest part.

Because the loss was his fault. It had been his choice.

And that was something that transcended the guilt he was comfortable with. It overrode the self-flagellation that made him feel most at ease.

"I missed you. And more than that, I wish like hell I hadn't stayed gone for as long as I did. I regret that. I missed so much of your life. So much of Callie's. So much of everybody's. I'd like to say I regret most that I left you with all that responsibility, but hell, I regret the most that we weren't close. That we have a relationship to rebuild now, because I shattered it. Because I didn't just..." He closed his eyes. "I lost my friends. And I felt helpless and responsible for that. But maybe feeling responsible was a way to find some place for all that anger to go. Because it's just such a helpless, infuriating feeling. Losing people you care about like that. I hated it. I still do. And I hate this. I hate that the end result of everything that happened was losing time with my family, even if it was my own choice. When I know how short and fragile everything is."

"Yeah," Boone said, looking down. "I mean, I get that. I'm mad at you about that. And I still feel some resentment sometimes toward... Wendy's ex, I guess. For all the years I couldn't have her, because he was wasting her time. But mostly... When you get something good, you kinda gotta just take it. I have Wendy now, so what's the point of being angry about all the years I didn't have her? What's the point of being full of resentment? I have what I want."

"I don't quite follow."

"You made your choice. I can't even say it was a bad one. Because who knows what would've happened to you, who knows if you could have healed the way you did, if you hadn't made the choice. You wouldn't have ever met your boys. That you don't regret, do you?"

"No," he said. "Of course not."

"Exactly. So... Yeah, parts of this were hard. And there

are always going to be things to regret. But those were the decisions you made. So here we are, all together now."

"Yeah. I guess we are."

"You like her," he said, gesturing toward Marigold.

"I... Of course I do. She's my friend. She's Jason's sister. There's a lot of baggage there."

Except that felt like the smallest piece of what they were. They understood each other. Because they had both been through difficult things. It was more bonding than baggage, and not in a traumatic way. It was something he would never be able to explain to another person. He wasn't sure he would ever fully be able to articulate it to himself.

"No. Come on. You know what I mean. You're into her."

Buck flashed back to kissing her. "Yeah," he said. "I am."

Because there was no point lying when he was sure his desire for her was written all over his face. When he was sure his brother knew him better than that.

In spite of the distance. In spite of the time they had spent apart.

"What are you going to do about it?"

"Are you asking about my sex life?"

"No. I don't give a shit if you're sleeping with her or not. What I want to know is—are you going to let yourself have her? I'm not talking about physical stuff."

Boone was talking about love.

And it was all fine and good for his brother to believe in that sort of thing. For himself.

But Buck... He couldn't see a way forward with love.

"I'm just… Whatever we can have, for as long as we can have it, that's what I'm here for," he said.

"Because?"

"The kids are dating," he said.

"Right. So you're going to give precedence to a couple of teenagers' first relationship over what could be the real thing?"

"No. I… That isn't it. There's no way to say this without sounding like a vampire in a teen movie. Okay? But there are just some things that can't be fixed. There are some scars that leave you too…messed up to move on from."

"Yeah. You're right. You do sound like a vampire in a teen movie. Ridiculous. The thing is, Buck, it's your life. I'm not really sure why you'd choose to live in hell when you're alive and could choose something different."

He grimaced. "It is not that simple."

"Well. I'm glad you're home. How about that? And someday, I hope all of you comes home."

"What does that even mean?"

"It means as long as you keep part of yourself hidden away, you're not really here. You're not really living. Enjoy your food."

And Boone walked away, leaving Buck standing there wishing his brother had just punched him in the face instead.

Chapter Twelve

The next few weeks passed in a level of bliss Marigold wasn't used to. She spent time with Lily, made plans for her new business expansion, did her job and always found time to make love with Buck while Lily was at school. And it was in those times, those stolen hours, that a part of herself began to grow again. A part that had been stunted, reviving itself in a way that she hadn't imagined was possible.

She felt lighter. She felt more herself. In touch with all the parts of herself, not just the part that was Lily's mom. Not just the part that was a businesswoman or a responsible citizen of Lone Rock. She was a woman. And in Buck's arms, she felt like one. Really. Truly. Wonderfully.

And when Lily came home saying they needed chaperones for the fall festival dance, Marigold felt honored. That her daughter wasn't embarrassed by her and actually wanted her to attend a school function. That felt amazing. Really and truly wonderful.

So she agreed. And the next day, when she was lying in bed with Buck, she found out that Colton had asked him to chaperone as well. Which meant they were the two primary chaperones of the fall festival dance.

"That's hilarious," he said, laying his head back against the pillow, naked and proud and glorious.

"Why?"

"Because it's so public, while we're sneaking around. We are not complying with the rules."

"We are also not teenagers," she said, swatting him on his broad chest. He really had the best chest. Hairy and muscular and yum.

"Right, right. Can't wait to stand there next to you, trying to be good and proper."

The idea sent a thrill through her.

"Yes. And we will be."

"Maybe I should bring you a corsage."

He rolled over so he was above her, and she arched up and bit his lower lip. "Maybe you should."

So when he did, she shouldn't have been surprised. They drove separately and met outside the school gym. He was dressed in a suit, and the sight made her heart drop into her feet. She was in a sparkly dress that went down to her knees, trying to look fancy, but not like she was trying to look young. Even though she was.

"Your corsage, madam."

"You're ridiculous," she said.

"Am I? Or am I romantic?"

She wasn't supposed to want him to be romantic. But it made her heart sing. It made everything inside of her lift.

She really did kind of want the romance.

And she didn't know what to do about that.

They walked into the gym together, and she had the corsage firmly on her wrist. Bright pink roses and baby's breath. She tried to imagine him actually going into a flower store and buying this, but he must've done it.

Colton had brought one for Lily. And she was almost entirely certain that Buck had insisted. She wasn't really sure if kids gave each other that kind of thing these days generally. But clearly Buck thought it was important.

"Wow," she said, surveying the scene that could best be described as teen hormones crashing into teen emotions. In other words, a lot of a lot.

"I don't miss being a teenager," he said.

Which was somewhat ironic, all things considered.

"Yeah. Not really."

"Even Marcus has a date," he said.

"He does?"

"Yeah. He was excited about it."

"That's cute."

"Sure. Cute. Terrifying. What was I thinking getting into kids at this level? Having to worry about sex and pregnancy and all that kind of stuff."

She barked a laugh. "I don't actually know. You're an idiot. Or a glutton for punishment."

"Do we have to worry about Colton and Lily sneaking off tonight?"

"No," she said. "She's actually meeting up with a group of her girlfriends afterward, and I have confirmed this with their mothers. Because obviously I'm well acquainted with subterfuge. It's one thing to say you have plans, but I require proof. Also, I can track her cell phone. It is so much harder to be a kid these days."

"Damn," he said. "What a nightmare. Your parents can actually verify where you are?"

"Yes. I mean, you could leave your phone at a different location, but they won't do that."

"No," he said, chuckling. "They won't. Imagine being that connected all the time. What's the fun in that? We used to get to run absolutely feral."

"Yeah. Look where that got both of us."

He lifted a shoulder. "Yeah. Fair." He cleared his throat. "My brother said the other day that you can't do too much second-guessing of your decisions. I mean, not when the decisions lead you to good places. I regret that I left home. But I don't regret adopting the boys."

She nodded. "Yeah. I get that. I regret my behavior after my brother's death. I don't regret Lily. And that's always a really tricky thing as a parent. To try to make it very clear to her that I want her to have different… different paths available to her than I did, but to also make it very clear that I don't regret being her mother."

"I don't envy you that."

"She's a good kid. I just have to be thankful for that every day. This has actually been…probably the most difficult part of our relationship. Because she's trying to be a grown-up, and I don't want her to be. And at the same time… *I'm* trying to be a grown-up."

"Yeah. Well. Do you regret that you…have to do this? Be a parent?" He looked at her, his eyes intense.

She shook her head. "Of course I don't. I'm happy."

"Me too."

They spent a portion of the evening guarding the punch bowl and dealing with some mild bullying and a little bit of drama around two girls who came in the same dress. But otherwise, it was a pretty quiet evening. It was strange to be in the gym of the old school. She had been a different person back then. So had he.

And they had never been in it together. But here they were now.

The DJ onstage announced it was time to play some oldies, and she died inside when the first song was one that had been popular when she was in middle school.

"Did you hear that?" she asked. "We're oldies."

"Well, I'm offended," he said. "But I have always liked the song."

"It's a good song," she said, as the sweet vocals filtered through the gym. There was nothing to dislike about Sixpence None the Richer, and this one had been popular at school dances back then for a reason. The demand to be kissed was of course inside half the kids in this gym. Now and then.

A universal need.

"I think we should dance," he said. "All the better to supervise these kids."

"Really?"

"Yes," he said. "Really."

He held his hand out, and...she didn't have the strength to say no. Because she wanted to touch him. She wanted to be held by him. She wanted him.

He pulled her up against his body, and she felt herself melt. They moved in time to the music, their eyes locked together, and she could no longer deny that she wanted romance. Or, maybe she didn't want it. But they were having it. It was happening. This wasn't friends with benefits. It was something more. And she wasn't sure if she had the strength to turn away from that. Because it was so beautiful.

He twirled her and brought her back to him, holding her like she was precious.

And all the years that she had spent feeling like someone who was on probation—like someone who didn't deserve everything, like someone who had damaged herself, and her life, with her choices—melted away. Because he didn't look at her like she was a consolation prize. Like he cared for her, but it was a shame she had been such a slut when she was a teenager. Like she was great, but it was a shame she came with her daughter.

Never. Not once.

He looked at her like she was precious. And it made her heart just about burst.

"Marigold," he whispered, against her ear. "I think this might be a date."

She pulled back just slightly and met his gaze. "Yes. I think it is."

Chapter Thirteen

Lily looked over at her mother and Buck. The suspicion that her mom had feelings for him had been getting more and more certain every week. Her mom said no, but she blushed when his name came up. She looked giddy whenever he called.

Lily recognized it, because it was how she felt when she thought about Colton. But…the more she thought about it, the more she was sure her mom wasn't going to do anything with Buck if Colton and Lily were dating. Because her mom had always sacrificed for her.

Lily was leaving for college anyway. She was seventeen. You didn't marry the first guy you ever made out with. The first guy you ever let get to second base. You didn't marry that high school boyfriend, because you had to go do things.

Her mom hadn't gotten to go do things. And she was counting on Lily to go away and make something of herself. She had sacrificed so much in order for Lily to do that. And now her mom was getting ready to sacrifice wanting the first guy that she had even shown any interest in for Lily's whole life because Lily happened to be dating his son. A dead-end relationship that she knew wasn't even half of what Buck and her mom could have.

She put her hand to her chest and wished it didn't feel like her heart was breaking and moved away from Colton, stepping outside the gym, trying to catch her breath.

She was grateful she had made plans with her friends. Grateful she had decided she wasn't going to do something crazy like sleep with Colton tonight.

Her eyes filled with tears, and she shook her head, didn't let them fall.

Colton followed her out the door. "What's wrong?"

"You see them?"

"Who?"

"Buck and my mom."

"Oh yeah. They were dancing. So?"

"She likes him. I mean… They like each other."

"You think so?"

"Yes. And… I think there's something going on between them. I have thought that for a while."

"Why didn't you say anything?"

"Because I thought I was being crazy. And… I didn't want to mess this up. Us. But the truth is… We can't be together."

He looked like she had hit him, and she felt horrible. She felt like the villain.

Breaking her own heart.

Breaking his.

"My mom has sacrificed everything for me. Absolutely everything. And I think your dad would make her happy. But she keeps telling me that nothing is going on between them, and she so clearly… I think she's in love with him. And she doesn't want to disrupt my life or my relationship with you, because if they get married, then I'm going to be your stepsister."

"Why are you saying this?"

"Because it's true. It's real. It's happening." She took a deep breath. "We're going to college anyway. We are not going to end up together, Colton. This was… It was great. And you were great. There's nothing wrong with you. But it's not the right timing. And I think… I think because of them it's never going to be."

"You're really breaking up with me at a dance?"

"We don't have to be broken up until after the dance ends," she said. "We could have one more dance."

Colton's face looked stony. "No. We can't."

"Please don't be mad at me. Please. I like you. I care about you. And if our parents end up together then…"

He swallowed hard. And it was like he suddenly saw all the potential problems with all of this. They could never get to where they hated each other. Not if they were going to be stuck together as part of the same family, forever.

"Okay."

"Let's go back to the dance."

"Sure."

But there was something terribly blank in his eyes. And when he touched her hand, it didn't feel the same.

But that was a good thing. It wasn't supposed to.

She had made the right choice.

Because her mom wouldn't tell her what was going on, she'd had to try to figure it out and handle it herself. Try to fix it.

So she had done the best she could.

Chapter Fourteen

Lily was safely off with her friends before the dance ended, and Marigold breathed a sigh of relief when the last of the kids filtered out of the gym.

She felt Buck approach, and she turned to him. Her heart lifted, lodging itself in her throat. He was just so… handsome. She wished she could see a way out of how complex all of this was. But there were just so many reasons for what was between them to not be the big romance. And yet it was beginning to feel like one.

She wasn't sure what to do about that. The best thing to do would be to stop sleeping with him.

Yet she didn't want to. Hadn't she done enough behaving?

She didn't want to behave.

She had lost this part of herself for so many years, and she felt like she was awash in new tones of color ever since the two of them had first kissed.

She couldn't go back.

"I told the boys I was headed to my parents' house. That I wouldn't be home."

"Oh."

"I lied to them," he said.

"You lied to them?"

"Yes. Because I'm a very bad man. And I would like to spend the whole night showing you exactly how bad."

That was so cheesy. She shouldn't respond. But she was responding to that. Because she knew about his brand of wickedness, and it lit her skin on fire. It lit her soul on fire.

"Are they going to be all right by themselves?"

"Colton is seventeen. They'll be fine. I just have to drop them back at home."

"Okay," she said.

"I'll meet you back at your place."

She drove home, giddy and fizzy. They had a whole night to themselves. The luxury was almost impossible to take on board. Normally, they only had stolen moments during the day.

She wanted to sleep with him. Share the bed with him all night. Let him hold her.

She had ordered some sexier underwear, since this new situation had developed where she actually needed it. So she took the extra time she had to herself to get a bit of a performance together. She found a red lace bra and panties, and put a red silk robe over the top of it. It was a little a cliché, but men were simple. Buck was very simple, in the best way. She didn't worry about being sexy enough for him. He seemed happy no matter what she was wearing, or not wearing.

She had never really been in… She hesitated to call this a relationship. But it was the closest thing. The same man, a man she talked to, a man she knew, a man who had gotten to know her body as she had gotten to know his.

When he knocked at the door, she hopped in place a couple of times, trying to get the excitement more reasonably distributed through her body so she wasn't shaking when she went to kiss him.

She opened the door. There he was. Tall and perfect and beautiful. The exact delivery she had been hoping for.

"I can't believe we have all night."

He stepped inside and closed the door behind him. He didn't grab her and kiss her like he normally did. He took his time. Slowly, he put his hat on the peg by the door, took his jacket off and hung it there too.

And she was mostly naked.

It was erotic, if a little bit irritating, because it seemed imbalanced.

But instead of commenting on it, she just untied her robe and let it drop down to the floor.

And she could see that whatever he had been intent on doing, he'd lost his resolve completely when he saw her body.

His eyes were like a blue flame, and she felt his own need echo inside of her.

"Well I'll be damned," he said.

"Do you like it?"

She sounded more hopeful than she had intended to. A little more insecure. She wasn't normally insecure. But she did want to hear how much he appreciated her. It was like he had opened up a well of need inside her that she hadn't known previously existed.

It just felt really good to have someone who seemed to want to spend time with her. To have someone in her life who thought she was beautiful. To be touched, casually and intimately. Intensely and softly. He was everything, all the time.

And she was used to carrying all the things by herself.

But not with him. Not with him.

He closed the distance between them and began to kiss her, deep and hot, carnal.

It didn't even feel strange anymore. To be everything—every part of herself—that she contained. To know she could have this wildness and still be the Marigold she wanted to be. To know she could be sexual and sensual and responsible and good all at once.

She began to unbutton his shirt, pushed it off his shoulders. She kissed her way down his body and knelt down in front of him, slipping his belt through the buckle.

He grunted as she exposed his hardness to her touch and then, leaned forward and took him in her mouth.

She felt wicked. In the very best way.

Luxuriating in this, in him.

She wanted to give to him.

It was like a dam had broken inside of her. And she knew one thing above all else. She didn't have a place inside her that was angry at him. Not anymore. She didn't have a place inside her that grieved her brother separately from everything else in her life. Just like she didn't have a place inside her that was only good and responsible or a secret chamber where she kept her sexuality. She was everything. Everything all at once. And only when the intensity of those emotions, the certainty of what she felt, was free to flow, to be, could she see the truth.

Yes. Everything was complicated. Yes, *they* were complicated. But she was falling in love with him all the same. It could never be physical only. Because she had too many feelings for him.

She had made him her bad object once.

She had been slightly concerned for a moment that she was just making him a good object, rather than a whole person. But that wasn't it. He wasn't the one who needed to change. She was. She had closed off so much of herself because of fear. She had been the best mother she could be. She loved her daughter. She put all her ferocity, all her care into that relationship. But she hadn't tried to make friends. She had never tried to have relationships. She had been so careful with her parents.

It was all just trying to protect herself. From bad feelings. From difficult feelings. Trying to be healed when… There was healing to be had, she believed that.

But perhaps more than healing, she wanted to be brave enough to try and dig deep and find a purpose in the tragedy that had happened. Not to make bland comments about how it was God's will, or it was Jason's time—she didn't believe that. It was a mistake. It was a bad thing that happened. And if she could go back and choose it all over again, of course she would never shorten her brother's life in the name of her personal growth.

But she didn't get to choose it.

What she got to choose was what she did with it now.

She wanted to love Buck.

She wanted to be a great mother.

She wanted to be a good daughter.

She wanted to be a businesswoman. Someone who mattered in the community.

She wanted to be everything. She wanted to be bold. She wanted to risk. She wanted to care.

She poured all of that into him now. Into pleasuring him.

Everything.

And right when he was on the brink, he gripped her and pulled her to her feet, branding her mouth in a searing kiss. "Marigold," he said, his eyes wild.

She was pretty sure she had done to him what had just happened to her. That all the walls were down, that everything was flooding out.

That he was everything.

The good man and the bad one. The one who had made mistakes and the one who had spent years trying to correct them. The one who had been made a scapegoat when he didn't deserve it. The one who had hurt his family. The one who had loved his family.

The boy she had been attracted to then. The man she loved now.

She took his hand and led him up the stairs.

Brought him into her bedroom.

They fell down onto the bed, and he stripped her the rest of the way, rolling her over so she was sitting on top of him. Then he handed her a condom packet.

She tore it open, rolling it over his hard length and positioning herself on top of him.

She took him in, inch by inch, relishing the feeling of joining, knowing that she cared for him. Or rather, enjoying the immense, incredible feeling of not trying to hold anything back.

She clung to his shoulders, clung to him. Rolled her hips in time with her need, riding them both to completion, their harsh cries of pleasure mingling together as they both found their release.

She collapsed over him.

"Stay with me," she said. "All night."

"Of course," he said.

The complicated stuff was just going to have to work out. It just was.

Because she wanted him.

The question was, how big of a risk was she willing to take to have it all?

The last thing Buck expected to see when they tumbled down the stairs the next morning to get coffee was Lily and Colton sitting there at the breakfast table, looking like two disapproving parents.

Marigold stepped behind him, holding her robe closed, and he felt like clutching his own nonexistent pearls at the fact that they had been caught by their children.

"Good morning," Lily said, looking sideways at Colton.

Colton took a sip of the coffee, looking at Buck disapprovingly. "You didn't come home last night," he said.

"No," Buck said. "But I told Marcus to let you guys know something came up."

"You did," Colton said. "You weren't honest about where you were. You said you had to go to Grandma and Grandpa's. Is this Grandma and Grandpa's, Buck?"

"It isn't," Buck said, giving his son the most deadpan stare he could manage.

"I didn't think so. It's very disappointing behavior."

"Well, very sorry for disappointing you."

"We just want to know that you're being safe," Lily said.

Marigold sputtered. "Excuse me?"

"Emotions can run high in these situations, and it's very important to know that you're making good choices. Your health and safety is very important. As is your future. Mom, you're about to start a business, and given that, you know it's not a good time for you to have a baby."

"A baby!" Marigold looked like she was going to faint away.

"Well, accidents happen," Lily said.

"And on that topic," Colton said. "Buck, anybody could see your truck was parked in the driveway all night. You know how the neighbors will talk. And it is much more difficult for the women in these situations than for the men. People are very judgmental."

"All right," Buck said. "That's it. Enough."

"Don't take that tone with me," Colton said. "Sorry," he said, "it was for the bit."

"Well the bit is *done,*" Buck said.

"You just should've told us," Lily said. "Instead, we had to figure it out by watching the two of you at the dance last night."

"Which anyone could have done," Colton said. "Because you were putting on a performance for our entire school. How do you think we feel about that?"

Marigold pushed forward. "I'm sorry," she said. "I didn't mean to…"

"Don't worry about it, Mom," Lily said. "I'm not mad. I just wish you would've told me."

"I thought it was too complicated."

"There's no complication," Colton said. "We broke up."

"What?"

"Yeah," he said, shrugging his shoulder. "A while ago. We're just friends now. And we're going to college at the end of the school year. It's not that deep."

Buck stared at his son. He didn't think Colton was being honest at all. There was a strange kind of detached way he was talking that Buck recognized a bit too clearly from when he had first met Colton at the ranch.

It was the way he responded to trauma. And Buck didn't like that at all.

"What we wanted to say," Lily added, "is that there's no reason you two can't…do your thing. Date. Whatever this is. You're adults. And yes, we wanted to give you a hard time, since you gave us a hard time too. But whatever reason you have for hiding it… You just don't need to anymore."

That was such a strange sensation. Getting a blessing from their kids. And yeah, he supposed that did mean they didn't have to hide it anymore. But that also meant they needed to come up with a different label for it. Which he had been pretty aware of for a while now. There were feelings between them, and those feelings transcended the physical. They had for a while. Last night… Last night had been transformative in a way he hadn't been anticipating. It had changed things.

But he still didn't know… He still didn't know what he wanted. Or what it meant.

He just knew that he cared about Marigold, and he wasn't ready to let go of whatever this was.

"Well," Colton said. "Lily and I will leave you to it."

"You will?" Buck asked.

"Yeah. We're going to go out and get pancakes. See you later."

Colton stood up, and Lily followed, and they walked out. Leaving Buck and Marigold alone.

"Well. I guess… We weren't being as secretive as we thought."

"I need to talk to her."

"You just did," Buck said.

"She can't just be okay with the fact that her and Colton broke up."

"Sure she can. They're young. Like she said, they're going to school."

"I just don't believe it."

"How about we deal with the two of us for five seconds. What about that?"

She turned to look at him. "And what? What are we?"

"I guess we have to answer that question. Because we don't have the excuse that we did fifteen minutes ago."

"What excuse is that?"

"That it's too complicated because of the kids."

He wasn't sure he wanted to go there. Wasn't sure he wanted to take the conversation in this direction, but he was doing it. Because he was pretty sure it wasn't fair to be bringing this up when he didn't think he could answer the question either.

Can't you?

"I keep thinking about it," Marigold said, looking at the back wall.

"What exactly?"

"Us. This." She shook her head. "We had a good reason to keep it a secret. There were a lot of complications. You went and talked to my parents. We discovered that wasn't really a complication. Our kids came here and talked to us, and now that's not really a complication. So where is the complication exactly?"

"I'm not following."

"It's us. It's us, or there isn't one. I don't know. But I realized something last night."

He felt everything in him go tense. "What's that?"

"I think I'm in love with you, Buck. And I say that as somebody who knows how scary life is. I say that as someone who has spent so many years protecting myself that I don't even remember what it's like to be…fearless. And young. My foundation, so much of me, is based on loss. And I told myself for a really long time that I was just being responsible. By not bringing men into my and Lily's lives. That I was being respectful and careful by not talking to my parents about you or Jason. You left town. I withdrew in a different way. I made myself into a different person, and I cut a lot of myself off. And last night it was like… It was like I realized that I was feeling everything for the first time."

His heart hammered.

Everything in him felt stuck. Sick. He didn't want to hurt her, not in any way. But he also didn't think he could give her what she was asking for. Because with love, came a set of responsibilities he had never once managed to live up to in his life.

He was trying. He had adopted the boys. But dammit, to throw a relationship on top of that? Another kid?

He had abandoned his family. Nothing in him was...

He didn't deserve this.

And above all else, he couldn't handle it.

"What exactly do you think you want?" He asked it carefully. Slowly. Because he was making assumptions. He was jumping to conclusions. And she didn't deserve that.

"Everything. Nothing less. I didn't want to fall in love with you, Buck. You are the most inconvenient person for me to fall in love with." Her eyes filled with tears, and he wished he could say something to make it better. Except he was the one making her cry. He was the one who was going to make it worse. He was the one who was going to break everything.

So there was nothing he could say. There was nothing he could do.

"Of course you didn't," he said, his voice rough. "Nobody would."

She shook her head. "No. It isn't because of you. It's because of me. Because I told myself you were absolutely the worst person to fall in love with, but what if my perspective was all wrong? It's a terrible thing, trying to figure out how to categorize your brother's death. Trying to figure it out while you're all laden down with the stuff life throws at you. And at the same time, people say all these things to you. Well-meaning people say the most horrendous things. About how it was meant to be. About how he's in a better place. But I always wanted him to be here with me."

"Of course you did," he said.

"It's just, because of that, I really resisted looking for meaning in what happened back then. Like finding any meaning there was a betrayal. Like it diminished the loss. But not accepting what it meant, that was just me fiercely holding on to pain I didn't need to hold on to. I think I can believe both things now. That Jason should be here, and that because he isn't here there were certain things I had to learn and accept. Certain ways I had to grow. And certain people I am connected to. Forever." She made eye contact with him, her gaze like an arrow. "You. I think you are one of the only people in the world who could possibly understand me. My pain, what I've been through. I think you're the only person, other than my parents, who felt the impact of that loss. But you do."

"Yeah. Because I'm complicit."

"You're not. And you know that."

He did. But something in him was desperately seeking a shield to throw in front of her words. And taking responsibility for her brother's death was a big, easily accessible shield.

She was quiet for a long moment. "I can't help but notice that you're not saying it back."

That stuck him, right in the gut. The truth of the matter was, he couldn't say it back. But he also couldn't deny that he did love her.

He loved her.

He had fallen in love with her over the course of these weeks, months. And it wasn't just working together, sleeping together, these family dinners, seeing her with his family. With his boys. It was everything.

It was the way she smiled, the way the sunlight caught her hair. It was the way she made him feel. Like anything was possible.

But he knew it wasn't.

Because he knew what he was.

He was the man who had left his family for twenty years. He was trying to make up for it. He was trying to be new, trying to be better, trying to be different. But he wasn't. Not yet. And he maybe never would be.

And so he couldn't say that he loved her. He couldn't promise her a future. He couldn't promise her anything.

"Now you don't have anything to say."

"I can't."

"You know, there was a man who once told me he paid close attention to what the universe was trying to say to him. To his intuition. The checks in his gut. Where is that man?"

"I'm listening to my gut," he said.

"And your gut says you can't be in love with me?"

"My gut says we can't make a future out of this. My gut says I went way too far off the path to get back on it now. I'm sorry. I wish things could be different. But I have Colton and Marcus and Reggie, and I am trying to make up for the fact that I have been a bad son and a bad brother for two decades. I am trying to make up for the fact that…"

"I don't believe that. I don't believe any of it. You know what I believe? You need your guilt. Because it's your security blanket. Without it, you're afraid of what you'll become. But I know you don't need it. You're a good man, Buck Carson. I don't care what anyone in this town used to say, and I don't care what my thirteen-year-old self said to you in the streets all those years ago. You don't need guilt. This is why you didn't want to accept my forgiveness. You wanted to come home and have everybody throw stones at you. All the better if your own family would've picked up the rocks. Because then you can insulate yourself with that guilt. You could say you were right to be gone. Because everybody hates you. Is it that bad to find out people are actually happy to see you? That we actually want you?"

"I just can't do this."

He turned away from her, and he walked to the door. He got his coat and his hat from the peg. And he felt like a damned coward. He felt like he was doing the same thing he had always done.

But sometimes it was for the best.

Because just like back then, he knew leaving was the right thing to do.

Was it the right thing to do?

He gritted his teeth, and he walked out the door.

But Marigold followed him.

He made his way to his truck and opened the driver's side door, but she kept on coming.

"You are a coward," she shouted.

"We don't need to perform this for the neighbors," he said.

"Why? Because we are so evolved now? Because we've changed? Because I'm not thirteen anymore, so I don't get to yell at you in the street? I will. If that's what it takes for you to understand. What's the point of growing up if you don't grow up? What's the point of all this?

Of being so good. Of both of us being so damned responsible. What is the point of any of it? I'm letting it all go. I'm giving it away. I'm not responsible. I'm not good. I am heartbroken. And I am angry at you. For throwing all of this away, for throwing us away. How dare you."

"You don't understand," he said, slamming the door shut again. "I'm trying to protect you. You're right, you have done a lot of work. And what am I? Nothing. No matter what I do I am never going to be able to erase the way I messed things up. My parents are old. My siblings grew up without me. They had to take care of everything while I was off licking my wounds. I didn't apologize to your parents, I didn't apologize to Ryan's parents, I didn't apologize to Joey's parents. All I did was take all my hurt and stuff it down deep inside of me. I made it all about me. That's who I am. When everything is terrible, I make it about me. And it is only my guilt that finally dragged me out of it. It is only my guilt that finally made me take a good, long, hard look at myself and say that if I was still breathing, I better the hell make it count, because my friends were dead, and I was wasting my chance at life. Yeah. Guilt pulled me out of rock bottom. And I'm sorry if you don't understand why that worked for me. But it did."

"You're more than that," she said. "This is your sign. This is your other opportunity. To look around at yourself, to look around your life and ask why are you breathing?"

"For those boys."

"Breathe for yourself too."

He shook his head. "I can't."

"You are the biggest catfish on the planet," she said. "Because you are so charming and so handsome, and it is fake. Inside, you are a mess. The same mess you were when you left. You haven't grown at all. You're just hiding behind something different. Now it's this facade of the benevolent martyr. How nice for us. And how nice for you. You can roam around in a philosophical hair shirt for the rest of your life and never have to take a risk again. Because you're already dying. So what are you afraid of? Living. That's what you're afraid of."

"Maybe," he said, feeling like he'd been stabbed straight through the chest. "But you know, a lot of people are afraid of bad things happening to them. I'm afraid of the way I seem to make bad things happen to other people. And I don't know what to do about that fear."

It was the truth, even if it was a little overdramatic, even if it didn't entirely make sense. He knew. He understood. He felt the truth of it, burning there at the center of his chest. There was something in him that was just rotten and wrong, and if he didn't control it… If he didn't control it, then everything would be ruined.

"Maybe it's best this way," he said. "Best if you don't understand. And you just hate me."

"We're business partners," she said, clearly exasperated, broken, and it was his fault.

"That's not going to change. I won't go back on my word."

"Is that the game you play? You make all these commitments that you can't get out of, and then you tell yourself that even if you withhold your heart, you're doing the right thing? Is that the point of you following fate?"

He knew it wasn't. He knew what she said wasn't totally true. Except, maybe when he had adopted the boys, he hadn't anticipated loving them like he did. Really loving them like his own sons.

But he just… He just couldn't do more.

"You'll thank me for this later."

She bent down and picked up a pebble, as he got into the truck, then threw it at the door as he pulled out. He heard it hit; it dented.

He unrolled his window. "Are you nuts?"

"If I am it's your fault!"

Well. That said it all. And that was why he had to go. So he kept on driving, until he couldn't see her anymore.

Chapter Fifteen

When Lily came home, she was the immediate and total focus of Marigold's feelings, because what else was she supposed to do with all the pain building up inside her chest.

Certainly not feel it.

She almost laughed at that. At herself for being so ridiculous.

At everything.

"You're really okay?"

"I said that I was," Lily said.

"Well, I just I know breakups can be hard and…"

Lily frowned. "Are you okay?"

She realized that she probably looked a mess, and that her mascara was running.

"I'm good," she said.

"Did something happen with Buck?"

"Lily… This isn't about me. It's about you. And the fact that you chose to do something rash because you were worried about me."

"That wasn't why. I was thinking about what you said. About the fact that I'm going off to school, and you're right. How am I supposed to go off and have new experiences if I'm obsessing about a guy back home. I like Colton, and I didn't want things to get dramatic between us. So now they don't have to. It's not a drama."

"Oh."

She wouldn't know what "not a drama" was like. Since every time she tried to feel something, apparently it was a drama. It ended with screaming in the streets.

"Lily... Buck and I broke up."

"You broke up?"

"Yes." She sighed heavily. "I wanted more than he was ready to give. And you know, this is why I worried about you. You and Colton. It isn't about maturity, it's about the fact that this kind of stuff can be really dangerous. I'm thirty-three, I should have it together a little more. It's not like I'm totally inexperienced with men."

Lily grimaced. Because what could be more horrifying than having to hear about your mother's past sexual experiences? Even if implied? Nothing.

But if Marigold had to be a cautionary tale, then she would be.

It would at least make this heartbreak feel like it had a point.

"Well, you know you were born somehow," Marigold said. "So don't grimace at me."

"I'm just... Mom, are you okay?"

"No," she said. "I mean, I'm going to get out of bed and I'm going to do things, and I'm going to be your mom, and I'm going to be myself, but I'm hurt. It's been really, really difficult these last couple of hours. So I don't know what it's going to be like going forward. I really thought we had something. I thought he was in love with me. Anybody can get hurt when there are bodies and hearts involved. And so if you take anything away from this, I just want you to take away that…this is why I was worried about you. Because it's hard for me to go through. And I would never want to see you in this kind of pain."

"I don't want to see you in pain either," Lily said. "How can he not be in love with you? You're the best and you're amazing. You are the sweetest, nicest, most caring person I know. You're the best mom. You have done more for me than I can ever thank you for. You're just… You're wonderful. And if he doesn't realize that, then he can go straight to hell."

Marigold should probably correct Lily for speaking out harshly, but she wasn't going to.

"I don't want you to be jaded, and I don't want you to be armored," Marigold said. "But I do want you to be aware that… Love can be… Well, it can be *this*."

"I'm sorry." Lily wrapped her arms around Marigold. "He should appreciate you."

"Thank you. I want you to remember too, Lily, that love can also be *this*." They parted for a moment, and she felt a little glimmer of hope inside her, a little shaft of light shining through the gross darkness. "We have had a lot of love. And we have a great life. Nothing was ever missing. How could it be, when I have you? The greatest daughter in the world. I'm so proud of you."

"Thanks, Mom," she said.

"I'm going to be okay."

"Are you going to date other men? Are you going to go wild when I leave?"

"Maybe," she said, trying to smile. "Probably not."

"It would serve you right if you did. I'm very sex positive, Mom. It's your body. You can do what you want with it."

She tried to contain her grimace. "Thank you. I didn't need to hear that."

"Well, I don't want to know about it. I'm just saying... Times have changed and women are allowed to express themselves that way."

"Thank you very much," Marigold said. "Someday, I will regale you with stories about how I am a slut of the old ways, my child. But you're not ready for that yet."

That earned her a look of horror, which she decided to call her one win for the day. Well, other than the fact that no matter what happened, Lily loved her. And so all wasn't lost. It couldn't be.

But when she left Lily downstairs, Marigold threw herself across the bed and wept. Because all might not be lost, but a big piece of her heart was.

And she didn't know if it was ever going to grow back.

He was trying to fix fences, but mostly, he was just hammering his thumb. He cursed and chucked the hammer across the field, and Colton picked it up and handed it to him. He looked up and saw that Reggie and Marcus were standing behind him.

"Here, you dropped this. Dumb ass," Colton said.

Buck looked up at his oldest son, who was glaring at him like he'd just clubbed a baby seal. "Excuse me?"

"You heard me," Colton said, his eyes full of storm. "I didn't stutter."

"What did I do?"

"You broke up with Marigold," Marcus said, stepping forward, even angrier looking than his brother.

Buck wasn't about to be lectured by a half-grown piglet who'd never even touched a woman. "Yeah. I did. For her own good."

Reggie howled. "For her own good! Do you hear yourself? You sound like a chump."

"Listen," Buck said, his voice hard. "Men and women are different and—"

"You sound like you have a *podcast*," his youngest added.

"What the hell does that mean?"

"Do you feel insulted?" Reggie asked.

"Yes."

Reggie narrowed his eyes. "Then you know what it means."

Buck stared at his boys. "I'm serious. She is an amazing woman. And she deserves somebody who... Who is better than me."

The three of them exchanged glances.

"She does? But we don't?" Marcus asked.

"That's *not* what I said," Buck said.

"It kind of is, though," Marcus said. "A little bit. Why are you not good enough for her, but *we're* supposed to live with you?"

Those little rats. That wasn't what he was saying at all, and it was different, and they ought to know it. He was sort of tongue-tied trying to figure out how to explain that it was different, but it was.

"I... It's *different*. Romantic stuff is different." He decided to go with that very articulate explanation.

"Is it?" Reggie asked.

"You're a smart-ass, shut up."

His words didn't have any heat; they sounded petulant even to him. And Reggie was not deterred.

"*Seriously*, Buck. You meet a nice woman. A beautiful woman. We all like her daughter—sorry Colton—and you break up with her. We could've had a *mom*."

It was the slight break in Reggie's voice at the end that got him.

That stabbed him clean through the chest. "That's not... That's not fair. You are an emotional terrorist," he said.

"Maybe you deserve it," said Marcus. "Maybe you deserved a little bit of emotional terrorism for the shit you put her through."

"I'm not trying to hurt anybody," Buck said. "I'm a mess, okay? That is a documented fact. In high school I drank too much, and I was adjacent to that awful accident. I frankly should've been in it. Everybody in town blamed me. Then I abandoned my family."

"So what? That's all you are? You just do stuff because you feel guilty and you feel like you have to make up for it?"

"Yeah. That's why I do stuff."

It was why he had to. To try and be better. To try and atone.

"Ah. So we're all part of your redemption scheme. You just feel guilty. See, you adopted a bunch of sad foster kids so you could try to right your balance with the universe." Reggie looked angry now. "Good thing my mom died, I guess, and my sister too. What a big help to you. It made it really easy for you to earn some points on that one. I was an extra sad case."

This was going all wrong.

"Reggie, that's not what it is."

They were all looking at him. All angry.

"I love you," Buck said. "I didn't expect it. I can be honest with you about that. I thought… I thought it would be like taking care of you as campers. But it's not. It hasn't been. I'm your dad. And I love you, and guilt has nothing the hell to do with it. You knuckleheads. You're not just mine right now, not just mine because…because I feel like a mess, and I wanted to do something to make myself feel better. You're mine because you were meant to be. Because the whole fucked-up road I took to get to Hope Ranch led me to you. And I was supposed to be there, even though a whole bunch of stuff around it wasn't supposed to happen. Adopting you three was one of the few good things I did. I listened to my gut. And then I ended up… You changed my life. If not for you, I wouldn't have come back here. I never would've reconnected with my family. That's not guilt. It's love."

Colton blinked, then looked away, a muscle in his jaw twitching. "Sounds to me like you don't really need the guilt."

And all Buck could do was sit there, shell-shocked. Because it was true. It wasn't guilt that kept him with the boys. It was love.

Guilt wasn't what kept him going.

He thought of his choice to leave his family. There had been misguided love there, even if the choice had been wrong. He had acted from a place of love. Flawed love. But…

Every day with the boys he saw what flawed love could do.

Why wasn't he willing to try that with Marigold?

Because you're afraid. Because everything she said is true.

His heart caught hard in his chest. Yeah. That was true. He was afraid. He was afraid of letting go of his guilt. There was a reason he hadn't gone to see Joey's and Ryan's parents. There was a reason he was holding on to those shields.

Because they protected him, not because they protected the people around him.

Because he was afraid he could never be worthy of her love, and if he accepted it and he lost it…

He had never felt weak. He had felt a lot of things, but never weak. Yet in this moment, that was how he felt. Like nothing more than a coward.

And that was unacceptable.

"I've got to fix it," he said.

"Great," said Marcus.

"But I've got to fix *me* first."

"Shit, bitch," said Reggie. "We don't have that kind of time."

"Maybe not all the way. But I have to… I have to do something."

"Maybe you should make a list. That's what my therapist used to say to do."

"Okay. I'll make a list."

So he did. He spent the day writing down what he needed to do, who he needed to talk to. He started at Joey's old house. Joey's mother let him in. His father had died five years earlier. She didn't condemn him.

Then he went to Ryan's place. And as he talked to Ryan's parents, he released the guilt. He realized he was the only one holding on to it.

And then it was time to go to his own parents' house.

"What brings you here?" his mother said, smiling.

"I want to say that I'm sorry. I really am so fucking sorry. I'm so sorry that I missed so many years. And I really want you to forgive me. Because I want to be different. I don't want to feel this way for the rest of my life. I want to be more than grief. And more than mistakes. And more than good deeds trying to cover up everything broken inside of me. I want to be better. And I want… I want to be able to love a woman the way that I should. I love Marigold. I want to have a future with her. A family. I messed up big-time with her. I realized not too long ago it's because I'm such a mess."

"Hell," his dad said. "Son. We are all a mess and none of us makes it through life without getting messier than we were when we were born. I spent years feeling regret over how you left. Wondering what I could've done better with you."

"So did I," his mother said.

"No," Buck said. "Don't feel bad. It was my decision to leave. I was the one who couldn't handle it."

"And I feel like, as your parents, we should have done

something different to make it so you knew you could stay." His dad cleared his throat. "That's life."

"What if we all just stopped blaming ourselves? Because there's no room for regret. I mean, I have it. A bunch of it. For all the time I missed, but…"

"But you have your boys."

"Yes. And I hope that I'll have Marigold. And if so, then what it took to get there… It would be worth it. Somehow all my bad decisions led me to the right place." He thought long and hard about that intuition in his gut. And he realized, that was the thing that had been leading him all along. More than a gut check. Divine intervention. Because it was nothing short of miraculous that with everything he'd done wrong, so much was right.

"I'm just thankful," he said.

"I think that's a pretty good start."

He nodded slowly. And when he went outside, the sun felt different. Warmer. He couldn't change his past. He couldn't go back and make better decisions. He could only make good ones going forward. And give thanks for the fact that he had been given so much in spite of himself.

Chapter Sixteen

Marigold was bustling around the new building, her dream significantly less beautiful than it had been only last week. What did it matter now?

This was the problem with love, she thought. With opening yourself up. Then beautiful new kitchens didn't feel as significant as they should.

She'd been dreaming of this, and now her dreams felt dim. Which infuriated her. Her dreams were not dim.

But for a moment, she'd thought it was possible to have it all.

Now anything else felt less.

Damn that man for making her life feel like less.

She was about to go into the back room when she heard the door open. Then she stopped and turned around, and there was Buck, standing there backlit against the sunlight.

Like a knight in shining armor.

A hero.

Light and color and everything she'd been missing, in his black Henley and his blue jeans, his cowboy hat on his head.

No. He ruined this, remember?

But she didn't care. Because she wanted him.

And because everything they'd talked about, everything they'd been working through these past few months, was all about the fact that you had to be able to move on from bad choices.

That the end wasn't final, if you didn't let it be.

"I need to talk to you," he said.

Her first instinct was to protect herself. "Why? Haven't you said everything there is to say?"

"No. Because last time we talked I left off something really crucial."

"What's that?"

"I love you. I loved you even when I was telling you no. You're right, I never said I didn't love you. I loved you that whole time. But I couldn't figure out how to keep myself safe and how to love you. That's what it comes down to. I told myself all kinds of things. That I didn't deserve love because of the way that I had abandoned my family. That I couldn't be trusted. But I spent twenty years disconnected from everyone and everything. On purpose. Until those boys came into my life, I had forgotten how to really love. I knew how to atone. I knew how to do good things because guilt motivated me. But those boys changed me. Yet with you, I tried to do the old things. I tried to revert to type. But having my boys look at me and ask if I only adopted them because I felt guilty… Hell no. Of course not. And that's another thing. I'm trying to be a role model here. I'm doing a bad job at it. Because what I'm showing is that if you make a mistake you have to make yourself pay for it for the rest of your life."

"You didn't make a mistake. You didn't cause that accident."

"I don't mean the accident. I mean leaving. I mean not staying. But I was too hurt. I was too messed up. I told myself that everybody would be better off without me. I believed it. Because I… I just hurt so damned bad. So much of this, is just actually being afraid of hurt. And not knowing how to share myself. Because what I know how to do is run away. I reverted to type. And I'm sorry. You didn't deserve that."

"Why don't you let me decide what I deserve?"

"But I want to take care of you. I want to be better for you. I want— I'm an idiot. Because the reason you came to my door that day had nothing to do with business. Or atonement. Or even sex. It was love. That was it. That was everything. From the first moment. The first moment I saw you. I just knew that I couldn't let you walk away from me."

"I love you."

"I love you too."

"I want it all," he said. "I want to get married. I want to move in together, I want to share space. But I do understand if you can't do that before Lily goes college."

She nodded slowly. "I'll have to talk to her. It is her last few months at home."

"Of course."

Because loving each other meant loving all of it. Loving him meant loving all his baggage, all the boys. And loving her was the same. And they both understood it. Because they understood each other.

She had thought for a long time that she was healed.

In some ways, she had been. Healed enough to do right by her daughter, healed enough to be a good mom. But she was finally healed enough to be herself.

And that was an incredible gift.

Epilogue

Welcome to Lone Rock...

The day Buck moved Marigold into his house they passed that familiar sign.

All of Marigold's belongings were in the back of the truck, and they were ready to start their new life together. They would be living in sin before the wedding. And Lily had said she didn't mind moving out to the ranch before graduation, which meant they were going to be one big happy family before she and Colton left for college. Reggie and Marcus especially had completely latched on to Marigold as their mother, and she was giving them absolutely everything.

He had never felt more in awe of how beautiful life could be. He had spent way too long thinking about how cruel it could be.

"You look happy," Marigold said.

"Of course I am," he said, slinging his arm over the back of the seat. "I'm in love."

And for the first time in twenty years, Buck Carson was well and truly home.

* * * * *

VEGAS VOWS, TEXAS NIGHTS

CHARLENE SANDS

Dedicated to my lifelong friends: Mary, Allyson and Robin. Decades of Forever Friends, keepers of memories, hearts of gold, in good times and in bad, they are always there. We are fortunate to have each other.

One

Las Vegas, Nevada

Katie woke slowly, snuggling into her cushy pillow, her eyes refusing to open. A warming ray coming through the hotel room window caressed her skin, telling her it was later than her usual 4:00 a.m. wake-up-and-bake time.

But she wasn't in Boone Springs today and Katie's Kupcakes and Bakery was closed this weekend. She'd planned a super fun bachelorette party for her best friend, Drea, and fittingly, she'd just had the best dream of her life. Though the details were fuzzy, she'd never woken up with such delicious contentment before. From head to toe, her entire body tingled.

A nudge to her shoulder popped her eyes open. *What the...?*

"Sorry," a deep male voice whispered from behind her.

Her eyes opened wider as she tried to make sense of it. She hadn't imagined or dreamed the voice, had she? No, she was fully awake now, and it had been real. She could feel the warmth of the sheets beside her. A hand brushed over her bare shoulder and she gasped.

Oh no. She recognized that voice.

Taking the sheets covering her bare body, she rolled over, hoping her mind had played a nasty trick on her. But that hope was dashed the second she laid eyes on *him*, Lucas Boone—her sister's ex-fiancé, the man who'd crushed Shelly's heart.

Her stomach began to ache.

She clutched the sheets to her chin and sat up. That's when her head started pounding. "Luke, what on earth?" Dizzy, she swayed and struggled to focus.

"Sweetheart, lay back down. You drank me under the table last night and my head's aching like a sonofabitch. Your hangover's got to be much worse than mine."

"My…hangover? Luke, damn it. Is that all you have to say? Look at us! We're in bed together. And unless I miss my guess, you're as stark naked under the sheets as I am."

He reached for the sheet.

"Don't you dare look," she warned.

He set the sheet back down. "I guess you'd be right."

Her cheeks burned. Being in bed with Lucas Boone was wrong on so many levels, she could hardly believe it. "What on earth did we do last night?"

Luke glanced at their shed clothes littering the hotel room and arched a brow.

"We couldn't have. I wouldn't… I couldn't…"

Goodness. She thought back to how Luke had called off the wedding to Katie's sister three days before the ceremony and had immediately enlisted in the Marines.

He'd claimed he wasn't ready to settle down and took all the blame upon himself, but that didn't make up for all the time he'd spent leading Shelly to believe they'd had a future together. That had been five years ago. Now Luke was living in Boone Springs again, the town founded a century ago by his ancestors. He was his brother Mason's best man, while Katie was maid of honor for Mason's fiancée, Drea. Unwittingly she and Luke had been thrown together in a joint bachelor/bachelorette party in Sin City. Vegas, baby. What happened here stayed here.

She thought about her sister again. How her scars remained. Poor Shelly faced the humiliation bravely but she'd never forgotten what Luke had done to her, how he'd betrayed her love and trust. She'd become bitter and sad and never let her mother, Diana, or Katie hear the end of how Luke had ruined her life. So the thought of Katie sleeping with Luke, her one-time friend, drunk or not, would be the worst of the worst.

Luke rolled over onto his side and braced his head in his hand, as if they were discussing what to have for breakfast. "What do you remember about last night?"

"What do I remember?"

"Yeah, do you remember leaving the party with me?"

She moved away from him as far as the bed would allow and thought about it. She remembered drinking and laughing and dancing with Luke most of the night. She'd felt guilty having so much fun with him, but they'd always gotten along, had always been friends until he'd backed out of the wedding.

The Boones had been good customers at her bakery. She and Luke also shared a love of horses and both volunteered at the Red Barrel Horse Rescue. Still, ever since his return from military service nearly a year ago, they'd been overly cautious with each other, their conversations often stilted and awkward. Katie, too, had been hurt when Luke had dumped her sister. Katie had also trusted him.

"I remember you offering to walk me back to my hotel." Which was only a few blocks away from the nightclub.

"We'd both had too much to drink."

The pain in her head was a reminder of that. "Yes."

Luke stared into her eyes; his were clear and deep blue. Kinda mesmerizing. "You pleaded with me not to take you back to your hotel. You didn't want the night to end. You...uh..."

Katie rubbed her aching head. This was getting worse by the second. "What?"

Luke remained silent.

"What did I say?" she demanded. She had to know, to make some sense out of this.

"You said you wanted what your friends had. You wanted someone to love."

"Oh God." She covered her face with her hands, her long hair spilling down. She was embarrassed that in her drunken state, she'd revealed her innermost secret desire. And to Luke no less. "And so we ended up in your hotel room?"

Luke flinched and his eyes squeezed shut. The concerned expression on his face really worried her. "Not exactly. We went somewhere else first."

"Another club?"

He shook his head. "Not according to this." He grabbed a piece of paper from his nightstand and gave it a once-over. "Another thing you said you wanted..." He handed her the paper.

She looked down at the bold lettering on the piece of parchment she held and her hand began shaking. A marriage certificate. Both of their names were listed and it had today's date. "You can't be serious."

"Hey, I don't remember much from last night either. My head's spinning like a damn top right now."

This was ridiculous. It had to be a bad joke. Where was the hidden camera? Someone was pranking her.

Yes, it was true she'd thought of her secret wishes, often. She'd wanted to find love and be married, though she'd never voiced those wishes to anyone. She didn't want her friends to worry about her or think she envied their happiness, but she wouldn't have told Luke that, would she? Certainly she wouldn't have acted upon it.

Yet, the proof was staring her in the face. Dated today, as in they'd gotten married after midnight, about the time they'd walked out of the club together. The facts added up, but she still had trouble digesting all of it.

"I can't believe this. No, this isn't happening." She lowered her voice. "We didn't...do anything else, did we?"

Was she being naive to think that she'd end up naked in bed with handsome, appealing Luke without having sex with him?

"I remember some things. From last night." The blue in his eyes grew darker, more intense. "Don't you?"

She didn't want to. She didn't want to think it possible to spend the night with the one man in the whole world who was off-limits to her. But darn it, vague memories started to breach the surface of her mind. Being held, being kissed, her body caressed, loved. She grimaced. Dear Lord, the memories were fuzzy, vague, but they were there.

"Oh no," she whispered. Tears touched her eyes. "Why didn't you stop it?" she asked.

It was unfair of her to throw this all on him. The way he flinched at her question said he thought so, too. "I... couldn't."

He couldn't? What did that mean?

"Katie, it's going to be okay. We're married. I didn't take advantage of you. I mean, from what I remember, you weren't complaining about any of it."

She gripped the sheets closer to her chest. "That's what you think I'm worried about? It's okay that we had sex because we're married? My God, Luke. Do you have any idea how bad this is? You were engaged to my sister! You practically left her at the altar. My mom and sister were devastated. I'm not worried about my virtue here. It's way bigger than that."

"Okay, okay. Calm down." Luke ran a hand down his face. "I'm going to take a shower and get dressed and we'll discuss it. Unless you want to go first?"

"No, no." Married or not, she wasn't about to let him see her naked. "You go first."

"Fine. And Katie…it really is going to be all right."

She frowned. The frown only deepened when Luke rose from the bed as if they'd been married for years and walked into the bathroom, giving her a stunning view of his broad shoulders, muscular arms and perfect butt.

Her heart pounded hard. She'd married a Boone, one of the richest men in all of Texas, the man who'd betrayed her sister, the man she'd tried hard to avoid since he'd come back and resumed his life in Boone Springs months ago.

As soon as she heard the bathroom door close, she rose and scrambled to gather up her clothes from the floor. That's when she spotted an open condom packet, the top torn off, the contents empty. Now there was actual proof they'd consummated the marriage, as if her own sated body wasn't already screaming that to her.

She dressed and waited for him. They had to resolve this immediately. She wasn't going home as Katie Boone. No, sir. When she heard the shower faucet turn off, she braced herself, finger combing her hair, straightening out her cocktail dress, her resolve as sharp as her annoyance.

The door opened and out walked Luke, his hair wet, his skin glowing in the morning light. He wore a soft white towel around his waist, but the rest of him was hard, ripped muscle and brawn.

Good Lord. Was he the man in her dreams?

No, he couldn't be. Just because they'd once been friends and they shared a love of horses didn't mean she'd ever think of him that way, even subconsciously.

"Luke, we need to talk."

He looked her up and down, his eyes raking over her black dress, and suddenly she felt amazingly warm. She shifted her attention to a drop of water making its way down his bare chest, tunneling through tiny hairs to drip past his navel and absorb into the towel.

Luke caught her eyeing him and smiled. "I need a cup of coffee. We both do. I'll order breakfast while you take your shower."

He seemed too accommodating, too casual, as if he also hadn't made the biggest blunder of his life. Where was his panic?

"And we'll resolve this then?"

He nodded. "We'll talk, I promise."

Thirty minutes later, Katie stepped out of the bathroom refreshed and feeling a little better about her predicament. Her stomach still churned, but her outlook wasn't nearly as bleak. They were in Las Vegas, after all. How hard would it be to dissolve their quickie marriage, to seek a divorce from a wedding that should never have happened? Surely there were hundreds of people who found themselves in the same situation after a wild night and too much drinking.

Luke waited for her at the rolling table that had been delivered by room service. Thankfully he was fully dressed now, in jeans and a navy shirt that made his eyes pop an even darker shade of blue. She had only the clothes she'd come with last night and her purse. Luckily her cell phone had enough charge for her to text Drea this morning telling her not to worry, she'd explain everything later.

Or not.

But she'd have to tell the bride-to-be something. They shared a hotel room and Drea had seen her leave with Luke last night and knew she hadn't returned to her room.

"Ready for breakfast?" Luke was already sipping coffee, the pot of steaming brew sitting on the table beside dishes of bacon, eggs, French toast, roasted potatoes and a basket of fresh pastries.

Ugh. None of it looked appetizing. She couldn't eat. "No, thanks. Coffee's good."

She grabbed the coffeepot and poured herself a cup, taking a seat facing him. She dumped in three sugar cubes and stirred, Luke giving her an arch of his brow. What could she say? She loved sweet comfort food and right now, sugar was her healing balm. His silent disapproval had her reaching for a fourth sugar cube, and she stared right at him as she dumped it into her coffee.

"You're not eating anything?" he asked.

"I'm not hungry, Luke. My head's still fuzzy."

"I thought the shower would help."

"The shower made me realize that if being in Vegas got us into this mess, then why can't being in Vegas get us out of it?"

Luke gave her a long stare and slowly shook his head. "What?"

"I want a divorce. Immediately. Surely there's someone in this city that can accommodate us."

Luke scratched his head, looking at her as if she were a child asking for the moon. "That's not possible, Katie."

"How can you say that? We haven't even tried. Look, I wasn't myself last night and you know it. How long have we known each other? Ten years?"

"Twelve and a half." She stared at him and he shrugged. "I have a good memory for dates. We met at the first anniversary of the Red Barrel Rescue."

Katie remembered that day. She'd chosen the rescue to be the subject of her high school term paper and had gone there not knowing what to expect. She'd taken one look at the beleaguered and maimed horses being cared for and had fallen in love. Luke had been a mentor of sorts, and through her, he'd met her sister, Shelly.

"And in all those twelve and a half years, have you ever known me to be impetuous or wild or, as you put it today, the kind of girl who could drink you under the table?"

"No." He scratched his head. "But then, I've never been with you in Vegas."

She rolled her eyes. "This is serious, Luke. I don't recall all that happened last night, but I do know we have to undo the problem as soon as possible."

"I…agree."

"You do? Good, because for a second there, I was starting to believe you didn't think this was a big problem."

"I can't get a divorce until I speak with my attorney. I'm sorry, Katie, but this isn't going to happen today."

"Why not?"

"Because it's more complicated than that. I'm a Boone, and that means divorce proceedings can get pretty nasty. My attorney isn't going to let me sign my name to anything until he sees it."

"Goodness, Luke, I don't want anything from you or your family. If that's what you're getting at, you can go straight to—"

"It's not me, Katie. It's just the way things are when you're…"

"Rich?"

"A Boone."

"How horrible it must be for you not knowing who you can trust. I suppose you had those very same issues with Shelly?"

"Let's leave your sister out of this."

"Easy for you to say." Katie's stomach burned now, the acid churning violently. This was not going well. He was being obtuse and the implication that she was somehow out for Boone money only ticked her off. "There's nothing we can do? Maybe if you give your attorney a call—"

Luke frowned. "I can't. He's out of the country on a personal matter."

"Personal matter? You could say this is your personal matter."

He sighed. "His mother is extremely ill and he's there to help get her affairs in order. That is, if the worst happens."

"Oh. I'm sorry to hear that. Can't you use someone else?"

Luke shook his head. "I'm afraid it doesn't work that way. At least not for me."

She jammed her hands on her hips and his attention immediately was drawn there. Gosh, how much of last night did he remember? He was looking at her differently than he ever had before. As if he was taking their marriage seriously, as if she was…his wife. "I can't go back to Boone Springs married to you, Luke."

"Looks like you're going to have to. Our flight leaves in a few hours."

Katie sighed and tears welled in her eyes. "I can't believe this."

He kept silent.

She had no choice but to relent. She saw no other way out. If she prolonged her stay here in Las Vegas, the entire wedding party would get suspicious. She didn't need that. She had to keep what happened between her and Luke quiet. She'd think of something before the Boone company plane took off.

"Fine. I'm not happy about this. If the truth comes out, I'm doomed. It'll ruin my relationship with my family. And who knows how this would affect my mama's health. Promise me that no one will know about this, promise me you'll keep our secret."

Luke touched her hand, his slight caress sweet, comforting and confusing as hell. "I promise, Katie. No one will know."

Luke waited until everyone boarded the Boone company plane, keeping his eyes trained on Katie. She took a seat by the bridesmaids in the back, all the girls huddling around the bride-to-be.

He couldn't keep from admiring Katie's beautiful blond hair tied up in a ponytail, the strands framing her face making her look wholesome and sweet. She was all those things, but last night at the club, he'd seen her flirty, passionate side. Mischief had glowed in her soft green eyes, especially while she'd been dancing in her sexy black dress. Now, in a denim jacket and jeans, she contrasted beautifully with the creamy leather seats and ambience of the custom designed plane.

She was his wife now. He could hardly believe it. He was actually married to Katie Rodgers. While Mason was engaged to Drea and his other brother, Risk, was engaged to April, Luke had inadvertently beaten his brothers down the aisle.

Katie glanced his way and their eyes met. He could look at her forever and never tire of it. But as soon as she caught him eyeing her, she turned away.

He smiled inside but didn't dare appear content around a quiet, sullen Katie. She was just cordial enough to her friends to ward off questions. She'd told everyone she'd gotten sick last night, barfing up her brains and Luke had taken her to urgent care in the wee hours of the morning to make sure she wasn't dehydrated. It was a feasible fib, one everyone seemed to believe, with the exception of his brothers. While Drea had thanked him for taking care of her best friend, both Risk and Mason had given him the stink eye.

Hell, he certainly hadn't planned any of this, but hearing Katie's softly spoken desire about wanting love in her life, wanting to be married, had reached down deep inside him and wrung out his lonely heart. He'd been drunk, too, and his willpower around her had been at an all-time low. She'd flirted with him, practically asked him to make love to her, and well…he didn't have much defense against that. Not with her.

The pilot, a navy veteran, came by to say hello to the passengers and make sure everyone was ready for takeoff.

Luke shook his hand. "Hey, Bill. Hope you didn't lose too much at the tables while you were here."

"Nah, my big gambling days are behind me. The penny slots are just my speed."

"I hear you," Luke said. He'd never been a gambler. He didn't like to play games he couldn't control. And he didn't like the odds in Las Vegas, with the exception of his recent marriage.

The odds of him marrying Katie had been slim to none. Yet he'd beat them and no one was more surprised than he was. Except Katie. He'd won the jackpot and now he had to convince his new bride being married to him wasn't a big fat mistake.

"Any time you want to come up and copilot, you know where the cockpit is," Bill said.

"Maybe later. Right now I'm still feeling the effects of last night's party." Luke grinned. "I'm afraid you're the designated driver today." He was in no shape to navigate anything, much less fly the friendly skies. He'd become a helicopter pilot while living on Rising Springs Ranch and had gotten his pilot's license in flight school during his stint in the service. Yet Mason had insisted he not pilot the plane so Luke could let loose and not have to worry about his alcohol consumption. His brother wanted everyone to have a good time.

"Sure thing. I'll see that you all have a good flight."

"Thanks, Bill."

Luke buckled up and glanced back at Katie. She was all set, looking like she'd just lost her best friend, even though Drea was sitting right next to her.

He sighed and as he turned his head around, he came eye to eye with Risk in the seat beside him. "Something going on between you two?" he asked.

He'd promised Katie he wouldn't give away their secret and he wouldn't betray that vow. "Who?"

"Don't be obtuse. You and Katie."

"No, nothing."

"I'm not judging," Risk said. "And if you do have something going with her, it'd be a good thing. I can read you like a book. You're hot for her."

Luke shot him a warning look.

Risk's hands went up. "I'm just saying, if you get together with her, you have my approval."

"Like I'd need it."

"Hey, just want to see you happy for once."

"You do know who she is, right?"

Risk smirked. "The best pastry chef in all of Texas. She'd keep us silly in gourmet cupcakes."

"She's Shelly's younger sister. And she barely tolerates me."

Years ago, Katie had dragged Shelly to a Red Barrel charity function and had introduced them. There'd been instant attraction between them and Luke had begun dating Katie's big sister. The engagement had seemed to fall right into place. Until the day Luke had woken up and realized he was making a big mistake.

"You two took off together last night," Risk said, "and today, you can't take your eyes off her."

"Leave it alone. Okay?"

Risk seemed to read the emotion on his face. "Okay,

I'll back off." He slapped Luke on the shoulder. "But if you run into a problem, I'm here for you."

"Appreciate that. Why aren't you hanging with your fiancée?"

"Seems the girls won't call it quits on their bachelorette party until the plane touches down in Boone Springs."

Risk eyed April, giving Luke a chance to seek out Katie again. And there she was, trying her best not to spoil everyone's fun, trying to smile and conceal the pain she must be going through. The thought that he was the cause of her pain ate away at him. It was the last thing he wanted. But he couldn't let her go. Not now.

She was the girl who shared a love of horses with him, the girl he'd danced with most of the night, the impossible girl who'd been in his dreams for the past five years.

He needed a chance with her, and this was the best he was going to get.

One chance.

Was that too much to ask?

Two

A Boone limo picked up the entire wedding party at the airport, taking everyone directly to their homes on the outskirts of town. Katie was among the last to be dropped off since she lived in the heart of Boone Springs, her apartment just above the bakery. It was a modest place, with one bedroom, one bath, but the rooms were spacious enough and her large home kitchen served as a backup when orders in the bakery exceeded their limit. That didn't happen often. Katie ran an efficient place and there was nothing like rolling out of bed at 4:00 a.m. and working in her jammies downstairs until the bakery opened at seven o'clock.

As the limo pulled up in front of the bakery, she was struck with a pang of relief. "This is my stop," she said to her friends remaining in the limo. "I hope you all had a great time."

Drea gave her a big hug. "It was wonderful. Amazing girl-bonding, my friend. Thanks for all you've done. Love you for it."

"Love you, too."

Katie glanced at everyone and waved a farewell. "All of you made the party for our dear friends something to remember."

"After last night, I've forgotten more than I remember," Mason said, smiling.

"You had the best time with your friends and family, especially with your fiancée." Drea gave him a quick kiss on the cheek. "Just ask me, I'll fill in the blanks."

Katie had some blanks she'd like to have filled in, too.

"One thing I do know, Luke and Katie worked hard on organizing this. Thank you," Mason said. "You two make a good team."

A rush of heat crawled up her neck. "Thank you. It wasn't that hard, really, and it was fun." The only difficult part had been working with Luke. *Her husband.* Oh God.

The limo driver grabbed Katie's bags and opened the door for her.

"I'll get off here, too," Luke told the driver.

Katie glared at him.

"It's a short walk to the office," he explained. "And I need to check up on something. Benny, if you could drop off my bags at the ranch I'd appreciate it."

The limo driver nodded. "Yes, sir."

Katie climbed out, Luke right behind her.

"I'll take those." He grabbed her bags from the driver's hand.

Katie noticed some raised eyebrows in the limo and wanted to melt right into the cement. What on earth was Luke doing? She didn't want to arouse suspicion. It was bad enough she'd had to lie to her best friend about where she'd been last night. But Luke was oblivious as to how his behavior appeared to everyone.

"Bye," Drea said. "Thanks again, hon. We'll talk soon."

"Okay," Katie said, giving her friend a smile.

When the limo drove off, she turned to Luke. "Give me my bags, Luke."

"I'll carry them up for you."

"That's not necessary."

"I know, but I'd like to."

"Why?"

"Your hangover is hanging on. You're pale and looking a little weak."

"The only reason I look ill is because of what happened between us. Makes me sick to my stomach."

His mouth twitched, but she wasn't at all sorry she'd been so crude. Well, maybe she was a little bit sorry. This was just as much her fault as it was his.

"All the more reason for me to help you. I feel responsible."

"Don't."

"I can't help it, Katie. C'mon, you need to rest."

She didn't like him telling her what she needed, but his jaw was set stubbornly and they couldn't stand here all day arguing. "Okay, fine."

He had the good sense not to gloat at winning the point. He nodded and walked over to the front door with her bags.

She opened up her shop and walked in first. The bakery had been closed for three days, yet the scent of vanilla, cinnamon and sugar flavored the air. The smell of home. She sighed and her body relaxed.

"Smells like you in here," Luke remarked, as if reading her thoughts.

"How's that?" she asked.

"Sweet."

She let his comment hang in the air for a moment. She didn't feel sweet right now. She felt horrible and guilty. She kept wishing she could escape from this horrible dream. Waking up wed to her sister's ex was truly a nightmare. And the sooner they rectified it, the better.

"The stairs are in the back, through the kitchen." She led the way and he followed.

He stopped to take a look at her baking area. "So this is where the cupcake magic happens. I've always wondered what this place looked like."

"Yep, this is it. This is where I spend a good deal of my life." She couldn't keep the pleasure out of her voice. She was proud of her shop, proud of what she'd accomplished. And she loved her work.

Luke took in the huge mixer, bowls and cupcake tins, the bins of flour and sugar and the industrial-size refrigerator. Yes, this was home to her.

"I see you here," Luke said, as if he was picturing her at work.

"It's not glamourous."

"I would imagine it's darn hard work. But work that you enjoy."

"True."

"Your bakery is the best in the county, everyone knows that. But I've only known you as a horse lover. You spend a lot of time at Red Barrel. How do you find time for both?"

"You run a multimillion-dollar company, how do you find the time?"

He grinned. "You're quick, I'll give you that."

"Apparently, not quick enough," she mumbled. Or else she wouldn't have gone to bed with him.

Luke ran a hand down his face. "I wasn't lying when I said it was mutual, Katie. I know that for a fact. Don't blame yourself too much."

She squeezed her eyes shut briefly and nodded. The man she knew at the horse rescue was gentle and caring and kind. He'd been her friend at one time and that was where it all got confusing. Because he had hurt her sister and maybe what Katie thought she'd known about him was all wrong. "Okay, can we just not talk about it?"

"Talk about what?" He played along. "You were going to tell me how you find time to work at the rescue."

"My workday ends early. And I think the work we do at the rescue is important. Those animals need help." She lifted a shoulder. "I don't date. Or at least I haven't for a while and so I have all kinds of—"

"You won't be dating, Katie."

She didn't like his tone, or the implied command. "Luke, for heaven's sake. You think I want to complicate my life even more?" She fisted her hands. "And you don't get to tell me what I can or cannot do."

"It may have been a hasty wedding, but you're my wife."

She wrinkled her nose. "Don't say that."

"I'm your husband."

"For a nanosecond. Remember, you promised that you'll look into a divorce as soon as possible."

"I said it and I will. But until that time…" Luke came closer, his incredible eyes soft on her. He took her hand and squeezed. "If you ever need anything, call me."

"You know what I want."

He smiled and his blue eyes darkened. "I know what you think you want."

"What does that mean?"

His hand gently wrapped around her neck, his fingertips urging her forward. Then he lowered his mouth to hers and kissed her. It was tender and sweet, not at all demanding, and the pleasure made it hard to pull away.

"I think you should leave," she murmured, pushing at his chest.

"I was just going."

When he backed away, she stared at him. There was a moment, one tiny second, when she saw something in him that made her happy, made her wish he didn't have to go.

"When you hear from your attorney, give me a call."

He nodded and walked out of the bakery.

Maybe it was a good thing she hadn't taken him up to her apartment.

"Here's your herbal tea, Mama." Katie handed her mother a mug and took a seat beside her on the living room sofa in the home Katie and her sister had grown up in on Blue Jay Avenue. The neighborhood was close-knit, just on the outskirts of Boone Springs, about a ten-minute drive from the bakery. She'd come here as soon as she'd unpacked her bags.

"Thanks, honey. I love the pomegranate and blackberry mix." Her mother blew on the steam and then sipped delicately. "Mmm. Tastes so good going down."

"It is good," she said, concerned over her mother's health.

Diana Rodgers had tired eyes that told of sacrifice and lack of energy. Her body was a bit broken from ill health. At the age of fifty-eight, she'd suffered a minor heart attack that had taken her away from the teaching job she'd loved. Taking an early retirement had never been in her plans. She'd been a single mother most of her life, working hard at the grammar school with special needs kids. But the job was stressful, and Diana often took her work home with her, a habit her cardiologist couldn't condone.

"So why aren't you joining me in a cup?"

"I will a little later. Right now, I just want to hear how you're feeling."

"You've only been gone three days, hon. I appreciate you coming over as soon as you got home, but I'm the same as I was before you left." Her mom waved her hand. "Enough about me, how was your trip?"

"It was…nice." Katie had trouble mustering up any enthusiasm. *Oh, and one little detail I forgot to mention… I married Lucas Boone.* "Drea and Mason enjoyed it very much. I think everyone did."

Her mother moved around in her seat a bit and her mouth twisted as it did every time the Boone name was mentioned. "Too bad Drea had to fall in love with *him*."

"Mom, Mason's a nice guy."

"He's rich and feels entitled, just like all the Boones."

She meant Luke.

That sick feeling in Katie's stomach acted up again. "Drea's happy and that's all that matters."

Her mother sipped her tea. "So, what did all you gals do at the bachelorette party?"

Katie shrugged. "The usual things. We saw the sights, ate like there was no tomorrow, had a spa day, went to a concert, and then on the last night the entire group got together for a party at a nightclub."

There. She'd given a short, encapsulated version of her long weekend. Enough said.

"You had to deal with Luke?"

Before she could answer, Shelly walked into the house, dropping her shoulder bag on the edge of the sofa. "What about loser Luke?"

Katie's heart started pounding. Shelly was still bitter. "Hi, sis. What are you doing here?"

"Checking in with Mom, just like you." Her sister, dressed in nurse's white, walked over to give her mother a kiss on the cheek. "Hi, Mom. How are you today?"

"Feeling pretty good. Your sister made me some tea. Would you like a cup, sweetheart?"

"Thanks, but I'm fine. Just thought I'd stop by here first, before heading home and changing clothes. Dr. Moore asked me and a few colleagues to attend his seminar tonight. I have to leave soon. So, what about Luke?"

"Nothing," Katie said.

"Your sister had to plan Drea's bachelorette party with him."

"We didn't plan the bachelorette party together. He was

in charge of entertaining the groomsmen. All we did was coordinate the party at the end of the weekend together."

"Ugh," Shelly said. "Poor you."

"It wasn't that bad."

"I feel sorry for any woman who gets involved with him," Shelly said flatly. "I should've known better."

"He wasn't ready for marriage," Katie said. God, they'd had this conversation for years. It was truly beginning to grate on her nerves. Shelly never was one for letting go. She'd never forgiven their dad for divorcing their mother. She'd never accepted their father's new wife. Clearly, a broken engagement, even if it was three days before the ceremony, was much better than a divorce later on.

"Why are you defending him?" Shelly asked.

"Maybe I just want you to move on with your life, Shel. Maybe I'm not defending him so much as I'm looking out for you."

Shelly sighed. "Okay, got it. Easier said than done."

"It's so nice to have both of my girls here with me today," her mother said softly.

"I wish I could stay longer," Shelly said. "But I'm meeting everyone at the hospital in an hour."

"That's fine, honey. You go on to the seminar. I'm proud of the way you girls are so conscientious about your work. That means you, too, Katie."

"I know, Mama." Her mother had always told her how proud she was of what she'd accomplished at the bakery. Her business was on solid ground now but it hadn't always been that way. Her mom had faith in her, had always given her support. "I'll stay and visit with you a bit longer."

"Wonderful." Shelly gave her a rare smile.

Her sister had had a rough time facing her friends after the marriage debacle and then to have her "almost" groom leave town for years, leaving her with no hope, no way to reconcile her sadness, no way to rant and rave at him. That was probably the greatest injustice. Shelly had never gotten the closure she'd needed.

After Shelly left, Diana got up to take her teacup to the kitchen. "I made soup, your favorite, chicken and dumplings. Will you stay and have some with me?"

"Sure, that sounds yummy."

Katie was beat, tired and nervous, but having comfort food and her mother's company would distract her from the giant mistake she'd made in Las Vegas last night.

Katie raced down the stairs, stubbing her toe on the last step. "Ow, damn it." As she entered the bakery, not even the soothing scents of all things sweet helped lighten her mood this morning. She'd overslept by an hour and now she was totally behind schedule. Gosh, she'd had so much on her mind, sleep had eluded her, and when she'd finally fallen asleep, it had been deep and heavy. She'd dreamed that a faceless beast was chasing her and she'd kept running and running until she'd woken up in a sweat.

Was that dream trying to tell her something?

She flipped on the light, tied on her lavender Katie's Kupcakes and Bakery apron and got to work, gathering up her ingredients, prepping her cupcake tins.

The Monday morning special was always a carrot zucchini cupcake infused with a light apricot filling. She called it her Start Smart Special, a healthier alternative to a sugary treat. It was a fan favorite for those guilty of indulging over the weekend.

Her assistant, Lori, knocked on the back door. Katie opened it to her smiling face.

"Hey, good to see you. How was your trip?" Lori asked, as she walked past her and took off her sweater.

"Uh, it was okay."

"That so? Just okay?" Lori sounded as if she had her doubts. They'd worked closely together for six years and knew each other pretty well. Now Lori was putting herself through college at night aiming for a degree in business, so the bakery hours were perfect for her. The shop closed at two in the afternoon. "Sounds like it wasn't fun. Did something happen?"

"No. Nothing. I'm just tired. I overslept."

"You never oversleep. Maybe you had *too* much fun in Vegas." Lori winked. If she only knew. "You're gonna have to give me deets. I've been cramming all weekend, stuck at my place, fantasizing about your fun weekend."

"There are no details." Katie shrugged. "We had a good time. Saw a show. Got massages, did some dancing. Usual stuff."

"You were excited about it when you left here. I thought for sure you'd have some good Vegas stories to entertain me with this morning."

Lori put on her apron and they began measuring out ingredients. She started on chocolate ganache cupcakes with marshmallow filling while Katie worked on the special. They had their routine down to a science and being behind schedule meant one or two cupcakes would have to get the boot.

"Sorry, Lori. Nothing much to report," she fibbed. "How about we eliminate anything pumpkin, since the fall season has been over for a while," she said, changing the subject.

"Good choice."

"And if there are any complaints, you know what to do."

"Always."

It was her motto to keep the customer happy by giving away a free cupcake or two to ward off hostility. Although that rarely happened with her regular Boone Springs customers. They were like family. She knew most of them by name, as well as where they lived and how many kids they had. She often catered birthday parties and other occasions.

While the cupcakes were baking, she worked on pastries, filling croissants, making cookies and cinnamon rolls. Between the two of them, working nonstop, they'd filled the bakery case shelves by 7:00 a.m. Coffee brewed and her regulars began popping into the shop.

By nine thirty, there was a lull and Katie flopped into a chair in the small lounge by the back door. Exhaustion set in and it wasn't just from lack of sleep, but acute mental fatigue over what happened in Vegas this past weekend.

Lori gave her a sympathetic look. "Why don't you go upstairs for an hour?" she suggested. "Get in a nap. I can handle things until it picks up again."

"Don't we have deliveries today?" Sometimes they'd get orders from companies or restaurants or clients celebrating big birthdays.

Lori scanned the list on the bakery wall. "It's Monday and pretty calm right now."

"Thanks, but I'll be fine in a few minutes. Just need to get a second wind."

The second wind didn't come and by closing time, Katie was truly beat. She had one delivery to make, a last-minute order for a private dinner party happening later tonight. They needed a dozen tiramisu and a dozen lemon raspberry cupcakes, and while Lori closed up shop, Katie arranged the cupcakes in a box and taped it shut.

"Let me take those for you," Lori said. "I can drop them off on my way home. This way you can go upstairs now and relax, put your feet up."

"I can't let you do that. You've got studying to do."

"It'll take me ten minutes, tops. It's my way of making up for all the days you let me off early when I had to cram for an exam. Say yes."

"You really are such a good friend. Yes. Thanks."

Lori smiled. "Welcome."

After Lori took off with the delivery, Katie climbed the stairs slowly and once inside her apartment, plopped down on her sofa. She turned on the television, struggling to keep her eyes open until she finally lost the battle.

Normally, Luke spent most of his time in the office in the main house at Rising Springs Ranch. He took a hands-on approach to running things on the property and had a good relationship with Joe Buckley, their ranch foreman. They worked well together and Luke knew Joe wouldn't let him down.

Today he was at the Boone Springs corporate office, sitting in a room with his name plaque on the desk, staring out the window.

He had Katie on the brain and he'd come into town today, just because he wanted to be close to her. Her bakery was only two blocks away, nestled in between a clothing boutique and a fabric store. Because of the location, the bakery got pretty good foot traffic. Even if it didn't, Katie would be successful, because her pastries were the best in the county and because Luke had made sure no Boone holdings would ever compete with her.

A little fact he'd kept secret.

While he was serving the country, he'd made his wishes known and his brothers had all been onboard. He'd put the Rodgers family through enough and they'd done what they could to make sure Shelly and her family wouldn't unintentionally suffer any hardships of their doing.

But for him, it had mostly been about Katie. Wanting to see her succeed, wanting her to have a good life. God, when he'd come back home, he'd wished she had married, or at the very least, been in a serious relationship. Knowing she was still single had made his return torturous, yet he'd managed to keep his distance when he saw her around town or when they volunteered at the horse rescue.

And then Vegas happened.

Frustrated, he forced himself to go over ranching reports he'd pulled up on his computer. He had to get some work done, had to feel productive today, instead of daydreaming about seeing Katie again.

A little after two in the afternoon, his cell phone rang. "Hey, Wes. How's it going?" Luke usually didn't hear from the manager of the horse rescue, so he knew this had to be important.

"Hey, Luke. Sorry for the call, but it's Snow. I'm sorry to say it might be her time. The ole girl isn't breathing real well. I've had Dr. Hernandez out. He gave her some painkillers, but that's about all he can do for her. Thought you'd like to know."

Luke's stomach churned. Snowball was a mustang who'd been severely abused and she'd come to the rescue at the same time he'd returned home. He and Katie both had sort of taken the mare under their wing. They had a soft spot for the old girl. She'd been recovering, but the abuse had taken its toll on her and unfortunately with some of the horses, there wasn't much else to do but ease their pain.

"Thanks, Wes. Sorry to hear that. I'll, uh, I'll come by. I want to see her."

"Thought you would."

"I'll let Katie know, too."

"I just called Katie. She didn't answer her phone. I left her a message."

"Okay, well, I'll try to get word to her somehow. I'll see you soon, Wes."

Luke hung up and rubbed at the corners of his eyes. Giving himself a moment to gather his thoughts, he shook his head. As much as he wanted to see Katie again, he didn't want to give her bad news.

Five minutes later, he was in his car, driving by the bakery. There was a Katie's Kupcakes Is Klosed sign on the window. Still, he parked the car in a diagonal spot right in front of the bakery and got out. He tried the shop's door handle. No luck. Then he cupped his hands to ward off the sun's glare and peered inside the window. Not a soul was around.

A car slowed on the street and a young girl called out, "Can I help you?"

He recognized her as one of Katie's employees, though he couldn't recall her name. She'd made a few deliveries to the Boone corporate office. "I'm looking for Katie."

"Hold on a sec." The young woman parked her car and walked over to where he stood by the door.

"I'm Lucas Boone."

She smiled as if to say she knew who he was; the Boones were usually recognized in town. "Hi, Lucas. I'm Lori. Do you need cupcakes or something? The bakery is closed."

"No, nothing like that. I need to see Katie. It's important. Has to do with the Red Barrel Horse Rescue."

"Oh… I see." The young woman nibbled on her lips.

"She's not answering her phone."

"No, she's probably resting up in her apartment. She was pretty exhausted today."

"It's really important. Can you help me?"

She thought it over for a few seconds. "I know your brother is marrying her best friend, Drea. So, I guess it's all right if I let you in."

"Thank you."

Lori put the key into the lock and opened the door. "I only came back because I left my textbook and notes here and I've got this big exam tomorrow night."

Luke nodded and she let him inside the empty bakery.

"I'll go upstairs and knock on her door," she said. "I'll let Katie know you're here."

And a few minutes later, Luke was face-to-face with a sleep-hazy Katie.

"W-what are you doing here?" Katie stood at her doorway, a plaid blanket wrapped around her shoulders, staring at Luke. She didn't think she'd see him again so soon. His head was down, a concerned look on his face. Her heart began to pound hard. "Lori said something about the rescue?"

"I got a call from Wes a little while ago. It's Snow. She's in bad shape."

The air left her lungs and her shoulders slumped. "Oh no. Not our girl."

"Yep. I'm afraid so." He rubbed the back of his neck. "Thought you'd want to know. Wes tried to call you."

"I—I was fast asleep. I didn't hear my phone."

"I'm on my way out to see her. Maybe for the last time."

Oh man. All she could think about was the raw deal Snowball had gotten, a life of abuse and pain. Her owner had neglected her and she'd come to the rescue undernourished, scarred and broken. It wasn't fair. They'd tried their best to save her, and now Katie wasn't about to let her take her last breaths alone. "I've got to see her, too."

"I'll take you."

"No, you go on." She ran a hand through her hair. She must look a mess. "I need to run a comb through my hair and freshen up."

"I'll wait."

"You don't have to."

"Katie, I'm here, my car's out front and we're driving to the same place. Let's not waste any more time when we can spend it with Snow. Just do what you have to do, I'll be waiting downstairs."

He was right. Snow was too important to her to quibble with him about driving arrangements. "Okay, fine. Give me a minute."

Five minutes later, she was dressed in jeans and a red shirt, her hair in a knot at the top of her head. She splashed water on her face and put on lip gloss to keep from biting her lips and then dashed down the stairs and out the door of the bakery.

Luke waited for her out front, leaning against his black SUV, his hands in his pockets, a pensive look on his face. Her stomach was still in a twist about her ultra-secret marriage to her sister's ex. And now, the sweet mare she'd tended for the past year might be dying.

"Ready?" Luke asked, opening the door for her.

"Yes... I think."

"Yeah, I know what you mean. Snow's a special one."

Katie climbed in and grabbed her seat belt while Luke closed the door and took a seat behind the wheel. They drove off in silence and as they approached the canyon, she shivered.

"Cold?" he asked.

"A little." She hugged her arms to her chest. "I forgot my jacket." She'd forgotten how chilly the canyon could get in the later hours of the day.

"I can warm you up real fast," he said, giving her a smile.

His dimpled grin brought heat to her body instantly. She flashed back to Vegas and those hours they'd spent in bed together.

He reached for the dials on his dashboard and soon a flow of warm air surrounded her. "Better?"

She nodded.

"I've got an extra jacket in the back. I won't let you freeze to death out here."

That he was talking about "letting" her do anything or

not gave her nerves a rattle. He wasn't really her husband—just thinking it seemed completely foreign to her—but he was taking care of her needs and that wasn't something she was used to, with any guy. "Thanks."

A few minutes later they approached Red Barrel Horse Rescue and Luke parked in the gravel lot in front of the small building that served as the office. "I'll go in and let Wes know we're here," he said. "You want to stay in the car and keep warm?"

"No, I'll go with you."

"Sure," he said. He stretched way back and grabbed two jackets from the back seat of his car. "Here you go."

He handed her a suede jacket lined with lamb's wool, while he took a lighter weight cotton one. They tossed them on, hers almost reaching her knees, and Wes came out of the office to greet them.

The men shook hands, then Wes gave her a gentle hug. "I knew you two would come out as soon as you heard. Snow's in the barn. I've made her as comfortable as possible."

Luke met her eyes, then looked back at Wes. "We'd like to see her now."

"You two know the way. Stay as long as you want."

"Thanks," Luke said, his hand closing over hers gently. They began walking toward the barn and Katie took note of all the other horses in the corrals on the property. They were the lucky ones who'd been given a second chance at Red Barrel. There were so many others who were sick and hungry running wild in the canyons.

Once they reached the wide wooden doors, Luke turned to her. "No matter what happens in there, just know we did the very best we could for her."

"I know that," she whispered. "It's just that she's a special one. And she's been through so much."

"Well then," he said, his eyes softening. "Let's make her final hours the best they can be."

She held on to a breath. And then exhaled. "Okay."

They walked out of the daylight and into the darkened barn. A cold shiver ran through her. It was definitely jacket weather in the canyon.

"There she is," he said, pointing to the largest paddock in the barn.

Katie moved closer to the stall and as she laid eyes on Snow, she clutched her chest. "Oh, sweet girl." It hurt so much seeing Snow weak, giving up the fight.

"She's down," Luke said. "But she's still with us."

"Yes, she still is. You've waited for us, haven't you, my pretty Snowball?"

Snow lifted her head and eyed them both before laying her head back down on a pillow of straw.

Katie took off her jacket and entered the stall, laying the jacket on the straw beside the mare. "Do you mind?" she asked Luke.

"Not at all," he said, doing the same with his jacket.

They lowered down and sat on the jackets next to Snow.

"Hey, girl. I'm here," she whispered in her ear. "You don't have to do this alone." Katie laid her hand on Snow's mane and used the gentlest touch to comfort her. "I know you're struggling to breathe. Just stay calm. I'm here."

Luke stroked Snow's flank and whistled a soft, mellow tune. He was actually pretty good and not only did the whistling relax the mare, it soothed Katie's nerves as well.

"That's nice," she said, closing her eyes. "How did you learn to do that?"

"A buddy of mine taught me when I was overseas."

Katie opened her eyes. "When you were in Afghanistan?"

He nodded. "We had time to kill when we weren't on

active duty. You know, something to fill the void from being away from home."

"Must've been hard."

"It wasn't a walk in the park," he said.

"Yet you signed up for it. When you had family here and a multimillion-dollar company to run. You didn't have to enlist."

"I felt like I did. I think the time away helped."

"Are you talking about my sister now?"

He nodded. "I never meant to hurt her. I know she hates me, but a lot of time has passed since we broke up."

"You mean, since you walked out on her? Humiliated her?"

"Yeah," he said, frowning. "If that's the way you want to put it."

"It's just that my family trusted you," she said, stroking Snow's mane. Luke hadn't stopped his caresses either. "And your decision sort of came out of left field."

"What can I say that I haven't already?"

Katie was at odds with her feelings. She wanted to support Shelly and their mom, but Luke had a point. He couldn't marry a woman he didn't love. It was just too bad he'd come to that conclusion right before the wedding was to take place.

"I know they hate me, Katie. But do you?"

The question took her completely off guard. "*Hate*'s a strong word."

"So you don't?"

"Let's just say I hate how things played out."

Luke nodded. "Fair enough."

"Speaking about the way things played out, any news from your attorney about our dilemma?"

Luke frowned. "No."

She drew a deep breath. "Too much to hope, I guess."

Snow became agitated, moving around on her bed of straw.

"I think you need to keep whistling," Katie said. "It really does help her."

Luke put his lips together again and the melodic sounds filled the barn. Soon, Snow calmed and her breaths came more evenly.

Afternoon gave way to evening, and the ole girl hung on. Snow's eyes were closed now, her breathing more labored. "That's my girl, Snow. Ease over the bridge now. You'll be in a better place soon." Katie bent to kiss her and stroked up and down her nose.

Luke took a break from whistling. "I remember when I first spotted her. She was covered with sores and bruises, yet she had soulful eyes. They were filled with such life, such hope."

"I was appalled at the way she'd been treated. For heaven's sake, the poor thing didn't have a name," Katie said.

"Yeah, I remember. Her coat was black underneath the dirt, and that circle of white on her forehead right smack between her ears couldn't be missed. It looked like she'd been struck by a fat snowball."

"And I named her Snowball."

"I named her Snowball," Luke said, raising his voice an octave.

She smiled, seeing the feigned indignation on his face. In truth, she didn't know who'd said it first, but they'd agreed on the name. "Okay, maybe we both named her Snowball."

Luke smiled, too. "I think that's the way it happened. Finally, we agree on something."

Katie liked this Luke, the one who showed compassion. A man who could laugh at himself and not put on airs. He was a zillionaire, yet he never seemed to flaunt it. "It's the magic of Snow. She's…"

They both gazed down at the mare. She was still. No longer breathing. "Oh no."

Katie looked at Luke as both their smiles faded. The mare had taken her last breath as they were conversing. Snow had heard them, recognized their voices and felt at peace enough to slip away without struggle.

Tears stung Katie's eyes.

Luke, too, was pinching the inner corners of his eyes.

"She's g-gone."

"She is," he said. He wrapped his arms around her shoulders, pulling her in close. "But she went knowing she was loved."

Katie couldn't hold back any longer. She nodded, bobbing her head as the truth of his words sank in. She wept quietly and turned to Luke, her tears running down her cheeks and soaking his shirt.

"It's okay, Katie. Don't cry, sweetheart."

"I knew this day would come, but I didn't think it would be so soon. I thought we'd have more time with her."

She had never owned a pet. She'd never had an animal to care for, to nurture and love, until she'd started working at the rescue. She loved all the horses here; they all had a story. But for some reason Snow was special. She'd touched Katie's heart and they'd shared a deep connection, a bond that she didn't have with any of the others. Katie had taken it as a personal challenge to make Snow's days comfortable.

Luke clearly felt the same way. His eyes moist, his expression sad, he couldn't mask his sorrow either. He brushed his lips across her forehead. She needed his warmth right now, his strength.

"There's nothing more we can do." His voice was shaky and he seemed reluctant to release her, to let go of the bond they'd shared. "We should go."

She nodded, wiping her face with the back of her hand

and then attempting to pat his shirt dry from her tears. "Sorry."

"Don't worry about it," he said softly.

"I hate to leave her."

"I'll let Wes know she's gone. He'll take good care of her from now on."

It was hard to let go. To say goodbye.

Luke rose and helped her up, entwining their hands. "Ready?"

"I think so." She glanced at poor Snow one last time, her heart breaking.

Luke picked up the jackets and brushed the straw off them. "Put this on. It'll be cold outside."

He gave the fallen horse one last glance, too, a look filled with sadness and regret as he grabbed a woolen blanket from the stall post and covered her body.

Katie slipped into his jacket and he clasped her hand again, his warmth and strength seeping into her. He led her out of the barn. "C'mon, sweetheart. Let me take you home."

She didn't mind the endearment this time; she couldn't fight it. Couldn't argue. She'd had a rough twenty-four hours and she was just too numb to think anymore. His shoulders were there for her to lean on, he seemed to know the right things to say and this one time she would accept what Luke had to offer.

Without guilt.

Three

Luke stood facing Katie at the threshold of her apartment. He'd insisted on escorting her upstairs after entering the bakery, probably because she couldn't quite get her emotions in check. She'd wept most of the drive home, little sobs that broke from her lips every time she pictured Snow lying still on the ground, lifeless. In the car, Luke had glanced at her often. She'd felt his concerned gaze but she couldn't look him in the eye. She didn't like showing her vulnerable side to anyone, but tonight she couldn't help it. Her emotions were running out of control.

"Are you going to be okay?" he asked her.

"I think so." She bit her lip. "You don't have to worry about me."

He stared into her eyes, then ran a hand down his jawline. "But I do."

"You have no obligation to me, Luke. Really, I'll be fine."

"Is that what you think this is?"

He said it softly, without condemnation, and suddenly she felt small and petty. "No, no. I'm sorry. I know you're just as upset as I am about Snow. Really, I'm glad we shared her last night together. You cared for her as much as I did. Gosh, I can't believe I'm speaking of her in the past tense."

"It's strange, huh?"

"Yeah."

She stared at him, so many thoughts racing through her mind. But mostly, she was glad he was there tonight, lending her comfort, helping her come to grips with losing Snow.

"It's been a long day. I should let you go, get some rest," he said.

"That sounds…good."

"Okay, well. Good night then."

He turned to leave and Katie blurted, "Luke, wait."

He turned, his dark brows lifting.

She took both of his hands in hers and gave a squeeze. "I just wanted to thank you for coming to get me today. It meant a lot to me to be there. Honestly, I don't know how I would've gotten through it all, if you weren't with me."

Then she reached up on tiptoes and pressed her lips to his cheek to give him a chaste peck, but suddenly she turned her head, he turned his, and their lips were locked in a real kiss. Luke made a sound from deep in his chest and a warm delicious sensation sparked inside her.

She might've kissed Luke dozens of times in Vegas, but she didn't remember any one of them. *This* kiss she'd remember. This kiss she didn't want to end.

A moan rose from her throat, one of need and want, and for a moment she flushed, totally embarrassed. But Luke didn't stop, he didn't hesitate to devour her mouth. He was all in, too, stirring her deepest yearnings to be held, to be comforted. She was hurting inside and this kiss was a balm to her soul.

He moved forward, backing her into the apartment, kissing her endlessly. She went willingly, relishing the taste of him, the raw pleasure he was giving to her. He tossed his jacket off and then removed hers without breaking the kiss. Then he cradled her in his arms, holding her so close to him that his need pressed against her belly.

A surge of heat raced through her. It was astonishing how quickly he made her come alive. She was glad of it, glad of the sensations rocking her body. In Luke's strong arms, she suddenly wanted what was forbidden to her.

"Luke," she said when the kiss came to an end.

He looked deep into her eyes. "Don't tell me to stop," he whispered, grazing his lips over hers again.

"I'm not, but maybe we should come up for air?"

The quick smile on his face devastated her. He was so darn handsome. Why did it have to be him? She took a deep breath, pausing for just a few seconds. "Okay, that's enough."

"You're good with this?" he asked, brushing a wayward strand of hair off her face. "Don't answer that," he murmured. "I already know you are."

He cupped her face in his hands and gazed into her eyes, before claiming her lips again. The absolute pleasure overwhelmed her, helping to ease the pain in her heart. It amazed her how easily she welcomed him, how much she wanted more of his kisses, more of him. Her insides heated, and a spiral of warmth traveled through her body, making her hot, needy.

"You feel it, too, don't you?" he whispered in her ear.

She shouldn't. But yes, yes. She did. "Yes," she said softly, hating to admit it, but she couldn't lie to him. Couldn't try to deny how his touch shockingly turned her on. How his kisses made her melt. How she wanted more.

This was all about Snow and the loss she felt. It had to be. Because no other reason would do.

Luke unbuttoned his shirt and tossed it off. He clasped her hand and set it flat on his chest. The taut muscles under her palm intrigued her and she moved her hand over him, gently mapping out the broad expanse of his chest. He was stunning, hard, firm, tough.

Electricity sizzled between them, an invisible connection pulling her closer, making her head swim. She pressed a kiss to his shoulder and felt him shudder.

"Katie."

Her name came from deep in his throat, not a plea, not a warning, but a mixture of awe and reverence that set off a barrage of tingles.

She hadn't had a man in her life for two years, and even that hadn't been anything serious, just casual dating. And now here she was with Lucas Boone, for heaven's sake, wanting him, needing his strength and compassion. Her body reacted to his, and she was sure it was mutual grief heightening the sensations, making a hard day a bit easier.

He began kissing her again, drawing her tight into his arms, his big hands caressing her shoulders, her back and then lower yet. Everything below her waist throbbed in the very best way.

She moaned, a guttural sound erupting from her throat that she didn't recognize as her own. Yet she relished the way Luke touched her, and soon his hands were caressing her chest, undoing the buttons on her blouse, pushing it off her. His eyes gleamed as he took in her small round breasts overflowing the cups of her bra.

"So beautiful," he murmured between kisses.

His praise brought more tingles, more heat. She was lost in the moment, totally and fully engaged. He removed her bra and cupped her breasts, taking one into his mouth, stroking it with his tongue gently, reverently, making her feel more alive than she'd ever felt before.

Soon she was wrapped in his arms and being carried into her bedroom. He didn't let up, didn't stop kissing her until he set her down, her boots touching the ground.

"Invite me in," he rasped.

That made her smile. "You're already here," she whispered.

His lips quirked up in a sexy way and she wouldn't have been able to deny him, even if she'd wanted to. "I guess I am." He kissed her again and before she knew it, the rest of her clothes were off and she lay waiting for Luke on the bed.

She had a moment of panic, the realization of what was happening finally dawning. This was Luke, her sister's ex, the man she'd accidentally married in Las Vegas. Yet she'd bonded with him tonight while they were saying goodbye to Snow and shared a deep loss together. It was complicated, and she'd deal with it later, but now... now she needed the comfort he provided. The thrills were an added bonus.

He came over her on the bed, gazing down, a hungry look in his eyes. "I don't take this lightly, Katie. I... This isn't—"

"I know," she said simply. "I know why this is happening."

"You do?"

"It's about Snow."

Luke stared at her for a long second. "Yeah."

Then he covered her body with his, stroking her below the waist until she whimpered in pleasure and then shattered into a hundred pieces. Now she knew what total bliss felt like and she basked in contentment. "Oh wow," was all she could say.

"Yeah, wow," Luke said, pressing tiny kisses along her

shoulder blades, allowing her time to enjoy the aftermath of her climax.

Then he brought his lips to hers again, and she welcomed it and invited him in with her body. He wasted no time shedding the rest of his clothes and sheathing himself in a condom. "I want you, Katie."

She knew. And so when he joined their bodies and gasped, she did, too. "Oh, Luke."

He filled her full and the need inside her grew as his thrusts deepened. Each movement heightened the intensity until she cried out. Luke seemed as lost as she was, moving inside her in a deliberate rhythm that lifted her hips and took her completely home.

He wasn't far behind. His thrusts grew harder, his face masked in pained pleasure and she kept pace with him, taking the ride with him, until he finally shuddered in release.

Moments later, he fell upon the bed next to her and cradled her in his arms. He kissed her forehead and kept her close, both of them too out of breath to utter a word.

Luke woke first, and Katie's sweet scent wafted to his nose. He felt her presence beside him on the bed, and when he opened his eyes and actually saw her snuggled in tight, her honey blond strands spilling onto her pillow, he smiled. She was his wife, and they'd made love last night like they belonged together. This was his honeymoon, all he'd ever wanted. All he'd ever needed.

How many lonely nights had he spent thinking about her? During his stint in the Marines, forbidden thoughts of her would creep into his mind. He'd felt terrible for hurting Shelly, for hurting the Rodgers family. But it would've been a whole lot worse, being married to one sister while secretly craving the other. Often, when he was alone with his thoughts in Afghanistan, he'd wondered if he'd been a damn fool for falling for a woman he'd never touched, never kissed. How would he know if they were compatible? What if the real thing didn't live up to the fantasy?

Now, he knew.

Oh boy, were they compatible. Katie *was* his real thing, his fantasy come true.

He stared at her, watching her take slow peaceful breaths. He should probably leave and let her come to grips with what happened alone. But he couldn't walk out on her. He couldn't leave without seeing her reaction. Was he a fool to hope that she'd be okay with what happened between them?

It was nearing 4:00 a.m. She'd soon be rising for work, but he needed a few more minutes to savor being in bed with her, to savor the sweet serenity of her body next to his, their warmth mingling.

Luke sighed and bent over to place a light kiss on her cheek.

"Mmm," she murmured in her sleep.

He smiled and gently moved a fallen strand of hair from her face. "My pretty Katie," he whispered, needing to touch her again.

She tossed around a bit and he backed off, turning to his side and bracing his head in his hand, content to just watch her sleep.

Too soon, the alarm clock on the nightstand blasted through the peace and Katie opened her eyes and found him beside her. "Hi," she said.

Her greeting surprised him.

"Morning, sweetheart."

Clearly, she wasn't thinking straight.

Luke reached over her to shut off the alarm and then pressed his luck, brushing his lips over hers. Her lips were warm and welcoming. For a second, he held on to hope. "Did you sleep well?"

She blinked and blinked again. "What the…" And then she darted up on the bed, a pained expression on her face. "Oh no."

She glanced down, obviously noting she'd slept in the nude. She grimaced as if her world was coming to an end and then covered up her perfect body.

"Katie—"

"Luke, this was only about Snow. We were both hurting last night, but I… I should've known better. I shouldn't have let my emotions overwhelm my judgment. We can't keep doing this."

"Seems to me, we *do* keep doing this. Must mean something."

"It does. It means I'm a numbskull."

"No, you're not. You're human, and you have real feelings that you can't chuck away or hide. It was good between us last night."

Katie stared at him as if remembering. She couldn't deny the sparks and fire they'd shared last night. For him, there was nothing better.

"Yes, but it can't happen again. We were both…lost."

He wasn't lost. He'd known exactly what he'd needed. And she did, too, but she wouldn't admit it.

She shrugged and a little pout curled her mouth up. "Poor Snow."

"Yeah. It was hard losing her, but you gave her the comfort she needed."

"You really think so?"

He nodded. "I think you're amazing."

"Don't say things like that. It's already complicated enough."

"What, I can't praise my wife?"

She gritted her teeth. "I…am…not…your…wife."

Luke's good nature faded. Why was the thought of being married to him so distasteful? Of course, he knew it was because of Shelly, but was that all it was? Her harsh tone spurred his temper. "Funny, but I have a document that says you are. And, sweetheart, we've consummated our marriage more than once already."

"Don't remind me," she said, rising from the bed, taking the sheets with her. But one corner of the sheet caught on the nightstand knob and jerked away from her body. She stood before him naked in all her glory.

She hoisted her chin. "I'm taking a shower. I'm already late getting to the bakery. You need to leave before Lori gets here, which is in less than an hour."

As she turned away, he focused on the curvy shape of her bare body, her rounded cheeks and the length of her long legs.

It was a freaking turn-on. His throat went dry and his body grew immediately hard. Hell, he wasn't getting out of this bed until he calmed down. He needed to think about cattle prices or something equally benign.

And ticked off as he was, he still couldn't help wondering what she would do if he followed her into the shower.

Katie set two pots of coffee brewing on the back counter of the bakery, behind the near empty bakery case. Normally, decaf was her speed, but this morning she needed a large jolt of caffeine, something that would make her think more clearly. Obviously, last night she'd had no clarity. Not one bit. All she'd had was grief and Luke's welcoming arms.

Spending the night with him had been a big mistake, but at the time she'd needed someone. No, not just someone... She'd needed Luke.

God, she didn't want to feel things for him that would cause a world of trouble. What she'd confessed to him in Las Vegas was true. She wanted someone in her life. She wanted a partner, someone to share moments with, someone who'd have her back. But it couldn't be him. Never him. Her mother's weak heart couldn't take it and Shelly would probably disown her as a sister. She held Luke responsible for her lack of trust in men and her generally bitter disposition.

Katie felt sorry for Shelly and was completely guilt-ridden about finding momentary pleasure in Luke's arms last night. He was the poison apple and she'd taken the forbidden bite.

Katie set out her utensils and staples: bowls, measuring cups, flour, sugar and eggs. She had begun measuring out her ingredients when the sound of boot heels clicking on the stairs reached her ears. Her nerves rattled a bit. It was Luke. Thank God, he was leaving.

"Coffee smells real good. Mind if I have a cup?" he asked.

She kept her head down, pouring sugar into the industrial-size bowl. "It's not ready yet."

"That's okay. I'll wait."

She glanced at the wall clock.

"Don't worry, I'll be out of your hair in a few minutes. I just want a little coffee before I head out. Lori will never know I was here."

"But I will," she muttered.

Luke chuckled.

"Don't laugh. None of this is funny."

He came up behind her, his nearness making her jittery. "Katie, I'm not laughing at the situation. I know this isn't easy on you. I'm laughing, because…well."

"What?" She turned to face him. He'd cleaned up nicely, his dark blond hair groomed and overnight beard extremely swoon-worthy.

He curled his hands around her waist and drew her in with those sky blue eyes. "You're cute when you're angry. Sexy, too."

"Hardly, Luke." She rolled her eyes.

"You doubt it, after last night?"

"Look, I know you think you're my husband and all, but from now on, I'd appreciate it if you didn't tell me I was amazing or sexy or cute. I'm none of those things...to you."

"Sounds like the coffee's ready." He ignored her comment and walked into the bakery.

She sighed. Maybe it was better not to argue with him. He would leave soon and she could go on with her baking.

"You want leaded?" he asked from the other room.

"God, yes," she called to him.

While he was pouring coffee, she combined all the ingredients for her base cupcake recipe and turned on the mixer. Then she started cutting up fruit for her fresh fillings; it was peaches and apples today.

Luke walked in with two steaming cups of coffee. "You take anything in it?"

"No, just black is fine," she said. She sampled too many of her sweets during the day to add any more sugar to her diet. She'd learned the hard way to always taste test her pastries before putting them on the shelves.

"I like watching you work," he said, handing her a cup.

She didn't know what to do with that comment. She clutched the cup to warm up her hands and wished he'd just leave.

"Do you get up at four every morning?"

She nodded. "If I want to open the bakery at seven, I do."

"It's a lot of work."

"It is, but Lori's a big help. Most mornings we're right on schedule."

He smiled, then sipped his coffee. He made her uncomfortable, eyeballing her the way that he was. She put her coffee down and got back to work.

"Okay," he said, taking a huge gulp. "It's time for me to get going, too."

"So soon?" she asked with a rise in her voice and once again, he chuckled.

"You know, I can stick around if it'd make you feel better."

"Out," she said, turning her back on him.

Luke didn't seem to take offense. Instead he roped his arms around her and she turned to frown at him. "What are you doing?"

"Giving you a goodbye kiss."

And then his mouth was on hers, and the melding of their lips felt like heaven on earth.

When the kiss ended, she backed away from him and pointed to the door. "Go."

He went.

She drew a deep breath and then let out a flustered sigh. Whenever the man kissed her, she felt helpless and needy.

It was all so terribly wrong.

Three days later, Drea entered the bakery just before lunch, a big smile on her face. Her bestie was smiling a lot lately and most of that had to do with Mason. Katie wasn't jealous of their happiness; she was thrilled for the two of them. It was just, at times, she thought she'd never meet the right guy, never know that kind of love.

She didn't get any encouragement from her sister and mom. They both thought a woman was better off without a man, but Katie didn't see it that way. She wasn't bitter or jaded, not yet anyway. But being around that sort of pessimism made it hard to keep a positive attitude.

Drea walked up to the counter and Katie greeted her. "Hi there. What brings you by so early this morning?"

"I have an invitation for you."

"Lunch? I'd love to." She wouldn't mind catching up with her friend.

"No, silly. Not lunch. Mason and I want to thank you for helping us plan the wedding and for being the best bachelorette party planner around. We want to take you to dinner tonight. Don't say no. We really, really want to do this."

Katie smiled. "Of course. I'd love to. Thanks."

"Can you be ready by six?"

"I can." She gave Drea a nod. Well, it wasn't lunch with her friend, but Mason was a pretty nice guy and Katie could use the distraction. "Where should I meet you?"

"Oh, no need for that. Luke will pick you up."

"Luke? Uh, why on earth?"

Drea shook her head. "Listen, I know he's not your favorite person, but you two seemed to get along just fine in Las Vegas."

The mention of Vegas brought up visions of their hasty drunken marriage and Katie's stomach squeezed tight.

"It's a thank-you dinner for him, too. We thought you wouldn't mind…much. I mean, you two have been working together at Red Barrel, right? And you seem cordial enough lately."

Oh gosh. Little did Drea know, Luke made her uncomfortable in too many ways to name. Being cordial to him in public was an act.

Yet Katie didn't want to come off as a scrooge. She didn't want to hurt Mason's feelings either, by refusing to break bread with his brother. What could she say? She was trapped, by no conscious doing by her friend. "No, that's fine. But maybe I should drive myself. You know, in case it's a late night. I wouldn't want to hold you guys up. You know I turn into a pumpkin by ten o'clock."

Drea laughed. "I promise Luke will have you home by ten."

"Can't we all go together?"

"We could, only Mason and I will be leaving earlier in the day for a final meeting with our wedding caterer and we didn't think you'd want to be dragged to that."

It was an impossible set of circumstances. Having maid of honor duties alongside Luke as best man, they were bound to be thrown together, but Katie hadn't seen this one coming. Not by a longshot. "Fine, have Luke pick me up. What should I wear?"

"Something dazzling. We're going to The Majestic."

It was a swanky non-Boone restaurant known for its classically romantic atmosphere on the outskirts of Boone County. "Nice," Katie said, feigning enthusiasm.

"Okay, great. We'll see you tonight." Drea clapped her hands. "I'm so excited. I've never been there before."

"Neither have I."

"It'll be a first for both of us then."

At noon, Katie and Lori were in the midst of their second rush hour, the first always coming around eight in the morning. This noon rush wasn't anything they couldn't handle, so when Shelly walked in with a man by her side, Katie greeted them both.

"Hi, Shel. Good to see you. What's up?" She darted a glance at the good-looking blond man standing beside Shelly.

"Katie, this is Dr. Moore. He's new in town and I told him about the best cupcakes in all of Boone County. Dr. Moore, this is my talented sis, Katie."

They exchanged greetings.

"Let me warn you, I have a sweet tooth," Dr. Moore said. "So you might be seeing me in here a great deal."

"Then you are my kind of person. Welcome. Do you have a favorite flavor?"

"I told him you make the best lemon raspberry cupcake

in the world." Shelly smiled and there was a light in her eyes that Katie hadn't seen in a long time.

"Sounds good to me. Love the shop, by the way," he said, admiring the pastel decor and dining area. He glanced at the bakery case. "And it looks like I'll be back to try everything you have in here."

"Good thing his brother is a dentist," Shelly said, teasing.

Katie chuckled. Her sister *never* teased, at least not recently, and it brought a lightness to Katie's heart. "I'd say so. So, will you two be eating here? We also have coffee, hot chocolate and chai."

"Another time. I'm afraid I have to get back to the hospital ASAP."

"Me, too," Shelly said.

"Okay then, let me box these up for you. And I'll throw in a few of my carrot zucchini specials and my newest creation, vanilla infused with peaches."

"That's very nice of you. Can't wait to try them later." His cell phone rang and he glanced at the screen. "Excuse me. I'm sorry, but I have to get this," he said, walking toward the front door. "Shelly, can you meet me outside?"

"Of course."

"Thanks again, Katie."

"Sure thing."

The second the doctor walked out, Katie couldn't hold her tongue. "He's really cute."

"I suppose."

"You mean to say you haven't noticed?"

Shelly caught her drift and rolled her eyes. "Oh, for heaven's sake. I was just being neighborly. Dr. Moore doesn't know too many people in town. I thought he'd like the shop and I wanted to introduce him to you."

"So, you're not interested in him? Because he seems

nice and you've never brought a guy into my shop before this."

"No, I'm not interested in him. Luke ruined me for all men, I'm afraid. So don't even think it."

"Shel, really. It's been years and it's time you moved on. Can't I think it a *little bit*?"

"Not even a smidge."

Katie sighed. She only wanted her sister to be happy. But it looked like Shelly was fighting it tooth and nail.

Katie selected the cupcakes from the bakery case and set them in the box, sealing it with two Katie's Kupcakes stickers. "Okay then. Here you go," she said, handing the box to Shelly.

"Thanks for the treats, sis."

"Shel?"

"What?"

"I like it when you come by to see me. You should do it more often."

Shelly's expression softened and there was beauty in her eyes and her smile just then. "I will. I promise."

Katie watched her sister leave and sighed. She had her own problems to deal with.

Tonight, she had a "date" with the man who'd broken her sister's heart.

Four

Luke scrutinized his reflection in the mirror after changing his shirt and tie several times trying to get the look just right. Normally, he didn't give two figs about looking sharp, but tonight he was going on a date with Katie. Well, not a date, but hell, the way his stomach was doing somersaults, it might as well be one. He hadn't seen her in three days. He'd kept himself busy, but no amount of work or play could keep him from thinking about her.

Once dressed, he headed to the parlor and found Aunt Lottie sitting on the sofa, all alone, sipping from a tumbler of bourbon. As soon as she noticed him, she gave him a wolf whistle and he chuckled. He never knew what she would do or say. She was genuine and quite a surprise and that's why all of his family loved her. But the desolate look he'd caught on her face moments before he entered the room tugged at his heart.

"You look handsome, Luke. Got a hot date?"

"Thanks. And you know I'm going to dinner with Mason and Drea tonight."

"And Katie, too? Is that why you've spruced up?"

"Never mind me. What's wrong, Aunt Lottie? And don't put me off. You've been unusually quiet lately. Is it Drew?"

She pursed her lips, but then finally nodded. "That man's got me all mixed up."

Drew MacDonald lived on the property now. He'd once been a land baron, with a ranch adjacent to Rising Springs, but he'd fallen on hard times when his wife Maria passed away. Lottie and Maria had been dear friends, and now years later, Drew and Luke's aunt were testing the waters of a relationship that unfortunately seemed to be drying up.

"It's clear you two care for each other."

"I suppose," she said. "But he's forever badgering me about this and that."

"That's nothing new. Even when Maria was alive, you two didn't much see eye to eye."

"Isn't that important though? Seems to me, a man and woman should have the same disposition."

"Boring."

"What?" she asked.

"Aunt Lottie, I know you. We all do. You have an adventurous nature. If you two got along like steak and potatoes, there wouldn't be any sparks. He's spirited, and you certainly are. Makes for a pretty lively union, if you ask me."

"I don't know. I always feel like I'm too much for him. Like he wants me to change."

"Does he tell you that?"

"No. But it's quite apparent to me."

Luke shook his head. "I don't know about that. I think he cares an awful lot for you. And you have deep feelings for him, too."

His aunt blinked. "The last time we were together was at the Founder's Day gala. We fought and he walked out."

Luke knew about the argument. Drew had been upset at Lottie for putting her life in danger, running into the street trying to save a wayward dog. And April, Risk's fiancée, had pushed her out of the way before a car almost hit her. It had all been caught on video and had made the news.

"That was a couple of months back."

"I know. Now, whenever we see each other on the ranch, it's awkward and we barely speak."

Luke took his aunt's hand. "You're a wonderful woman and I'll always have your back, but I can see Drew's point of view, too. He doesn't want you taking unnecessary risks."

"I made it all these sixty-two years."

"But he lost a wife. He's probably very sensitive about this stuff."

Lottie nodded. "How'd you get so smart about these things?"

"I wouldn't say I'm smart. I have issues." The biggest one being he'd married a woman who wanted out, as quickly as possible. And he was dragging his feet. "But I had a lot of time to think when I was in the service. Four years' worth. I guess you could say I see the big picture now and something's telling me that you two should go for it."

"You really think so?"

He nodded. "Yes, I think so. You're both being stubborn."

"I'll keep that in mind. Thanks," she said, giving him a kiss on the cheek. "Now, go. Have a great time with your Katie."

His aunt gave him a coy look. Sometimes he wondered if she had uncanny powers of perception.

"I'm going. I'm going."

From the minute Katie stepped into The Majestic, she felt transported into another era. The black-and-white-checkered floors, the elaborate table dressings with fine bone china and tiered, flickering candles gave way to sophistication and romance from a time long ago.

"You fit in this place, Katie," Luke said. "Especially tonight. I like your hair up like that."

She didn't want to hear his compliments. When he'd picked her up at her bakery apartment, he'd given her compliment after compliment, making her head swim, giving her ego a boost. True, she'd gone all out, putting her hair up in a messy bun, dressing in a long sleek black gown with a slit up the side and a thin rope of delicate rhinestones stitched into a sloping neckline. She'd bought the dress at an estate sale in Dallas. It was a gown she'd had to have, yet she'd never believed she'd have a place to wear it. Until tonight.

"This place is beautiful," she said, in awe of her surroundings.

Boone County appealed to many, but this place was one of a kind and definitely catered to the rich and fabulously famous.

"Like I said, you fit in perfectly."

She took his arm and stared into his deep blue eyes. Wearing a slate gray suit, his dark blond hair smoothed back showing off his strong jawline, he wasn't exactly hard on the eye. But that was shallow of her. He was much more than that. Mostly, he was off-limits. "Thank you. But please don't say nice things like that. This situation is hard enough."

She hoped her plea would set him straight. After hearing Shelly's bitter comment today about Luke ruining her for all men, Katie had to keep a firm resolve. There was too much at stake and she had to admit that Luke's compliments were charming her. Making her want things she had no right wanting.

"I'm only speaking the truth," he said in his defense.

"You see, that's what I mean." She squeezed her eyes closed for a moment. "Just don't. Please, Luke."

His eyes shuttered yet he didn't answer her.

The maître d' greeted them. "Mr. Boone, so good to see you again. Please, follow me. I believe your brother and his fiancée are waiting for you."

Luke pressed a hand to her back and guided her farther into the restaurant. It was only a moment before she spotted Drea and Mason sitting at a corner table overlooking the patio gardens. Thank goodness. She needed reinforcements tonight. Drea would make the perfect buffer.

The maître d' showed them to the table and pulled out a chair for her. She took her seat and Luke sat down next to her, his scent, his presence looming. She'd been intimate with him and was beginning to learn his mannerisms, like how his eyes turned a darker shade of blue when he was turned on, and how his mouth twitched when he tried to hide a smile, and how when he was exasperated, he'd run a hand along his jawline. She'd seen that one a lot since Las Vegas.

"Hi, you two." Drea smiled at them.

Mason reached over to shake Luke's hand. "Glad you both could make it."

"Thanks for the invite," Luke said.

"Yes…thank you," Katie added, though she'd rather muck a barn stall than spend any more time with Luke.

"Isn't this place spectacular?" Drea asked. "I feel like I'm in a 1940s movie or something."

"I feel the same way," Katie said.

"The food here is top-notch," Mason said. "The owner, Billy Meadows, was a friend of our father's. I think Henry Boone would've loved to top this place in grandeur, but Dad wasn't the greedy type. He saw his competition as a good thing."

"It's good for the town, too," Katie said. "Having choices, that is."

The Boone brothers gave each other a quick glance. Katie wondered what that was all about, but quickly Luke changed the subject. "So, your wedding is in less than a month. Hard to believe. If there's anything I can do for you guys, let me know."

"Same here," Katie interjected.

"Don't you worry, Katie my friend," Drea said. "I have a list of things I need help with. My final gown fitting is coming up and the bridesmaids' dresses are in."

"Exciting. Sign me up," Katie said.

"Aren't you helping Aunt Lottie with the bridal shower?" Luke asked her.

"Yes. And I'm looking forward to that. It's next weekend." Drea wanted a couples shower, and that meant more contact with Luke, but oh well, there was nothing Katie could do about it. Once the wedding was over, and Katie and Luke were properly divorced, she wouldn't have to spend any time with him.

"I feel bad taking you away from Red Barrel," Drea said. "I know you like to spend your free time there and it seems like I'll be usurping all of it."

"I...don't mind." The reminder of the rescue disheartened Katie. She hadn't been back since Snow died. "It's part of my MOH duties."

"That's maid of honor, in case you two didn't catch on," Drea added.

Mason smiled at her. "We're not that slow. I knew what it meant."

"Good thing you did. Because I had no idea," Luke said.

"You're not up on wedding speak, bro." Then Mason turned to Katie. "You looked sad when Drea mentioned the rescue. So sorry. Luke told me you lost a precious mare not too long ago."

"Yes. It was hard. She was a special one."

Drea's voice softened. "I've already told you how sorry I am that you lost Snow."

Luke touched her hand and she gazed into his eyes, seeing the compassion there. "She's at peace now."

Katie nodded, then pasted on a big smile. She wasn't here to bring everyone down. Yet the reminder of losing Snow, combined with her sister's bitterness today, gave her a stomachache. "I'm fine, really. Drea, I've been your friend since third grade and I'm looking forward to every minute of helping you with your wedding plans, so don't you worry about putting me out. We've fantasized about this day for as long as I can remember."

Drea blew her an air-kiss. "I know we have. And your day will come, too, and when it does, I'll be right there for you."

Katie's cheeks heated and she felt like such a fraud, sitting here next to her best friend and lying through her teeth. She couldn't even spare Luke a glance for fear of giving herself away.

Luckily, the waiter approached with menus and took their drink orders.

"Nothing for me please. Just water." She couldn't take a drink, not with her stomach in turmoil. And she'd sort of sworn off alcohol ever since Las Vegas.

Once the drinks were served, Mason asked everyone to raise their glasses. "Thank you both for coming. We wanted to show our appreciation for giving us a wonderful party in Las Vegas. Everyone had a good time, thanks to you both. Drea and I really appreciate your love and support. So, here's to a loving family and lasting friendships."

Everyone clinked their glasses and sipped. Then Drea gave Luke a kiss on the cheek and turned to give Katie a big hug and kiss, too.

"It was my pleasure," Katie said.

"Yeah," Luke said. "My pleasure, too. It was a great time for everyone."

Katie didn't have the heart to agree with him. It would be the biggest lie of all.

Musicians set up beyond the dance floor and began playing tunes her grandparents had probably loved. It was lively, big band stuff that seemed to bring out the best in people. After the waiter came by to take their orders, Mason grabbed Drea's hand and pulled her onto the dance floor. Drea turned to give Katie a helpless look as if to say sorry for leaving her alone with Luke.

"Would you like to dance?" Luke asked, after a minute of silence.

She shook her head. "No, thanks." She didn't want Luke holding her, touching her. They'd done too much of that already. Her stomach still churned and the only thing that would make it better was to be free of Lucas Boone. When she was sure Mason and Drea were well beyond hearing distance, she whispered, "I need an update on...on our divorce."

"What?" Luke leaned closer to her and she repeated what she'd said into his ear. His pure male scent filled her nostrils, and her mind flashed to the night they'd shared together. She wished those memories would fade, but every time she was close to him, they became sharper.

"I don't have an update. My attorney is still out of the country."

"Shh." Why was he using his regular speaking voice? "Surely there's something we can do," she said quietly.

Luke took her hand. "Sorry, Katie."

She didn't want his apologies, she wanted action. She could try to find an attorney herself, but unless she ventured to Willow County or some other town, she feared news would get out. It was the curse of living in a small town: the gossip hotline was long. Luke had promised her his attorney would use great discretion and she believed that, because nobody wanted to cross a Boone.

She pulled out of his grasp, but not before Drea and Mason returned to the table and eyed their linked hands. *Oh boy.*

Mason's brows rose, but dear Drea pretended not to notice.

After dinner was served, the conversation around the table was pleasant and engaging. Mostly they talked about wedding plans and the building of Mason and Drea's new home on Rising Springs Ranch property.

"Katie's going to help me design our kitchen," Drea said. "She's the expert in that area."

Katie had felt Luke's eyes on her most of the night and the look of admiration on his face right now made her uneasy. "I'm hardly an expert."

"You know more than a thing or two about kitchens, Katie. Admit it."

Mason spoke up. "She's right, Katie."

"Just take the compliment," Drea said, grinning.

Katie nodded, giving in. "O…kay, if you insist."

Luke laughed and she eyed him carefully. "What's so funny?"

His lips went tight and he shook his head. "Nothin'."

She was afraid he would say she was cute or something equally as revealing, so she dropped it. But she knew his laugh now and when it was aimed at her.

Dessert and coffee were served. The pastries, pies and cakes were beautiful, but Katie had barely eaten her dinner so the thought of dessert didn't sit well. Beef Wellington had sounded good on the menu, but as soon as the dish arrived, Katie had lost her appetite. She'd been feeling queasy lately, and for good reason. She'd married the enemy and the nightmare was continuing. She felt out of control, restless and confused about her feelings for Luke.

"I'll sit this one out," she said politely.

"Too much cupcake sampling at the bakery?" Drea asked.

"Uh, yeah. I'm really full," she said, and Drea gave her a look. She was astute enough not to ask her what was wrong, but she had no doubt her friend would be questioning her about it later on. "But you go on. Enjoy. Everything looks delicious."

After dessert, Mason and Drea took to the dance floor again. Her friend knew enough not to try to coax her out there with Luke. Thank goodness.

She glanced at her watch and noted the time. "Luke, it's after nine."

"Yeah," he said. "I know. You've been checking your watch every five minutes since we got here."

"I have not."

"You have." He ran his hand down his face in his classic frustrated move and it irritated her no end.

"Lucas Boone, exactly what is it you want from me?"

That stumped him for a second. He blinked his eyes and then stared at her. "You would be surprised."

Her heart started racing. "Would I?"

"I have absolutely no doubt you would, so let's drop it." He rose. "Grab your purse. I'll take you home now."

They waited until the dance ended to say goodbye to Drea and Mason. "Thank you for this evening, it was wonderful," Katie said.

"I'm glad you enjoyed it," Mason answered.

She hugged Drea goodbye, too, and then she and Luke were off.

The drive home was quiet, uncharacteristically so. Luke didn't spare her a word or a glance and she felt the tension down to her toes. "Are you mad at me?" she asked.

He inhaled a breath and shook his head. "No."

"Is that all you're going to say?"

"Yep. That's all." He kept his gaze trained on the road.

She folded her arms around her middle, and her stomach knotted up. She'd almost forgotten how unsettled it felt. It was all this stress, and she was put off that Luke, regardless of his denial, was angry with her. If anyone had a right to be angry, it was her. "Well, maybe I'm mad at you."

"What?" This time he did take his eyes off the road. He had an incredulous look on his face. "I'm not the one who spoiled the evening for Mason and Drea. They were trying to do a nice thing. And you refused to participate."

"I didn't refuse to participate. I just didn't want to… be with you. And for some reason, you don't seem to understand that."

"Oh, I get it all right. But couldn't you have shown some appreciation to my brother and Drea? You wouldn't dance, wouldn't eat. Why was that, *wife*?"

He said that just to rub salt in her wound. "Don't be an ass, Luke. I could never be your wife. And you know darn well I didn't spoil anything."

Her belly clenched and her face pulled tight as she absorbed the pain. "Uh." She glanced out the window, hiding her discomfort, hoping Luke wouldn't catch on.

"What's wrong?"

"Nothing." She wouldn't look at him.

Luke steered the car onto the side of the road and parked along the highway.

"What are you doing?" she asked, breathless.

"What's wrong with you?"

"I told you, nothing is wrong with me." Once again, her stomach rolled and she bit her lip. She didn't want to get sick in front of him. They were in semidarkness, the moonlight casting them in shadows. "But I would appreciate it if you took me home."

"Can we just talk a minute?" he asked.

"I'm not feeling well, okay? It's all this stress. I'm worried sick about my mother and sister finding out about… about what happened. And being with you makes me go a little nutty."

"Katie," he said, his voice ultra-soft now. "I'm sorry you're not feeling well. Why didn't you say something before?"

"I didn't want to ruin the evening. But according to you, I'm guilty of that, too."

"Katie," he whispered. "I was just being—"

"A jerk?"

"Okay," he said, defeat in his voice. "I was a jerk. Of course you didn't spoil anything. So I make you nutty? Do you hate me that much?"

"Luke, I don't hate you. I never did. Maybe my problem is that… I like you. And it's impossible."

"You like me?" His voice rose, filled with hope.

"Luke, we've been… Well, you know. I keep asking myself why I let that happen. True, it was grief over Snow, but—"

"How much do you like me?"

He was crazy to think anything could ever come of the two of them, yet he was asking as if there was a chance. "Not enough to destroy my sister and hurt my mother." Her stomach cramped and she put her hand on it. "Oh."

"Katie?"

"Luke, please, take me home."

Concern entered his eyes. "Okay, just sit back and try to relax. I'll get you home quickly, sweetheart."

She wasn't his sweetheart. She wasn't his anything, and she hoped this little talk would convince him of that.

A short time later, he pulled up in front of the bakery. "Hold on a second," he said and got out of the car to open the door for her. He took her hand and helped her out.

"Thanks for the ride." She turned away from him, but he didn't release her hand.

"I'll make sure you get in safely."

The front door was ten feet away. "I'll be fine."

"I'll walk you," he said stubbornly and he walked beside her as she made her way to the front of the bakery.

She unlocked the door and took a step inside.

"Katie?"

"What?" She turned to him.

His eyes were soft on her, his expression etched in concern. "Are you feeling any better?"

"A little."

He tipped her chin up and planted a sweet tender kiss to her lips. It instantly warmed her insides, soothing her. "Get some rest. I'll check on you tomorrow."

Before she could say "Don't," he had turned away and hopped into his car. A dreamy feeling flowed through her body as if she was floating.

Until she realized that Luke had just kissed her on the public street.

And someone might have seen them.

She took a peek, noting the sidewalks were empty, and there were no cars in sight, yet her belly twisted up again. And all feelings of warmth quickly evaporated.

Early the next morning, Luke pulled up in front of the bakery, wondering if he was making a mistake by showing up here. He had Katie on the brain, and just remembering how she'd looked in that sexy gown last night, how delicious her lips tasted when he'd given her a goodbye kiss, gave him some hope that she wouldn't mind him checking in on her.

She'd admitted she liked him. He'd been floored hearing those words come out of her mouth. It was more than he'd expected, more than he'd thought possible. It was a start. Keeping away from her for the past five years had been hard on him, but Las Vegas had changed all that.

He got out of the car and entered the bakery, disappointed to see her assistant behind the counter helping customers. He was hit with a knot of apprehension. Was Katie still feeling poorly?

And just then she walked out of the kitchen and into the bakery. They made eye contact. There was a spark in her eyes, a light that she quickly extinguished. But he'd seen it and she couldn't deny that for that one second, she'd been happy to see him.

He took a seat in a café chair and waited, watching Katie and Lori efficiently handle the morning rush. Finally, once the crowded bakery thinned out, Katie walked over to him. "I hope you're here to give me news…about you know what," she whispered.

She was speaking about the divorce.

"No change on that, I'm afraid."

She pursed her lips. "Then why are you here?"

He shrugged. "For coffee."

She tapped her foot. "Can I get you anything else?"

"Just coffee for now."

She hesitated. "Don't you have a coffee cart at Boone Inc.?"

"We do, but as you can see, I'm not at Boone Inc. at the moment. I'm here."

She sighed. "I'll get it for you." She turned to leave.

"Katie," he said firmly.

She gave him a deadpan look.

"How are you feeling?"

"I'm fine. Now will you go?"

"Coffee, please."

She gave her head a shake and left only to return a moments later holding a steaming cup of coffee. "Here you go." She set the cup in front of him.

"Sit with me."

"I can't, I'm working."

"Just for a minute." He pointed around the shop. "The place has emptied out."

"Only if you promise to leave as soon as you're through."

"Fine."

She sat down facing him, and once up close, he noticed the fatigue on her face and how her eyes were rimmed with red. She'd been moving slowly around the bakery. "How are you feeling?"

"I feel...good."

She was lying. "Don't take this the wrong way, but you look sluggish this morning."

"What every girl wants to hear. Thank you for that."

He shook his head. The woman was constantly sparring with him. Today, it wasn't cute or funny. "How's your stomach?"

"Luke, you don't have to check up on me. I'm perfectly capable of taking care of myself. So please, have your coffee and leave."

"Is that any way to speak to a customer? One you actually like."

She sighed. "Luke, I'm beginning to regret telling you that."

"Just for the record. I like you, too. A lot."

"Shh." She glanced at the door.

What was she so afraid of? Was she expecting to see her sister or mother walk in this morning? Was that it? Diana and Shelly had to know he and Katie had wedding business to discuss. They were both helping Aunt Lottie put on the bridal shower for Drea and Mason. Luke and Katie had been thrown together lately and it shouldn't be a crime that the two of them spent some time together.

He sipped his coffee. "Mmm, perfect."

"I'll tell Lori you enjoyed it. She makes a mean cup."

"So, I'll see you at the bridal shower on Saturday. Are we all set for that?"

"I am. I'm making the cake and helping with some of the activities."

"I'm good on my end, too." He actually wasn't asked to do much, just help the day of the shower behind the scenes. "I can pick you up and bring you out to the ranch."

"That's silly. You live at the ranch. You don't need to come all the way out here to pick me up. I'll manage."

She was good at shooting him down.

"I am sorry, you know," he said. "I don't like being the source of your stress. But I can't do anything about that right now."

"I'll...try to remember that. So no more sudden visits to the shop?"

"I can't promise that. I might have a craving."

Katie gave him a hard stare.

"For a cupcake."

She nibbled on her lip, trying to keep from saying something. Whatever it was, he was sure he didn't want to hear it. He finished his drink, then rose and reached out to help her up, but she ignored his outstretched hand.

"Just try to rest. Feel better, Katie."

The genuine concern in his voice caused a momentary tug in her heart. The truth was, she hadn't had anyone care about her this way in a long time. And it felt sort of nice. This was what she'd longed for, what she'd revealed to Luke in Las Vegas. She wanted more out of life. She wanted a partner, someone to share things with. She'd neglected that part of her life to make the bakery a success. Now, she had a thriving business, but no one to share it with.

Perhaps she should start dating again.

And then she remembered...she couldn't date anyone. She was married to Lucas Boone.

Three days later, Lottie opened the front door of the ranch house at Rising Springs to face Drew MacDonald. He was the last person she was expecting this morning and her heart did a little flip seeing him looking so handsome with a salt-and-pepper beard, his graying, windswept hair and his workout clothes the same shade of jade green as his Irish eyes.

It had been awkward between them lately but she wanted to rectify that. They were all going to be family as soon as Mason and Drea, Drew's daughter, were married. And this weekend, Lottie was throwing the two lovebirds a couples bridal shower.

"Hi, Drew. I didn't expect to see you this morning."

Suddenly, she remembered what she must look like. She was cooking up a storm, baking apple cobbler and cookies for her nephews. Not only were her clothes a mess, but she probably had flour on her face and in her hair.

"I didn't come to see you."

"Oh."

"I mean, I'm happy to see you and all, but Luke asked me to stop by some time this morning. He needs a bit of advice about a company I used to deal with. Anyway, I decided to stop by after my walk."

"I see. I'm glad you're still taking walks, Drew."

"I enjoy it. But I sure liked it better when I had a walking partner." He gave her a direct look.

Warmth rushed up her cheeks. The man could always make her blush. "You need that much motivation?"

"No, ma'am. Just liked the company." And before she could react, he took a deep breath. "Something smells awfully good in here."

"I'm baking, in case you can't tell." She gestured to her

smudged clothes. "Apple cobbler and lemon supreme cookies. I'll send some home for you and Drea."

"Thanks. I'd never refuse any of your baking, Lottie. Though I'd probably have to walk farther every day just to burn off the calories."

"I don't think apple cobbler would do you any harm. You're, uh, looking fit these days."

They stared at each other for a few beats of a minute. "Well, if Luke's home, maybe I could see him now?"

"Oh, right. Sure, he's in the office. You know where it is. Go on in."

"Thanks. Oh, and it was nice talking to you this morning."

"Same here, Drew."

After he turned and walked down the hallway, she smiled. It seemed they could have a civil conversation if they put their mind to it. She went back to baking and thinking about Drew, her heart lighter than it had been in a long while.

An hour later, she came downstairs after taking a quick shower and changing her clothes. She wore a soft pink bell sleeve blouse. It worked well with her rosy complexion, and silly her, she found herself dressing to impress. She gave a quick knock on the office door and then entered.

Luke was sitting in front of his laptop computer, Drew nowhere in sight. "Hi, Aunt Lottie. What's up?"

"Oh, I thought you were having a meeting with Drew?"

"I was. He left a little bit ago." Luke grinned. "Don't you look pretty today. I thought you were baking."

"I was and I'm finished now. I meant to send Drew home with some cobbler and cookies for Drea."

"Just for Drea?" he asked, his mouth twitching.

She chuckled. She'd been caught. "Well, for both of them."

"So, what's stopping you? Take it over to them. I'm sure they'd appreciate it."

"You think so?"

"I know so. Drew loves his sweets."

"That is true." She mulled it over for half a second. She hadn't gotten all dressed up for nothing. "Okay, I think I will."

Luke smiled the smile of a matchmaker. The only thing missing was him rubbing his hands together gleefully. "Good idea."

And a few minutes later Lottie was set with a canvas tote containing the lemon cookies and a covered dish of still warm cobbler. She took off on foot; the extra bit of exercise today would do her good. Her heart was aflutter, thinking about Drew and how much he was beginning to mean to her.

As she approached the MacDonald cottage, Drew opened his front door and out stepped a pretty, dark-haired woman she'd never seen before. The two embraced in a passionate hug that lasted far too long. And then the woman took his face in her hands and kissed him right smack on the mouth.

Shocked, Lottie froze for a moment, not believing what she was seeing. She stood on the road, bag in hand, ready to make nice with Drew, and now she was hit with raw pangs of jealousy. She couldn't watch any longer. She turned on her heels and made fast tracks away from the cottage before Drew could see her.

Goodness, what an idiot she was. Had she been naive to think that Drew didn't have other options when it came to women? He'd straightened himself out, was ruggedly handsome and had a good heart, for the most part. She'd always thought of him as hers in an odd sort of way. Had he led her on all these years? Or had she been blind to his needs?

Either way, she was roaring mad at him and his sweet-talking ways.

As her anger raged, she picked up her pace, walking as fast as her legs would take her. Running from the hurt, from the loss, from the betrayal as tears trickled down her face.

Five

"I'm here, Mama," Katie called as she unlocked the door and entered her mother's house Thursday afternoon.

She didn't find her right away. But soon Shelly appeared, coming in through the sliding back door. "Mom's in the backyard, getting some fresh air."

"That's a good idea. It's a beautiful afternoon. How're you doing, sis? Staying for dinner?"

"No, sorry. I hope you're okay with making Mom dinner without me. I'm… I'm going to a seminar tonight. It includes dinner."

"That's no problem, but another seminar? You know what they say, too much work and not enough play…"

Shelly smiled. "If I'm dull, then I'm dull. I happen to love my work."

"I get it. I love my work, too." Then Katie grinned. "Is a certain Dr. Moore going to this event?"

"Take that grin off your face, brat. And actually Dr. Moore is giving the seminar, part two of his Cardiology in the Twenty-first Century lecture. So of course he's going to be there."

"Now the evening's sounding more interesting." Katie smiled again.

Her sister picked up a pillow and tossed it at her, just like when they were kids. Katie was too fast for her. "You missed me."

"Only because I wasn't really trying."

There was a breezy lightness to Shelly tonight that she hoped would continue.

"So, Katie, any chance we can go shopping with Mom on Saturday? I have the day off and I thought it'd be nice to get her out of the house. You know, have a girls' day."

"Oh, that's a great idea, but I can't do it Saturday. It's Drea and Mason's bridal shower."

Shelly's perpetual frown reappeared. So much for light and breezy. "Oh, right. That's if Mason decides to show up for it. Boones are notorious for disappointing their fiancées."

"Shel, give it a rest, okay? Drea's crazy about him."

"Yeah, well, I was crazy about Luke and look how that turned out. I mean, he was an amazing boyfriend and fiancée until he wasn't."

"I know it hurt you, but you can't change the past," Katie said, trying to get through to her sister. Trying to ease her own conscience, too.

"I know that. But I also know I can't suppress my emotions."

"But you're suppressing living your life."

Shelly gave her head a tilt. "You really think so?"

"I absolutely do. You have a lot to offer someone. You should be open to that."

"Well, it's not as if anyone's busting down the door to get to me."

"How about you taking a chance. Walk out the door and find what you're looking for."

"I'm…scared."

Katie winced. It was hard seeing her big sister admit that. She took Shelly's hands in hers and squeezed. "Shel, you're strong enough to deal with anything that comes your way. You're a fantastic person, a wonderful nurse. You make people feel better, you care. People look up to you, they value your judgment. Never doubt that. I think that you'll find what you're looking for if you give yourself a chance."

Shelly drew a breath. "Maybe." She nodded. "I'll try. And thanks, sis. You're the best."

The conversation made Katie ache inside for the pain her sister had gone through. Hearing her admit that she'd been crazy about Luke was like a dagger to her heart.

Because Katie was starting to have real feelings for Luke.

And they were getting stronger every day.

Saturday morning, Katie rose extra early to get a head start on baking so she'd have enough time to put the finishing touches on the bridal shower cake. Though cakes weren't her specialty, she knew enough about them to design a one-of-a-kind cake for Drea and Mason that resembled the home they were building on Rising Springs land. It took a great deal of thought, but the cake when finished would be spectacular.

Halfway through the decorating, fatigue set in, and she took a seat to rest. She'd been stressed out lately, and for good reason, but she'd never felt so tired before. Her mother told her she was taking on too much, that she needed extra help running the bakery, but Katie didn't think that was it.

"You look as green as this pistachio icing," Lori said,

picking up a freshly frosted tray of cupcakes. "Are you feeling poorly?"

"I think I'm just tired. I worked hard on the cake last night and didn't get much sleep. I probably should've closed the shop today, so I could concentrate on Drea's shower."

"Why don't you go up to your apartment and get some rest? I'll finish up with the cupcakes, so you can be fresh for the bridal shower."

Normally, Katie wouldn't think of it, but her tummy was aching, the same queasy feeling she'd been having for days now. "I'll go up for an hour if you don't mind."

"Go, I've got things covered here."

"I have no doubt. You could run this bakery with your eyes closed. I'll be back soon."

"Take your time," Lori said.

"Thanks." Katie climbed the stairs to her apartment and once inside, her stomach cramped tight and she couldn't fight the nausea. "Oh no." Her hand on her belly, she dashed to the bathroom and made it just in time. When she was through, she sat down on the tile floor next to the toilet until her tummy settled down.

Where had that come from? She thought back to what she'd eaten these past few days but nothing struck her as odd. Could it be stress and fatigue causing such a disruption to her health?

She rose and took a shower, then tucked herself into bed. She'd rest for just a few minutes and then get up to put the finishing touches on the cake.

The sound of birds tweeting broke into her sleep. Katie opened her eyes and listened again. Those weren't real birds, it was her cell phone chirping. She grabbed it off the nightstand. Her eyes widened when she saw the time and she jolted out of bed, panicked. It was nine o'clock!

She was supposed to be at the ranch in half an hour. The shower was starting at noon.

The text read, Drea's sending me to pick you up. Stay put.

It was from Luke.

Oh God. She was late. She took a few minutes to dress and comb her hair and then raced downstairs. "Lori, I'm so sorry," she called out. She didn't have time to deal with Luke coming to get her. Actually, with the way she was feeling, she really could use his help.

"Hey, no problem," Lori said, coming into the work area. "It's slow right now, but I was beginning to worry. Are you feeling better?"

Gosh, she didn't have time to feel bad. She had to finish the cake and get to Rising Springs. "Yes, I'm better. The rest did me a world of good but I've got to finish the cake. Should only take a few minutes."

Katie pulled the cake out of the fridge and spent the next twenty minutes piping the perimeter and adding the names. When all was said and done, the two-tiered cake looked like a picture of serenity and love.

"There," she said, with a heavy dose of pride and relief.

"It's beautiful." Luke had sneaked up beside her. She hadn't heard him enter but she appreciated the compliment.

"Thanks."

"A lot of work?"

"Yes," she replied. "But worth the effort."

"Funny, that's how I feel about you."

Katie turned to find a twinkle in his eye. "Luke."

He grinned. "C'mon. Let's get our butts to the house before the shower starts without us."

"You really didn't have to come."

"Drea insisted, and who am I to argue with my future sister?"

"Riiiight."

She wouldn't tell him she was glad he'd come to the rescue, that she had been sluggish lately and she hoped once they settled their "marriage" problem, her tummy aches would disappear.

Luke had driven with extra caution while Katie sat in the back seat of his roomy SUV with the double-tiered cake beside her. And now, thanks to Luke carefully carrying it inside, the cake sat on the kitchen counter, ready to be revealed once the shower began.

As Katie put up snow-white paper wedding bells along the perimeter of the spacious patio overhang, Luke held the ladder for her, watching her carefully. "You sure you don't want me to do that?" he asked her, for the second time.

"Not at all. These have to be spaced just right and hung a certain way."

"And a mere man can't figure it out?"

She laughed. She was having fun decorating for her best friend's shower and she didn't want anyone to take the joy away. "I think not."

"That's okay, I'm enjoying the view from down here anyway."

Katie immediately grabbed at the back of her dress, making sure she was well covered. The dress was tight enough to cling to her legs. But she noticed it was fitting a little more snugly around her waist than she'd remembered. She had to stop eating her own cupcakes. "You can't see anything, Luke, so stop teasing."

"Everything I do see, I like."

She gave him a look. "Shh."

"I meant the decorations are looking real pretty. Everyone's doing a great job."

She shook her head at him. He was so full of it. But in a sweet way that made her…nutty.

From her vantage point on the ladder, everyone was

pitching in and doing a great job. Risk and April were arranging the table flowers. April was an expert at staging homes so her expertise was spot on. The next home she would permanently stage would be at Canyon Lake Lodge, the old manor that Risk had bought for them to live in once they renovated it. The two were going to run the lodge together.

Drea and Mason were locked in an embrace watching the lily pads they'd set afloat in the pool drift off. Their happiness was contagious. Katie could be happy for them, and for this day. It was a dream come true for Drea, who'd been through so much in the past.

"Okay," Katie said, draping the last of the wedding bells. "I think I'm done."

She lowered herself down from the ladder and was hit with a bout of dizziness. Her head swam for a moment and Luke was right there, taking her hands, staring into her eyes. "Katie?"

"Whoa," she said. "That was weird."

"What happened?"

"Nothing." She gave her head a gentle shake. "I think I came down the ladder too fast. Got a little light-headed. I'm fine now."

He stepped closer to her. "Are you sure?"

"Yes," she said automatically. She stepped back from him, breaking their connection. She didn't want him worrying over her. She didn't want to see concern on his face or hear it in his voice. It was all too confusing.

Lottie approached with a gracious smile. "Katie, the cake is amazing. I can't wait for the guests to see it. We'll bring it out soon to show off your beautiful work."

"Thanks, Lottie. I'm—"

"She worked hard on it, Aunt Lottie." There was possessive pride in Luke's voice that had Lottie darting inquisitive glances between them.

"I can see that."

"It was a labor of love," Katie said.

Lottie patted her hand. "I bet you have a lot of love to give, Katie."

"I'm sort of married, uh…" She hesitated when Luke's eyes went shockingly wide. "To my job. I mean, right now I'm concentrating on the bakery. I haven't had time for anything else," she said quietly.

"Well, when you find the right one, you'll know it. There's no rush."

Katie nodded. "I agree. No rush at all."

Drew walked up and smiled at everyone. "Katie, I just saw the cake. You've outdone yourself."

"Thank you."

"I bet it tastes as good as it looks."

"Hope so."

"Drew's got a sweet tooth," Luke said good-naturedly. "I bet you enjoyed Aunt Lottie's cobbler the other day, too. Did you leave any crumbs for Drea?"

Drew's brows furrowed. "Cobbler? If you mean the day I stopped by to see you, Luke, I left your place before getting a chance to dig in."

"But she brought you some that day, didn't you, Aunt Lottie?"

Luke's aunt bit her lip and shook her head. "No, I never made it over."

She didn't give Drew a glance, and her expression was tight. After that, Lottie excused herself to speak with the caterer and Drew walked off in the other direction. Katie thought for sure something was up between the two of them.

She looked at the string and tape and scissors she'd left lying around. "Okay, well, I'd better clean up my mess. The guests will be arriving soon."

"I'll help," Luke said.

Katie couldn't shake the guy. He turned up beside her at every turn. It made mush of her nerves because she was getting used to him being around. She scooped up her mess before Luke could grab anything. "I've got this," she said. "But Mason might need your help. You should check with him."

"In other words, you want me to get lost."

She smiled.

And Luke took the hint. "I'll see you later."

"Okay," she said brightly and once he walked off, Katie entered the house and took a seat in the kitchen. Her tummy was still a bit unsettled and her energy was sapped.

She couldn't wait for the shower to begin and end. All she could think about was getting back into bed and sleeping.

Katie squinted into the bright May sunshine as she stepped out into the Boones' beautifully groomed backyard that they'd spent hours decorating. Everything had turned out perfectly. Drea's dream of true love and marriage was coming true.

The guests filed in as music played over hidden speakers. She watched as groups mingled and enjoyed appetizers and drank wine. Some of the girls in attendance were her friends, too, many of them either married, engaged or escorted by a boyfriend. She sighed and put on a happy face to mingle as well and catch up on their news.

Once the luncheon was served, everyone took their seats. Katie sat at the Boone table. Everyone was paired off with their counterparts, leaving her sitting next to Luke. Funny how it always worked out that way.

He seemed perfectly content with the arrangements and all she could do was smile and have a good time, for Drea's sake. Most of the guests played a silly game of who knew the bride and groom the best, and Katie ended up winning the bride half of the game.

Drea and Mason opened their gifts, and then Katie was asked to cut their cake, but not before a dozen pictures were taken of it. Katie was showered with compliments, which gave her spirit a lift. She found herself smiling and laughing a lot throughout the day.

"I'm glad to see you so happy," Luke whispered in her ear as they sipped coffee.

"I'm happy for Drea."

"Me, too. For Mason. The guy's gaga over his fiancée."

"As well he should be. Drea is awesome."

"So are—"

She put a finger to his lips to quiet him, and then realized what she'd done and quickly removed it, but not before a few heads turned her way. Oh God, had they seen her trying to silence his compliment?

Luke didn't let it faze him. He bit into a forkful of cake. "This is delicious."

She shot him a warning look, but that never seemed to work with him. "Thanks."

As the shower was winding down, Katie decided to remove herself from his presence. "Excuse me. I'm needed in the kitchen, and no, I don't need any help."

She escaped him and entered the kitchen, offering to help, but Lottie shoed her away. "You've done enough. The staff will take care of cleanup. Honestly, I think that's the best marble cake I've ever eaten. It's beautiful on the inside and out. You're a genius."

Drew walked into the kitchen and added, "That you are, Katie girl. I had seconds and would go back for thirds if I was twenty years younger."

Lottie feigned a smile and turned her back on him.

"Thank you both," Katie said. "Lottie, if you really don't need my help, I'll go outside and talk to Drea."

"Good idea," Lottie said. "Go have fun. I'll be out in a second."

* * *

Lottie watched Katie leave and then turned to Drew. "Honestly, I don't need any help here. You should go back outside, too."

"Kicking me out?" His mouth quirked up.

Lottie sighed. "No, you can stay or you can go. Do whatever you want, Drew."

Drew frowned. "Lottie, what the hell is wrong with you? You haven't spoken to me all day. Did I do something wrong, again?"

He was annoyed at her? Did he think she was a fool? The image of Drew kissing that woman on his porch flashed in her mind and anger roiled in her stomach. It was time to confront him. There was no other way. "Not at all. I mean, kissing a woman behind my back isn't wrong. Not if you read from the book of Drew MacDonald."

"What are you talking about?"

"I saw you, Drew. The other day, I was bringing you a dish of cobbler and I… I saw a woman coming out of your house. You two were very cozy. I guess I've been mistaken about the two of us. There is no us."

Drew's green eyes sparked and she couldn't tell what he was thinking. "There is no us?" He took her hand and tugged her close. "Lady, you have no idea."

Then he cupped her face in his hands and laid a kiss on her lips. Her heart fluttered and her mind dizzied as delicious sensations sped through her system. She kissed him back, trying to keep pace with his passion, his ardor.

She couldn't seem to get enough of him, and he must've been feeling the same way. He pulled her into his arms and she went willingly. His kisses went deeper, longer and nothing, nothing she'd experienced in this world had ever felt better. "Drew," she murmured.

He kissed her again, the melding of their mouths seamless and perfect.

Then he broke away and her eyes popped open. She stared at him and he said with a rasp, "Now, tell me there is no us."

"But the woman?"

"I'm her AA sponsor and she needed a one-on-one talk. Whatever you saw was gratitude. *She* kissed me and I set her straight right after that. My goodness, Lottie, she's half my age."

"So, you're not—"

"After the way we just kissed, you have to ask?"

Then he turned his back on her and walked outside. She touched a finger to her mouth, his taste still tingling on her lips.

On the drive home after the shower, Luke kept glancing at Katie. She sat in the passenger seat of his car, struggling to keep her eyes open as she laid her head against the headrest. Snuggled into her jacket, she looked warm and cozy and so peaceful, her body sinking into the contours of the seat.

He tried not to utter a sound as he drove along the quiet road, and before too long, she fell asleep. Luke drove on, feeling the rightness of this moment in his bones. He and Katie. There was no other woman in the world for him and as each day passed, the feeling grew stronger and stronger.

While she was hoping for a quick divorce, he was stalling...perhaps wrongfully so, but all those years while he was in Afghanistan serving his country, he'd felt hollow and empty inside. It was the worst feeling in the world, that aloneness, that feeling that aside from his brothers, there was no one waiting for him back home. Now, he had what he'd always wanted. It would be hard giving it up.

He could tell she was bone tired by the way she was huddled between the seat and the window, her breaths as noisy as they were weary.

Katie was a force, a dynamo in a very understated way. She'd made Katie's Kupcakes a success. And all the while, she'd continued supporting Red Barrel, donating her time and energy to neglected and abandoned horses. She was a great friend, a wonderful daughter and an ultra-loyal sister.

Luke sighed. He wanted to reach out and hold her hand, but that might wake her. That might put her on alert and it was the last thing he wanted, to make her wary, to have her erect walls that would keep him out. No, he was content to have her near him, to watch her sleep. Too soon, he would have to part ways with her.

Once they reached her street, Luke steered his car to the back door of her shop and parked. She'd want him to use discretion so the people strolling along the sidewalk wouldn't see him trying to get a sleepy Katie out of his car.

He didn't give two figs about being seen with her, so this he did for her.

"Sweetheart," he said gently, taking her hand trying to rouse her.

She didn't wake readily, only curled deeper into the comfort of her jacket.

"Katie, honey, you're home. You need to wake up."

She mumbled something incoherently and continued to sleep.

"Okay," he said on a whisper. "Looks like you need Prince Charming, only I don't see him anywhere around here."

He smirked at his bad joke and then got out of the car. When he opened her passenger side door, he hoped the cooler air would jostle her awake. When that didn't happen, he scooped her up in his arms, taking her handbag along with him.

"Luke," she breathed out and the sound of her sultry voice nearly did him in. His wholesome Katie was a very sexy temptation.

"I've got you."

He managed to dig the keys out of her purse, and once inside the bakery, he climbed the stairs to her apartment. Sleep tousled and still drowsy, she was light in his arms and relaxed enough to lie against his chest as he opened her apartment door. He carried her inside and wanted so much to deposit her onto her bed and lie down next to her.

Once in her living room, he set her on her feet and held on as she gained her footing. "Katie?"

She opened her eyes and gazed up at him. "Sorry. I was just so tired. I don't know why… I've never been that tired before."

Touching her cheek, Luke brushed a honey blond strand of hair off her face. "It's not a problem," he said quietly. "You've had a lot on your plate, sweetheart."

"I guess that must be it." The apartment was cool and dark and Katie looked so tempting, so soft. "Did I sleep all the way home?"

"Not all the way."

She covered her face with her hands. "Oh gosh. I'm so embarrassed. You're always seeing me at my worst."

"That's an impossibility, Katie."

"Luke," she warned, but with a smile on her face.

Yeah, he knew the drill. She was constantly giving him warnings. Yet Katie didn't know how hard it was standing this close to her while she looked so damn tousled and sexy. She had no idea how hard it was for him to say goodnight when he was legally married to her. He summoned up his willpower. "I'd better get going. Let you get some rest."

Was that a twinge of disappointment in her eyes? "It's probably for the best."

"Yeah," he said, hating to go. He touched a finger to her cheek and then kissed her there, softly, tenderly. "Good night then." He turned away from her, leaving her looking a little bit lost in the middle of the room.

When he was halfway to the door, she called to him. "Luke?"

He spun on his heels and faced her.

She took a big swallow. "Don't go."

Oh God. He drew breath into his lungs and approached her. "Why?"

"I mean you can go if you want to, but I'm just saying I'm not as tired now and if you'd like to stay for coffee or a drink, that would be nice. But you don't have to, you can always—"

"I'll stay."

"You will?"

He nodded. She had no idea how much he'd wanted to hear those words.

"But if I do, I'd want—"

"I, uh, sort of know what you want, Luke." She squeezed her eyes closed briefly.

He scratched his head. She was just so adorable. "I was going to say I'd want a cupcake with that coffee. If it's not too much trouble."

A look of relief swept over her face. "No, not at all. I'm your go-to for all things cupcake."

His go-to for all things, period.

"Just kick me out when you want me to leave," he said. They'd lingered after the bridal shower, Katie going gaga over Drea's gifts and talk of the wedding, while he had beers with both of his brothers, but it was still early in the evening.

She chuckled. "Don't worry. I will."

He didn't want to dwell on how easy it was for her to reject him, time and again. "So, are you always this peppy after a long nap?"

"I don't know. I usually don't take naps," she said as she walked into the kitchen and flipped on the light. She arranged half a dozen mouthwatering cupcakes on a dish and put them on the table, then began making coffee. "Have a seat."

Luke opted not to sit at the table. He leaned against the kitchen counter, watching her work. It smelled good in her kitchen, like sugar and warmth. "I plan on going to the rescue tomorrow. Haven't been back since Snow passed."

"Neither have I," she admitted. She stopped pouring ground beans into the coffee maker and bit her lip. "It's gonna be hard going back."

"Yeah. But there are so many other horses who need attention. After the wedding, I'm going to look into raising funds for Red Barrel. I've already spoken to Wes about it. They could use more financial support."

"It's a good idea, but I know your family—you, mostly—have been donating on a regular basis."

"How do you know that?"

"I hear things and that's all I'm going to say."

"You like keeping secrets, is that it?"

Her eyes grew as round as the cupcakes on the platter. "I certainly do not. I'm a very honest person and I hate secrets. You're the one making anonymous donations to the rescue and secretly marrying the first girl too drunk to know better." She blinked several times.

"First of all, sweetheart, it's not a crime to make a private donation once in a while. And second of all, you're not the first girl."

"Oh."

"You're the only girl."

She met his eyes and whispered, "Don't, Luke."

"Why'd you really invite me in tonight? And I want the honest truth."

She put her chin up, as if refusing to answer, but he stared at her for a long time and then her eyes fluttered and finally she admitted, "I get lonely...sometimes."

His heart pulled tight and he touched a finger to her

cheek, the skin smooth and soft there. "You don't ever have to be, not when I'm around."

She took a hard swallow, her eyes filled with regret. He hated seeing her looking so torn and scared. He couldn't have her afraid of him. She had to know he was her safe space. Leaning against the counter, he took her hand and brought her into the cradle of his arms. Her body pressed against his and all his willpower dashed out the window. *Oh man.*

"You don't have to say those things," she said quietly. "You're not really my husband."

"We have a marriage license to prove it," he said, kissing her forehead.

"It's just paper. It's not real."

"It's not just paper, sweetheart. And that's why you're fighting it so much."

"We've had this argument before," she said softly.

"Let's not have it again." And then he brushed his lips over hers and made love to her mouth until the coffeepot sizzled and the cupcakes were long forgotten.

Katie didn't want to have this uncanny, impossible attraction to Lucas Boone. Her brain was telling her no, no, no, while all other parts of her body screamed out yes. She'd never been in this kind of dilemma before. Usually she'd follow reason, but Luke had turned her rational thinking upside down.

Now, after abandoning the coffee and cupcakes, both stood naked and aroused in her bedroom facing each other. It was a blur how quickly they'd shed their clothes and wound up in here. One earthquake of a kiss was all it had taken. They were cast mostly in shadow with only a glimmer of moonlight peeking in through the shutters.

"I want to know all of you," Luke said, taking her hand

and kissing the inside of her palm. "I want you to know all of me, too."

Katie drew breath into her lungs. It seemed the harder she pushed him away, the more she thought about him, the more she wanted him. And now she was giving in to her true feelings, too tired to fight them any longer.

She knew what he wanted and as she touched him, caressed him, she could only relish his groans of pleasure, his quick breaths. It was too good, too delicious, the sensations wrapping them both up causing heat to climb rapidly.

And when she was through pleasuring him, he kissed her long and hard and then moved her onto the bed and returned the favor.

She was out of her mind with one burning hot sensation after another. He was a master with his mouth, his hands. He knew not only where to touch her, but how to touch her, making her feel worshipped and treasured. His kisses made her pulse with lust and need. Then when his broad, powerful body covered hers, sheathed in protection and moving deep inside her thrust after thrust, she cried out his name and climaxed to the highest peak.

It was beautiful. It was perfectly amazing. And scary as hell.

Minutes later, Luke tucked her close, spooning her, his breath soft on her neck. He reached around to cup her breast with one hand and fondle her with his masterful fingers.

"You're beautiful this way," he said, kissing her shoulder.

"What way?" she asked, smiling. She was still blissfully coming down from her release.

"Naked."

She laughed.

He kissed her again. "But I also like it when you're relaxed like this."

"Hmm. We do well like this," Katie admitted.

"Excuse me, did I just hear you say you think we're good together?"

"I wouldn't go that...far. Oh." He strummed his thumb over her nipple, sending immediate heat down to her belly. He was relentless, toying with her body, his hand stroking over places that could make her weep in pleasure.

"You wouldn't?" He brought his mouth to her shoulder and kissed her again and again. She squeezed her eyes tight. "Tell the truth."

"We can't be...together, Luke."

"Seems like we are together, sweetheart. And it's no use trying to deny it."

She turned to face him. She had to keep her resolve firm or they'd all live to regret it. "Luke, let's not argue about this. Not tonight. Can we change the subject?"

He paused, masking his feelings with a blank stare, which was fine with her. She didn't want to delve too deeply into his emotions. Or hers, for that matter. "What would you like to talk about?"

She turned onto her back and focused on the delicate patterns created by moonlight on the ceiling. "How about your father?"

"My father?" She'd surprised him, but she'd always been curious about Henry Boone. He'd been legendary, but she was curious about something that was said about him.

"Yes," she said. "He had a reputation for being sort of a... Well, there's no other way to say this. It was rumored he was quite ruthless in business."

"That's what happens when you're wealthy. People start thinking the worst of you."

"Really?"

"Happened a lot in my family. Before Drea learned the truth, she believed my father swindled Drew out of his ranch, Thundering Hills. Yet, all my father was trying to do was protect her from the truth. Drew had gone through quite a rough patch after his wife died and he'd made a secret deal with my dad to buy his ranch and put the money away for Drea's education. Drea wasn't told the truth until she fell in love with Mason."

"It was hard on Drea when her mom died. So, when you were talking with Mason the other night at dinner about how your father welcomed competition, you were speaking the truth?"

"Yes, my father was a fair man...to an extent. He always protected the town and made sure that the townsfolk came before dollar signs. It's how Boone Springs has thrived."

"And you and your brothers follow in his footsteps?"

"We try."

"I've always felt blessed that my shop has done so well. I thought for sure another bakery would've opened up by now. We're a growing community and—"

"You don't have to worry about that, Katie."

"What?" There was something in his tone, a finality in his voice, that worried her. She nibbled on her lip.

"You're the best baker in Texas."

"I'm sure I'm not. But just then, you seemed so confident. What are you not telling me?"

"Nothing, sweetheart. Just drop it."

"Luke, there's five bakeries in Willow County and I always wondered why I'm lucky enough to have a monopoly on the bakery business in Boone Springs."

"The grocery stores sell baked goods."

"Not the same thing. I've been in business almost seven years and in all that time, no one has tried to open a bakery that I know of. I think I'll ask April why that is." April, soon to be Risk's wife, was a Realtor. She knew both Willow and Boone counties very well. "She should know."

"Maybe, or maybe you should just count your lucky stars."

"What does that mean?"

"Nothing, sweetheart. Just don't involve April in this."

"In what?" Luke was being obtuse, deliberately trying to hide something. He kept his lips buttoned up tight.

When he reached for her, she pulled away. "Tell me."

He sighed and scrubbed his jaw. "You know the Boones own more than half of the properties in town."

"Yes, common knowledge. So?"

"So, we have a plan for the town, and each one of us has input."

"Okay?"

"That's it, Katie."

Baffled, she shook her head. "What's it?" Then a thought flashed in her mind and she couldn't let it go. She had to find out the truth no matter how the notion sickened her. "Are you saying the Boones have made sure I've had no competition?"

"Not the Boones. Just me," he said on an uncharacteristic squeak.

"Just you?" She didn't understand. Luke was confusing the hell out of her. "Why on earth would you do that?"

"It's not a bad thing, Katie. We've only had two inquiries and, well, they found better deals elsewhere."

"Because you made sure of it." Katie's emotions ran rampant. Anger, disappointment, betrayal. All of it made her heart ache. She rose from bed and threw on her clothes quickly.

"Katie."

"Get dressed, Luke. Right now."

As she watched him put on his clothes, she shook uncontrollably. Now that he was dressed and she didn't have to look at his striking body, she tried to make sense of this. She stood across the bed from him. "When did you do this? And I want the absolute truth?"

"Five years ago."

"Five," she whispered. *Five.* Frustrated, tears welled in her eyes. "Why, Luke? I don't understand."

"Don't you, Katie? Don't you know?"

She shook her head. She had no clue. Five years ago, he was dating her sister. Five years ago, he'd abandoned her sister. Five years ago, he'd joined the Marines.

Luke walked around the bed and came to face her. He placed his hands on her shoulders and she was forced to look into his melt-your-heart blue eyes. "Katie, I'm in love with you."

"No!"

"I am. And I've been in love with you for a very long time."

Oh God. She was afraid to ask. "H-how long?"

"More than five years now. When I realized I loved you, I had to back out of the wedding. I had to. I knew it was crazy and impossible. And so... I left town."

"That's why you joined the service?" She trembled from head to foot.

"Yes," he said on a long breath as if he was finally relieved to confess it. He stroked her arms up and down.

And then it all dawned on her and she flipped his arms off her and backed away. She was the reason Shelly's heart had been broken. "Oh no. Oh no. Oh no." She couldn't believe this. She couldn't comprehend what he was saying. But she knew deep down in her heart it was true. It all made sense now. "I never encouraged you."

"You didn't have to, Katie. You were just you."

"God, Luke. This is making me sick. Really sick. You have no idea how hurt Shelly was, how hard those first few years were for her. And now I find out it's all because of me! I'm to blame for all her pain." Tears streamed from her eyes now, big salty drops spilling down her cheeks.

"Nobody's to blame, Katie. You can't help who you fall in love with."

"Obviously you couldn't. And I'm not forgetting your duplicity about the bakery either. My goodness…you are certainly not like your father. You don't play fair."

Luke's eyes grew hot and he clenched his teeth. "All I wanted was for you to have a good life, Katie. I wanted you to be happy, to be successful."

"And you didn't think enough of me to let me go after that success on my own."

"My God, woman. You are being irrational."

"I'm being real, Luke. And honest. I don't want you to love me. I want a divorce as quickly as possible. And I want you to leave."

Luke looked her square in the eyes. "Fine."

"Well, good. Now go."

"I'm gone," he said.

After he slammed the door behind him, Katie's stomach gripped tight and she raced to the bathroom, throwing up into the toilet until there was nothing left.

Six

Katie stared at the stick in her hand, looking at it hard and praying the results would miraculously change, but that was too much to hope for. The stick wasn't changing, nor had it changed the last two times she'd taken the pregnancy test this week. The nausea, her late period and three pregnancy tests weren't wrong. She was going to have Luke's baby.

Luke, the guy who'd proclaimed his love for her last week. Luke, the guy who'd made sure her bakery wouldn't fail, regardless of her talent. Luke, the guy who'd caused her family undue heartache.

She fought the guilt that was eating away at her. What would Shelly think? What would she say?

Katie searched her mind, struggling with her memory, trying to recall her interactions with Luke back when he and Shelly were dating. Had Katie somehow given him the wrong idea? Had she done anything to encourage him? She wasn't a flirt. She'd never been good in that department.

No incidents came to mind, except her times working with him at the Red Barrel and sharing their love of horses.

It was hard to believe any of this, but now reality was staring her in the face on that stick.

Trembling, she touched a hand to her belly. Where could she turn? Who could she confide in? Drea was going to be married into the Boone family in a few weeks. Katie couldn't tell her best friend, could she? She certainly couldn't tell her sister or her mother, that was for sure. The news could very well send her mama back into the hospital.

"Oh, Katie, what are you going to do now? You're pregnant." Saying those words out loud, no matter how quietly, had impact. It made it real and there was no going back, no way to fix this.

She stared at herself in the bathroom mirror. How much longer could she hide her fatigue and nausea? And soon, she'd have a baby bump to hide as well. She had always wanted children, she wanted this one. It wasn't the baby's fault she'd gotten into this complicated mess. The child would be loved. Always loved.

A knock on her door made her jump. She tossed the box into the trash and straightened up her appearance.

"It's me, Drea," her friend called out.

Katie squeezed her eyes closed. Was it that time already? She was supposed to be dressed and ready to go with Drea for the final fitting on her wedding gown, but she was moving slowly this afternoon. "Coming," she said.

She opened the door and Drea took in her appearance. Oversize sweats weren't what she usually wore to go out. And well, Katie's face probably blended in with the shabby chic color on her walls. Only the paint was in style, and Katie was anything but.

Drea's big smile faded. "Katie, are you okay? You look a little...under the weather."

Of course her friend would think that. Perky Katie was

always ready for anything. She worked ten hours a day and ran around town like a spark was lit under her butt. She could juggle her career and her volunteer work and still have energy to spare.

"Nope, I'm fine," she said. "Come in."

"Okay, but we don't have to rush. We don't need to be at Clara's Bridal for an hour."

That sounded good to her. She still needed to get dressed and rushing around wasn't in the plan. "I've made a pot of jasmine tea. Would you like some?"

"Yes, sounds wonderful."

"Want anything to go with it?"

"No cupcakes for me. Remember, I have to get into my wedding gown today." Drea made herself comfortable at the kitchen table and Katie brought over her rose-patterned teapot. She sat down, too and poured the tea. "You have such a sweet expression on your face right now. I think love has gone to your head."

"I have to keep pinching myself that I'm getting such a great guy. Say, when we're through at Clara's, would you like to have dinner at the ranch with all of us?"

It was the last thing she wanted to do. She hadn't seen Luke in a week, and she'd rather it stay that way. After their last encounter, she'd contacted an attorney about the divorce, but that was just in the early stages. At least she was doing something about it. "Uh, I don't think so, but thanks anyway."

Drea pierced her with a curious look. "You look about as glum as Luke does. What's with the sour puss, my friend? Is something going on between the two of you? Because if it is, I'm here to listen."

Luke was in a bad mood lately? Why? Because she'd tossed him out of her apartment when he'd shocked her with his declaration of love? How on earth did he expect her to absorb that news? And now her best friend was asking probing questions.

"Oh, would you look at the time? I'd better change my clothes and get ready. Don't want to be late. I'll just be a few minutes."

Katie escaped Drea's questioning stare and walked into her bedroom. Her shoulders slumped and all the energy seemed to drain from her body. What in the world was she going to do?

"One thing at a time," she whispered. And right now, she had to put on a happy face and be the best maid of honor she could possibly be.

She took some time to gather her thoughts and then put on a floral sundress. She tossed her arms through a cropped sunny yellow sweater and slipped into a pair of pumps. Next, she rimmed her lips with rosy gloss and colored her lids with eye shadow, hoping to hide her pale complexion. Then she scooped her hair up in a twisty bun and was good to go.

On a deep sigh, she walked out of the bedroom. "I'm ready," she called out and found Drea just coming out of the bathroom.

"Apparently that's not all you are," she said, sympathy touching her eyes. She lifted the empty pregnancy test box. "I wasn't snooping, honest. But I saw this in your trash can, honey. Are you?"

Katie squeezed her eyes closed. She hadn't wanted to tell anyone, not yet. But now she was trapped and maybe that wasn't such a bad thing. She needed a friend, someone to confide in. "I am. I mean, I think so. Three pregnancy tests wouldn't lie, would they?"

"Do you have other symptoms?"

Katie nodded.

Drea walked over to her and gave her a big hug. "Oh,

Katie." The embrace lasted a long time and then Drea broke away. "Can you tell me about it?"

"We have to go to your fitting. It's important."

"You're more important. I'll change the appointment for tomorrow, not to worry." She pulled out her phone and called the bridal shop. They seemed to be accommodating her, and Katie felt terrible letting her friend down this way.

After she ended the call, Drea took her by the hand. "Now, come sit down on the sofa and talk to me." They sat facing each other. "I have a feeling Luke is the father. Am I right?"

"Yes, you're right," Katie said. "It's a long story."

"I'm here to listen. You can trust me."

"Luke doesn't know. And he can't know. Not until I can divorce him."

Drea blinked several times, shock stealing over her face. "Divorce him? Katie, you married Luke?"

She nodded, her emotions a wreck. Tears built up behind her eyes. "It's not what you think. It's worse. And I have to swear you to secrecy, Drea. Nobody else can know right now."

"Not even Mason?"

Several tears spilled down her cheeks. "You see, that's why I couldn't tell you. I don't want to put you in a compromising position. You shouldn't have to keep secrets from your fiancé."

"I, uh, I promise I won't say anything…until you tell me I can. Right now, you need my help and I need to be here for you." Drea took her hands and gave a gentle squeeze. "I want to help."

Katie nodded. "T-thank you. I know this isn't e-easy for you."

"I'm going to be fine, it's you I'm worried about. Now start from the beginning and tell me everything."

Katie started talking, the words spilling out of her mouth

easily now that she was finally able to unburden herself and share her innermost secrets with her best friend.

Luke sat as his desk at Boone Inc. staring at the computer screen, too absorbed in what he was about to do to concentrate on work. He glanced at his watch. It was almost time for him to end his marriage to Katie. However short-lived, he'd loved thinking of her as his wife. But that would be over soon. His attorney was due any second now.

Luke rose from his desk and walked over to the stocked bar in the corner of his office. He picked out the finest bourbon on the shelf and poured himself a drink. He needed fortification today to go through with this. It was what Katie wanted and the last thing she'd said to him as he'd walked out her door. She didn't want his love. She wanted a divorce.

And now he was about to grant her wish.

He took a large gulp. The alcohol burned this throat going down, but it also helped soothe his wrecked heart. He couldn't hold on to Katie if she didn't want him. Didn't love him.

Only, he believed she did. She was just too frightened to admit it.

Katie wasn't easy. She wouldn't have made love to him if she wasn't emotionally involved. He knew by the way she sizzled from his touch, the way she'd kissed him back so passionately she'd nearly bowled him over. The way she'd granted him her body so generously when he'd worshipped her. It wasn't just sex between them but if she refused to admit her feelings, what else could he do?

Every bone in his body rebelled at what was about to happen, but he cared about her enough to let her go. To free her from their secret marriage so she wouldn't lose the love of her sister, her mother.

The knock on the door came too quickly. He swallowed

another swig of his drink. "Come in," he said, setting the tumbler down on his desk. He stared at the door as if it'd bite him and was relieved to find his brother Risk walking in instead of Carmine Valencia, his attorney.

"Hey," Risk said.

"Hey back at ya. What's up?"

"Nothing much. April's out with the rest of the bridesmaids, going for fittings or something. Want to have lunch at the Farmhouse Grill? My treat. I have a few hours to kill and I'm craving their pulled pork sliders."

Luke shook his head. He'd deliberately set his appointment with Carmine in the Boone Inc. offices rather than at Rising Springs. It wouldn't do to parade his lawyer in front of his relatives. "Sorry, no can do. I have an appointment in a little while."

"Someone more important than your brother?" Risk chuckled and then glanced at the near empty bourbon tumbler on his desk. "You're drinking this early? Whenever I used to drink before four, it had something to do with a woman."

"Those days are over for you. Lucky you."

Risk moved farther into the room and pinned him with a sober look. "Hey, why the bitterness? What's going on?"

Luke sighed. "Nothin'."

"Something. Who is she?"

"Mind your beeswax, Risker."

"Using my childhood name that always got on my nerves? Okay, now I know there's something wrong."

"Listen, Carmine will be here any second. So, I can't have lunch with you. Sorry, bro."

"Carmine, as in your personal attorney?"

"Yep."

"Are you okay? You've been quiet and, well, grumpy this past week or so."

Luke put on a smile. "I'm fine. Just let it be, Risk. Will you?"

His brother eyed him, concern in his expression. It was hard to fool his brothers. "Yeah, but..."

"I know. If I need your help, I'll ask. But trust me, this isn't anything you can fix."

Nobody could.

Luke's mood was about to go from gray to black. As soon as Valencia walked into the office and started the divorce proceedings.

Two days later, Luke drove to Red Barrel Rescue. In many ways the rescue had rescued him, giving him an outlet for his loneliness. Giving him a chance to think without anyone asking questions or judging him. Helping heal the neglected and sickly horses put life in perspective. It gave him balance and helped him recover from the hard times he'd had in Afghanistan, the soldiers who'd been left behind. While he was in the Marines, he'd longed for home, for Katie, and the hardest part of it all was not being able to tell another soul what he was going through. He'd kept his secret love for her locked away.

And now after making arrangements with his attorney, the divorce was in motion.

Even though Katie didn't want anything from him, he'd made a few stipulations that he believed to be fair. He wasn't going to leave Katie in the lurch. If she wanted a divorce, she'd have to agree to his terms.

Luke parked his truck and waved at Wes, who was in one of the corrals trying to calm a horse. The horse snorted and paced back and forth, a frightened look in her eyes. Wes wasn't making too much progress with her.

Luke walked over to the fence and Wes approached. "Hello, Luke."

He gave Wes a nod. "Looks like you've got a new guest."

"We do. She's a feisty one. Mustang. Probably lost her

way coming down from the hills. Either that or someone figured she was too wild to deal with and left her stranded. She was brought in two days ago."

"Does she have a name?"

He laughed. "Katie stopped by yesterday for a bit. She named her Cinnamon."

Luke smiled as he watched the mare huff and stomp around the far side of the corral. "That sounds about right."

"Katie tried to work with her a bit, but it was no use. The mare wouldn't let her get close. I don't know which of the two females was more stubborn. Anyway, Katie didn't look so good, so I sent her home."

Luke swiveled his head toward Wes. "How so?"

"She looked worn out, sort of drained. Never seen her look that way before. That girl does too much."

"She loves coming here." Luke always liked watching her work with the animals, whether it was to exercise them around the corrals, or bathe and groom them, or give them the loving caresses they needed. He enjoyed working beside her, seeing her energy and compassion. But it worried him a bit that she was fatigued. He wondered if she'd feel better once she received his divorce papers. It hurt to think it, but being rid of him might just be good for her health.

"We love having her here. Hell, she once told me this place was like her second home."

"I believe that." He sighed. He hadn't laid eyes on Katie in nine days and he missed her like crazy. "Well, I'm here and have a few hours. Put me to work."

Wes gave it some thought. "Pepper's up next. She could stand to take a dozen turns around the corral with the lead rope. After that, all the horses are due for their feed."

"You got it. No mucking for me today?"

"You feel like mucking?"

"Nobody feels like mucking." Except he wouldn't mind

yielding a hoe and working up a sweat in the stables. Anything to take his mind off Katie.

After several hours of hard work at Red Barrel, Luke arrived home after eight and headed straight for the shower. He'd mucked after all, needing the hard work, needing to blow off steam, and now his whole body ached. He walked into the shower and lingered, the hot spray raining down his shoulders and chest.

But every time he closed his eyes, he saw Katie. He wanted her here, with him now, giving both their bodies a good washing and afterward...

Luke shook his head, trying to clear his mind of her. He had to get a grip.

The shower door latched behind him as he got out and dried off. He put on his jeans and a T-shirt and wandered downstairs. The house was unusually quiet for this time of night. No lights were on anywhere, which was how he liked it. Quiet and dark, like his mood. His stomach growled. He hadn't eaten lunch or dinner today and he needed sustenance.

As he headed toward the kitchen, he heard Drea conversing with someone and stopped just short of the doorway, not wanting to interrupt.

"I'm sneaking a bite of lemon chiffon pie," he heard her say quietly.

He realized Drea was speaking on the phone. He turned around to leave, and then Drea said, "Whoops. Sorry, Katie. I shouldn't mention food when you're nauseous. I heard the nausea and fatigue will pass after your first trimester. It's still so hard for me to wrap my head around. You're going to have a baby."

Luke's eyes opened wide. He slumped silently against the wall, shocked at what he was hearing.

"No, I promised you, I won't tell a soul," Drea whispered so quietly he could barely hear. "Not until you're ready."

Luke backed away from the kitchen doorway, his mind racing. Katie was pregnant? She was going to have his baby. Climbing the stairs, he tried not to make a sound. Once he reached his bedroom, he lowered himself down on the bed. After the shock wore off, pure joy filled him up.

It was what he'd dreamed about for so many nights. To have a family with Katie. To *be* a family. Luke closed his eyes, absorbing the news.

But his joy only lasted an instant. Why hadn't she told him? How long had she known? She'd pressed for a divorce over and over again. Did she hate him that much to deny him their baby? Or was it fear that kept her from revealing the truth to him?

No wonder Katie had been tired lately. No wonder she'd been emotional. He'd seen a subtle change in her lately, but he'd always thought it was their secret marriage causing her stress. Well, stress or no stress, Luke wasn't giving her a divorce. Not now. Not when there was a baby to consider.

His baby. His child. A Boone.

Thoughts ran rampant in his head. Should he confront her? Make her fess up? Prod her into a confession?

He was no bully. He wanted Katie to tell him on her own. He wanted to be a part of the pregnancy, a part of the birth of his child. Did he have it in him to wait it out? Hell, he didn't know. He needed advice and he needed it quick. There was only one person who would know what to do.

Aunt Lottie.

The next morning, Luke put on his walking shoes and caught Aunt Lottie just as she was about to take her morning walk. "Mind if I join you today?"

His aunt tried to hide her surprise. "Sure, I'd love that." She eyed him curiously but with a smile on her face.

"Thanks."

"I remember a time when you three young boys would hike way up to the ridge with me. I loved taking you for walks."

"And you'd turn your head and pretend not to see us all roll down the grassy hill and crash into each other." The image made him smile. "It's a good memory."

"It is."

He opened the door for her and they made their way down the road. His aunt was always stylish no matter what she was doing. Today, she wore a dark raspberry jogging suit, her blond hair pulled back in a perky ponytail, her shoes sparkling clean as if she'd never worn them a day in her life, while he knew better.

"It's hard to believe Mason is getting married in a week," she said. "I know your folks will be dancing at their wedding."

"They will, if Mom has anything to say about it."

Aunt Lottie looked off in the distance. "I miss them."

"Me, too."

They were quiet for a while, and then when they were far away from the house, and out of earshot of the crew, Aunt Lottie spoke up. "As much as I love having your company on this walk, I know something's troubling you, Luke. Care to share it with me?"

"Aunt Lottie, you're sure perceptive."

"I just know you boys. And unless I miss my guess, this has something to do with that adorable girl, Katie."

Luke drew breath in his lungs. "It does. I married her."

"You married her?" His aunt stopped walking and tried her best poker face, but the shock in her voice gave her away.

"When we were in Vegas. It's the cliché drunken-vows-at-the-Midnight-Chapel sort of deal. Nobody knows. Well, one other person knows, but I'm in terrible need of advice."

Aunt Lottie nodded her head. "Why do I think you're not too sorry about this marriage?"

"Because I'm not. I'm in love with Katie."

"Oh dear," she said. "I see the problem. Katie's family won't abide that."

"They have no love for me, as you know. But actually, that's not the problem. The real problem is that I just found out by total accident, that...that Katie is pregnant."

"Pregnant? Oh my." Aunt Lottie smiled. "It's a blessing, Luke. Babies are little miracles. But does that mean she hasn't told you?"

"Right, she hasn't told me. I just found out last night by overhearing a conversation. And well, Katie's been pressing me for a divorce. She's worried about her family's reaction and what the news of our secret marriage would do to her mother's health.

"Honestly, Aunt Lottie, I think Katie is running scared. I know there are strong feelings there. She's just afraid to admit it. Now I don't know what to do. I've spoken to my attorney about filing for a divorce, putting the wheels in motion because Katie wanted to have this whole thing behind her. Unfortunately, my attorney is too efficient, and the papers have already been sent. But I won't sign them. I won't divorce her now that she's carrying my child. But do I confront her about the baby?"

"Oh dear. Luke, I understand your impatience. But Katie is in a tough spot right now. She's probably as confused as you are. Don't put more pressure on her. Give her time to sort it out in her head. She'll do the right thing."

He ran a hand through his hair and sighed. "That's easier said than done."

"I know." She turned to him, wrapping her arms around his shoulders, lending support and love. "Be patient with her. In the end, she'll be grateful for it. And one more thing."

"What is it?"

"Don't you dare divorce that girl."

He laughed, feeling a lightheartedness he hadn't felt in a long while. "I don't plan to."

Katie fumed, staring at the divorce papers she'd received by special messenger today. She couldn't believe the terms Luke expected her to agree to. What was with that man, anyway? Their marriage wasn't real. It had been a big fat mistake. She'd told him she wanted nothing from him, not one thing. But did Luke listen? No. He'd had his attorney draw up papers that went totally against her wishes.

She wouldn't agree to his crazy terms. She picked up her phone and tapped out a text to him.

I need to see you, right away.

Her text was answered five minutes later. I can be there in half an hour.

She didn't want Luke coming up to her apartment. She'd been getting curious looks from Lori lately, but her friend and employee was too discreet to question her. Aside from that, Katie didn't want reminders of the last time they'd been together in her apartment.

She didn't love the idea of meeting him in a restaurant either. There were too many people who might overhear their conversation. She couldn't believe she'd had to resort to so much secrecy lately.

Not here, she texted. Meet me at Red Barrel in an hour.

Luke's text came in fast. I'll be there.

A short time later, Katie's anger still simmered just under the surface as she drove up to the rescue. She parked her car next to Luke's steel gray truck in the back of the parking lot. Apparently, he'd gotten here early and as she scanned the area, she found him leaning against the barn wall, the sight of him making her heart beat harder. Angry or not, whenever she spotted him, her initial reaction was breathless attraction, one she couldn't quite seem to shake. It ticked her off that her body betrayed her mind.

She hadn't seen him in over a week, but now his eyes held hers from across the yard, watching her every move. She grabbed her skinny briefcase out of the car, one that made her look professional. Luke pulled away from the wall, his tan hat low on his forehead, his swagger making her swallow down hard. Dressed in jeans, a tan chambray shirt and snakeskin boots, he epitomized Texas, the image of a man who knew strength and power.

He approached her, his intense sky blue eyes trained on her. She held firm, trying not to let her heart overrule her mission here.

"Katie, it's good to see you."

She swallowed. "Hello, Luke."

"You want to talk?"

"Yes, I do."

"There's no one in the barn right now."

Privacy was of the utmost importance to her and the barn would provide that. It was a slow time for the rescue. Most of the volunteers had already gone home. And Wes was usually in the office by now, finishing up on business.

"Let's go," she said.

"How are you feeling?" Luke asked as they headed for the barn.

"Me? I'm fine."

"It's just that you've been feeling tired lately."

"No more than usual," she fibbed.

Luke nodded and was quiet until they entered the barn. Once inside she stopped, shaking her head at his gesture for them to sit on a bale of hay.

He frowned and faced her.

She pulled out the divorce papers and held them tight in her hands. "This is not what we agreed on."

"What's wrong?"

"What's wrong is that you are proposing to give me half a million dollars and then pay monthly alimony of three thousand dollars! I can't take that. I told you I wanted nothing and I meant it. I do fine on my own. At least I thought the bakery was doing well until I found out why."

"You'd be successful regardless. Can't you forget about that?"

"No, I can't. I feel terribly betrayed. I feel like a fraud, like my hard work didn't mean anything, I was pretty much ensured a monopoly in Boone Springs. The idea keeps me up at night."

"Katie, dammit. You need to rest."

Her jaw dropped. Was he kidding? He was responsible for many of her sleepless nights. "Then stop making me crazy. I don't need your help or your money."

His mouth grew tight for a few seconds, his face tensing up. And then all of a sudden, his eyes softened, the dark blue hue turning lighter, brighter. A big smile graced his face. "You know something, you're totally right, sweetheart." He took the divorce papers out of her hand. "This is all wrong."

He tore the paper down the center, then neatly placed the two pieces together and tore them again. "Here you go," he said, giving the squares back to her.

She stared at the ripped papers in her hand. "What are you doing?"

"I'm trying to give you what you want."

"No… I don't think that's it. You gave in too easily. What are you up to?"

"Nothing at all. You didn't want what I was offering. We have no deal now."

"For heaven's sake, Luke. It's not a deal, it's a divorce."

"One in the same."

A grotesque shrieking sound coming from outside interrupted them. It was so loud and ungodly, she had to find out what it was. She ran to the barn door and looked outside to the corral.

A giant hawk was swooping down on Cinnamon, winging over the horse inches from her head. The mare backed up and huffed, whinnying in panic as the bird continued to terrorize her. The hawk didn't back down. It kept on swooping and screeching at the horse.

Katie raced to the fence and screamed at the hawk. "Go! Get out of here!" She called to Luke, "He's relentless!"

Luke ran past her and the next thing she knew, he was behind the butt end of a rifle, taking aim.

"You're not going to shoot him, are you?"

He took his shot, the sharp snap of gunfire exploding in her ears. The hawk flew away, leaving the mare in peace finally.

"You didn't miss, did you?"

"Nope, wasn't trying to kill it. Just scare the damn thing away."

"I've never seen anything like that. Have you?"

"It's nothing more than a mama protecting her young, I'd imagine. There must be a nest around here. Or maybe one of her young'uns fell from the nest and Mama took it out on the closest one around."

"Cinnamon?"

"Just speculating."

She pointed at the rifle Luke held in one hand. "Where did you get that?"

"From my truck. I didn't see Wes's car and figured he was gone. It was up to me to take care of it."

"Well, that you did." She swallowed. "Could you please put it away?"

Surprise registered on his face. "Sure thing. I'll be a minute."

He turned and walked off, and Katie took a good look at the mare. She was still, motionless as if the hawk had put her in a state of shock. Maybe it was the loud ring of the rifle as well.

Katie opened the corral fence, looking into the mare's eyes. She didn't flinch, didn't seem to mind her approach. "Easy, girl, I'm coming," she said. She took several more steps toward Cinnamon. "That's it. Good girl."

She was making progress, speaking to the mare as she inched closer and closer.

"Katie, get out of there. Now." Luke's voice came from behind.

"Be quiet. She's letting me approach."

"You don't need to approach her. She's a wild one," he said through gritted teeth. Katie didn't dare turn to look at him. He was following her around the corral fencing.

"Not now, she's not. Stay put, Luke."

"Like hell I will."

"She'll spook if you try to come in and you know it."

"Are you *trying* to give me a damn heart attack?"

She smiled. He was being melodramatic. Katie knew horses just as well as anyone in Boone Springs, and she knew this one was ready to make friends.

"There, there, girl," she said softly. She put out her hand. "We're gonna be friends, you and me."

The horse snorted.

Katie waited and finally Cinnamon took a step toward her and then another step. The horse kept her eyes trained on her. Katie did the same. They were forming a bond, trusting each other, although tentatively.

Finally, the horse halted, going as far as she trusted, and Katie took the final step toward her. Inching closer, she touched her palm to the mare's nose. The mare held still as Katie stroked her up and down. "You're a good girl, aren't you?"

"Katie, you proved your point. Now get out of there." Luke's voice was low and strained.

"I know what I'm doing," she murmured.

Just then a blue jay flitted over Cinnamon's head. After what she'd just been through with the hawk, the horse spooked and kicked up her front legs. She came down hard and slammed into Katie's side. The jolt tossed her onto the packed ground. "Ow!"

"Dammit." Luke catapulted over the fence and scooped her up. "You are insane," he said, as he carried her out of the corral. He latched the gate, gave one deadly look over his shoulder at Cinnamon and headed to the barn.

The sun was setting now, casting long shadows on the land. Whatever sunshine was left didn't follow them into the barn. Katie could only make out the lines of fury around Luke's mouth, the dangerous slant of his eyes.

"You can put me down now," she said quietly.

"Can I?" His voice was harsh, impatient. "Maybe you'll decide to do another fool thing, like chase after a mountain lion or wrestle a bear."

"Luke."

"Hell. Are you hurt?" He kept her close and let her down slowly, her body brushing against his. Once her boots hit the ground, he probed her shoulders, her arms, gently applying pressure to her rib area. "Any pain here?" he asked.

"No."

Reaching behind her, he checked her spine and lower back, then laid his hands on her buttocks. "Here?"

She cleared her throat. "Nothing hurts."

Yet his touch was familiar, comforting and welcome. She couldn't lie to herself anymore. Her body came alive under his touch.

"Thank God for that. You could've been crushed."

"But I wasn't."

"Pure luck." His anger mingled with a look of genuine relief. "Don't worry me like that again."

Katie absorbed his words. She should be spitting mad at him for making demands he had no right making, yet she wasn't mad at all. His concern touched her deeply. She couldn't remember feeling this way about anyone before or having someone care so much for her. She approached him and laid her head on his chest, enjoying the sweet sensations rushing through her. She'd never admit it to him, but when the mare bucked up and then came down, Katie froze, knowing she was going to get shoved. And she'd sent up prayers that the jolt wouldn't harm the baby she carried.

She'd been lucky her prayers were answered.

Luke stroked her back, letting his hands glide up and down, easing the rough knock she'd taken. It felt right all of a sudden, more right than it should, and she gave in to the comfort.

He tipped her chin up and claimed her mouth in an inspiring kiss. He tasted delicious and her yearnings heightened, her breaths came faster. Luke broke off the kiss and grabbed her hand. "Come with me," he said.

He tugged her to the back of the barn and grabbed a quilted horse blanket. Throwing it down over a bed of straw, he straightened it out a bit, then lay down, bringing her with him.

She turned to him. "What about Wes?"

"He's gone. I told him earlier I'd lock up for him if he had to leave. We're alone here."

They weren't entirely alone. An image flashed in her mind of the three of them becoming a family, her, Luke and their baby. Tears burned behind her eyes. She wanted to tell him so badly about his child, about him becoming a father. But she held back. Call her a coward, but she wasn't ready for the backlash. She wasn't ready to own up to the truth. He'd expect something from her, something she couldn't really give.

She was silent for a few seconds and then Luke asked, "Sweetheart, you sure you're not hurt?"

She took his face in her hands and pressed a kiss to his lips. "No, I'm not hurt, Luke."

Then she unfastened his shirt, one snap at a time, eager to touch his skin, kiss his powerful chest. And fall deep into oblivion until the stars faded in the night sky.

Luke shed his clothes quickly, with Katie not far behind. Then he covered his body over hers, warming her up, kissing her senseless. He loved this woman and had wanted to die a thousand deaths when he saw that wild mare nearly stomp the life out of her. Katie had been lucky and he hoped to heaven she'd take better precautions next time. If not for her, for their baby.

Surely, she wouldn't do anything to endanger their child, but for a moment there, back in the corral, Luke hadn't been sure. He'd nearly blurted out that he knew about the baby, and only stark fear from seeing that mare knock Katie to the ground had shut him up.

He wanted her to come to him with the truth on her own. He didn't want to bully it out of her. Aunt Lottie had told him to be patient, and he was trying. Really trying.

Her little moans brought him back to the moment and he kissed her again, weaving his hands in her long silky blond hair. She was sweet and gentle and beautiful everywhere. He treasured every morsel of her body, caressing her breasts, their undeniable softness arousing the hell out of him. Next, he lay his palm on her belly and sweeping joy entered his heart, thinking of the child they'd both created. But he didn't linger there. He moved his hand past her navel to stroke her inner folds. She was soft there, too, and her heat caused his breath to speed up and his body to grow painfully hard.

"Katie," he murmured, finding her sweet spot. He caressed her there, over and over, her body moving wildly until she whimpered and cried out his name. There was no better sound. Then he sheathed himself and rose over her, joining their bodies.

"Ah, Katie. You feel so good."

Minutes later, he found his release, and the joy and peace that went along with it.

Katie had to be his.

There was no other way.

Seven

Katie woke with a blissful humming in her heart. The first image that came to mind was being with Luke last night. Having him inside her, and how he'd thrilled her with his masterful thrusts until they both came apart.

She sighed deeply. Then her alarm chimed, giving her notice it was time to rise and shine. Well, she didn't know about the shine part, but she rose from her bed. Luke had warned her last night she'd be sore today from the fall she took and he'd been right. Her shoulders and arms ached, but nothing hurt more than her rear end.

She readied a bath, throwing in a bath bomb scented with lavender. When she'd undressed and was just about to put her toes in to check the water, her phone pinged.

It was a text from Luke.

How are you feeling this morning? Are you sore?

Yes, a little bit. I'll live. Why are you up at this hour?

It was just after four. Luckily, so far she wasn't nauseous, but the day was young.

Thinking of you. I can come by and rub the soreness away.

Katie smiled. Wouldn't you just love that.

So much.

Sorry, have to go. Just getting in the tub.

Want company?

No thanks. Go back to sleep.

I'll dream of you. In the tub.

Katie signed off and set the phone down, the sweet humming in her heart speeding up. Last night, Luke had charmed her and she wasn't sure it was deliberate on his part, but rather an organic charm, like the way his blue eyes often set on her, as if he treasured her. She also felt it in the way he protected and cared for her.

Yet, he'd gone against her wishes for a simple divorce. She'd said she wanted nothing from him. And she didn't. She'd have to fight him on that. She wouldn't take a dime of Boone money. When they divorced, it should be as if they'd never married. A clean slate. She'd never be his wife in the real sense.

Yet, he was relentless in his pursuit, making her forget all the valid reasons she had to push him away. Her sister, her mother's health, the bakery deception.

After last night, they hadn't spoken of divorce again. Luke had simply walked her back to her car and given her a quick kiss on the lips, making her promise to get to sleep as soon as possible. He'd followed her home, just to make sure she'd arrived safely.

Of all the men in the world, why did it have to be Luke?

She stepped into the tub and slid down, luxuriating in the sweetly scented water, letting the heat soak away her soreness.

She thought about the baby she carried, just a tiny speck of life that would change her whole world. And she also thought about her carelessness in the corral. She couldn't afford another mistake like that and she was grateful Luke had been there. Grateful nothing worse had happened. She'd never take a chance like that again.

Hours later, Katie stood behind the bakery case and greeted one of her first customers of the day. "Hello again," she said.

"Hi, Katie. Remember me? Davis Moore."

Katie sure did remember him. He'd come into the bakery with Shelly one day. "I do, Dr. Moore."

"Call me Davis."

"All right. What can I do for you today?"

"I'm here for a dozen of your best cupcakes. Give me a variety of them, please."

"Okay, sure. That's easy enough."

"And throw in a few of Shelly's favorites. I think she said lemon raspberry."

"Yes, that's right. She loves them."

"Well, good."

She studied the good doctor. He was tall and nice looking and seemed pleasant enough. "So how is Boone Springs treating you so far?" she asked.

"I like it just fine. The people are friendly. And the work is satisfying."

"I'm glad to hear that."

She packed up the box and he paid for the cupcakes. And then he stood there, hesitating.

"Is there anything else I can get you?" she asked.

"Uh, well." He glanced around the shop. Other than a few customers sitting at the café tables, it was just the two of them. "Shelly's been so kind to me, making me feel welcome and all, I want to do something nice for her. Do you know her favorite flowers?"

"Not roses," she blurted. Shelly had had a fascination with roses and they'd ordered hundreds of snowy white roses for her wedding to Luke. Ever since then, she abhorred every kind of rose. "But I know she likes lilies."

"Lilies. Okay. Thanks for the tip. I might've blundered with the roses otherwise."

"I'm sure she'll appreciate the thought."

"Thanks."

"Hey, Davis?" She stopped him as he was scooping up the box, about to leave. "I just want to tell you Shelly really admires you. The flowers will make her happy."

A big smile graced his face, and his eyes were twinkling. "Good to know."

Well, wasn't that interesting? Katie didn't mind nudging the good doctor in Shelly's direction. She hadn't told Davis Moore anything that wasn't true and if only her stubborn sister would open herself up to let someone in, Shelly might find some happiness one day.

Three days later, Katie sat in her mother's kitchen trying to disguise her queasiness. "Mama, you didn't have to cook for us." Her stomach turned just at the smell of the spaghetti and meatballs. She wasn't eating heavy meals lately, but she couldn't talk her mother out of it. It was Katie's favorite dish and her mom worked so hard at preparing it.

"I want to cook for my daughters for a change. You girls

are always cooking for me. You're on your feet all day long. And goodness, Katie, you've been looking tired lately."

"I've noticed it, too," Shelly said, putting out pasta bowls. "You're looking pale. Not getting enough sleep? Or are you doing too much for Drea's wedding? There's always something happening. Can't miss it in the headlines. Whenever a Boone sneezes, the local papers feel the need to report it. They're holding the rehearsal dinner at The Baron."

"Yes, that's on Friday night."

"Soon it will be all over," Shelly said, "and you won't have any reason to deal with Luke. It must be so awkward for you."

"It…is. But we've—"

"You've what?" her mother asked, sitting up straighter in her chair. Her mother appeared healthier today, which also meant she was more engaged in the conversation.

"We've, uh, found a way to deal with each other. He's… not a bad person, Mama."

"Says who? Any man who breaks my daughter's heart isn't getting nominated for sainthood, I can assure you. We all embraced him and he turned his back on us."

"Mama, he didn't turn his back on you," Shelly said. "He turned away from me. He didn't love me enough."

Katie's chest tightened. She felt guiltier than ever, because she'd been actually entertaining thoughts of a life with Luke. But once again, her family brought her back to reality. If they ever found out the true reason Luke left Shelly—because he was in love with her—and that she was now carrying his child, all hell would break loose.

Funny, when she was around all this negativity, her situation looked grim, but when she was with Luke, she could envision a happy life together.

It was all so very confusing.

"That man doesn't know what he's lost," her mother said.

"I don't think he cares," Shelly said.

"He cares," Katie blurted.

Both heads turned to her. "What?" her sister asked.

"I mean, Luke isn't a horrible person. He knows he hurt you, hurt us all, and he's sorry about it."

"And you know this how?"

"I've spent time with him, remember? At the rescue and in preparing for Drea's wedding. But he didn't want to… Oh, never mind."

Katie could tell by their narrow-eyed expressions they weren't buying any of this. And they were looking at her like she was being a traitor to the Hate Lucas Boone Club.

"You're right. There's no need to spend another second speaking of him," her mother said.

Katie wanted to skulk in the corner but she wouldn't because she was too darn curious about Davis Moore. She took a pasta plate to the stove and dished up a generous amount for her mother. "Here you go, Mama. The least I can do is serve you."

"Thank you, sweetie." Her mom smiled and it brightened her face. Katie remembered a time when her mom smiled a lot. That was a long time ago.

Once they were all sitting and Katie was pushing her pasta around the plate, she casually mentioned Shelly's new friend. "Davis Moore came into the shop the other day, Shel. Seems he does have quite a sweet tooth."

Shelly stopped eating, the fork halfway to her mouth. "I suppose he does."

"Did you get the lemon raspberry cupcakes he bought specifically for you?"

"Yes, I did."

"He seems like a nice guy. He's settling into Boone Springs well, or so he says. I guess you've been showing him around town?"

"Yes, some. He's quite remarkable, actually. Has a long list of accomplishments in—"

"He's handsome," Katie said.

"Katie, are you interested in him?" her mother asked.

Shelly squared her a look and Katie tortured her for a few seconds. "Me? No, Mama. I think you're asking the wrong daughter."

"Shelly?"

"Mama, it's nothing. I mean, I like him and he did send me a beautiful bouquet of lilies the other day as a thank-you. But we're just friends."

"I think he wants to be more than friends, Shel."

"Why, what did he say?"

"All good things," Katie answered.

Shelly blushed and her mother gave her an approving look.

It was progress, albeit very little.

But both of them still had no use for Lucas Boone and nothing Katie could say would change that.

Luke knew the exact moment Katie entered the rehearsal dinner at The Baron Hotel's Steak House because the entire dining room seemed to light up. Or maybe it was just him. Everything seemed brighter when Katie was around. She stole his breath wearing a one-shoulder black dress and tall heels, her blond hair up in a messy bun with wisps of hair framing her face.

He sighed. She still hadn't told him about the baby and his patience was coming to an end. He couldn't see any physical evidence of her pregnancy yet, but he knew their child was growing in her belly.

Didn't she know how much he'd want to be a part of it? How much he would cherish their time together until the baby came? He thought for sure they'd gotten closer after the night in the barn, but after that one text, she'd never returned any of his other calls or texts.

She was avoiding him.

Risk stood beside him as the bridesmaids entered the restaurant. They were all giggles and laughter, and right in the middle of it all was the happy bride-to-be, Drea. Soft music played in the background as the rest of the wedding party filed in.

"Guess everyone's here," Risk said. "What happens now?"

"Now we have drinks and food and Drew makes a speech."

"Isn't he doing one tomorrow?"

"Nope, that's my job," Luke said.

"I suppose Katie's giving one, too?"

"I suppose."

"Don't tell me you don't know every little thing about her, bro. She's on your radar twenty-four-seven."

"I'm in love with her, Risk. So yeah, she's on my radar. And that's just between you and me."

"Okay. Wow. Want to talk about it?"

"There's nothing to say. You know the situation with her family."

"Yeah… I do. Man, oh man. Does she feel the same way about you?"

Luke shrugged. "She's trying her best not to but yeah, I think she does."

Risk gave him a sharp slap on the back. "Hang in there, and try not to look like you're going to your own execution. For Mason and Drea."

Luke nodded. "I'll do my best."

He wandered over to Aunt Lottie. She looked brilliant tonight in a sleek sapphire pantsuit. She always wore the most exotic jewelry from her many adventures around the globe. Today her necklace made of gold and Asian sculpted jade caught his eye. "Aunt Lottie, you're looking mighty pretty tonight."

"Thank you, Luke. That's nice to hear."

"Would you like a drink?" he asked.

"I would love one."

He guided her over to the bar. "What would you like?"

"Wine sounds wonderful. A hearty pinot," she told the bartender.

"I'll have your best rye," Luke said.

"Yes, sir."

Once the drinks were in their hands, Luke walked with Aunt Lottie over to a corner of the room. "How's your… situation, Luke?" she asked quietly, sipping her wine.

"She still hasn't told me. I have to admit, it angers me. She's denying me my rights."

"But you don't blame her, do you?"

"I'm trying not to. She's the *one*, Aunt Lottie. I can't stand just waiting around for her to come to her senses." Luke took a swig of his drink, the whiskey going down smoothly.

"Being patient isn't easy, especially when you know the truth. I'm excited for you as well. I almost can't wait myself. You'll be the first one in the family to become… Well, you know."

He nodded, searching the room and finding Katie in conversation with both of his brothers. She would talk to them but not him. A surge of jealousy had him gulping down his drink.

"She's a pretty one, isn't she?" Aunt Lottie remarked.

"Beautiful."

His aunt touched his arm. "Be patient. It hasn't been that long. And I'm sure Katie is mixed up right now, trying to work things out in her head."

"I hear you," he said. "I just wish she would trust what she feels. Trust me."

Drew walked up then, and Aunt Lottie gave him a warm smile. "Hello, Drew. Are you ready for the big day tomorrow?"

"I am. How about you?"

"Yes, of course. You know how I feel about Drea. She's like the daughter I never had. I'll be very happy seeing Mason and Drea say their vows."

"It'll be a good day. Well, I'll talk to you later. Didn't want to interrupt your conversation."

"It's okay, Drew." Luke kissed his aunt's cheek. "You stay and talk to Aunt Lottie. I'm about ready for another drink. Excuse me."

Lottie watched Luke walk off, wondering if she'd given him the right advice. She'd certainly botched her own love life, so who was she to give him guidance on his?

She turned to Drew. "You look nice this evening."

In his dark suit and string tie held with a sterling silver and turquoise clasp, Drew had never looked more appealing to her. His snowy hair and slight beard were groomed perfectly, giving him an air of sophistication.

"Thank you. Same goes for you," he said. "I like that color blue on you."

She smiled. "Thank you. Are you nervous about your speech?"

"I'm not much for public speaking."

"I think you'll do fine. After all, you'll be talking about Drea."

"And what a lousy father I've been."

"That's past history. Drea adores you."

"She didn't always."

"She does now and that's what you have to focus on."

"I guess so. I appreciate the pep talk. Well, just wanted to say hello. I'll be getting to my seat. Looks like dinner's about to be served."

"Sure, okay," she said, deflated. Why didn't she tell him she adored him, too? Why didn't she apologize for believing he'd been interested in another woman? The man had been nothing but true blue and honest with her, and yet she'd managed to alienate him. After the way he'd kissed her the other day, she had no doubt about his feelings for her or her feelings for him.

She just wished she had the nerve to tell him.

Before it was too late.

Katie sat next to Luke at the rehearsal dinner. There was no escaping it. Mason was paired up with Drea, Risk with April, and she didn't want to make a big deal of changing seats.

The truth was, she was falling for Luke, and the more time she spent with him the harder it would be to say goodbye. They couldn't be a couple. They couldn't stay married.

But when the baby came, she wouldn't deny Luke his rights. Her child needed both a father and mother. She'd been deprived of that in her own childhood, and sure, she'd faired okay, but it was hardly ideal. Her child deserved better than having come from a broken home, even before he or she was born.

Unfortunately, right now it was the only way forward. After the wedding, she'd have no reason to see Luke. She'd tell him in her own way and in her own time and…she'd have to confess to her family, too. She wasn't looking forward to that. She kept praying a solution would miraculously present itself.

The impossibility of it all hit her and tears moistened her eyes.

"What's wrong, sweetheart?" Luke whispered ever so closely in her ear.

She shook her head, summoning strength. "Nothing,"

she whispered, making sure no one was observing their exchange. She faked a smile. "I'm fine."

And then Luke's hand found hers under the table. The comfort he lent felt good even if he was the last person who should make her feel anything. But his encouragement, his compassion, seeped into her and soothed her raw nerves. She had to think about the baby and what was best. When she was with Luke, she had trouble thinking of anything else but being with him…as a family.

And yet her worry about her mom and sister always seemed to ruin that fantasy.

Mason stood up then and thanked everyone for being a part of the wedding. He'd put gifts on the table and encouraged the groomsmen to open their small blue boxes. Luke was forced to let go of her hand to open his gift. She was hit with a wave of relief and sadness at the same time as he broke their connection.

"Gold cuff links," he said, glancing at her.

She smiled. "Those will look good on you," she said. "They're very nice." And they probably cost a fortune.

At times, she forgot about the Boone wealth and what it meant. But Luke wasn't defined by his wealth. He was down to earth and kind and generous. He ran Rising Springs Ranch, shared the corporation with his brothers and owned half the town.

He was a man's man, a guy any girl would love to have by her side.

Tears touched her eyes again. She was being hormonal, her elevator emotions going up and down.

"Hey, if you don't stop looking so sad, I might have to kiss you into a better mood," Luke said softly.

She gasped and eyed him, giving him a don't-you-dare look.

"Smile, Katie."

"For Drea and Mason?" She glanced over to where they

sat at the table. They were busy eating their salads and chatting with each other, happiness on both of their faces.

He shook his head. "For me."

Goodness, what was with his ego? "I have no smiles for you," she said through tight lips.

Luke grinned. "Katie, you're forgetting about the work we did at the rescue," he said loud enough for others to hear, if they were so inclined. "You were very diligent."

Her nerves rattled. Of course, no one would know what they were talking about, but she knew, and it was a visual she couldn't get out of her head. Being naked in the barn with Luke and having him make love to her had been exciting. He'd always managed to draw her out of her wholesome shell and make her do wild and sexy things. "I… know. Sometimes I get carried away."

Luke stared into her eyes. "But it's very much appreciated."

Heat rushed to her face. "Is it?"

"Yes, you have a knack, with stallions especially, that's really inspiring."

She rolled her eyes, hiding a smile. There were no stallions at the rescue right now. "You give me too much credit."

"Doubtful."

Just then, Drea rose from her seat. "I, too, want to thank all of you for being a part of our special day. I can't wait until Mason and I become man and wife with all of you very special people in attendance. And I have gifts for my wonderful bridesmaids, too."

She walked around the room, giving the girls beautiful embossed gift bags made of soft lavender linen, the same color as their gowns. When she got to Katie, she kissed her cheek. "Thank you for everything, my bestie. This one is special, just for you. Because you're my maid of honor."

"Thank you," Katie said, giving Drea a smile straight from the heart.

"Please open your gifts," she said to everyone.

Katie opened hers by pulling a drawstring and then reached inside. She pulled out a black velvet box and opened the lid. "Ah! This is beautiful." She lifted out a gold-and-diamond drop necklace. She was touched and truly surprised. She'd never owned anything this exquisite before. "I don't know what to say."

"Say you'll wear it tomorrow."

"Try to stop me." She hugged the necklace to her chest.

Drea grinned. "I had help picking it out."

"Mason?"

She shook her head. "Luke. Actually, he has pretty good taste."

"You picked this out?" she asked him.

He nodded. "It looked like you. Bright and sparkly."

She blinked and didn't know what to say. He was constantly surprising her.

"I will treasure it," she told Drea.

An hour later, Katie walked out of the restaurant and heard footsteps hitting the ground behind her. "Katie, wait up."

She sighed, stopped and turned around to Luke. "What is it?"

"Let me walk you to your car."

"That's not necessary."

"No, but I'd like to." His jaw set tight and it was no use arguing.

"Suit yourself," she said lightly and as she began walking again he fell in step beside her. He was quiet, pensive, and she didn't know what to make of his mood.

Once she reached her Toyota in the parking lot, she spun around to face him. "Well, here I am."

"I can see that."

"Thank you for walking me. Now it's time for me to get going."

"Where to?"

"Home to pick up my things and then I'm spending the night at Drea's cottage. We're getting our hair and makeup done there in the morning. Drew's getting the place ready for us right now."

He nodded.

"I really should get going."

A tick worked in his jaw. "Katie, where do we go from here?"

There was an urgency about him that she didn't quite understand. Why was he being so persistent? "Luke." She glanced around. There were a few people getting into their cars near her. "This is hardly the time or place."

"Then you tell me a good time and place and I'll be there."

She sighed. "I don't know. We have issues. And I can't think about them at the moment. Why are you bringing this up now?"

"Because you've been avoiding me. You haven't been answering my calls or texts. I didn't want to say anything tonight, but at some point you're gonna have to face reality."

"And what reality is that?"

Luke's eyes narrowed. He opened his mouth to say something, then closed it again.

"Look, I just needed a…break," she said.

"From what?"

"From…you."

His lips went tight and the look in his eyes darkened. "From me?"

"Yes, if you must know. I can't think when you're around."

"That's right, I make you crazy."

"Yes, yes, you do and it's horrible."

His brows rose in surprise and a hurt look crossed his features. "Fine. I'll give you all the space you need," he said, his tone sullen.

"You don't have to get mad."

"I'm not mad," he said, his voice a harsh rasp. He opened her car door and gestured for her to get in. She slid into the driver's seat, giving him a last look.

Then he slammed the car door.

And refused her another glance.

Eight

Katie cried on the way to the MacDonald cottage. She wanted to shed all her tears before she spent the night with Drea. This was to be their special before-the-wedding slumber party. Just the two of them, like they'd planned since they were kids. She wouldn't spoil the fun by being a miserable companion.

But she'd hurt Luke, made him angry. And she didn't feel good about any of it: the divorce, her deception about the baby. She wasn't lying when she told Luke he made her crazy. He did, because he was the right man for her, under the wrong circumstances.

Why did it have to be him? Recently, she'd asked that of herself every single day. She couldn't take it any longer. She didn't want to hurt the people she cared about. It was time to own up to the truth. She would reveal her secrets and finally deal with the consequences.

After the wedding.

With that thought in mind, her tears stopped flowing. At

least she had a plan now and it made her feel one thousand percent better. As she entered the gates of Rising Springs Ranch, she stopped the car and tidied herself up, wiping her tears and putting on a fresh coat of lip gloss. Tonight, she would be the best, best friend to Drea she could be and they would have a fun time.

Katie started her car up again and slowly drove down the road past the main house heading to the cottage. With her maid of honor dress and shoes in the back seat as well as her toiletries, she was totally prepared.

What she wasn't prepared for was seeing the flames up ahead, blazing bright and licking the night sky.

Her throat tight, she drove farther down the road and immediately stopped when she spotted Lottie and Drea with looks of horror on their faces. She parked the car on the side of the road and ran to them, the acrid smell of soot and ash filling her lungs.

"Oh no!" Half of the cottage was on fire. "What happened?"

Drea was shaking uncontrollably. "Oh, Katie. My d-dad's in there. I don't know how it h-happened. But he left the dinner early to come home and fix up the house for us."

"Luke's gone in after him," Lottie cried out.

"Luke? Oh my God. How long has he been in there?"

"He ran in as soon as he spotted the flames. Firefighters are on the way, but Luke refused to wait."

Katie's heart raced. This couldn't be happening. Not to Drew and Luke. Her Luke. She'd never forgive herself if something happened to him. She should've told him…she loved him. She did. She loved him, but was too frightened to confess. And now she was scared to death she'd never get the chance to tell him.

He needed to know she was carrying his baby. She needed him to know he was going to be a father. Maybe he wouldn't have taken such a chance with his own life.

But Luke was tough, a Marine, and of course he'd head straight into a burning house to save a friend.

She closed her eyes and prayed for both of them.

She couldn't lose Luke now, not when she was finally able to admit her true feelings for him.

The wind shifted and they were blasted with heat, forcing them to step back several yards. To think, Luke was in there, trying to save Drew. Smoke billowed up and they waited impatiently, holding hands, tears spilling down their cheeks.

From a distance, sirens could be heard. The fire engines were on the property now, but Katie kept her eyes trained on the front of the house. "Luke, please, please be okay," she whispered.

And then from out of the smoke and flames, Luke staggered down the steps, his face a mass of black soot, as he half walked, half dragged Drew with him.

"Thank God!" Lottie exclaimed, running over to the fence and opening it.

Both men looked worse for wear, but they were alive and breathing on their own.

"Daddy, are you okay?" Drea ran over to help.

"He will be," Luke said. "I found him knocked out on the floor by the back door. He's got a big knot on his forehead."

Drew looked up and gave his daughter half a smile. "One of the candles I set out for you gals got too close to your curtains and caught fire. I went running through the house to get the hose and tripped over a box of your softball trophies," he told her.

Drea's face paled. "Oh, Daddy. I'm so sorry."

"I wanted to surprise you and Katie with the trophies. I've been cleaning them up and damn fool that I am, I didn't quite…" He began coughing hard, his face turning red from the exertion.

"It's okay, Dad. No more talking right now."

Katie glanced at Luke. He looked exhausted, too, and coughed every now and then. She wanted to run over to him and hug him tight, but the firefighters had just pulled up and were shouting orders. Paramedics took Drew and Luke to their van for observation, while the firefighters set their hoses up to battle the flames.

Katie stood by the van, watching them tend to Luke. Every so often, he would glance her way and she'd smile and wave, wiping tears from her eyes. She'd been given a second chance with him and she wasn't going to blow it.

Lottie and Drea stood by Drew's side as he was being examined. "You really should go to the hospital for a complete checkup," the paramedic was saying.

"You said I'm fine. I don't need any more checking up."

"I said there's no sign of smoke inhalation. But that needs to be confirmed."

"My daughter is getting married tomorrow, and I need to be there."

"Dad, it won't take too long," Drea said.

"I'm just fine, Drea."

Lottie touched the paramedic's arm. "Let me speak to him, please."

"Okay, ma'am. I'll be back in a few minutes after I call this in."

Lottie smiled at Drew. "You had me in tears." She walked over to him, arms extended, and gave him a big hug. "I've never been so frightened in my life. To think you might've died in that house. And I can't have that. I can't lose you. I can't stand the thought of us not being together a moment longer. Drew Joseph MacDonald, I love you very much. And if you'll have me, I want to marry you."

Drew blinked and rubbed his sore head. "Did I hear you right? You want us to get married. Maybe I did hit my head too hard."

"Yes, yes and no. Yes, you heard me right. Yes, I want to marry you. And no, you didn't hit your head too hard. At least I hope not. You'd better say yes, because I'm not going to let you alone until you do."

"Promise?"

"I promise."

Drew smiled. It was a whopper, and Lottie smiled right back at him.

Katie and Drea exchanged glances. Drea had prayed for her father to find happiness. Now her prayers were being answered.

"I love you, Lottie. And I'm honored to marry you," he said. "Don't know if I'll have a house for us to live in though."

"We'll figure it out. It'll be our little adventure."

"Now you've got me looking forward to having an adventure with you."

"Oh, and one more thing, Drew," Lottie said. "You need to be checked out tonight at the hospital."

"No, I don't—"

"You do. And so does Luke. But don't worry, I'll go with you and make sure you get to the wedding on time."

"Bossy woman."

"You love it."

He grinned and pulled her close. "Guess I do."

And then he kissed her.

Once the paramedics were through checking over Luke, Katie walked over to him, put her arms around his neck and kissed him solid on the mouth. She didn't care who witnessed it, or what they thought. She just wanted Luke, period.

He snuggled her close, his eyes gleaming. "Are you going to propose to me?" he asked.

She brought her mouth to his and kissed him again. "Silly man. I'm already your wife."

"But you don't want to be."

"I'm rethinking that, Luke." She smiled at him and he blinked.

"You are?"

She nodded.

Luke's expression changed and his mouth spread into a grin.

Katie put her hands on his soot-stained face, looked into his blue eyes. "You saved Drew's life. It was a brave thing to do, but it scared me half to death."

"I just reacted. I couldn't let him die inside the house. I had to go after him."

"You risked your life."

"It was worth it. And there's an added plus."

"Oh yeah? What would that be?"

"You're here with me. And your eyes have a certain gleam. Sort of like the way you'd look at Snow, or one of your delicious cupcake concoctions."

"You do realize you just compared yourself to a horse and a cupcake," she said softly, admiring his handsome face and thinking of what might have happened to him.

He chuckled. "Katie, you're too much." He bent his head and kissed her, and it was better than anything in the world. But he needed more medical attention and she needed to wrap her head around loving him. She backed away, imploring him, "Be patient with me. For just a little while longer."

Before he could respond, Drea walked up with Drew and Lottie, all three holding hands. Drea stepped up. "I'll never forget what you did tonight, Luke." She was obviously rattled, the prospect of losing her dad keeping tears in her eyes. "You're a good man."

They embraced, Drea hugging him tight.

"Does that mean I'll be your favorite brother-in-law from now on?"

Drea smiled. "Risk would have to do something pretty great to top this. Saving my dad, that's a pretty high bar."

Drew walked over to him. "Let me shake your hand, Luke." Then he swiped the air and put his hand down. "Forget that." He wound his arms around Luke and gave him a big manly hug. "Thank you, son. I wouldn't be here if it weren't for you."

"You're welcome, Drew."

"I don't know what else to say. You risked your life to save mine. I'll be grateful to you for the rest of my life."

"No need for that," Luke said humbly. "Just make Aunt Lottie happy."

"I plan to." Drew gazed at Lottie with love in his eyes. It was beautiful to witness.

Lottie gave Luke a big hug, too. "Don't know what I would've done if I lost you both. You're like a son to me and I love you very much."

"Love you, too, Aunt Lottie."

"So then you'll get checked out at the hospital?"

"I'll make sure of it," Katie intervened.

Luke grabbed her hand. "You'll go with me?"

"Yes."

And if Shelly got wind of it, she'd have to tell her the truth. But luckily, she happened to know Shelly wasn't working tonight. She was taking her mother over to her friend's house for a nice long visit. It bought Katie a little time to reveal the truth.

When Mason and Risk showed up, everyone turned to them and filled them in on what had happened. They'd stayed behind to have drinks at The Baron before coming home.

As the fire was quelled, leaving only half of the three-bedroom cottage standing, everyone right then and there decided the wedding would go on as planned. It was set and ready to go.

They had something else to celebrate, too.

Drew and Lottie's engagement.

"I'm sorry for the way things turned out tonight, Drea." Katie handed her friend a glass of white wine. She happened to know this brand of pinot grigio was her favorite. The Boones had offered them the entire east wing of the second floor of their ranch house for tonight. They sat facing each other on the twin-size beds in one of the guest rooms. "Your dad's home is nearly destroyed."

"He'll rebuild, Katie. It'll give him and Lottie a chance to build something to their liking. Besides, I think my dad's happier than he's ever been. He and Lottie have been tiptoeing around each other for years. Now they'll finally settle down together. And he got a clean bill of health, thanks to Luke. If he hadn't rushed in to save Dad, the smoke would've gotten him before the fire did."

"Yeah, Luke's amazing. I'm happy he checked out just fine at the hospital, too. In that respect we were very lucky."

Drea smiled. "I saw you two kissing."

"I finally realized I love him. He's my guy."

"So, are you going to tell him everything?"

"I plan to. Very soon. I couldn't stand the thought of something happening to him before I had a chance to tell him he was going to be a father. It really put things in perspective for me. Our child deserves a loving home."

"I'm excited for you."

"Thanks." She bit her lip. "It's strange how things turn out sometimes, isn't it?"

"What do you mean?"

"Well, you hated Mason for what you thought he'd done

to your father. And I wasn't too keen on Luke, for what he did to Shelly. Now we're both in love with a Boone."

"You married one."

"And you're about to." Katie sipped her sparkling cider. "Let's not forget how much April disliked Risk when he first came back into her life, too. Their fake engagement led to the real thing."

Drea took a sip of wine. "Well, there's just something about those Boone brothers."

"I'll drink to that." She finished off her cider. "Oh my gosh, I just realized you probably lost a lot of your things at the cottage, too."

"I did, but I have what I need. I've been staying with Mason at the house, so half my stuff is here now."

"You're not panicked so I take it your wedding dress is safe and sound."

"Lottie picked it up for me from the bridal salon. It's here, at the house. She was going to bring it by the cottage in the morning."

"Thank goodness. Tomorrow is going to be a special day."

"You know, I wouldn't mind if you decided to wander over to the west end of the floor tonight, hon. Risk is at April's tonight and Mason decided to spend the night at The Baron."

"Because the bride and groom shouldn't see each other before the wedding?"

"Right…and we like the tradition. But tradition doesn't dictate anything about the best man and the maid of honor not seeing each other."

"Really…hmm. I wouldn't want to desert you."

"I'm starting to get super tired." Drea put her arms up and yawned. "And I need my beauty sleep."

"You're such a bad liar. But I would love to check in on him. Make sure he's okay."

Drea pointed toward the door. "Go."

"Gosh, now I'm getting thrown out of your room."

"Only because you've got something much better waiting for you across the hall."

Katie stood. "How do I look?" She fussed with her hair and straightened her dress.

"You could be wearing rags and Luke would think you were beautiful. You look great." Drea shooed her away. "It's down the hall and the last door on your right."

Katie blew her a kiss and made her way down the long hallway on bare feet, eager to see Luke again.

She knocked on his bedroom door three times. No answer. He was probably sleeping. Her desire to check in on him was stronger than her worry about waking him up, so she put her hand on the doorknob and opened the door.

As she stepped inside, she told herself she had a perfect right to check on her husband. He could've been injured or killed tonight running into those flames. But as she looked around, she found his bed was still made. Had he gone somewhere at this hour of night? She turned to leave, her hand reaching for the doorknob.

"Katie, where do you think you're going?"

She froze for a second and spun around. Luke was just stepping out of the bathroom, a towel draped below his waist. Moonlight glistened on his wet hair. Drops of water cascaded down his shoulders, falling onto his granite-hard chest. She itched to touch him there, to devour him and show him how much she loved him even though she had yet to tell him. "Luke, I didn't think you were here."

"I'm here." He smiled wide.

"Y-yes, you are."

He sauntered over to her. "Some nights I like to shower in the dark, with just the moonlight streaming in. It's quiet and peaceful that way."

"Oh... I didn't know."

"There's lots of things you don't know about me, sweetheart. I can't wait for you to learn all of them." He moved closer, the scent of his lime soap wafting to her nose.

"I came to check on you."

He opened his arms wide. "I'm healthy, Katie."

Her gaze flew below his waist and the bulge hidden under the towel. "That might be an understatement, Luke."

He laughed, a mischievous sound that got her juices flowing.

"You sure you're not tired, because I don't have to stay—"

"You're joking, right?"

She smiled at him. "Y-yes, I think I am. I don't want to leave."

Luke opened his arms and she stepped into them. Someone up above was granting her wishes, because as his arms wrapped around her and snuggled her close, her every dream was coming true. There was only one tiny flaw in her plans to be with him tonight, but she shoved thoughts of her family aside. She wanted to be fully in the moment. And as Luke's lips touched hers, his hard body pressing against her and his desire under the thin towel barrier reminding her of the thrills to come, she washed away everything and everybody but what was happening between them tonight.

"Katie." His voice held awe and wonder. "This is where you're meant to be."

She overflowed with emotion. It was almost too much for her, this roller coaster of a night. She shook, unable to control herself. "Luke, just kiss me and keep on kissing me."

He gripped her head in his hands and crushed his lips over hers, his expert mouth making every bone in her body melt. She could faint from the delicious sensations he aroused. And soon her dress was off and they were on the bed, under the covers, Luke worshipping her body.

His heat was contagious. She was nearing combustion, but she held on, wanting to enjoy every minute of this night with him. A night filled only with desire. No problems, no issues, just two people expressing their love in the most potent way.

Katie's body erupted first, her orgasm reaching new heights. "Luke," she cried out.

And he was there with her, rising above, his hard body tightening up, his powerful thrusts and groans of pleasure beautiful to behold. He held her tight as his release came and she kissed him until his breaths steadied and they both fell back onto the bed.

"Wow," he said, as he ran his hand up and down her arm. "Just checking that you're real."

"I'm real. Realer than real, after that."

He laughed and kissed her shoulder. "Stay with me tonight. Be my wife in all ways."

"I will," she answered, wanting that so badly, too.

Luke looked at the empty place beside him on the bed and smiled at the note Katie had left for him this morning on her pillow.

Dear Husband,
Sorry, had to leave early. Today is all about Drea and Mason. See you soon.
Your Wife

Luke rose from the bed, breathing in Katie's pleasing scent. In his humble opinion, she always smelled delicious and today was no exception. He couldn't believe she was finally his, after all his years of trying to do right by her, of trying to deny his feelings.

She hadn't said the words he wanted to hear. She hadn't confessed her love or told him about their baby yet, but they had made great progress. Finally, Katie thought of him as her husband. She'd come to him last night, and all it had taken was him racing into a house on fire for her to realize she cared about him.

He stepped into the shower, letting the water rain down his body, wishing Katie was here. It'd been a fantasy of his, to have her all soapy and wet with him, but they had time for that. Today, his brother was getting married, and Luke had the honor of being his best man.

He dressed in jeans and a T-shirt, and glanced out the window to the yard below. A team of event workers were constructing an open-air tent to house two hundred and fifty guests. A dance floor was going up as well as tables and chairs. Mason and Drea had opted to speak their vows on the steps of the gazebo Mason had built in the backyard.

Rising Springs Ranch had hosted many events, but this was the first wedding, and the Boones were doing it big.

Luke walked down the hallway and across the bridge that led to the east wing of the house. He heard the girls giggling, Drea and Katie giddy with excitement over the wedding. Warmth spread through his heart as he made his way downstairs.

In the kitchen, Aunt Lottie was drinking coffee with Drew. Early risers. "Mornin'," he said to them. Lottie and Drew had eyes only for each other.

Then Drew sat up straighter. "Luke, boy, how are you feeling this morning?"

"I'm feeling fit. How about you?"

"I'm…doing fine. Lottie's making sure of it. She won't hear of me worrying about losing my place, not today. Much of what I lost can be replaced but today is Drea's special day. And as long as she's happy, I'm happy."

Luke gazed at the loving look on Aunt Lottie's face

and knew instantly these two people were right for each other. "Congratulations again. Seems we've got another wedding coming up."

"Yep, but we're happy to focus on this one today. Drew's giving away his daughter."

"Now, Lottie, I'm not keen on that phrase. I'm not giving Drea to anyone."

Lottie laughed. "What would you call it then?"

"I'm allowing Mason the privilege of marrying my daughter."

"And Mason knows it, too," Luke added. "When's he getting here?"

"Not until just before the ceremony."

Luke poured himself a cup of coffee and looked under the covered dishes to see the brunch Jessica had made for the bridesmaids. "Wow, that's a lot of food for the girls."

"I agree, so help yourself, and then vamoose for a few hours. The girls need to get all dazzled up. Myself included."

"And men tend to ruin their party? Is that what you're saying, Aunt?"

"Something like that."

Luke got the hint. "I'll eat fast and then be on my way."

He had something he needed to do at Red Barrel Rescue anyway.

Something that would make Katie happy.

Katie stared at Drea in the oval mirror in her room, noting the gleam in her eyes, the joy on her face. All the bridesmaids had already gone downstairs, giving her and Drea some alone time.

"Drea, you are beautiful. I can't even describe how amazing you look. Now I know what they mean when they say blushing bride. That's you, and guess what? It's time to go downstairs."

"It is," she said dreamily. "I'm...a little nervous."

"No need to be. I've got your back."

"Thanks, hon." Drea gave her a peck on the cheek, making sure she didn't smudge her pale pink lipstick. "And you look amazing, too. I love your hair like that." Katie's hair was pulled up in a very loose updo, with blond curls framing her face. "The band of flowers in your hair makes you look like a princess."

"It's a miracle what a hair and makeup artist can do with a hot mess like me."

"Shush, none of that. You're not a hot mess as far as I'm concerned. You're a beautiful mommy-to-be."

Katie turned sideways and glanced at her reflection in the mirror. "Do you see a baby bump?"

Drea grinned. "Not yet, but it'll be here soon enough."

Katie sighed. She still had trouble believing she was having a baby, and then her crazy symptoms would appear to remind her. Today, she'd been lucky: no nausea. Only bliss this morning, waking up next to Luke. She had him on the brain, but she had to remember that this day was all about Drea and Mason. "I hear the violinist playing. It's time to go."

"Okay," Drea said. "You first. I'll be right behind you."

As Katie walked out the back door and down the path leading to the gazebo, she found Mason waiting for his bride, an eager look in his eyes. Katie didn't linger on Mason but rather on the guy standing next to him, his best man, the man she'd married weeks ago. And didn't Luke look smoking hot in his tuxedo?

Katie couldn't seem to look away until the music stopped for a beat, and then the familiar wedding march began to play. Drea stood beside her father, their arms entwined. She was holding a bouquet of white gardenias and roses. Everyone stood and then Drea made the walk down the aisle.

Katie teared up, her emotions running high. This was a monumental day. Her bestie was marrying a great guy. And before she knew it, they spoke sweet, funny, loving vows to each other and were then pronounced husband and wife. It was a glorious ceremony and Katie's tears flowed freely, from happiness for a change.

Mason and Drea were met with great applause and they waved to their friends and family as they made their first walk as a married couple down the aisle. Next it was Katie and Luke's turn to leave, and she met him in front of the flower-strewn gazebo. He took her hand possessively as they made their way up the aisle and away from the seated guests. Once they reached the reception tent, he stopped and quickly kissed her, his eyes beautifully blue and twinkling. "You look gorgeous."

"So do you, Lucas Boone."

His grin made her dizzy. "I expect to dance with you all night long."

"Don't I get one dance with the groom?"

His mouth twisted adorably. "One, since it's my brother."

Photographers were snapping photos and a videographer was recording the entire event. Katie had a mind to release Luke's hand and hoped the kiss wasn't captured on film. These photos were bound to make the newspapers in Boone County. But as she pulled her hand away slightly, Luke tightened his hold, making it clear he wasn't going to play that game anymore.

It meant she'd have to speak with her mother and sister soon. Like tonight after the wedding, or tomorrow, at the latest.

Chandeliers hung from the high beams and the drapes were parted in strategic places to give the tent an airy feel in the late afternoon. Hors d'oeuvres and champagne were passed around by white-jacketed waiters and Mason and

Drea took their places at the head table beside Risk and April. Mason waited until his guests were all inside the reception area before he picked up a microphone.

"May I have your attention please? First of all, I want to thank you all for coming and sharing our special day with us," he said. The crowd settled and all looked his way. "I have an announcement to make. Actually, it's really a wedding present for my bride."

Surprised, Drea gave him a curious look, though her eyes were still glowing.

"Tonight, our musical entertainment will be provided by The Band Blue."

Sean Manfred walked into the tented area, along with the rest on his band.

Drea looked from Sean to Mason, and then tears flowed down her cheeks. "Mason, how did you manage this?"

"He didn't have to twist my arm very hard, Drea," Sean said. "Congratulations to both of you."

Drea gave Sean the biggest hug and turned to Mason. For him, she had a major kiss. It was all so touching and sweet. The Band Blue had played a part in getting Mason and Drea together when they'd all worked on a fund-raiser for the Boone County Memorial Hospital. And now here they were after winning their first Grammy, playing at Drea and Mason's wedding.

"Pretty cool," Luke said to Katie.

"It's a wonderful surprise. Did you know?"

He nodded. "I knew. I helped Mason arrange it. It's what best men do, right?"

"Yes, but it's quite a secret to keep."

"No bigger than our secret."

"Yeah, about that, we should talk. After the wedding?"

He played with a strand of her hair, distracting her with the loving way he was looking at her. "I'm all in."

Nine

The Band Blue captured the guests' attention, their country pop music less drawl and more beat. Most of the wedding guests got up and danced like it was the best party they'd ever attended and some stood by in awe just watching the band do their thing. It was almost as if they were attending a concert.

Luke hadn't been joking when he said he'd dance with Katie all night long. She'd never had so much fun, but she wasn't at all sorry when The Band Blue began singing a slow, sexy ballad.

"Twinkle toes, let's dance to this slow one," Luke said.

"Thought you'd never ask," she teased.

She walked into his arms and rested her head on his shoulder. Two hundred and fifty guests had seen them stick together like glue this evening. They'd seen the way Luke looked at her when she was giving her funny little toast and they'd seen the way she hung on his every word when he'd given his toast to the happy couple.

She was sure it would get back to her sister, but there was nothing she could do about it. She couldn't hide her feelings for him anymore and slow dancing with him had lots of pluses. Like breathing in his swoon-worthy masculine scent, being held in his strong, powerful arms and enjoying his occasional and surprising kisses.

The crud would hit the fan later, but right now she wasn't going to think about that. She wanted to celebrate her best friend's wedding without fear or trepidation.

She lifted up on her toes and gave Luke a sweet kiss on the mouth.

He brought her tighter into his embrace. "What was that for?"

She gazed into his eyes. "Just because."

"That's a good enough reason for me."

He always made her smile. Well, not always, but recently she found herself breaking free of the binds of obligation to Shelly and her mom.

"This is probably the best wedding I've ever attended," she said dreamily.

"You mean, ours wasn't this good?"

"Ours? It's not even a blip on my radar."

"I know." He kissed the top of her head. "I'll make that up to you one day."

She gazed at him, finally finding the courage she needed. "Luke, will you come with me?"

"Sure, where are we going?"

"To the gazebo. It should be quiet there. And well, the reception's almost over. We'll be back in time for the last dance."

Luke took her hand and led her down the pathway leading to the gazebo. The sun was just descending, the sky to the west ablaze with hues of pinks and oranges. Once they reached the gazebo, she walked up the steps and took a seat. Luke sat directly beside her.

She got right down to business. "I don't know where to start, but yesterday when I found out you were inside Drew's house with fire all around you, I couldn't deny my feelings for you any longer. I love you, Luke. I don't know when it happened or why. Lord knows, I have half a dozen reasons not to care for you but I do. Very much."

His eyes closed, as if he were treasuring her words, as if he was trying to lock this memory away. He'd been patient with her. And obstinate and persistent. But she loved him, all of him, and she was glad to finally tell him.

"Katie, I've waited five long years for this. I love you. I've already told you but it wasn't the way I wanted to tell you. Not in the heat of an argument like that."

"I kicked you out of my house when you told me."

"I know. And I'll admit now, I overstepped my bounds by denying you competition at the bakery. It's just the way I love. I protect the people I care about."

"But you won't do anything like that again, will you?"

"I promise you, I won't."

She smiled and Luke ran his hands up and down her arms, soothingly, sweetly, and then he kissed her and kept on kissing her until she could barely breathe. She put a hand on his chest. "There's more."

"Tell me more." His eyes glistened as he gave her his full attention.

"I'm, uh… I'm…pregnant. You're going to be a father."

There, she'd said it. Telling him only made it seem more real.

"Ah, Katie." Tears misted in his eyes. "This is the best news," he said, relieving her qualms. She'd had no idea if he even wanted children. It had never been a topic of conversation. Why would it be, when all she'd been focusing on lately was divorcing him?

"So then, you're okay with it?"

"I'm…blown away. Did you worry I wouldn't be happy about this?"

"I didn't know how you felt about children in general. I've never seen you around them, but I see how compassionate you are around horses and all animals really, so I was hoping this wouldn't rattle you."

"I'm on top of the world right now. You and I created a baby, sweetheart, and I'll love that child as much as I love you. I don't care when or how it happened, it's a blessing."

"I think so, too," she said softly. "But I've always used protection. I'm fuzzy about our wedding night in Vegas."

"Me, too. I, um, I would never put you at risk, Katie. Not consciously. I hope you know that."

"I do. I guess we both blurred out."

"Yeah"

"It's just…well, I'm going to have to face my sister and mom very soon."

"The sooner the better, Katie. And I'll be with you every step of the way."

"T-thanks. But this is something I have to do on my own. Tomorrow. I'm gonna tell them tomorrow. Right now, I think we should get back to the wedding."

"I could sit here all night with you, but you're right." He cupped her face, laid a solid, delicious kiss on her lips and then stared into her eyes. "We should get back."

Hand in hand, they made their way down the gazebo steps approaching the twinkling lights of the tent, just as April came out to greet them holding a cell phone. "Katie, I think this might be important. Your phone's been ringing on the table almost nonstop."

"Oh, okay. Thanks, April." She glanced at her recent calls. "It's from Shelly. I'll be just a minute. Please excuse me." Alarmed, Katie hid her concern from Luke and April. Shelly knew where she was tonight and she wouldn't call unless it was super important.

"Want me to stay?" Luke asked.

"No, you go on. I'm sure it's nothing."

April hooked Luke's arm. "Come on, Luke. You owe me a dance."

Reluctantly Luke was led away and Katie paced back and forth until her sister picked up.

"Shelly? It's me. What's wrong?"

The news was not good. Katie's mom was in the hospital. This time it wasn't her heart, but a case of pneumonia and it was bad enough for Shelly to take her to the emergency room.

Katie took a minute to absorb it all, her heart beating fast, and then she went back to the reception to seek out Luke. She found him just finishing a dance with April. Grabbing his arm, she took him off to the side. "I have to leave. My mom's very ill. She's in the hospital. Will you please tell Drea and Mason I'm sorry, but I have to go?"

"I'll go with you," he said immediately.

"No."

"No? Katie, I'll drive you."

"Goodness, Luke. Don't you get it? I can't show up at the hospital with you."

"Are we back to that?"

"I'm sorry. But I'm going. By myself."

Luke's mouth hardened to a thin line and that stubborn tick twitched in his jaw.

She couldn't deal with him right now. She had to get to the hospital.

Katie sat by her mother's hospital bed, watching her sleep. Her breathing seemed labored right now and she hated seeing her hooked up to all that equipment. Outside in the hallway, she heard Shelly's voice and turned just in time to see her sister speaking to Davis Moore. When they were through talking, Dr. Moore took hold of Shelly's hand and promised to check in with her later.

Shelly gave the good doctor a hero-worship smile, one only a sister would recognize, and kept her eyes trained on him as he walked away.

If her mother wasn't so ill, Katie might find that amusing.

Shelly walked into the room and laid a hand on Katie's shoulder. "You must've come straight from the wedding."

"Your call scared me so I didn't bother to go home to change."

"I'm glad you're here."

She put her hand over the one Shelly had placed on her shoulder. "Of course I'd come."

"You look pretty," Shelly said. "That color suits you."

What? No snide remark about the Boones or the wedding?

"Thank you." Katie rose from her chair to face Shelly. "How's Mom doing?"

"Things have calmed down now. She had a fever when I brought her in and her coughing was bad."

"Thank goodness you were with her tonight."

"I, uh, wasn't. I was out, but I called to check on her and heard her hacking away. I knew it wasn't good. Davis thought that I should take her straight to the emergency room."

Davis? Shelly must've been out with him tonight. And hopefully not at a seminar. "I didn't realize Mom was ill."

"It came on suddenly. She was having trouble breathing and with her fever spiking, I didn't want to take any chances. She's where she needs to be at the moment."

Katie nodded, tears welling in her eyes. Her mother looked pale and so still. Fear stuck in her throat. She couldn't lose her mother. She was too young. She was going to be a grandmother.

Katie's stomach churned, her emotions roiling. Though her eyes burned, she wouldn't cry. She needed to be strong. "Do...do you think she's going to be okay?"

"Pneumonia is never good in an older person, but Mom should be able to recover from this now that she's being monitored," Shelly said in her nurse voice. "I do want to warn you, Mom's health isn't the best in general, so it may take a long time for her to get better."

Katie sighed, pain reaching deep into her heart. "Just as long as she does."

"It's important that she stay calm. She'll be medicated throughout the night. You don't have to stay, Katie. I'll call you if anything changes."

"No, I'm not going home. When Mom wakes up, I want to be here."

"Okay, sis. But at least go home and change your clothes. It gets chilly at night on the hospital floors. You'll freeze in that dress."

Katie hesitated a moment. "I don't want to leave Mom."

"I'll stay until you get back. Mom won't be alone."

"Okay, if you promise."

"Go, little sis. And of course I promise. You can always count on me."

Katie took those words to heart. Her older sister had always been her friend, had always had her back. She'd been someone she could rely on for all their years.

Katie's heart sank even further with guilt. She was torn up inside, worried sick over her mother and worried about Shelly's reaction to her news. All her life, she'd never wanted to let anyone down. And now, it seemed, she was letting down everyone she cared about. "I'll be back in fifteen minutes, at the latest."

She gave her mother an air-kiss and then walked out of the hospital room feeling a sense of desperation and sadness. She hated seeing her mother looking frail and weak.

As she walked toward the elevator, she pulled out her cell phone, ready to let Drea and Luke know what was going on. The screen went black. "Shoot." She was out of charge. Of course. She'd used her phone all day long during the wedding, taking pictures and texting Lori about bakery issues, never realizing she'd need it tonight.

Making her way through the lobby, she found her car easily in the parking lot and drove to her apartment. The drive only took five minutes. As she pulled into her parking space at the back end of the bakery, a car followed her and parked directly next to her. It was Luke.

She got out of her car, and so did he. She met him in front of her back door.

"Katie, I texted and called you and then I started to worry," he said. "What's going on?"

"Luke, I'm in a hurry right now."

"And you couldn't call me?"

"My cell has no charge. It died just as I was texting you and Drea. My mother's really ill right now. I only came home to change my clothes so I can sit with her during the night."

"I'm sorry to hear that. What's wrong with her?"

"Pneumonia. I'm so worried. They've got her hooked up to all these machines. It's scary to look at."

"Ah, that's too bad. Let me help. What can I do?"

He reached for her, and she scooted away. "Nothing. There's really nothing you can do. My mom's recovery could take weeks. Maybe longer. Shelly is waiting for me at the hospital right now."

He ran a hand through his hair. "Katie, why do I get the feeling you're pushing me away again?"

"I'm…not. I just can't focus on more than one problem at a time."

"I'm your problem?"

"You know what I mean. I'm really sorry, but I have to get upstairs."

"Okay, go. But you know how to reach me if you ever need anything."

"I do. Thanks."

She sidestepped him and went to the back door.

"Charge your phone, Katie," he said as he climbed back into his car.

"I will. I'll text you tomorrow."

Luke didn't look happy. He was right—she'd pushed him away. She couldn't afford having him around. How would she explain it? It was the same old same old, except now her mother was in even worse shape than before.

She raced up her stairs and shed her pretty maid of honor gown, throwing on a pair of comfy black leggings and a big cozy gray sweatshirt. She wrapped her feet up in a pair of warm socks and put on tennis shoes.

She had always thought falling in love would be easy and fun and thrilling. Well, loving Luke had caused her nothing but indecision and pain. It wasn't supposed to be this way. She did love him. The thought of not having him in her life destroyed her.

And she feared if she pushed Luke too far, he'd never come back.

When Luke returned to the ranch, he found his family sitting at a table under the tent, drinking a final toast to Mason and Drea. All the guests were gone. The caterers and waiters were just leaving and the tent was due to be taken down tomorrow.

The lights still twinkled, clashing with his dark mood.

He brought over a bottle of Jack Daniels from the bar and sat next to Risk.

All eyes were on him, including his Aunt Lottie's and Drew's.

"How is Katie's mother?" Drea asked.

"She's in the hospital with pneumonia."

"Oh no. Poor Diana. First a heart attack and now this. Is she bad?"

"According to Katie, she is. She's worried sick." Luke slouched in the chair and sipped from the bottle, raising a few eyebrows. He didn't care. He needed his family to know the truth. It was time. "My wife doesn't want me there."

His brothers exchanged glances and then Mason asked, "I'm sorry, did you say wife?"

"Yep. I married Katie in Las Vegas." He sipped from the bottle again.

"What," Mason asked, "are you talking about?"

"I'm married to Katie. It's true."

"I'm in shock," Risk said, glancing at April.

"No more than she was when she woke up next to me in Vegas."

"Wow, bro. You got married during my bachelor party?" Mason said.

"Yeah, I did."

"Okay. Well, Katie is a great person." Mason put out his hand and they shook on it. "Congratulations."

"Same here," Risk said, slapping him on the back. "Congrats."

Luke frowned. "Don't get carried away. It's not a marriage made in heaven. It was one of those too-drunk-to-know-any-better moments. Immediately, Katie demanded a divorce." He gulped down another swig of whiskey, finally feeling the effects of the alcohol.

"Well, I think you and Katie are meant for each other. You two make a great couple," April said sweetly.

It only made him feel worse. "She thinks her mother and Shelly would never accept it. She swore me to secrecy. She didn't want the word to get out. The truth is, I love her and she loves me. But it's taken a lot of persuasion on my part to get her to admit it." He gave everyone at the table an equal glance. "I'm sorry I haven't told you before this."

"So why now?" Aunt Lottie asked.

"Why now?" He gave them all another look. "Because Katie is pregnant. We're having a baby."

"Wow! This is amazing. The best wedding present you could have given us," Mason said, pulling Luke up and hugging him. "And I didn't think anything could top you getting The Band Blue here."

Drea stood, too, and they embraced. "I'm so happy for you and Katie."

"I can't believe it. This is wonderful news," April said.

Risk pulled him in for a hug. "Wow, you sure know how to liven up a party. Congrats." He slapped him on the back. "Hey, I'm gonna be an uncle."

Tears swam in Drea's and April's eyes. "We're gonna be aunts," they said at the same time as if just realizing it, and then everyone laughed.

When the laughter died down, Luke shook his head, grateful for their encouragement. "And now for the hard part. I'm gonna have to swear you all to secrecy. Just until Katie feels like she can share the news with Diana and Shelly. Right now, she won't hear of it. And she's doing her best to push me away, too."

"Why?" April asked. "If she loves you?"

"It's what women do sometimes," Lottie said sagely, glancing at Drew.

April nodded. "Yeah, I guess I did that with Risk, too."

"And I did that to Mason," Drea said. "But we all had good reasons, at the time. Just don't give up on her. She does love you."

"How can you be so sure of that?" Mason asked his new wife.

Drea kissed his cheek and said softly, "Best friends

know these things." Then she turned to Luke. "I'm sure of it."

"Thanks, and don't worry. I've been very patient with Katie. She was ready to tell her family the truth until Diana got sick. I won't let her push me too far away. I have a plan."

"A Boone with a plan? Just make sure it doesn't backfire," Aunt Lottie said.

He'd had the same thought. But he had to try something. His patience was at an end.

Katie was on a roll this morning. She'd finished baking cupcakes and frosted one hundred of them in less than an hour in her work kitchen. They were now ready to go in the dessert case.

"Lori, cupcakes are up."

"Coming," Lori called from the bakery. "I'll be right there."

Katie washed the bowls and utensils, and when Lori walked in she grabbed one of the large cupcake tins. "Wow. Working fast."

"I have to. I'm going to stop by the hospital to check on my mom after the morning rush. Thank you for holding down the fort for me this week."

"Of course. How's Mama doing today?"

"Getting better every day. Her doctor says she's out of danger."

"All good news."

"I know. Thank goodness. Her fever is gone and if it stays normal for one more day, they'll release her."

Katie had closed the bakery for the first three days while her mother was fighting pneumonia and had taken turns with Shelly to sit with her at the hospital. She reopened her shop once her mom's recovery took a good turn.

"That's great, Katie. It's been a hard week for you."

"As long as my mom gets to come home, it's all worth it."
"I'll keep good thoughts for her."
"Thanks."

Once Lori walked out, Katie checked her cell phone. No texts yet from Luke. He usually texted her first thing in the morning and then at night before bed. He always asked about her mother's health, and made sure she was feeling okay, too. She hadn't seen him since the wedding and it was killing her. She really missed him, but not enough to ask him to come over.

She couldn't take the pressure right now and she understood that this wasn't the way Luke wanted it. He wanted to be let into her heart and her life. She wasn't sure if Luke was trying to abide by her wishes by staying away, or if he was really angry with her. Maybe a little bit of both.

"Oh God," she murmured. She didn't want to push him away like this, but what choice did she have?

The morning rush was intense, Katie and Lori working their butts off, trying to accommodate all the customers' orders. Davis Moore walked in and Katie waved to him.

He gave her a quick smile. "Hi, Katie."

"Hi, Davis. Are you here for your usual?"

He'd become a regular customer and she had gotten to know him a bit. "Actually, I'm surprising the entire floor with your cupcakes this morning. Can you pack up two dozen for me to take back to the staff?"

"Sure." She turned to Lori. "We can do that, right?"

Lori nodded, getting two big boxes ready.

"Be sure to include Shelly's favorite, lemon raspberry," he told her. "Put in two of those. Your sister got me hooked on them, too."

"Shelly's good for business."

He grinned. "She's good all the way around."

Katie paused momentarily, holding back a wide smile. "I agree."

"Your mom's making progress on her recovery. I checked in on her this morning."

"Thank you. It makes me feel good knowing she's getting expert care. Actually, I'll be leaving here in just a few minutes to visit her."

"I wouldn't rush. She's got a visitor right now."

"Oh yeah? Do you know who it is?" Katie asked, making conversation as she totaled up the bill at the cash register.

"Well, someone told me it was Shelly's ex. He walked in with a big bouquet of tulips for your mom."

Katie nearly swallowed her tongue. Luke had gone to see her mother with a bouquet of her favorite flowers? "Davis, you know what? These cupcakes are on the house. As a thank-you to you and the rest of the staff."

"Well, that's nice of you—"

"Lori will finish up your order." Katie removed her apron and grabbed her purse. "I actually can't wait to see Mama another minute. I'll be back later," she told Lori. "Bye, Davis."

Then she dashed out the door, her stomach gripping tight. It wasn't morning sickness making her ill. It was a heavy dose of dread.

What in hell was Luke up to?

Ten

Luke hoped he wasn't making a big mistake. He stood outside Diana Rodgers's hospital room and took a breath. Holding a bouquet of Diana's favorite flowers in one hand, he gave her door a little tap with the other.

After a brief pause, she said, "Come in."

Her voice sounded strong. According to Katie, Diana was doing well. She'd make a full recovery and might even go home tomorrow. *Here goes*, he thought. He'd gotten the okay from Diana's nurse to pay her a visit.

He walked through the slightly open door and found her sitting up in bed. She glanced at him and the softness in her eyes disappeared. "Luke, what are you doing here?"

"May I come in?"

"You already have."

He nodded and set the tulips down on the bedside table. "For you."

Grudgingly, she glanced at the flowers. "They're lovely."

"I remembered your favorite."

She half smiled. "If only you'd remembered to marry my daughter."

Luke stared at her, understanding her wrath. "I came to speak with you, Diana. If you would hear me out."

"Haven't we said all there is to say years ago?"

"No, I don't think so."

Diana looked better than he expected. Her face hinted at a rosy sheen, her hazel eyes were bright and she seemed to have attitude, which he remembered about her. She was never a pushover.

"If you want me to leave, I will. But first, I want to say I'm glad to see you're making a full recovery. You look good."

"Thank you for that." She folded her arms over her chest.

"I'm here to speak to you about Katie."

"Katie? What about Katie?" Diana's eyes shifted warily.

"Well… Katie and I have been friends now a long time."

"I know. She always defends you."

"She does?" That made him smile. "I suppose I'm not your favorite person. But I'm here to explain about what happened. You see, I did love Shelly. I thought she was right for me and I was right for her. I suppose I'll always hold a special place in my heart for her."

"She was sick for months after you broke off the engagement. She crawled into a shell and didn't come out for a long time."

Luke pulled up a chair and took a bedside seat. "I'm sorry about that. But you might say I did the same by joining the Marines. I was hiding out, too, in my own way."

"And what were you hiding from?"

"My feelings. You see, I didn't mean it to happen and I certainly didn't want it to happen, but I fell deeply in love—"

"With another woman?" she asked quietly.

"Yes. I fell hard. I couldn't help it. This girl was everything I was looking for. She was bright and independent and funny. We shared the same interests and—"

"My Katie?"

"Yessss." Luke closed his eyes briefly, then opened them to look straight at Diana. "I'm in love with Katie. It's the real reason I left town. I didn't want to come between Katie and her sister. I left my family, my work, all the things I loved, to keep peace in your family. She never knew. She never encouraged me."

Diana bit her lip and then sighed. "Now that explains it. We couldn't figure out why you broke up with Shelly days before the wedding. And you didn't stick around long enough to work things out with her. You left her high and dry."

"I know. I've apologized to her and to you. Many times. And well, I did a good job of staying away from Katie when I returned home to Boone Springs, except for the time we'd spend at Red Barrel together. Katie was the perfect protective sister. She never gave an inch and I accepted that. But then we were thrown together for Mason's wedding."

"And?"

"And I fell in love with him, Mama."

Katie entered the room and set a hand on Luke's shoulder. She gave him a look that said she'd take it from here *and don't you dare argue*. He wouldn't dream of it.

"You love Luke?"

"I do, Mama. He's a good man."

Her mother continued to nibble on her lip. "What about Shelly?"

"I'll speak with her tonight."

"Brave."

"I'm not, Mama. I should've told you the whole truth

myself. You see, Luke and I got married in Las Vegas during the bachelorette party weekend. A little too much tequila at night makes a girl do silly things. I was beside myself and panicked when I woke up seeing that marriage license. I was worried sick about how you and Shelly would take it."

"She tried to divorce me," he said. "But I stalled her."

"You stalled her until she fell in love with you?" Diana asked.

"Yes." He kissed the top of Katie's hand and looked into her beautiful eyes. She'd finally come around and nothing made him happier. "I couldn't let her go a second time. I love her too much."

"Mama, I finally realized my love for Luke when he ran into that burning house and saved Drew's life. He could've been killed in that fire and all of a sudden, everything became clear to me."

"I see. I read about your heroics in the newspaper, Luke. It was courageous of you. And what you sacrificed to spare Shelly's feelings is commendable. You stayed away from home for four years. You did an honorable thing. It makes me feel a little bit ashamed about how I've treated you."

"Don't be. I understand."

"You can't help who you fall in love with, Mama."

"I guess not."

"There's more," Katie said.

Luke stood up, grateful that Katie was finally revealing the entire truth. He wrapped his arm around her shoulder and brought her in close, showing solidarity.

"We're going to have a baby, Mama," she said. "You're going to be a grandmother."

Diana's eyes went wide for a few seconds, as if sorting out the words in her head, and once the shock wore off, a big smile graced her face. "You're pregnant?"

"Yes, Mama. And you're going to be the best Grammy ever."

"That's wonderful news, sweetheart. I can hardly believe my little girl is going to be a mother. And I'm going to be a grandmother." Diana put out her arms, and Katie ran into them. "All I've ever wanted is for my girls to be happy."

"I am, Mama. I'm very happy."

"Then so am I."

When Katie backed away, Diana stretched out her arms again. "Luke?"

He walked over to her and she hugged him tight. He'd always liked Diana, and she'd treated him like part of the family when he was with Shelly. Was it possible to regain that bond again? "I guess…you're my son-in-law now."

"Guess so."

"Well then, welcome to the family, Lucas Boone," Diana said. "In a million years, I never thought I'd say those words to you."

Luke felt a thousand times better than when he'd first walked in here. "Neither did I."

Katie knocked on Shelly's apartment door. She'd had this place ever since college; it was in a nice neighborhood surrounded by parks and gardens. Shelly had done well for herself. She'd become a highly respected nurse and was on her way to bigger things professionally. While Katie nurtured horses and all animals, Shelly loved patient care. She had a nurturing spirit, too, and it had taken her a long time after her breakup to get back to a good place in her life again.

Katie's nerves rattled as she waited for Shelly to answer the door. She prayed that her news wouldn't set her sister back. That had been her greatest fear of all—that her sister would be crushed all over again.

When Shelly opened the door, she seemed surprised. "Katie? I was just going to the hospital to give you a break. What is it? Is something wrong with Mom?"

"No, nothing's wrong with Mom. She's actually feeling much better."

"Oh good. For a second there, I got worried."

"Can I come in?"

Shelly's brows furrowed and she stepped aside to let Katie in. "That expression on your face has me puzzled. You look...scared. Are you shaking?"

"I, uh. Shelly, we need to talk."

"Okay," she said. "What's up?"

Katie's legs went weak and she took a seat on the living room sofa. She'd rehearsed what she would say to Shelly many times, but as hard as this confession was in her head, it was ten times harder in person. "I have something to tell you, Shel. But first I want you to know I love you very much and I'd never intentionally hurt you."

"Of course, I know that. Same here. Please tell me what's on your mind, because I'm starting to get a weird vibe here."

"Weird? No, that's not the word I'd use."

"Katie, you're being cryptic."

"Okay, okay. It's just hard to begin. It's about... Luke."

Shelly blinked a few times. "What about Luke?"

"I, uh, he's my... Remember, I love you."

She nodded.

"Well, when Luke came back home from overseas last year, we started bumping into each other at the rescue. It wasn't a friendship really, but we shared a mutual love for horses and we worked together there at times. But it never went beyond that. I swear to you. Then in Vegas, during the party for Mason and Drea, Luke and I both got blistering drunk. Luke offered to walk me back to the hotel.

Only we didn't quite make it back. Instead…we went to the Midnight Chapel and…got…married."

Shelly's eyes nearly bulged out of her head. "You got married? Am I hearing correctly? You and Luke are married?"

Bile rose in her throat. The last thing she wanted was to cause her sister grief. She took a breath and went on, "I t-tried to get a divorce, but Luke kept stalling me, saying his attorney wasn't available. And I didn't know what to do. Shel, I was panicked. We hid it from everyone. I just wanted the ordeal to be over. Luke and I were thrown together a lot because of Drea's wedding. And when Snow died, we bonded over that. And well, Luke shared with me the real reason he couldn't marry you. It killed me to hear it. But you have to know the whole truth. Luke had fallen in love…with me," she whispered.

Shelly seemed unusually calm, but Katie didn't take that as a good sign. "Luke fell in love with you?"

"Again, Shel, I never encouraged him back then. We were friends. He was going to be my brother-in-law. And well, that's when he decided to break up with you and join the Marines. He didn't want to hurt you anymore than he had. He left his home and family so that he wouldn't come between us. He kept away for four years and when he returned home… Well, you know the rest. I'm so sorry, Shelly. I didn't want this to come between us. Ever."

"Well, what did you think would happen? That I'd be jumping for joy?"

"No, just the opposite. That's why this is so hard."

"I was a mess after he dumped me. And you're telling me you knew nothing about this?"

"I truly didn't. I swear. I was just as shocked when he told me the truth as you are now. And I didn't want any part of it. I fought my feelings for him."

Shelly ground her teeth, trying for restraint but Katie

knew that look. Her sister wanted to scream to high heaven at the injustice of it all. How could she blame her? She'd held on to her bitterness for all these years. *"Your feelings for him?"*

Katie sighed deeply. "Yes, I have feelings for Luke. I love him. I mean, I didn't know that I'd fallen in love with him, until he ran into a burning building to save Drew MacDonald's life. After that, I realized how much he meant to me. How much I cared for him. How much it would hurt if I lost him."

"And so, you threw your sister under the bus for a guy."

Her words cut deep, but Shelly's anger seemed to lessen, and was there actually space between her tight lips now? Was she making a joke?

Katie reached for her sister's hands and hung on tight.

"Your hands are freezing," Shelly said. "You're really tortured about this, aren't you?"

"Of course I am." Katie held back a sob.

"I hate seeing you in such pain."

"And I hate knowing I've caused you pain. I know you have no use for Luke."

"You shouldn't have to choose between us."

"But you only have horrible things to say about him, Shel. And I know this is awkward as hell, but… I don't know what to do."

Shelly sat quietly for a while, holding her ice cold hands, thinking. Seconds seemed like hours, but then her sister released a big breath.

"You *know* what to do," Shelly said firmly. "You love him and he loves you. There's nothing to do except make a life with him. Look, I know I've been bitter, and I've been difficult. I was hurt, but I finally realized that I didn't want a man who didn't love me like crazy. What kind of marriage would that make? Luke wasn't right for me. Not the way…"

"Davis is?" Katie asked, hopefully.

Shelly sighed. "We're getting closer every day. He's amazing."

"The feeling is mutual, on his part. Whenever he comes into the bakery, he finds a way to tell me just that."

Shelly had a dreamy look on her face. "He does?"

"Yep. Every single time."

"We have the same interests and, well, we're taking it slow, but I've never felt this way about anyone before. Davis always makes me feel special."

"That's wonderful, Shelly. I'm really happy for you." Katie nibbled on her lips, hesitating. "But I have another bit of news. I'm afraid there's more."

Shelly tilted her head. "Can I handle more news?"

"Gosh, I hope so. This is important." She laid a hand on her abdomen, a protective gesture that any woman would pick up on, especially a nurse.

The words wouldn't come. This news could crush her sister and ruin their relationship for good.

But it seemed she didn't have to speak the words. Shelly's eyes riveted to her stomach and *she knew*. "You're pregnant."

Goodness, this was difficult. "H-how do you feel about becoming an aunt?"

"An aunt. Katie?"

"Yes, I'm, uh, we're going to have a baby, Shel. I hope this isn't too much for you, because I'm really gonna need you. I need my big sis."

"My gosh, Katie. This is a lot to take in."

"I know," she squeaked, and gave Shelly her best little sister pout. It used to work when they were kids. "But I hope you can, 'cause I'm gonna really need you."

Shelly's shoulders relaxed and her expression changed. "You know what? I'm through being miserable. It's like meeting Davis has shined a bright light inside me. So, yes, of course I'll be there for you. You're my baby sister."

Tears dripped freely down Katie's face as she gave her sister a gigantic heartfelt squeeze. "Oh Shel, this means everything to me. Thank you."

"Have you told Mom?"

"Yes, just before I spoke with you," Katie said. "She's gonna be a grandma, and that makes her happy. I think she's accepted Luke, too. She said she just wants her girls to be happy."

Shelly smiled for the first time since Katie walked into the apartment. "Then, I think she's gotten her wish."

When Katie arrived home, she slumped on her bed, drained of energy. It had been an emotional day and all she could think about was getting into bed and falling asleep. It didn't matter it was only six in the evening, she was bone weary.

Her cell phone buzzed and buzzed and she dug into her purse. It was Luke. Immediately, she smiled. Her husband was calling.

She chuckled and then answered the phone. "Hi," she said.

"Hi."

Just hearing his voice brought her peace.

"How did it go with your sister?"

"It was difficult, but Shelly will come around. She's in love with someone and I think it's going to be okay."

Luke released a big sigh. "Glad to hear it, sweetheart. That makes this day perfect. Well, almost perfect. If you look outside now, you'll see there's a car waiting for you out front."

"A car? Luke, what are you up to?"

"You'll see. The driver knows where to take you. Trust me, Katie."

She took a deep breath. "Can I have twenty minutes? I need to shower and change."

"Okay, but remember I'll be waiting."

After she hung up the phone, she took a quick shower and put on her favorite floral sundress, one that wouldn't be fitting her too much longer. She tossed a short denim jacket over the dress and then slipped her feet into a pair of tan leather boots. Then she brushed her hair to one side and let it flow down her shoulders. She stared into the mirror for a second, wondering how on earth she'd gotten to this point in her life. This time, her thoughts weren't filled with dread and fear but with hope and promise.

The "car" Luke had sent was a limousine. Of course. At times she forgot how incredibly wealthy he was. The driver opened the door for her and she climbed in the back seat and stretched out.

"Miss, there's food and snacks and apple cider in case you get hungry," the driver said.

"Why, where am I going? Is it far?"

"Not too far. Mr. Boone wanted to make sure you were comfortable."

"I am, thank you. So, you can't tell me where you're taking me?"

"And ruin the surprise?" he asked with a grin before closing her door.

Surprise? Goodness, she didn't know how much more her heart could take today, but she leaned back, closed her eyes and relaxed. Luke had asked her to trust him. And she did.

A short time later, the limo turned down the path toward Red Barrel Horse Rescue. Katie sat up straighter in the seat and peered out the window. Her curiosity aroused, she scanned the area. There was no sign of Luke. The driver parked in front of the office and then got out to open the door for her. "Miss, Mr. Boone is waiting for you in the barn."

She glanced over to the big red barn and saw Luke approaching, wearing his black Stetson and a stunning dark suit, a string tie at his neck. Her heart raced. He was handsome and wonderful and all hers. She picked up the pace and soon she was in his arms, his mouth devouring hers, laying claim, making every bone in her body melt.

"Luke," she murmured between kisses. "What's this all about?"

Luke kissed her one last time. "Come with me."

He placed his hand on her back and led her into the barn. She gasped when she saw what he'd done. A dozen arrangements of flowers and tiny white lights surrounded a round linen-clad table set for two. Sparkling cider sat in a bucket of ice. The whole place appeared magical. "This is beautiful."

"I hoped you'd like it."

"But what are we—"

Luke dropped to one knee and took her hands in his. "Katie, I want to do this right. I want you to have all the things a bride should have, including a proper proposal."

"Oh, Luke." Tears swam in her eyes.

"I brought you here because this is where I fell in love with you. We have good memories here, you and me. It's fitting that this is the place I bare my soul to you. Katie Rodgers Boone, I'm crazy in love with you and have been for a long time. You're the only girl for me and I'm asking if you'll have me for your husband. To live and love with me for the rest of our lives. Will you, Katie?"

He reached into his pocket and presented her with a ring. Not just any diamond ring—this one was designed with emerald and marquise cuts of diamonds in the shape of a barrel. Red rubies surrounded the whole ring. "Do you see it?" he asked.

Tears streamed down her face now. Her every dream was coming true. "I see it. It's very special. And I see you for the good and honorable man that you are. I love the ring and yes, yes, yes. I'll have you for my husband, if you'll have me as your wife."

A smile spread across his face and he rose up. "Are you joking?" he teased as he placed the ring on her finger. Then he kissed her, a good, long, joyful kiss that warmed her heart. "You're all I've ever wanted. You, me and our baby, Katie, we'll be a family. I can't wait. But for now, I'm grateful our families know about us. We can stop pretending."

"Yes, I'm glad about that, too. I love you very much and now I get to show it."

"There's more."

"There always seems to be with you."

He chuckled and took her hand again. As they walked out of the barn, the sky was a shock of tangerine and pink hues, as if Mother Nature had summoned up such wonder for this moment.

"Katie, I said I didn't want you to miss out on being a bride. So today I'm giving you your wedding present."

"It's not necessary. You've already given me too much."

"Not even close, sweetheart. And I think you're going to like this gift." He led her to Cinnamon's corral. The horse looked her way, those big brown eyes capturing her attention. "I made arrangements to adopt her. She'll be yours."

"Really?" She'd never dared to dream of having a horse of her own. She loved every horse at the rescue, even the feisty ones, but she had a feeling Cinnamon was extra special. "She'll be mine…"

"Yes. And when she's ready, we'll take her to Rising Springs. I've already contacted a trainer to work with her."

"Luke, I don't know what to say but thank you." She buried her face in his shoulder and hugged him tight. "This is all so very much."

He put his hand over her belly. Any day now, the evidence of their love would be pushing the limits of her body and bumping out. "I love this little one already," he said.

She placed her hand over his. "Me, too."

He spoke softly, his arm snugly around her. "We should go in and have our dinner. Gotta keep the baby nourished."

"We do," she said. "And afterward?"

He kissed her, leading her inside. "Afterward, we'll have a proper start to our honeymoon, making hay inside the barn."

Katie laughed as Luke closed the big barn doors.

She was one lucky girl. Waking up wed to the Texan sure had its perks.

Epilogue

Three months later

Drew and Lottie stood before the minister in front of the backyard gazebo on Rising Springs Ranch, saying heartfelt vows of love and devotion. Luke looked on with Katie beside him. Her peach chiffon bridesmaid dress rounded over her growing belly, and her expression was light, bright and happy. The sight of her carrying their child always put a smile on his face and reminded him of his great fortune having married her.

Drea stood as Lottie's maid of honor and Mason as Drew's best man. Risk and April were also in the wedding party, along with a few of Drew and Lottie's good friends.

"I do," said Lottie, staring blissfully into Drew MacDonald's eyes. Drew was eager to repeat those same vows to her. The wedding was a family affair with fewer than thirty people in attendance. It was how Drew and Lottie wanted it. Only the most special people in their lives had received an invitation.

Theirs was the final piece of the puzzle that was the Boone family.

Drew's cottage was under repair, with the addition of new rooms and a modern kitchen for Lottie. The renovations gave the whole place a face-lift and soon, their Tuesday night poker games would resume there.

Mason and Drea had just moved into their newly built home on the property. Word had it that Drea was eager to start a family and Mason was more than willing to oblige.

Risk and April were just finishing the work at Canyon Lake Lodge, hoping to open their new venture this June. The Boones would receive the first invitation to test out the lodge, before paying customers made reservations.

Luke and Katie were living at the ranch, his wife delegating duties between Lori and a new hire at her shop. She didn't want to give up Katie's Kupcakes entirely, and on her workdays they stayed at Katie's apartment. Things would get a little more complicated when their baby came, but they'd work it out. He had no doubt.

"You may kiss the bride," Minister Gavin declared.

Drew landed a passionate kiss on Lottie's lips, one that made the minister turn a shade of bright red. He pronounced them husband and wife and the couple turned to their guests.

"Ladies and gentlemen, I give you Mr. and Mrs. MacDonald."

Luke took Katie's hand and squeezed it tight as applause broke out for the newly married couple. Katie gazed at him, her pretty green eyes clear and full of love.

As the wedding party and guests dispersed, heading toward the reception area, Luke tugged Katie away to a private corner of the yard. "What is it?" she asked.

"Just wanted a kiss, the good kind."

She laughed and then obliged him, her mouth sweet on his. The touch of her lips never failed to make him fall even harder in love with her. "I love you," he said from deep in his heart.

"I love you right back, Luke," she said sweetly. "And you still make me nutty."

"I still do?"

"Yes, you still do, and I wouldn't have it any other way."

* * * * *

THE SEAL'S SECRET HEIRS

KAT CANTRELL

To Cat Schield. Thanks for all the collaboration and for being my guide into the TCC world!

One

Royal, Texas was the perfect place to go to die.

Kyle Wade aimed to do exactly that. After an honorable discharge from the navy, what else lay ahead of him but a slow and painful death? Might as well do it in Royal, the town that had welcomed every Wade since the dawn of time—except him.

He nearly drove through the center of town without stopping. Because he hadn't realized he was *in* Royal until he was nearly *out* of Royal.

Yeah, it had been ten years, and when he'd stopped for gas in Odessa, he'd heard about the tornado that had ripped through the town. But still. Was nothing on the main strip still the same? These new buildings hadn't been there when he'd left. Of course, he'd hightailed it out of Royal for Coronado, California, in a hurry and hadn't looked back once in all his years as a Navy SEAL. Had he really expected Royal to be suspended in time, like a photograph?

He kind of had.

Kyle slowed as he passed the spot where he'd first kissed Grace Haines in the parking lot of the Dairy Queen. Or what used to be the spot where he'd taken his high school girlfriend on their first date. The Dairy Queen had moved down the road and in its place stood a little pink building housing something called Mimi's Nail Salon. Really?

Fitting that his relationship with Grace had nothing to mark it. Nothing in Royal proper anyway. The scars on his heart would always be there.

Shaking his head, Kyle punched the gas. He had plenty of time to gawk at the town later and no time to think about the woman who had driven him into the military. His shattered leg hurt something fierce and he'd been traveling for the better part of three days. It was time to go home.

And now he had a feeling things had probably changed at Wade Ranch—also known as home—more than he'd have anticipated. Never the optimist, he suspected that meant they'd gotten worse. Which was saying something, since he'd left in the first place because of the rift with his twin brother, Liam. No time like the present to get the cold welcome over with.

Wade Ranch's land unrolled at exactly the ten-mile marker from Royal. At least *that* was still the same. Acres and acres of rocky, hilly countryside spread as far as Kyle could see. Huh. Reminded him of Afghanistan. Wouldn't have thought there'd be any comparison, but there you go. A man could travel ten thousand miles and still wind up where he started. In more ways than one.

The gate wasn't barred. His brother, Liam, was running a loose ship apparently. Their grandfather had died a while back and left the ranch to both brothers, but Kyle had never intended to claim his share. Yeah, it was a significant inheritance. But he didn't want it. He wanted his team back and his life as a SEAL. An insurgent's spray of bullets had guaranteed that would never happen. Even if

Kyle hadn't gotten shot, Cortez was gone and no amount of wishing or screaming at God could bring his friend and comrade-in-arms back to life.

Hadn't stopped Kyle from trying.

Kyle drove up the winding lane to the main house, which had a new coat of paint. The white Victorian house had been lording over Wade land for a hundred years, but looked like Liam had done some renovation. The tire swing that had hung from the giant oak in the front yard was gone and a new porch rocker with room for two had been added.

Perfect. Kyle could sit there in that rocker and complain about how the coming rain was paining his joints. Maybe later he could get up a game of dominos at the VA with all of the other retired military men. *Retired*. They might as well call it dead.

When Kyle jumped from the cab of the truck he'd bought in California after the navy decided they were done with him, he hit the dusty ground at the wrong angle. Pain shot up his leg and it stole his breath for a moment. When a man couldn't even get out of his own truck without harm, it was not a good day.

Yeah, he should be more careful. But then he'd have to admit something was wrong with this leg.

He sucked it up. *The only easy day was yesterday.* That mantra had gotten him through four tours of duty in the Middle East. Surely it could get him to the door of Wade Ranch.

It did. Barely. He knocked, but someone was already answering before the sound faded.

The moment the door swung open, Kyle stepped over the threshold and did a double take. *Liam*. His brother stood in the middle of the renovated foyer, glowering. He'd grown up and out in ten years. Kyle had, too, of course, but it was still a shock to see that his brother had changed from the picture he'd carried in his mind's eye, even though their faces mostly matched.

Crack!

Agony exploded across Kyle's jaw as his head snapped backward.

What in the… Had Liam just *punched* him?

Every nerve in Kyle's body went on full alert, vibrating with tension as he reoriented and automatically began scanning both the threat of Liam and the perimeter simultaneously. The foyer was empty, save the two Wade brothers. And Liam wasn't getting the drop on him twice.

"That's for not calling," Liam said succinctly and balled his fists as if he planned to go back for seconds.

"Nice to see you, too."

Dang. Talking hurt. Kyle spit out a curse along with a trickle of blood that hit the hardwood floor an inch from Liam's broken-in boot.

"Deadbeat. You have a lot of nerve showing up now. Get gone or there's more where that came from."

Liam clearly had no idea who he was tangling with.

"I don't cater much to sucker punches," Kyle drawled, and touched his lower lip, right above where the throb in his jaw hurt the worst. Blood came away with his finger. "Why don't you try that again now that I'm paying attention?"

Liam shook his head wearily, his fists going slack. "Your face is as hard as your head. Why now? After all this time, why did you finally drag your sorry butt home?"

"Aww. Careful there, brother, or people might start thinking you missed me something fierce when you talk like that."

Liam had another thirty seconds to explain why Kyle's welcome home had included a fist. Liam had a crappy right hook, but it still hurt. If anything, Kyle was the one who should be throwing punches. After all, he was the one with the ax to grind. He was the one who had left Royal because of what Liam had done.

Or rather *whom* he'd done. Grace Haines. Liam had broken the most sacred of all brotherly bonds when he messed around with the woman Kyle loved. Afghanistan wasn't far enough away to forget, but it was the farthest a newly minted SEAL could go after being deployed.

So he hadn't forgotten. Or forgiven.

"I called your cell phone," Liam said. "I called every navy outpost I could for two months straight. I left messages. I called about the messages. Figured that silence was enough of an answer." Arms crossed, Liam looked down his nose at Kyle, which was a feat, given that they were the same height. "So I took steps to work through this mess you've left in my lap."

Wait, he'd gotten punched over leaving the ranch in his brother's capable hands? That was precious. Liam had loved Wade Ranch from the first, maybe even as early as the day their mother had dropped them off with Grandpa and never came back.

"You were always destined to run Wade Ranch," Kyle said, and almost didn't choke on it. "I didn't dump it on you."

Liam snorted. "Are you really that dense? I'm not talking about the ranch, moron. I'm talking about your kids."

Kyle flinched involuntarily. "My...what?"

Kids? As in children?

"Yes, kids," Liam enunciated, drawing out the *i* sound as if Kyle might catch his meaning better if the word had eighteen syllables. "Daughters. Twins. I don't get why you waited to come home. You should have been here the moment you found out."

"I'm finding out *this* moment," Kyle muttered as his pulse kicked up, beating in his throat like a May hailstorm on a tin roof. "How...wha..."

His throat closed.

Twin daughters. And Liam thought they were *his*? Someone had made a huge mistake. Kyle didn't have any children. Kyle didn't *want* any children.

Liam was staring at him strangely. "You didn't get my messages?"

"Geez, Liam. What was your first clue? I wasn't sitting at a desk dodging your calls. I spent six months in...a bad place and then ended up in a worse place."

From the city of Kunduz to Landstuhl Regional, the US-run military hospital in Germany. He didn't remember a lot of it, but the incredible pain as the doctors worked to restore the bone a bullet had shattered in his leg—that he would never forget.

But he was one of the lucky ones who'd survived his wounds. Cortez hadn't. Kyle still had nightmares about leaving his teammate behind in that foxhole where they'd been trapped by insurgents. Seemed wrong. Cortez should have had a proper send-off for his sacrifice.

"Still not a chatterbox, I see." Liam scrubbed at his face with one hand, and when he dropped it, weariness had replaced the glower. "Keep your secrets about your fabulous life overseas as a badass. I really don't care. I have more important things to get straight."

The weariness was new. Kyle remembered his brother as being a lot of things—a betrayer, first and foremost—but not tired. It looked wrong on his face. As wrong as the constant pain etched into Kyle's own face when he looked in the mirror. Which was why he'd quit looking in the mirror.

"Why don't you start at the beginning." Kyle jerked his head toward what he hoped was still the kitchen. "Maybe we can hash it out over tea?"

It was too early in the morning for Jack Daniel's, though he might make an exception, pending the outcome of the conversation.

Liam nodded and spun to stride off toward the back of the house. Following him, Kyle was immediately blinded by all the off-white cabinets in the kitchen. His brother hadn't left a stone unturned when he'd gotten busy redoing the house. Modern appliances in stainless steel had replaced the old harvest gold ones and new double islands dominated the center. A wall of glass overlooked the back acreage that stretched for miles until it hit Old Man Drucker's property. Or what had been Drucker's property ten years ago. Obviously Kyle wasn't up-to-date about what had been going on since he'd left.

Without ceremony, Liam splashed some tea into a cup from a pitcher on the counter and shoved the cup into his hand. "Tea. Now talk to me about Margaret Garner."

Hot. Blonde. Nice legs. Kyle visualized the woman instantly. But that was a name he hadn't thought about in—wow, like almost a year.

"Margaret Garner? What does she have to do with any—"

The question died in his throat. *Almost a year.* Like long enough to grow a baby or two? Didn't mean it was true. Didn't mean they were his babies.

It felt like a really good time to sit down, and he thought maybe he could do it without tipping off Liam how badly his leg ached 24-7.

He fell heavily onto a bar stool at the closest island, tea forgotten and shoulders ten pounds heavier. "San Antonio. She was with a group of friends at Cantina Juarez. A place where military groupies hang out."

"So you did sleep with her?"

"Not that it's any of your business," Kyle said noncommitally. They were long past the kiss-and-tell stage of their relationship, if they'd ever been that close. When Liam took up with Grace ten years ago, it had killed any fragment of warmth between them, warmth that was unlikely to return.

"You made it my business when you didn't come home to take care of your daughters," Liam countered, as his fists balled up again.

"Take another swing at me and you'll get real cozy with the floor in short order." Kyle contemplated his brother. Who was furious. "So Margaret came around with some babies looking for handouts? I hope you asked for a paternity test before you wrote a check."

This was bizarre. Of all the conversations he'd thought he'd be having with Liam, this was not it. *Babies. Margaret. Paternity test.* None of these things made sense, together or separately.

Why hadn't any of Liam's messages been relayed? Probably because he hadn't called the right office—by design. Kyle hadn't exactly made it clear how Liam could reach him. Maybe it was a blessing that Kyle hadn't known. He couldn't have hopped on a plane anyway.

Kyle couldn't be a father. He barely knew how to be a civilian and had worked long and hard at accepting that he wasn't part of a SEAL team any longer.

It was twice as hard to accept that after being discharged, he had nowhere to go but back to the ranch where he'd never fit in, never belonged. His injury wasn't supposed to be a factor as he figured out what to do with the rest of his life, since God hadn't seen fit to let him die alongside Cortez. But being a father—to twins, no less—meant he had to think about what a busted leg meant for a man's everyday life. And he did not like thinking about how difficult it was some days to simply stand.

Liam threw up a hand, a scowl crawling onto his expression. "Shut up a minute. No one wrote any checks. You're the father of the babies, no question."

Well, Kyle had a few questions. Like why Margaret hadn't contacted him when she found out she was pregnant. While Liam had little information on his whereabouts,

Margaret sure knew how to get in touch. Her girlfriend had been dating Cortez and called him all the time. She'd known exactly where he was stationed.

It was nothing short of unforgivable. "Where's Margaret?"

"She died," Liam bit out shortly. "While giving birth. It's a long story. Do I need to give you a minute?"

Kyle processed that much more slowly than he would have liked. Margaret was dead? It seemed like just yesterday that he'd spent a long weekend with her in a hotel room. She'd been a wildcat, determined to send him back to Afghanistan with enough memories to keep him warm at night, as she'd put it.

He was sad to learn Margaret had passed, sure. He'd liked thinking about her on the other side of the world, living a normal life that he was helping to secure by going after bad guys. But they'd spent less than forty-eight hours together and had barely known each other, by design. He wasn't devastated—it wasn't as if he'd lost the love of his life or anything. Not like when he'd lost Grace.

"We used protection," he muttered. As if that was the most important thing to get straight at this point. "I don't understand. How did she get pregnant?"

"The normal way, I imagine. Moron." Liam rolled his eyes the way he'd always done when they were younger. "Do you have any interest whatsoever in meeting your daughters?"

Kyle blinked. "Well…yeah. Of course. What happened to them after Margaret died? Who's taking care of them?"

"I am. Me and Hadley. Who's the most amazing woman. She's the nanny I hired when you didn't respond to any of my calls."

Reeling, Kyle tried to gather some of his wits, but they seemed as scattered and filmy as clouds on a mild spring day. "Thanks. That's... You didn't have to. That's above the call of duty."

Liam crossed his arms, biceps rippling under the sleeve of his T-shirt. "They're great babies. Beautiful. And I didn't do it for you. I did it because I love them. Hadley and I, we're planning to keep on taking care of them, too."

"That's not going to happen. You've spent the last ten minutes whaling on me about not coming home to take responsibility for this. I'm here. I'm man enough to step up." He set his jaw, which still throbbed. "I want to see them."

The atmosphere fairly vibrated with animosity as they stared each other down, neither blinking, neither backing down. Something flickered through Liam's gaze and he gave one curt nod.

"Fine." Liam called up the stairs off the kitchen that led to the upper stories.

After the longest three minutes of Kyle's life, he heard footsteps and a pretty, blonde woman who must be the nanny came down the stairs. But Kyle only had eyes for the pink bundles, one each in the crook of her arms.

Sucker punch number two.

Those were real, live, honest-to-God babies. What the hell was he thinking, saying that he wanted to see them? What was that supposed to prove? That he didn't know squat about babies?

They were so small. Nearly identical. Twins, like Kyle and Liam. He'd always heard that identical twins skipped generations, but apparently not.

"What are their names?" he whispered.

"Madeline and Margaret Wade," the woman responded, and the babies lifted their heads toward the sound of her voice. Clearly she'd spent a lot of time with them. "We call them Maddie and Maggie for short."

Somehow that seemed perfect for their little wrinkled faces. "Can I hold them?"

"Sure. This is Maggie." She handed over the first one and cheerfully helped Kyle get the baby situated without being asked, which he appreciated more than he could possibly say because his stupid hands suddenly seemed too clumsy to handle something so breakable.

Hey, little girl. He couldn't talk over the lump in his throat, and no one seemed inclined to make him, so he just looked at her. His heart thumped as it expanded, growing larger the longer he held his daughter. That was a kick in the pants. Who would have thought you could instantly love someone like that? It should have taken time. But there it was.

Now what? What if she cried? What if *he* cried?

He'd hoped a flood of knowledge would magically appear if he could just get his hands on the challenge. You didn't learn to hack through vegetation with a machete until you put it in your palm and started hacking.

"You can take her back," he said gruffly, overwhelmed with all the emotion he had no idea what to do with. But there was still another one. Another daughter. He found new appreciation for the term *double trouble*.

"This one is Maddie," the woman said.

Somehow, the other pink bundle ended up in his arms. Instantly, he could tell she was smaller, weighing less than her sister. Strange. She felt even more fragile than her sister, as if Kyle should be careful how heavily he breathed or he might blow her to the ground with an extra big huff.

Equal parts love and fierce devotion surged through the heart he'd already thought was full, splitting it open. She'd need someone to look out for her. To protect her.

That's on me. My job.

And then being a father made all the sense in the world. These were his girls. The reason he wasn't dead in a foxhole flopped out next to Cortez right now. The Almighty got it perfectly right some days.

"And this is Hadley Wade, my wife," Liam broke in with

the scowl that seemed to be a permanent part of his face nowadays. "We still introduce ourselves in these parts."

"It's okay," Hadley said with a hand on Liam's elbow. Her palm settled into the crook comfortably, as if they were intimate often. "Give him a break. It's a lot to take in."

"I'm done." Kyle rubbed his free hand across his military-issue buzz cut, but it didn't stimulate his brain much. He contemplated Hadley, the woman Liam had casually mentioned that he'd married, as if that was some small thing. "I don't think there's much more I can take in. I appreciate what you've done in my stead, but these are my girls. I want to be their father, in all the ways that count. I'm here and I'm sticking around Royal."

That hadn't been set in his mind until this moment. But it would take a bulldozer to shove him onto a different path now.

"Well, it's not as simple as all that," Liam corrected. "Their mama is gone and you weren't around. So even though I have temporary custody, these girls became wards of the state and had a social worker assigned. You're gonna have to deal with the red tape before you start joining the PTA and picking out matching Easter dresses."

Wearily, Kyle nodded. "I get that. What do I have to do?"

Hadley and Liam exchanged glances and a sense of foreboding rose up in Kyle's stomach.

With a sigh, Liam pulled out his cell phone. "I'll call their social worker. But before she gets here, you should know that it's Grace Haines."

Grace. The name hit him in the solar plexus and all the air rushed from his lungs.

Sucker punch number three.

Grace Haines had avoided looking at the date all day, but it sneaked up on her after lunch. She stared at the letters and numbers she'd just typed on a case file.

March 12. The third anniversary of the day she'd become a Professional Single Girl. She should get cake. Or a card. Something to mark the occasion of when she'd given up the ghost and decided to be happy with her career as a social worker. Instead of continually dating men who were nice enough, but could never live up to her standards, she'd learn to be by herself.

Was it so wrong to want a man who doted on her as her father did with her mother? She wasn't asking for much. Flowers occasionally. A text message here and there with a heart emoticon and a simple thinking of you. Something that showed Grace was a priority. That the guy noticed when she wasn't there.

Yeah, that was dang difficult, apparently. The decision to stop actively looking for Mr. Right and start going to museums and plays as a party of one hadn't been all that hard. As a bonus, she never had to compromise on date night by seeing a science fiction movie where special effects drowned out the dialogue. She could do whatever she wanted with her Saturday nights.

It was great. Or at least that was what she told herself. Loudly. It drowned out the voice in her heart that kept insisting she would never get the family she desperately wanted if she didn't date.

In lieu of a Happy Professional Single Girl cake, Grace settled for a Reese's Peanut Butter Cup from the vending machine and got back to work. The children's cases the county had entrusted to her were not going to handle themselves, and there were some heartbreakers in her caseload. She loved her job and thanked God every day she got to make a difference in the lives of the children she helped.

If she couldn't have children of her own, she'd make do with loving other people's.

Her desk phone rang and she picked up the receiver, accidentally knocking over the framed picture of her mom and dad celebrating their thirtieth wedding anniversary at a luau in Hawaii. One day she'd go there, she vowed as she righted the frame. Even if she had to travel to Hawaii solo, it was still Hawaii.

"Grace Haines. How can I help you today?"

"It's Liam," the voice on the other end announced, and the gravity in his tone tripped her radar.

"Are the girls all right?" Panicked, Grace threw a couple of manila folders into her tote in preparation to fly to her car. She could be at Wade Ranch in less than twenty minutes if she ignored the speed limit and prayed to Jesus that Sheriff Battle wasn't sitting in his squad car at the Royal city limits the way he usually did. "What's happened to the babies? It's Maddie, isn't it? I knew that she wasn't—"

"The girls are fine," he interrupted. "They're with Hadley. It's Kyle. He came home."

Grace froze, mid-file transfer. The manila folder fell to the floor in slow motion from her nerveless fingers, opened at the spine and spilled papers across the linoleum.

"What?" she whispered.

Kyle.

Her first kiss. Her first love. Her first taste of the agonizing pain a man could cause.

He wasn't supposed to be here. The twin daughters Kyle Wade had fathered were parentless, or so she'd convinced herself. That was the only reason she'd taken the case, once Liam assured her he'd called the USO, the California base Kyle had shipped out of and the President of the United States. No response, he'd said.

No response meant no conflict of interest.

If Kyle was back, her interest was so conflicted, she couldn't even see through it.

"He's here. At Wade Ranch," Liam confirmed. "You need to come by as soon as possible and help us sort this out."

Translation: Liam and Hadley wanted to adopt Maddie and Maggie and with Kyle in the picture, that wasn't as easy as they'd all assumed. Grace would have to convince him to waive his parental rights. If he didn't want to, then she'd have to assess Kyle's fitness as a parent and potentially even give him custody, despite knowing in her heart that he'd be a horrible father. It was a huge tangle.

The best scenario would be to transfer the case to someone else. But on short notice? Probably wasn't going to happen.

"I'll be there as soon as I can. Thanks, Liam. It'll work out."

Grace hung up and dropped her head down into the crook of her elbow.

Somehow, she was supposed to go to Wade Ranch and do her job, while ignoring the fact that Kyle Wade had broken her heart into tiny little pieces, and then promptly joined the military, as if she hadn't mattered at all. And somehow, she had to ignore the fact that she still wasn't over it. Or him.

Two

Grace knocked on the door of Wade House and steeled herself for whatever was about to happen. Which was what she'd been doing in the car on the way over. And at her desk before that.

No one else in the county office could take on another case, so Grace had agreed to keep Maddie and Maggie under the premise that she'd run all her recommendations through her supervisor before she told the parties involved about her decisions. Which meant she couldn't just decide ahead of time that Kyle wasn't fit. She had to prove it.

It would be a stringent process, with no room for error. She'd have to justify her report with far more data and impartial observations than she'd ever had to before. It meant twice as many visits and twice as much documentation. Of course. Because who didn't want to spend a bunch of time with a high-school boyfriend who'd ruined you for dating any other man?

Hopefully, he'd just give up his rights without a fight and they could all go on.

The door swung open and Grace forgot to breathe. Kyle Wade was indeed home.

Hungrily, her gaze skittered over his grown-up face. *Oh, my.* Still gorgeous, but sun worn, with new lines around his eyes that said he'd seen some things in the past ten years and they weren't all pleasant. His hair was shorn shorter than short, but it fit this new version of Kyle.

His green eyes were diamond hard. That was new, too. He'd never been open and friendly, but she'd burrowed under that reserve back in high school and when he really looked at her with his signature blend of love and devotion—it had been magic.

She instantly wanted to burrow under that hardness once again. Because she knew she was the only one who could, the only one he'd let in. The only one who could soothe his loneliness, the way she'd done back then.

Gah, what was she *thinking*?

She couldn't focus on that. Couldn't remember what it had been like when it was good, because when it was bad, it was really bad. This man had destroyed her, nearly derailing her entire first year at college as she picked up the broken pieces he'd left behind.

"Hey, Grace."

Kyle's voice washed over her and the steeling she'd done to prepare for this moment? Useless.

"Kyle," she returned a bit brusquely, but if she started blubbering, she'd never forgive herself. "I'm happy to see that you've finally decided to acknowledge your children."

Chances were good that wouldn't last. He'd ship out again at a moment's notice, running off to indulge his selfish thirst for adventure, leaving behind a mess. As he'd done the first time. But Grace was here to make sure he didn't hurt anyone in the process, least of all those precious babies.

"Yep," he agreed easily. "I took a slow boat from China all right. But I'm here now. Do whatever you have to do to make it okay with the county for me to be a father to my daughters."

Ha. Fathers were loving, caring, selfless. They didn't become distant and uncommunicative on a regular basis and then forget they had plans with you. And then forget to apologize for leaving you high and dry. Nor did they have the option to quit when the going got tough.

"Well, that's not going to happen today," she said firmly. "I'll do several site visits to make sure that you're providing the right environment for the girls. They need to feel safe and loved and it's my job to put them into the home that will give them that. You might not be the best answer."

The hardness in his expression intensified. "They're mine. I'll take care of them."

His quiet fierceness set her back. Guess that answered the question about whether he'd put up a token fight and then sign whatever she put in front of him that would terminate his parental rights. The fact that he wasn't—it was throwing her for a loop. "Actually, they're mine. They became wards of the state when you didn't respond to the attempts we all made to find you. That's what happens to abandoned babies."

That might have come out harshly. So what. It was the truth, even if the sentiment had some leftover emotion from when Kyle had done that to her. She had to protect the babies, no matter what.

"There were…circumstances. I didn't get any of Liam's messages or I would have come as soon as I could." His mouth firmed into an inflexible line. "That's not important now. Come in and visit. Tell me what I have to do."

"Fine."

She followed him into the formal parlor that had been restored to what she imagined was Wade House's former glory. The Victorian furniture was beautiful and luxurious, and a man like Kyle looked ridiculous sitting on the elegantly appointed chair. Good grief, the spindly legs didn't seem strong enough to support such a solid body. Kyle had gained weight, and the way he moved indicated it was 100 percent finely honed muscle under his clothes. He'd adopted a lazy, slow walk that seemed at odds with all that, but certainly fit a laid-back cowboy at home on his ranch.

Not that she'd noticed or anything.

She took her own seat and perched on the edge, too keyed up to relax. "We'll need to fill out some paperwork. What do you plan to do for employment now that you're home?"

Kyle quirked an eyebrow. "Being a Wade isn't enough?"

Frowning, she held her manila folder in front of her like a shield, though what she thought it was going to protect her from, she had no idea. Kyle's diamond-bit green eyes drilled through her very flesh and bone, deep into the soft places she'd thought were well protected against men. Especially this one.

"No, it's not enough. Inheriting money isn't an indicator of your worth as a parent. I need to see a demonstration of commitment. A permanency that will show you can provide a stable environment for Maddie and Maggie."

"So being able to buy them whatever they want and being able to put food on the table no matter what isn't good enough."

It was not a question but a challenge. She tried not to roll her eyes, she really did. But if you looked up "clueless" in the dictionary, you'd see a picture of Kyle Wade. "That's right. Liam and Hadley can do those things and have been for over two months. Are you prepared for all the special treatments and doctor's visits Maddie will require? I have to know."

Kyle went stiff all at once, freezing so quickly that she got a little concerned. She should really stop caring so much but it was impossible to shut off her desire to help people. This whole conversation was difficult. She and Kyle used to be comfortable with each other. She missed that easiness between them, but there was no room for anything other than a professional and necessary distance.

"Doctor's visits?" Kyle repeated softly. "Is there something wrong with Maddie?"

"Maddie suffers from twin-to-twin transfusion syndrome. She has some heart problems that are pretty serious."

"I...didn't know."

The bleakness in his expression reached out and twisted her heart. She wanted to lash out at him. Blame him. Those girls had been fighting for their lives after Margaret died, and where was Kyle? "Just out of curiosity, why did you come home now? Why not two months ago when Margaret first came looking for you? Or for that matter, why not when she first found out she was pregnant?"

She cut off the tirade there. Oh, there was plenty more she wanted to say, but it would veer into personal barbs that wouldn't help anything. She had a job to do and the information-gathering stage should—and would—stay on a professional level.

Besides, she knew he'd been stationed overseas. He probably hadn't had the luxury of jetting off whenever he felt like it. But he could have at least called.

Crossing his arms, he leaned back against the gold velvet cushions of the too-small chair, biceps bulging. He'd grown some interesting additions to what had already been a nicely built body. Automatically, her gaze wandered south, taking in all the parts that made up that great physique. Wow, had it gotten hot in here, or what? She fanned her face with the manila folder.

But then he eyed her, his face a careful mask that dared her to break through it. Which totally unnerved her. This darker, harder, fiercer Kyle Wade was dangerous. Because she wanted to understand why he was dark, hard and fierce. Why he'd broken her heart and then left.

"You got me all figured out, seems like," he drawled. "Why don't you tell me why I didn't hop on a plane and stick by Margaret's side during her pregnancy?"

Couldn't the man just answer a simple question? He'd always been like this—uncommunicative and prone to leaving instead of dealing with problems head-on. His attitude was so infuriating, she said the first thing that popped into her head.

"Guilt, probably. You didn't want to be involved and hoped the problem would go away on its own." And that was totally unfair. Wasn't it? She had no idea why he hadn't contacted anyone. This new version of Kyle was unsettling *because* she didn't know him that well anymore.

Really, she wasn't that good at reading people in the first place. It was a professional weakness that she hated, but couldn't seem to fix. Once upon a time, she'd thought this man was her forever after, her Prince Charming, Clark Gable and Dr. McDreamy all rolled into one. Which was totally false. She'd bought heavily into that lie, so how could she trust her own judgment? She couldn't. That's why she had to be so methodical in her approach to casework, because she couldn't afford to let emotion rule her decisions. Or afford to make a mistake, not when the future of a child was at stake.

And she wouldn't do either here. Maddie and Maggie deserved a loving home with a family who paid attention to their every need. Kyle Wade was not the right man for that, no matter what he said he wanted.

"Well, then," he said easily. "Guess that answers your question."

It so did not. She still didn't know why he'd come home now, why he'd suddenly shown an interest in his daughters. Whether he could possibly convince her he planned to stick around—if he was even serious about that. Kyle had a habit of running away from his problems, after all.

First and foremost, how could she assess whether the time-hardened man before her could ever provide the loving, nurturing environment two fragile little girls needed?

But she'd let it slide for now. There was plenty of time to work through all of that, since Maddie and Maggie were still legally in the care of Liam and Hadley.

"I think I have enough for now. I'll file my first report and send you a copy when it's approved." She had to get out of here. Before she broke down under the emotional onslaught of everything.

"That's it, huh? What's the report going to say?"

"It's going to say that you've expressed an interest in retaining your parental rights and that I've advised you that I can't approve that until I do several more site visits."

He cocked his head, evaluating her coolly. "How long is that going to take?"

"Until I'm satisfied with your fitness as a parent. Or until I decide you're unfit. At which point I'll make recommendations as to what I believe is the best home for those precious girls. I will likely recommend they stay with Liam and Hadley."

Without warning, Kyle was on his feet, an intense vibe rippling down his powerful body. She'd have sworn he hadn't moved, and then all of a sudden, there he was, staring down at her with a sharpness about him, as if he'd homed in on her and her alone. She couldn't move, couldn't breathe.

It was precisely the kind of focus she'd craved once. But not now. Not like this.

"Why would you give my kids to my brother?" he asked, his voice dangerously low.

"Well, the most obvious reason is because he and Hadley want them. They've already looked into adoption. But also because they know the babies' needs and have already been providing the best place for the girls."

"You are not taking away my daughters," he said succinctly. "Why does this feel personal?"

She blinked. "This is the opposite of personal, Kyle. My job is to be the picture of impartiality. Our history has nothing to do with this."

"I was starting to wonder if you recalled that we had a history," he drawled slowly, loading the words with meaning.

The intensity rolling from him heightened a notch, and she shivered as he perused her as if he'd found the last morsel of chocolate in the pantry—and he was starving. All at once, she had a feeling they were both remembering the sweet fire of first love. They might have been young, but what they'd lacked in experience, they made up for in enthusiasm. Their relationship had hit some high notes that she'd prefer not to be remembering right this minute. Not with the man who'd made her body sing a scant few feet away.

"I haven't forgotten one day of our relationship." Why did her voice sound so breathless?

"Even the last one?" he murmured, and his voice skittered down her spine with teeth she wasn't expecting.

"I'm not sure what you mean." Confused as to why warning sirens were going off in her head, she stared at the spot where the inverted tray ceiling seams came together. "We broke up. You didn't notice. Then you joined the military and eventually came home. Here we are."

"Oh, I noticed, Grace." The honeyed quality of his tone drew her gaze to his and the green fire there blazed with heat she didn't know what to do with. "I think we can both agree that what happened between us ten years ago was a mistake. Never to be repeated. We'll let bygones be bygones and you'll figure out a way to make this pesky custody issue go away. Deal?"

A mistake. Bygones. Her heart stung as it absorbed the words that confirmed she hadn't meant that much to him. Breaking up with him hadn't fazed him the way she'd hoped. The daring ploy she'd staged to get his attention—by letting him catch her with Liam, a notorious womanizer—hadn't worked, either, because he hadn't really cared whether she messed around with his brother. The whole ruse had been for naught.

Stricken, she stared at him, unable to look away, unable to quell the turmoil inside at Kyle being close enough to touch and yet so very far away. They'd broken up ten years ago because he'd never seemed all that into their relationship. Hadn't enough time passed for her to get over it already?

"Sure. Bygones," she repeated, because that was all she could get out.

She escaped with the hasty promise that she'd send him a set schedule of home visits and drove away from Wade Ranch as fast as she dared. But she feared it would never be fast enough to catch up with her impartiality—it had scampered down the road far too quickly and she had a feeling she wasn't going to recover it. Her emotions were fully engaged in this case and she'd have to work extra hard to shut them down. So she could do the best thing for everyone. Including herself.

Kyle watched Grace drive away through the window and uncurled his fists before he punched a wall. Maybe he'd punch Liam instead.

He owed his brother one, after all, and it sure looked as though Liam was determined to be yet another roadblock in a series of roadblocks standing between Kyle and fatherhood. Most of the problems couldn't be resolved easily. But Liam wanting Kyle's kids? That was one thing that Kyle could do something about.

So he went looking for him.

Wade land surrounded the main house to the tune of about ten thousand acres. There was a time when a scouting mission like this one would have been no sweat, but with a messed-up leg, the trek winded Kyle about fifteen minutes in. Which sucked. It was tough to be sidelined, tough to reconcile no longer being in top physical condition. Tough to keep it all inside.

Kyle found Liam in the horse barn, which was situated a good half mile away from the main house. *Barn* was too simplistic a term to describe the grandiose building with a flagstone pathway to the entrance, fussy landscaping and a show arena on the far end. The ranch offices and a fancy lounge were tucked inside, but he didn't bother to gawk. His leg hurt and the walk wasn't far enough to burn off the mad Kyle had generated while talking to Grace.

Who was somehow even more beautiful than he recalled. How was that possible when he'd already put her on a pedestal in his mind as the ideal? How would any other woman ever compare? None could. And the lady herself still got him way too hot and bothered with a coy glance. It was enough to drive a man insane. She'd screwed him up so bad, he couldn't do anything other than weekend flings, like the one he'd had with Margaret. Look where that had gotten him.

Grace was a great big problem in a whole heap of problems. But not one he could deal with this minute. Liam? That was something he could handle.

He watched Liam back out of a stall housing one of the

quarter horses Wade Ranch bred commercially, waiting until his brother was clear of the door to speak. He had enough respect for the damage a spooked eleven-hundred-pound animal could do to a man to stay clear.

"What's this crap about you wanting to adopt my kids?" he said when Liam noticed him.

Liam snorted. "Grace must have come by. She tell you to sign the papers?"

No one ordered Kyle around, least of all Grace.

"She told me you've got your sights set on my family." He crossed his arms before he made good on the impulse to smash his brother in the mouth for even uttering Grace's name. She'd meant everything to Kyle, but to Liam, she was yet another in a long line of his women. "Back off. I'm taking responsibility for them whether you like it or not."

Sticking a piece of clean straw between his back teeth, Liam cocked a hip and leaned against the closed stall door as if he hadn't a care in the world. Lazily, he rearranged his battered hat. "Tell me something. What's the annual revenue Wade Ranch brings in for stud fees?"

"How should I know?" Kyle ground out. "You run the ranch."

"Yeah." Liam raised his brows sardonically. "Half of which belongs to you. Grandpa died almost two years ago, yet you've never lifted a finger to even find out what I do here. Money pours into your bank account on a monthly basis. Know how that happens? Because I make sure of it. I made sure of a lot of things while you ran around the Middle East blowing stuff up and ignoring your responsibilities at home. One of those things I do is take care of Maddie and Maggie. Because you weren't here. Just like you weren't here to take on any responsibility for the ranch. I will not let you be an absentee father like you've been an absentee ranch owner."

"That's a low blow," Kyle said softly. Liam had always

viewed Kyle's stint as a SEAL with a bit of disdain, making it clear he saw it as a cop-out. "You wanted the ranch. I didn't. But I want my girls, and I'm going to be here for them."

Wade Ranch had never meant anything to him other than a place to live because it was the only one he had. Then and now. Mama had cut and run faster than you could spit, once she'd dumped him and Liam here with her father, then taken the Dallas real estate market by storm. Lillian Wade had quickly become the Barbara Corcoran of the South and forgot all about the two little boys she'd abandoned.

Funny how Liam had been so similarly affected by dear old Mama. Enough to want to guarantee his blood wouldn't ever have to know the sting of desertion. Kyle respected the thought if not the action. But Kyle was one up on Liam, because those girls were his daughters. He wasn't about to take lessons from Mama on how to be a runaway parent.

"Too little, too late," his brother mouthed around the straw. "Hadley and I want to adopt them. I hope you have a good lawyer in your back pocket because you're not getting those girls without a hell of a fight."

God Almighty. The hits kept coming. He'd barely had time to get his feet under him from being sucker punched a minute after crossing the threshold of his childhood home, only to have Liam drop twin daughters, Grace Haines and a custody battle in his lap.

They stared at each other, neither blinking. Neither backing down. They were both stubborn enough to stand there until the cows came home, and probably would, too.

Nothing was going to get fixed this way, and with Grace's admonition to prove he was serious about providing a stable environment for Maddie and Maggie ringing in his ears, he contemplated his mule-headed brother. He wanted help with the ranch? By God, he'd get it. And

Kyle would have employment to put on his Fatherhood Résumé, which would hopefully get Grace off his back at the same time.

"Give me a job if it means so much to you that I take ranch ownership seriously. I'll do something with the horses."

Liam nearly busted a gut laughing, which did not improve Kyle's grip on his temper. "You can feed them. But that's about it. You have no training."

And Kyle wasn't at 100 percent physically, but no one had to know about that. His injuries mostly didn't count anyway. It just meant he had to work that much harder, which he'd do. Those babies were worth a little agony.

"I can learn. You can't have it both ways. Either you give me a shot at being half owner of Wade Ranch or shut up about it."

"All right, smart-ass." Liam tipped back his hat and jerked his chin at Kyle. "We got a whole cattle division here at Wade Ranch that's ripe for improvement. I've been concentrating on the horses and letting Danny and Emma Jane handle that side. You take over."

"Done."

Kyle knew even less about cows than he did babies. But he hadn't known anything about guns or explosives before joining the navy, either. BUD/S training had nearly broken him, but he'd learned how to survive impossible physical conditions, learned how to stretch his body to the point of exhaustion and still come out swinging when the next challenge reared its ugly head.

You had to start out with the mind-set that quitting wasn't an option. Even the smallest mental slip would finish a man. So he wouldn't slip.

Liam eyed him and shook his head. "You're serious?"

"As a heart attack. I'll take my best shot at the cattle side of the ranch. Just one question. What am I aiming at?"

"We have a Black Angus breeding program. Emma Jane—she's the sales manager I hired last year—is great. She sold about two hundred head. If you want me to call you successful, double that in under six months."

That didn't sound too bad, especially if there was a sales manager already doing the heavy lifting. "No problem. Now drop the whole adoption idea and we'll call it even."

"Let me see you in action, and then we'll talk. I have yet to see anything that tells me you're planning to stick around. If you take off again, the babies will be mine anyway. Might as well make it legal sooner rather than later." Liam shrugged. "You made your bed by leaving. So lie in it for a while."

Yeah, except he'd left for very specific reasons. He and Liam had never been close, and Kyle hadn't felt as if he was part of anything until he'd found his brothers of the heart on a SEAL team. That's where he'd finally felt secure. He could actually care about someone again without fear of being either abandoned or betrayed.

He'd like to say he could find a way to stay at the ranch this time. But what had changed from the first time? Not much.

Just that he was a father now. And he owed his daughters a stable home life. They were amazing little creatures that he wanted to see grow up. With the additional complications of Maddie's health problems, he couldn't relocate them at the drop of a hat, either.

"I'm not going anywhere," Kyle repeated for what felt like the four hundredth time.

Maybe if he kept saying it, people would believe him. Maybe he'd believe it, too.

Three

Kyle drove into town later that night on an errand for Hadley, who had announced at dinner that the babies were almost out of both diapers and formula. She'd seemed surprised when he said he'd go instead.

Of course he'd volunteered for the job. They were his kids. But he'd made Hadley write down exactly what he needed to buy, because the only formula he'd had exposure to was the one for making homemade explosives. List in his pocket, he'd swung into his truck, intending to grab the baby items and be back in jiffy.

But as he pulled into the lot at Royal's one-and-only grocery store, Grace had just exited through the automatic sliding doors. Well, well, well. There was no way he was passing up this opportunity. He still had a boatload of questions for the girl he'd once given his heart to, only to have it handed back, shredded worse than Black Angus at a slaughterhouse.

Kyle waited until she was almost to her car, and then

gingerly climbed from his truck to corner her between her Toyota and the Dooley in the next spot.

"Lovely night, isn't it, Ms. Haines?"

She jumped and spun around, bobbling her plastic sack full of her grocery store purchases. "You scared me."

"Guilty conscience maybe," he offered silkily. No time like the present to give her a chance to own up to the crimes she'd committed so long ago. He might even forgive her if she just said she was sorry.

"No, more like I'm a woman in a dark parking lot and I hear a man speaking to me unexpectedly."

It was a perfectly legitimate thing to say except the streetlight spilled over her face, illuminating her scowl and negating her point about a dark parking lot. She was that bent up about him saying *hey* outside of a well-lit grocery store?

He raised a brow. "This is Royal. The most danger you'd find in the parking lot of the HEB is a runaway shopping cart."

"You've been gone a long time, Kyle. Things have changed."

Yeah, more than he'd have liked. Grace's voice had deepened. It was far sexier than he'd recalled, and he'd thought about her a lot. Her curves were lusher, as if she'd gained a few pounds in all the right places, and he had an unexpected urge to pull her against him so he could explore every last change, hands on.

Okay, the way he constantly wanted her? *That* was still the same. He'd always been crazy over her. She'd been an exercise in patience, making him wait until they'd been dating a year *and* she'd turned eighteen before she'd sleep with him the first time. And that had been so mind-blowing, he'd immediately started working on the second encounter, then the third. And so on.

The fact that he'd fallen in love with her along the way

was the craziest thing. He didn't make it a habit to let people in. She'd been an exception, one he hadn't been able to help.

"You haven't changed," he said without thinking. "You're still the prettiest girl in the whole town."

Now why had he gone and said something like that? Just because it was true didn't mean he should run off at the mouth. Last thing he needed was to give her the slightest opening. She'd slide right under his skin again, just as she'd done the first time, as if his barriers against people who might hurt him didn't exist.

"Flattery?" She rolled her eyes. "That was a lame line. Plus, I already told you I'd handle your case impartially. There's no point in trying to butter me up."

Oh, so she thought she was immune to his charm, did she? He grinned and shifted his weight off his bad leg, cocking his right hip out casually as if he'd meant to strike that stance all along. "I wouldn't dream of it. That was the God-honest truth. I've been around the world, and I know a thing or two about attractive women. No law against telling one so."

"Well, I don't like it. Are you really that clueless, Kyle?"

The scowl crawled back onto her face and it tripped his Spidey-sense. Or at least that's what he'd always called it. He'd discovered in SEAL training that he had no small amount of skill in reading a situation or a person. Before then, he'd spent a lot of time by himself—purposefully— and never paid much attention to people's tells. Honing that ability had served him well in hostile territory.

So he could easily see Grace was mad. At *him*.

What was that all about? She was the one who'd dumped him cold with no explanation other than she wanted to concentrate on school, which was bull. She'd been a straight-A student before they'd started dating and maintained her grade point average until the day she graduated a year after he had. Best he could figure, she'd wanted Liam instead and hadn't wasted any time getting with his brother once she was free and clear.

"You got something to say, Grace?" He crossed his arms and leaned against her four-door sedan. "Seems like you got a bee in your bonnet."

Maybe Liam had thrown her over too quickly and she'd lumped her hurt feelings into a big Wade bucket. And now he was giving her a second shot to spill it. He just wanted her to admit she'd hurt him and then say she was sorry. That she'd picked the wrong brother when she'd hooked up with Liam. Then maybe he could go on and meet someone new and exciting who didn't constantly remind him that Kyle, women and relationships didn't mix well. Maybe he'd even find a way to trust a woman again. He could finally move on from Grace Haines.

She licked her lips and stared at the sky over his shoulder. "I'm sorry. I'm not handling this well. The babies are important to me. All my cases are, but because we used to date, I want to ensure there's no hint of impropriety. All the decisions I make should be based on facts and your ability to provide a good home. So please don't say things like you think I'm pretty."

Something that felt a lot like disappointment whacked him between the eyes. She had yet to mention the episode with Liam. Maybe she didn't even know that Kyle had seen them together, or didn't care. No, he'd never said anything to her about it, either, because some things should be obvious. You didn't fool around with a guy's brother. It was a universal law and if he had to spell that out, Grace wasn't as great a girl as he'd always thought.

"Well, then," Kyle said easily. "Maybe you should transfer my case to someone else in the county, so you don't have to deal with my brand of truth."

She probably didn't even remember what she'd done

with Liam and most likely thought Kyle had moved on. He *should* have moved on. It was way past time.

She shook her head. "Can't. We're overloaded. So we're stuck with each other."

Which meant she'd checked into it. That was somehow more disappointing than her skipping over the apology he was owed.

No matter.

Grace was just a woman he used to date. That's all. There was nothing between them any longer. He'd spent years shutting down everything inside and he'd keep on doing it. Nothing new here.

And she had his babies and their future in the palm of her hand. This was the one person he needed on his side. They could both stand to act like adults about this situation and focus on what was good for the children. It would be a good idea to do exactly as he suggested to her and let bygones be bygones. Even though he hadn't meant a word of it at the time.

"You're right. I'm sorry, too. Let's start over, friendly-like." He held out his hand for her to shake.

She hesitated for an eternity and then reached out to take it.

The contact sang through his palm, setting off all kinds of fireworks in places that had been cold and dark for a really long time. Gripping his hand tight, she met his gaze and held it.

The depths of her brown eyes heated, melting a little of the ice in his heart.

Her mouth would be sweet under his, and her skin would be soft and fragrant. The moon had risen, spilling silver light over the parking lot, and the gentle breeze played with her hair. The atmosphere couldn't be more romantic if he'd ordered it up. He barely resisted yanking her into his arms.

Yeah, he was in a lot of trouble if he was supposed to keep this friendly and impartial. She was his babies' caseworker. But the fact of the matter was that he had never gotten over Grace Haines. He could no sooner shut down his feelings about her than he could pick up her Toyota with one hand. And being around her again was pure torture.

The next morning, Kyle woke at dawn the way he always did. He'd weaned himself off an alarm clock about two weeks into BUD/S training and hadn't ever gone back.

He lay there staring at the ceiling of his old room at Wade House. Reorientation time. *Not a SEAL. Not in Afghanistan. Not in the hospital*—which had been its own kind of nightmare. This was the hardest part of the day. Every morning, he took stock, so he'd know who and where he was. Then he thanked God for the opportunity to serve his country and cursed the evil that had required it.

This was also the time of day when he made the decision to leave the pain pills in the bottle, where they belonged.

Some days, that decision was tougher than others. There was a deep, dark place inside that craved the oblivion the drugs would surely bring. That's why he'd never cracked open the seal on the bottle. Too easy to have a mental slip and think *just this once*. That was cheating, and Kyle had never taken that route.

Today would not mark the start of it, either.

Today did mark the start of something, though. A new kind of taking stock about the things he was instead of the things he wasn't. *A father. A cattle rancher.* He liked the sound of that. It was nice to have some positives to call out. He needed positives after six months of hell.

Of course, Grace would be watching over his shoulder, and Liam was going to be smack in the middle of Kyle's steps toward fatherhood *and* ranching. The two people he distrusted the most and both held the keys to his future.

He rolled from bed and pulled on a new long-sleeved shirt, jeans and boots. Eventually, his wardrobe would be work-worn like Liam's, but for now, he'd have to settle for looking like a rhinestone cowboy instead of a real one. Coffee beckoned, so he took the back stairway from the third floor to the ground floor kitchen, albeit a bit more slowly than he'd have liked.

Hadley had beaten him to the coffeepot and turned with a smile when he entered. "Good morning. Sleep well?"

"Fine," he lied. He'd lain awake far too long thinking about how this woman and his brother wanted to take his kids away. "And you?"

"Great. The babies only woke up once and thankfully at the same time. It's not always like that. Sometimes they wake up all night long at intervals." She laughed good-naturedly and lowered her voice. "I think they plan it out ahead of time just to make me nuts."

Guilt crushed Kyle's lungs and he struggled to breathe. Some father he was. They'd agreed the night before that Hadley would continue in her role as Maddie and Maggie's caretaker until Kyle got his feet under him, but it didn't feel any more right this morning than it had then. His sister-in-law was getting up in the middle of the night with his kids, scant hours after he gave Liam and Grace a big speech about how he was all prepared to step up and provide a loving environment.

No more.

"I appreciate what you're doing for my daughters," he rasped, and cleared his throat. "But I want to take care of them from now on. I'll get up with them at night."

Hadley stared at him. "You have no idea what you're talking about, do you?"

"Uh, well…" Should he brazen it out or admit defeat?

God Almighty, he hated admitting any kind of weakness. But chances were good she'd already figured out he wasn't the brightest bulb on the board when it came to babies. "I'm going to learn. Trial by fire is how I operate best."

"They're not going to pull out AK-47s, Kyle." Hadley hid a smile but not very well and handed him a cup of steaming coffee. "Sugar and creamer are on the table."

"I like it black, thanks." He sipped and added *good coffee* to his list of things he was thankful for. "Tell me the things I need to know about my kids."

"Okay." She nodded and went over a list of basics, which Kyle committed to memory. Eating. Bathing. Sleeping. Check, check, check. Stuff all humans needed, but his little humans couldn't do these things for themselves. He just had to help them, the way he would a wounded teammate.

"Can I see them?" he asked. Felt weird to be asking permission, but he didn't want to mess up anything.

"You can. They're sleeping, but we can sneak in. You can be quiet, right?"

"Quiet enough to take out a barracks full of enemy soldiers without getting caught," he said without a trace of irony. Hadley just smiled as though he was kidding.

He followed Hadley to the nursery, a mysterious place full of pink and tiny beds with bars. The girls were asleep in their cribs, and he watched them for a moment, his throat tight. Their little faces—how could anything be that tiny and survive? A better question was, how did your heart stay stitched together when it felt as if it would burst from all the stuff swelling up inside it?

"I was their nanny first, you know," she whispered. "Before I married Liam."

What did a nanny even do? Was she like a babysitter and a substitute mom all rolled up into one? If so, that seemed like a bonus, and he'd be cutting off his nose to spite his face to relieve her of her duties. She could keep on being the nanny as far as he was concerned, as long as Grace was okay with it. She must be. Liam had hired Hadley, after all, and Grace seemed pretty impressed with them as a team.

"I'm not trying to take away your job," he mumbled.

Did she see it as a job? If she and Liam wanted to adopt the girls, she'd obviously grown very attached to them. Was it better to cut off their contact with the babies instead? Get them used to the idea?

If so, he couldn't do it. It seemed unnecessarily cruel and besides, he needed the help.

"I didn't think you were. It's admirable that you want to care for them, but there's a huge learning curve and they won't do well with a big disruption. Let's take it one step at a time."

He could do that. You didn't drop a green recruit into the middle of a Taliban hotbed and expect him to wipe out the insurgents as his first assignment. You started him out with something simple, like surveillance. "Can I watch you feed them?"

"Sure, when they wake up."

They tiptoed from the room and Kyle considered that a pretty successful start to Operation: Fatherhood.

Next up, Operation: Do Something About Grace. Because he'd lain awake last night thinking about her more than he'd wanted to, as well. Somehow, he had to shut down the spark between them. Or hose it off with a big, wet kiss.

Grace sat in her car outside of Wade House and pretended that she was going over some notes in her case file. In truth, her stomach was doing a cancan at the prospect of seeing Kyle again, and she couldn't get it to settle.

She'd gone a long time without seeing him. What was so different now?

Nothing. She was a professional and she would do her job. *Get out of the car*, she admonished herself. *Get in there and do your assessment.* The faster she gathered the facts needed to remove the babies from Kyle's presence and provide a recommendation for their permanent home, the better.

Hadley let her into the house and directed her to the second floor, where Kyle was hanging out with the babies. Perfect. She could watch him interact with them and record some impartial observations in her files.

But when Grace poked her head into the nursery with a bright smile, it died on her face. Kyle dozed in the rocking chair, Maddie against one shoulder, Maggie the other. Both babies were asleep, swaddled in soft pink blankets, an odd contrast to Kyle's masculine attire.

But that wasn't the arresting part. It was Kyle. Unguarded, vulnerable. Sweet even, with his large hands cradled protectively around each of his daughters. He should look ridiculous in the middle of a nursery decorated to the nth degree with girlie colors and baby items. But he looked anything but. His powerful body scarcely fit into the rocking chair, biceps and broad shoulders spilling past the edges of the back. He'd always been incredibly handsome, but on the wiry side.

No more. He was built like a tank, and she could easily imagine this man taking out any threat in a mile-wide radius.

It was a lot more affecting than she would ever admit.

And then his eyelids blinked open. He didn't move a muscle otherwise, but his keen gaze zeroed in on her. Fully alert. Those hard green eyes cut through her, leaving her feeling exposed and much more aware of Kyle than she'd been a minute ago. Which was saying something, given her thoughts had already been pretty graphic.

It was heady to be in his sights like that. He'd always

looked at her as if they shared something special that no one else could or would be involved in. But he'd honed his focus over the years into something new and razor sharp. Flustered, she wiggled her fingers in a half wave, and that's when he smiled.

It hit her in the soft part of her heart and spread a warmth she did not want to feel. But oh, my, it was delicious. Like when he'd taken her hand in the parking lot last night. That feeling—she'd missed it.

She'd lain awake last night imagining that he'd kissed her the way she'd have sworn he wanted to as they stood under that streetlight. It was all wrong between them. Kissing wasn't allowed, wasn't part of the agenda, wasn't what should happen. But it didn't stop her from thinking about it.

She was in a lot of trouble.

"Hi," she murmured, because she felt that she had to say something instead of standing there ogling a gorgeous man as he rocked his infant daughters against an explosion of pink.

"Hi," he mouthed back. "Is it time for our visit already?"

She nodded. "I can come back."

She didn't move as he gave a slight shake of his head. Carefully, he peeled his body from the chair, not jostling even one hair on the head of his precious bundles. As if he'd done it a million times, he laid first one, then the other in their cribs. Neither one woke.

It was a sight to see.

He turned and tiptoed toward the door, but she hadn't moved from her frozen stance in the doorway yet. She should move.

But he stopped right there in front of her, a half smile lingering on his lips as he laid a hand on her arm, presumably to usher her from the room ahead of him. His palm was warm and her skin tingled under it. The feeling threatened to engulf her whole body in a way that she hadn't been *engulfed* in a long time.

Not since Kyle.

Goodness, it seemed so ridiculous, but the real reason it hadn't been hard to stop dating was because no one compared. She was almost thirty and had only had one lover in her life—this man before her with the sparkling green eyes and beautiful face. And she'd take that secret to the grave.

Her cheeks heated as she imagined admitting such a thing to a guy who had likely cut a wide swath through the eligible women beating a path to his door. He hadn't let the grass grow under his feet, now, had he? Fathering twins with a woman he'd written off soon after spoke loudly enough to that question.

If she told him, he'd mistakenly assume she still had feelings for him, and that wasn't exactly true. She just couldn't find a man who fit her stringent criteria for intimacy. Call it old-fashioned, but she wanted to be in love before making love. And most men weren't willing to be that patient.

Except Kyle. He'd never uttered one single complaint when he found out she wasn't hopping into his bed after a few weeks of dating. And oh, my, had it been worth the wait.

The heat in her cheeks spread, and the tingles weren't just under his palm. No, they were a good bit more in a region where she shouldn't be getting so hot, especially not over Kyle and his brand-new warrior's body, laser-sharp focus and gentle hands.

Mercy, she should stop thinking about all that. Except he was looking at her the way he had last night, gaze on her lips, and she wondered if he'd actually do it this time—kiss her as he had so many times before.

One of the babies yowled and the moment broke into pieces.

Kyle's expression instantly morphed into one of concern as he spun toward the crib of the crying infant. Maddie. It was easy to tell them apart if you knew she was the smaller of the two girls. She'd worn a heart monitor for a long time but Grace didn't see the telltale wires poking out of the baby's tiny outfit. Hopefully that meant the multiple surgeries had been successful.

"Hey, now. What's all this fuss?" he murmured, and scooped up the bundle of pink, holding her to his shoulder with rocking motions.

The baby cried harder. Lines of frustration popped up around Kyle's mouth as he kept trying different positions against his shoulder, rocking harder, then slower.

"You liked this earlier," he said. "I'm following procedure here, little lady. Give me a break."

Grace hid a smile. "Maybe her diaper is wet."

Kyle nodded and strode to the changing table. "One diaper change, coming up."

He pulled a diaper from the drawer under the table, laid the baby on the foam pad, then tied the holding straps designed to keep Maddie from rolling to the ground with intricate knots. Next, he lined up the baby powder and diaper rash cream, determination rolling from him in thick waves. When the man put his mind to something, it was dizzying to watch.

With precision, he stripped the baby out of her onesie and took a swift kick to the wrist with good humor as he changed her diaper. It didn't help. The baby wailed a little louder.

"No problem," he said. "Babies usually cry for three reasons. They want to be held. Diaper. And…" A line appeared between Kyle's brows.

Then Maggie woke up and cried in harmony with her sister.

"Want me to pick her up?" Grace asked.

"No. I can handle this. Don't count me out yet." He nestled the other baby into his arms, rocking both with little murmurs. "Bottle. That was the other one Hadley said. We'll try eating."

Bless his heart. He'd gone to Hadley for baby lessons. He was trying so hard, much harder than she'd expected. It warmed her in a whole different way than the sizzle a moment ago. And the swell in her heart was much more dangerous.

The bottle did the trick. After Kyle got both girls fed, they quieted down and fell back asleep in their cribs. This time, he and Grace made it out of the room, but when they reached the living area off the kitchen, *flustered* was too kind a word for the state of her nerves.

Kyle collapsed on the couch with a groan.

"So," she croaked after taking a seat as far away from him as possible. "That was pretty stressful."

"Nah." He scrubbed his face with his hand and peeked out through his fingers. "Stressful is dismantling a homemade pipe bomb before it kills someone."

They'd never talked about his life in the military—largely because he was so closemouthed about it—and judging from the shadows she glimpsed in his expression sometimes, the experience hadn't softened him up any, that was for sure. "Is that what you did overseas? Handle explosives?"

Slowly, he nodded. "That was my specialty, yeah."

He could have died. Easily. A hundred times over, and she'd probably never have known until they paraded his flag-draped coffin through the streets of Royal. The thought was upsetting in a way she really didn't understand, which only served to heighten her already-precarious emotional state.

He'd been serving his country, not using the military as an excuse to stay away. The realization swept through her, blowing away some of her anger and leaving in its place a bit of guilt over never acknowledging his sacrifices in the name of liberty.

"And now you're ready to buckle down and be a father."

It seemed ludicrous. This powerful, strapping man wanted to trade bombs for babies. But when she recalled the finesse he used when handling the babies, she couldn't deny that he had a delicate touch.

"I do what needs to be done," he said quietly, and his green eyes radiated sincerity that she couldn't quite look away from.

When had Kyle become so responsible? Such an *adult*? He was different in such baffling, subtle ways that she kept stumbling in her quest to objectively assess his fitness as a parent.

"Did you give any thought to our discussion yesterday?" she asked.

"The job? I signed on to head up Wade Ranch's cattle division. How's that for serious?"

Kyle leaned back against the couch cushions, looking much more at home in this less formal area than he'd been in the Victorian parlor yesterday, and crossed one booted foot over his knee. Cowboy boots, not the military-issue black boots he'd been wearing yesterday. It was a small detail, but a telling one.

He'd quietly transitioned roles when she wasn't looking. Could it mean he'd been telling the truth when he'd said he planned to stay this time?

"It's a start," she said simply, but that didn't begin to describe what was actually starting.

She'd have to adjust every last thing she'd ever thought about Kyle Wade and his ability to be a father. And if she did, she might also have to think about him differently in a lot of other respects as well, such as whether or not he'd grown up enough to become her everything once again. But this time forever.

Four

Kyle reported to the Wade Ranch cattle barn for duty at zero dark thirty. At least he'd remembered to refer to the beasts as cattle instead of cows. Slowly but surely, snippets of his youth had started coming back to him as he'd driven to the barn. He'd watched his grandfather, Calvin Wade, manage the ranch for years. Kyle remembered perching on the top rail of the cattle pen while Calvin branded the calves or helped Doc Glade with injured cows.

Things had changed significantly since then. The cattle barn had been rebuilt and relocated a half mile from the main house. It was completely separate from the horse business, and Liam's lack of interest in the cattle side couldn't have been clearer. His brother had even hired a ranch manager.

Kyle could practically hear the rattle of Grandpa rolling over in his grave.

He'd always insisted that a man had to manage his own business and Calvin hadn't had much respect for "gentleman" ranchers who spent their money on women and whiskey and hired other men to do the work of running the ranch. Clearly Liam hadn't agreed.

The red barn dominated the clearing ahead. A long empty pen ran along the side of the building. The cattle must be roaming. Kyle parked his truck in a lot near a handful of other vehicles with the Wade Ranch logo on the doors. Easing from the cab, he hit the ground with bated breath. So far, so good. The cowboy boots were a little stiff and the heel put his leg at a weird angle, but he was going to ignore all that as long as possible.

He strolled to the barn, which had an office similar to the one in the horse barn. But that's where the similarities ended. This was a working barn, complete with the smell of manure and hay. Kyle had smelled a lot worse. It reminded him of Grandpa, and there was something nice about following in Calvin's footsteps. They'd never been close, but then Kyle had never been close with anyone. Except Grace.

The ranch manager, Danny Spencer, watched Kyle approach and spat on the ground as he contemplated his new boss.

"You pick out a horse yet, son?"

Kyle's hackles rose. He was no one's son, least of all this man who was maybe fifteen years his senior. It was a deliberate choice of phrasing designed to put Kyle in his place. Wasn't going to work. "First day on the job."

"We ride here. You skedaddle on over to the other barn and come back on a horse. Then we'll talk."

It felt like a test and Kyle intended to pass. So he climbed back into his truck and drove to the horse barn. He felt like a mama's boy driving. But he was in a hurry to get started and walking wasn't one of his skills right now.

Maybe one day.

Liam was already at the barn, favoring an early start

as well, apparently. He helped Kyle find a suitable mount without one smart-alecky comment, which did not go unnoticed. Kyle just chose not to say anything about it.

A few ranch hands gathered to watch, probably hoping Kyle would bust his ass a couple of times and they could video it with their cell phones. He wondered what they'd been told about Kyle's return. Did everyone know about the babies and Margaret's death?

Sucker's bet. Of course they did. Wade Ranch was its own kind of small town. Didn't matter. Kyle was the boss, whether they liked it or not. Whether he had the slightest clue what he was doing. Or not.

The horse didn't like him any better than Danny Spencer did. When he stuck a boot in the stirrup, the animal tried to dance sideways and would have bucked him off if Kyle hadn't kept a tight grip on the pommel. "Hey, now. Settle down."

Liam had called the horse Lightning Rod. Dumb name. But it was all Kyle had.

"That's a good boy, Lightning Rod." It seemed to calm the dark brown quarter horse somewhat, so Kyle tried to stick his boot in the stirrup again. This time, he ended up in the saddle, which felt just as foreign as everything else on the ranch did.

The ranch hands applauded sarcastically, mumbling to each other. He almost apologized for ruining their fun—also sarcastically—but he let it go.

Somehow, Kyle managed to get up to a trot as he rode out onto the trail back to the cattle barn. It had been a lifetime since he'd ridden a horse and longer than that since he'd wanted to.

God, everything hurt. The trot was more of a trounce, and he longed for the bite of rock under his belly as he dismantled a homemade cherry bomb placed carefully under a mosque where three hundred people worshipped. That he understood at least. How he'd landed in the middle of a job managing cattle, he didn't.

Oh, right. He was doing this to prove to everyone they were wrong about him. That he wasn't a slacker who'd ignored messages about his flesh and blood. That Liam and Grace and Danny Spencer and everyone else who had a bone to pick with him weren't going to make him quit.

When he got back to the cattle barn, Danny and the cattle hands were hanging around waiting. One of the disappointed guys from the horse barn had probably texted ahead, hoping someone else could get video of the boss falling off his mount. They could all keep being disappointed.

"One cattle rancher on a horse, as ordered," Kyle called mildly, keeping his ire under wraps. Someone wanted to know what he really thought about things? Too bad. No one was privy to what went on inside Kyle's head except Kyle. As always.

"That'll do," Danny said with a nod, but his scowl didn't loosen up any. "We got a few hundred head in the north pasture that need to be rounded up. You take Slim and Johnny and ya'll bring 'em back, hear?"

"Nothing wrong with my ears," Kyle drawled lazily. "What's wrong is that I'm the one calling the shots now. What do you say we chat about that for a bit?"

Danny spat on the ground near Lighting Rod's left front hoof and the horse flicked his head back in response. Kyle choked up on the reins before his mount got the brilliant idea to bolt.

"I'd say you started drinking early this a.m. if you think you're calling the shots, jarhead."

Kyle let loose a wry chuckle, friendly like, so no one got the wrong idea. "You might want to brush up on your insults. Jarheads are marines, not SEALs."

"Same thing."

Neither of them blinked as Kyle grinned. "Nah. The marines let anyone in, even old cowhands with bad attitudes. Want me to pass your number on to a recruiter? I'll let you go a couple of rounds with a drill sergeant, and when you come back, you can talk to me about the difference between marines and SEALs all you want. Until then, my last name is Wade and the only thing you're permitted to call me is 'boss.'"

Spencer didn't flinch but neither did he nod and play along. He spun on his heel and disappeared into the barn with a backhanded wave. Kyle considered it a win that the man hadn't flipped him a one-fingered salute as a bonus.

Now that the unpleasantness was out of the way, Kyle nodded at the two hands the ranch manager had singled out as his lieutenants, one of whom had fifty pounds on him. That one must be Slim. It was the kind of joke cowboys seemed to like. Kyle would probably be *jarhead* until the day he died after a recounting of his showdown with Danny Spencer made the gossip rounds.

"You boys have a problem working for me?" he asked them both.

Slim's expression was nothing short of hostile, but he and Johnny both shook their heads and swung up on their horses, trotting obediently after Kyle as he headed north toward the pasture where the cattle he was supposed to herd were grazing.

Then he just needed to figure out how to do it. Without alienating anyone else. Oh, and without falling off his horse. And without letting on to anyone that his leg was on fire already after less than thirty minutes in the saddle.

The north pasture came into view. Finally. It was still exactly where it had been ten years ago, but it felt as though it had taken a million years to get there, especially given the tense silence between Kyle and the two hands. Cattle dotted the wide swath of Wade land like black shadows against the green grass, spread as far as the eye could see, even wandering aimlessly into a copse of trees in the distance.

That was not good. He'd envisioned the cattle being easy to round up because they were all more or less in the same place. Instead, he and the hands had a very long task ahead of them to gather up the beasts, who may or may not have wanted to be gathered.

"How many?" he called over his shoulder to Johnny.

"A few hundred." Johnny repeated verbatim the vague number Danny Spencer had rattled off earlier.

He'd mellowed out some and had actually spoken to Kyle without growling. Slim, not so much. The man held a serious grudge that wouldn't be easily remedied. No big thing. They didn't have to like each other. Just work together.

"How many exactly?" Kyle asked again as patiently as possible. "We have to know if we have them all before we head back."

Johnny looked at him cockeyed as if Kyle had started speaking in tongues and thrown around a couple of snakes in the baptismal on a Sunday morning. "We just round 'em up and aim toward the barn. Nothing more to it than that."

"Maybe not before. But today, we're going to make sure we have full inventory before we make the trek." Kyle couldn't do it more than once. There was no way. "Liam didn't happen to invest in GPS, did he?"

Slim and Johnny exchanged glances. "Uh…what?"

"Satellite. RFID chips. You embed the chips in the cow's brand, for example, and use a GPS program to triangulate the chips. Technology to locate and count cattle." At the blank looks he received in response, Kyle gave up. "I'll take that as a no."

That would be Kyle's first investment as head of the cattle division at Wade Ranch. RFID chips would go a long way toward inventorying livestock that ran tame across hundreds of acres. That was how the military kept track of soldiers and supplies, after all. Seemed like a no-brainer to do the same with valuable livestock. He wondered why Liam hadn't done it already.

"All right, then." Kyle sighed. "Let's do this."

The three men rode hard for a couple of hours, driving the cattle toward the gate, eventually feeling confident that they had them all. Kyle had to accept the eyeball guesstimate from Slim and Johnny, who had "done this a couple of times." Both thought the number of bodies seemed about right. Since Kyle wasn't experienced enough to argue, he nodded and let the experts guide them home.

It was exhausting and invigorating at the same time. This was his land. His cattle. His men, despite the lack of welcome.

But when he got back to the cattle barn, Liam was waiting for him, arms crossed and a livid expression on his face.

"What now?" Kyle slid from his horse, keeping a tight grip on the pommel until he was sure his leg would support him.

"Danny Spencer quit." Liam fairly spat. "And walked out without even an hour's notice. Said he'd rather eat manure than work for you. Nice going."

"That's the best news I've heard all day." God's honest truth. The relief was huge. "He doesn't want to work for me? Fine. Better that he's gone."

Liam pulled Kyle away from the multitude of hands swarming the area by the barn, probably all with perked-up ears, hoping to catch more details about the unfolding drama.

"It's not better," Liam muttered darkly. "Are you out of your mind? You can't come in here and throw your weight around. Danny's been handling the cattle side. I told you that. This is his territory and you came in and upset the status quo in less than five minutes."

Kyle shook his head. "Not his territory anymore. It's mine."

"Seriously?" Liam's snort was half laugh and half frustration. "You don't get it. These men respect Danny. Follow him. They don't like you. What are you going to do if they all quit? You can't run a cattle division by yourself."

Yeah, but he'd rather try than put up with dissension in the ranks. Catering to the troops was the fastest way to give the enemy an advantage. There could only be one guy in charge, and it was Kyle. "They can all quit then. There are plenty of ranch hands in this area. I need men who will work, not drama queens all bent out of shape because a bigger fish swam into their pond."

"Fine." Liam threw up his hands. "You have at it. Don't say I didn't warn you. Just keep in mind that we have a deal."

His brother stomped to his truck and peeled out of the clearing with a spray of rock. Kyle resisted the urge to wave, mostly because Liam was probably too pissed to look in his rearview mirror and also because the hands were eyeing him with scowls. No point in being cocky on top of clueless.

His girls were worth whatever he had to do to figure this out.

Johnny approached him then. Kyle had just about had enough of cattle, his aching leg, difficult ranch managers and a hardheaded brother.

"What?" he snapped.

"Uh, I just wanted to tell you thanks." Johnny cleared his throat. "For your service to the country."

The genuine sentiment pierced Kyle through the stomach. And nearly put him on the ground where a day of hard riding hadn't. It was the first time anyone in Royal had positively acknowledged his time in the military. Not that he'd been expecting a three-piece band and a parade. He'd rather stay out of the spotlight—that kind of welcome was for true heroes, not a guy who'd gotten on the wrong end of a bullet.

Nonetheless, Kyle's bad day didn't seem so bad anymore.

"Yeah," he said gruffly. "You're welcome. You know someone who served?"

Usually, the only people who thought about thanking veterans were those with family or friends in the armed forces. It was just a fact. Regular people enjoyed their freedom well enough but rarely thought about the people behind the sacrifices required to secure it.

Johnny nodded, his eyes wide and full of grief. "My dad. He was killed in the first Gulf War. I was still a baby. I never got to know him."

Ouch. That was the kicker. No matter what else, Kyle and this kid had a bond that could never be broken.

Kyle simply held out his hand and waited until Johnny grasped it. "That's a shame. I'm sorry for your loss. I stood in for great fallen men like your dad and helped continue the job he started. I'm proud I got to follow in his footsteps."

The younger man shook his hand solemnly, and then there was nothing more to say. Some things didn't need words.

Kyle hit the shower when he got back to the house. When he emerged, Liam and Hadley asked if they could take the babies for a walk in their double stroller before dinner, and would he like to come?

A walk. They might as well have asked if he'd like to fly. He'd have a hard time with a crawl at this point. After the fishhooks Johnny had sunk into his heart, he'd rather be alone anyway, though it killed him to be unable to do something as simple as push his daughters in a stroller. He waved Liam and his new wife off with a smile, hoped it came across as sincere and limped into the family room to watch something inane on TV.

There was a halfway decent World War II documentary on the History Channel that caught his interest. He watched it for a few minutes until the doorbell rang.

"That was fast," he said as he yanked open the door with a grin he'd dare anyone to guess was fake, expecting to see Liam and Hadley with chagrined expressions because they'd forgotten their key.

But it was Grace. Beautiful, fresh-faced Grace, who stood on the porch with clasped hands, long brown hair down her back, wearing a long-sleeved sweater with form-fitting jeans. It was a hard to peel his eyes from her. But he did. Somehow.

"Hey, Kyle," she said simply.

His smile became real instantly. Why, he couldn't say. Grace was still a bundle of trouble tied up with a big old impossible knot. But where was the fun in leaving a tangle alone?

They'd agreed to forget about the past and start over. But they hadn't fully established what they were starting, at least not to his satisfaction. Maybe now would be a good time to get that straight.

"Hey, Grace." He crossed his arms and leaned on the door frame, cocking his busted leg to take the weight off. "What can I do for you?"

The sun shone behind her, close to setting for the day, spilling fiery reds and yellows into the deep crevices of the sky. As backdrops went, it wasn't half-bad. But it wasn't nearly as spectacular as the woman.

"We had an appointment. Earlier."

Kyle swore. He'd totally forgotten. Wasn't that just

dandy? Made him look like a stellar father to blow off his daughters' caseworker.

Fix it. He needed Grace's good favor.

"But you were off doing cowboy things," she continued. Her voice had grown a little breathy as if she'd run to the door from her car. But the scant distance between here and there sure didn't account for the pink spreading through her cheeks.

"Yep. Someone advised me I might want to find permanent employment if I hoped to be a daddy to my girls. Sorry I missed you." He raised a brow. "But it's mighty accommodating of you to reschedule, considering. 'Preciate it."

Good thing she hadn't wandered down to the barn so she could witness firsthand his impressive debut as the boss.

"No problem," she allowed. "I have to do the requisite number of site visits before I make my recommendations and I do want to be thorough."

Maybe there was room to get her mind off her recommendations and on to something a little more pleasant. *Before* she made any snap judgments about his ability to recall a small thing like an appointment with the person who had the most power to screw up his life. Well, actually, Grace was probably second, behind Kyle—if there was anyone who got the honor of being an A1 screwup thus far in this custody issue, it was him.

"Why don't we sit for a minute?" He gestured to the porch rocker to the left of the front door, which had a great view of the sunset. Might as well put Liam's revamp of the house to good use, and do some reconnaissance at the same time. Grace had to provide a report with her recommendations. He got that. But he wanted to know more about the woman providing the report than anything else at this moment.

"Oh." She glanced at the rocker and then over his shoulder into the interior of the house. "It would probably be best if I watched you interact with the girls again. Like yesterday. That's the quickest way for me to see what kind of environment you'll provide."

"That would be great. Except they aren't here. Liam and Hadley took them for a walk before dinner." Quickly, before she could ask why he hadn't joined them, he held up a finger as if a brilliant idea had just occurred to him. "Why don't you stay and eat with us? You can see how the Wade family handles meals. Meanwhile, we can hang out on the porch and wait for them to get back."

"Um…"

He closed the front door and hustled her over to the bench seat with a palm to the small of her back. To be fair, she didn't resist too much and willingly sank into the rocker, but as soon as he sat next to her, it became clear that *he* should have been the one resisting.

The essence of Grace spilled over him as they got cozy in the two-seater. It was too small for someone his size and their hips snugged up against each other. The contact burned through his jeans, sensitizing his skin, and as he tried to ease off a bit, his foot hit the porch board and set the rocker in motion. Which only knocked her against him more firmly so that her amazing breasts grazed his arm.

Actually, the rocker was exactly the right size for Kyle and Grace. Sitting in it with her might have been the best idea he'd ever had in his life.

Her fresh, spring-like scent wound through his head. They'd sat like this at her mama's house, but in the living room while pretending to watch TV on a Saturday night. It passed for a date in a place like Royal, where teenagers could either get in trouble sneaking around the football stadium with filched beer or hang out under the watchful eye of the folks. Usually Kyle and Grace had opted for the latter, at least until her parents went to bed. Then they got down to some serious making out.

He'd never been as affected by a woman as he'd been by this one. Even just a kiss could knock him for a loop. The memories of how good it had been washed through him, blasting away some of the darkness that had taken over inside. She'd always been so eager. So pliant under his mouth.

All at once, he wondered if she still tasted the same, like innocence laced with a warm breeze.

"Grace," he murmured. Somehow his arm had snaked across the back of the rocker, closing the small gap between them.

Grace's brown eyes peeked out underneath her lashes as she watched him for a moment. Maybe she was wondering the same. If that spark would still be there after all this time.

"How long will it be until Liam and Hadley are back with the girls?" she asked, her voice low.

"Later. Don't worry. We won't miss them."

"I, uh…wasn't worried."

She licked her lips, drawing his attention to her mouth, and suddenly that was all he could see. All he could think about. Her lips had filled out, along with the rest of her face. She'd grown into a woman while he'd been away, with some interesting new experiences shining in her eyes.

All at once, he wanted to know what they were.

"I've been wondering," he said. "Why did you become a social worker? I seem to recall you wanted to be a schoolteacher way back."

That was not what he'd meant to ask. But she lit up at the question. And the sunset? Not even a blip in his consciousness. Her face had all the warmth a man would ever need.

"I did. Want to," she clarified. "That's what I majored in. But I went to do my student teaching and something just didn't work right. The students weren't the problem. Oh, they were a bit unruly but they were fourth graders. You gotta expect some ants in the pants. It was me. There was no…click. You know what I mean?"

"Yeah." He nodded immediately. Like when he hit his stride in BUD/S training on the second day and knew he'd found his place in the world. "Then what happened?"

"I volunteered some places for a while. Tried to get my feet under me, looking for that click. Then my mom calls me and says a friend of hers needs a receptionist because the girl in the job is going out on maternity leave. Would I do her a huge favor for three months?"

As she talked, she waved her hands, dipping and shaping the air, and he found himself smiling along with her as she recounted the story. Smiling and calculating exactly what it would take to get one of those hands on his body somewhere. He wasn't picky—not yet.

"Turns out Sheila, my mom's friend, runs an adoption agency. She's been a huge mentor to me and really helped me figure out what I wanted to do with my life. See, I love children, but I don't like teaching them. I do like helping them, though. I ended up staying at the agency for four years in various roles while I got my master's degree at night."

"You have a master's degree?" That revelation managed to get his attention off her mouth for a brief second. Not that he was shocked—she'd always been a great student. It was just one more layer to this woman that he didn't know nearly well enough.

"Yep." She nodded slowly. "The county requires it."

"That's great."

"What about you? I know you went into the military but that's about it. You went into the navy, Liam said."

"I did." He shifted uncomfortably, as he did any time his years in Afghanistan came up among civilians. The top secret nature of virtually every blessed op he'd completed was so ingrained, it was hard to have a regular conversation with anyone outside of his team. "Special operations. It's not as glamorous as the media makes it out to be. I sweated a lot, got really dirty and learned how to survive in just about any conditions. Meanwhile, I followed orders and occasionally gave a few. And now I'm home."

Something flashed deep in her eyes and she reached out. Her palm landed on his bare forearm, just below the rolled-up sleeve of his work shirt. "It doesn't sound glamorous. It sounds lonely."

"It was," he mumbled before he'd realized it. Shouldn't have admitted that. It smacked of weakness.

"I'm sorry." Her sympathy swept along his nerve endings, burying itself under his skin. The place she'd always been.

The place he'd always let her be. Because she soothed him and eased his loneliness. Always had. Looked as if for all the things that had changed, that was one constant, and he latched on to it greedily.

"It's over now."

His arm still stretched across the back of the seat. The slightest shift nestled her deeper against him and a strand of her glossy hair fell against her cheek. He wasted no time capturing it between his fingers, brushing it aside, and then letting his fingers linger.

Their gazes met and held for an eternity. A wealth of emotions swirled in her eyes.

Her skin was smooth and warm under his touch. She tilted her face toward his fingers, just a fraction of a movement. Just enough to tell him she wasn't about to push him away.

He slid his fingers more firmly under her chin and lifted it. And then those amazing lips of hers were within claiming distance. So he claimed them.

Grace opened beneath his mouth with a gasp, sucking him under instantly. Their mouths aligned, fitting together so perfectly, as if she'd been fashioned by the Almighty specifically for Kyle Wade. He'd always thought that. How was that still true?

The kiss deepened without any help on his part. He couldn't have said his own name as something raw and elemental exploded in his chest. *Grace.* The feel of her—like home and everything that was good in the world, blended together and infused into the essence of this woman.

He wanted more. And he couldn't have stopped himself from taking it.

Threading both hands through her hair, he cupped her head and changed the angle, plunging into the sensation. Taking her along with him. She moaned in her chest, and answering vibrations rocked his.

She clung to him, her hands gripping his shoulders as if she never wanted to let go. Which was great, because he didn't want her to.

Her sweet taste flowed across his tongue as he twined it with hers, greedily soaking up everything she was offering. It had been so long since he'd *felt*. Since he'd allowed himself to be so open. Hell, he hadn't *allowed* anything. She'd burrowed into his very core with nothing more than a kiss, and he'd had little to say about it.

And then she was gone. Ripped away.

She bolted from the rocker, her chest rising and falling as she hugged the split-pine railing surrounding the porch with her back. "I'm sorry. I shouldn't have done that."

"But you did." Ruthlessly, he shut down all the things she'd stirred up inside, since it appeared as if she wasn't up for seconds.

"I got caught up. That can't happen again."

Her expression glittered with undisguised longing, and no, he hadn't imagined that she'd welcomed his kiss. That she'd leaned into his touch and begged for more. So why was she stopping?

"I heartily disagree." He smiled, but it almost hurt to paint it on when his entire body was on fire. And this woman was the only one who could quench the flames. "It's practically a requirement for it to happen again."

"Are you that clueless, Kyle?"

Clueless. Yeah, he needed to catch a couple of clues apparently, like the big screaming back-off vibes Grace was shooting in his direction.

"I'm your daughters' caseworker," she reminded him with raised eyebrows. "We can't get involved."

His body cooled faster than if she'd dumped a bucket of ice water on his head. "You're right."

Of course she was right. When had he lost sight of that? This wasn't about whether she was interested or not; it was about his daughters. What had started out as a half-formed plan to distract her from work had actually distracted *him* far more effectively.

And he wanted to do it again. That was dangerous. She could take his girls away at the drop of a hat, and he couldn't afford to antagonize her. Hell, she'd even told him she had to treat the case as objectively as possible, and here he was, ignoring all of that.

Because she'd gotten to him. She'd dug under his skin without saying a word. Talk about dangerous. He couldn't let her know she had that much power over him, or she might use it to her advantage. How could he have forgotten how much better it was to keep his heart—and his mouth—shut? That's why he stuck to weekend hookups, like the one he'd had with Margaret. No one expected him to spill his guts, and then he was free to leave before anyone got a different idea about how things were going to go.

That was the best he could do. The best he *wanted* to do. But he couldn't ditch Royal this time around when things got too heated. He'd have to figure out how to get past one more tangle in the big fat knot in his chest that had Grace's name all over it.

She thought he was clueless? Just a big dumb guy who couldn't find his way around a woman without a map? Fine. It served his purpose to let her keep on thinking that, while he flipped this problem on its head.

"Sorry about that, then." He held up his hands and let a slow grin spread across his face. "Hands off from now on."

Or at least until he figured out which way the wind blew in Grace's mind about the custody issue. He couldn't afford to antagonize her, but neither could he afford to let her out of his sight. Once he had curried her good favor and secured his claim on his children, all bets were off.

And when she mumbled an excuse about having other dinner plans, he let her leave, already contemplating what kind of excuse he could find to get her into his arms again, but this time, without any of the emotional tangle she seemed to effortlessly cause.

Five

The kiss had been a mistake.

Grace knew that. She'd known *while* she was kissing Kyle. The whole time. Why, for the love of God, couldn't she stop thinking about it?

She'd kissed Kyle lots of times. None of those kisses was seared into her brain, ready to pop up in her consciousness like a jack-in-the-box gone really wrong. Of course, all her previous Kyle kisses had happened with the boy.

He was all man now.

Darker, harder, fiercer. And oh, how he had driven that fact home with nothing more than his mouth on hers. The feel of his lips had winnowed through her, sliding through her blood, waking it deliciously. Reminding her that she was all woman.

Telling her that she'd yet to fully explore what that meant.

Oh, sure, she'd kissed a few of the men she'd dated before she'd become a Professional Single Girl. But those chaste, dry pecks hadn't compared with being kissed by someone like Kyle.

She couldn't do it again. No matter how much she wanted to. No matter how little sleep she got that night and how little work she got done the next day because she couldn't erase the goose bumps from her skin that had sprung up the instant Kyle had touched her.

When Clare Connelly called with a dinner invitation, Grace jumped on it, nearly crying with relief at the thought of a distraction. Clare was a pediatric nurse who'd cared for the twin babies in the harrowing days after their premature birth, and she and Grace had become good friends.

Grace arrived at the Waters Café just off Royal's main street before Clare, so she took a seat at a four top and ordered a glass of wine while she waited. The café had been rebuilt as part of the revitalization of the downtown strip after the tornado had tried to wipe Royal off the map. The owners, Jim and Pam Waters, had nearly lost everything, but thanks to a good insurance policy and some neighborly folks, the café was going strong. Grace made it a point to eat there as often as possible, just to give good people her business.

Clare bustled through the door, her long blond hair still twisted up in her characteristic bun, likely because she'd just come from work at Royal Memorial. Grace waved, and then realized she wasn't alone—Clare had her arm looped through another woman's. Violet McCallum, who co-owned the Double M Ranch with her brother, Mac.

Wow, Grace hardly recognized her. Violet looked beautiful and was even wearing a dress instead of her usual boots and jeans. It had been a while since they'd seen each other. Not since they'd all met at Priceless, the antiques and craft store owned by Raina Patterson, to indulge in a girls' night of stained glass making, which had been so much fun that Grace had picked it up as a new hobby.

"I had to drag her out of the house," Clare said by way of greeting, laughing and pointing at Violet. It was a bit of a joke among the three ladies as Violet and Grace had done something similar for Clare when she'd been going through man troubles. "I hope you don't mind."

"Of course I don't. Hi, Violet!" Grace jumped up and embraced the auburn-haired woman. Violet gave her a one-armed hug in return and scuttled to a seat.

Grace and Clare settled into their own seats. Grace signaled the waitress, then leaned forward on her forearms to speak to Violet across the table. "What are you using on your skin? Because I'm investing in a truckload. You look positively luminous!"

Violet flinched and gave Grace a pained smile, which highlighted dark shadows in her friend's eyes. "Thanks. It's, um…my new apricot scrub. I'll text you the name of it when I get home."

"Sure," Grace said enthusiastically, but it felt a little forced. Something was off with Violet but she didn't want to pry. They'd been friends a long time. If Violet wanted to share what was up, she would. "Give me your hand, Clare. Dinner can't officially start until we ooh and aah over your ring!"

A smile split Clare's face, and she stuck her hand out, fingers spread in the classic pose of an engaged woman. "Stand back, ladies. This baby will blind you if you don't give it the proper distance."

Clare had recently gotten engaged to Dr. Parker Reese, a brilliant neonatal specialist at Royal Memorial, where they both worked. Their romance had been touch and go, framed by the desperate search for Maddie's mother after the infant had been abandoned at a truck stop shortly after her birth. Margaret Garner had then gotten into her car and given birth to Maggie a little farther down the road, ultimately dying from the traumatic childbirth. So the twins had ended up separated. When Maggie ultimately went home with Liam and Hadley, they were unaware she had a sister. Thankfully, they'd eventually realized Maddie and Maggie were twins and thus both belonged with the Wades.

Of course, that had all been before Kyle had come home.

And that was a dumb thing to start thinking about. Grace pinched herself under the table, but it didn't do any good. The kiss popped right back into her mind, exactly the thing she was trying to avoid thinking about.

Kyle was a difficult man to forget. She should know. She'd spent ten years trying to forget him and had failed spectacularly.

"Tell us about the wedding," Grace insisted brightly. Anything to take her attention off Kyle.

Clare gushed for a minute or two until the harried waitress finally made her way over to the three ladies. The ponytailed woman in her early twenties pulled a pen from behind her ear and held it expectantly over her order pad.

"Sorry for the wait, ladies," she apologized. "We're short-staffed today."

"No problem," Grace tossed out with a smile. "This Chardonnay is fabulous. Can you bring two more glasses?"

"No!" Violet burst out, and then her eyes widened as all three of the other women stared at her. "I, uh, didn't bring my driver's license, and I know you have to see my identification, so no drinking for me. Water is fine anyway. Thanks."

"It's okay, Ms. McCallum," the waitress said cheerfully. "I know you're over twenty-one. You were two years ahead of my sister in high school and she's twenty-four. I'd be happy to make an exception."

Violet turned absolutely green. "That's kind of you. But water is fine. Excuse me."

All at once, Violet rushed from the table, snatching her

purse from the back of the chair as she ran for the rear of the restaurant toward the bathrooms. In her haste, she knocked the straight-backed chair to the floor with a crash that reverberated in the half-full café. Conversations broke off instantly as the other customers swiveled to seek out the source of the noise.

Violet didn't pause until she'd disappeared from the room. *What in the world?*

"I practically had to force her to come tonight," Clare confessed, her voice lowered as she leaned close to Grace and waved off the beleaguered waitress, who promised to come back later. "I guess I shouldn't have. But she's been holed up for a few weeks now, and Mac called me, worried. He mentioned that she'd been under the weather, but he thought she was feeling better."

That was just like Violet's brother, Mac McCallum. He was the kind of guy Grace had always wished she'd had for a big brother, one who looked out for his sister even into their adulthood. Back in high school, he'd busted Tommy Masterson in the mouth for saying something off-color about Violet, and the boys in Royal had learned fast that they didn't cross Mac when it came to Violet.

"We should go check on her," Grace said firmly. Poor thing. She probably had a stomach flu or something like that, and they'd let her run off to the bathroom. Alone. "Friends hold each other's hair."

When Grace and Clare got to the restroom, Violet was standing at the sink, both hands clamped on the porcelain as she stared in the mirror, hollow eyed, supporting her full weight on her palms as if she might collapse if the vanity wasn't there to hold her up.

"You didn't have to disrupt your dinner on my account." Violet didn't glance at the other two women as she spoke into the mirror.

"Of course we did." Grace put her arm around Violet

and held her tight as she stood by her friend's side, offering the only kind of support she knew to give: physical contact. "Whatever it is, I'm sure you'll feel better soon. Sometimes it takes a while for the virus to work through your system. Do you want some crackers? Cold medicine? I'll run to the pharmacy if need be."

A brief lift of Violet's lips passed as a smile. "You're so nice to offer, but I don't think what I've got can be fixed with cold medicine."

She trembled under Grace's arm. This was no garden-variety stomach bug or spring cold, and Grace was just about to demand that Violet go see a doctor in the morning, or she'd drag her there herself, when Clare met Violet's eyes in the mirror as she came up on the other side of their friend.

"You're pregnant," Clare said decisively with a knowing smile. "I knew it. That night at Priceless... I could see then that you had that glowy look about you."

Oh. Now Grace felt like a dummy. Of course that explained Violet's strange behavior and refusal to drink the wine.

Shock flashed through Violet's expression but she banked it and then hesitated for only a moment. "No. That's impossible."

"Impossible, like you're in denial? Or impossible, like you haven't slept with anyone who could have gotten you pregnant?"

"Like, impossible, period, end of story, and now you need to drop it." Violet scowled at Clare in the mirror, who just stuck her tongue out. "It's just an upset stomach. Let's go back to the table."

With a nod that said she was dropping it but didn't like it, Clare hustled Violet to the table and ordered her hot tea with lemon, then ensured that everyone selected something to eat in her best mother-hen style.

The atmosphere grew lighter and lighter until their food came. They were just three friends having dinner, as advertised. Until Clare zeroed in on Grace and asked point-blank, "What's going on with you and Kyle Wade?"

Grace nearly choked. "What? Nothing."

Heat swept across her cheeks as she recalled in living color exactly how big a lie that was.

"Funny," Clare remarked to Grace. "I'd swear I heard mention of a highly charged *encounter* with Kyle in the parking lot of the HEB the other night. Care to fill us in?"

Violet perked up. "What's this? You're picking up with Kyle again?"

"Over my dead body!" That might have come out a little more vehement than she'd intended. "I mean…"

"I haven't seen him yet," Violet said to Clare as if Grace hadn't spoken. "But when I went to the bank yesterday, Cindy May said he's filled out and pretty much the stuff of centerfold fantasies. 'Smoking hot' was the phrase she used. Liberally."

Clare waggled her brows at Grace. "Spill the beans, dear."

Heat climbed up her cheeks. "I don't have any beans to spill. His daughters are on my case docket, and we ran into each other at the grocery store. This is Royal. It would be weird if I *hadn't* run into him."

"I haven't run into him." Violet sipped her tea. "Clare?"

The traitor shook her head. "Nope."

"Well, the Kyle train has left the station and I was not on board. I don't plan to be on board." Grace drained her glass of wine and motioned for another one the moment the waitress glanced her way. Wow, was it hot in here, and she was so thirsty. "Kyle Wade is the strong, silent type, and I need a man who can open his mouth occasionally to tell me what I mean to him. If that's not happening, I'm not happening. But it doesn't matter because nothing is going on with us. He's trying to be a father and I'm working to figure out how to let him. That's it."

All at once, she realized she'd already made up her mind about his fitness as a parent. Kyle was trying. She'd seen it over and over. What could she possibly object to in his bid for custody? Nothing. Any objections would be strictly due to hurt feelings over something that happened a decade ago. It was time to embrace the concept of bygones and move on.

"Men are nothing but trouble," Violet muttered darkly.

"That's not true," Clare corrected. "The right man is priceless."

"Parker is one in a million and he's taken. Unless you're willing to share?" Grace teased, and tried really hard to shut down the uncomfortable squeeze of jealousy surrounding her heart.

Clare had met her Dr. McDreamy. Grace had nothing. A great big void where Kyle used to be, and nothing had come along in ten years that could fill it. Well, except for the one man whom she suspected would fill that hole perfectly. She just had no desire to let him try, no matter how much she wanted a husband and family of her own.

Eyebrows raised, Clare cocked her head at Grace. "So you're sticking by your single-girl status, huh?"

She didn't sound so convinced, as if maybe Grace had been kidding when she'd vowed to be a Professional Single Girl from now on.

"I've been telling you so for months," Grace insisted. "There's nothing wrong with high standards and until I find someone who can spell *standards*, it's better to be on my own."

Actually, her standards weren't all that high—a run-of-the-mill swept-off-her-feet romance would do just fine. If she was pregnant and in love with a man who desperately loved her in return, she'd consider her life complete.

"Hear, hear." Violet raised her mug of hot tea to click it against Grace's wineglass. "I'll join your single girl club."

"Everyone is welcome. Except Clare." Grace grinned to cover the heaviness that had settled over her heart all at once. There wasn't anything on her horizon that looked like a fairy-tale romance. Just another meeting with a man who was driving her crazy.

Grace drove to Wade Ranch the next day without calling and without an appointment.

She didn't want to give Kyle any sort of heads-up that she was coming or that she'd made a decision. Hopefully, that meant she could get and keep the upper hand.

No more sunset conversations that ended with her wrapped up in Kyle's very strong, very capable arms.

No matter what. No matter how much she'd been arguing with herself that maybe Kyle had changed. Maybe *she* had changed. Maybe another kiss, exactly like that first one, would be what the doctor ordered, and then she would find out he'd morphed into her Prince Charming.

Yeah, none of that mattered.

Kyle and his daughters—that was what mattered. That morning she'd spent two hours in a room with her supervisor, Megan, going over her recommendation that Kyle be awarded full and uncontested custody of his children. With Megan's stamp of approval on the report, Grace's role in this long, drawn-out issue had come to a close.

Hadley answered the door at Wade House and asked after Grace's parents, then let Grace hold the babies without Grace having to beg too much. She inhaled their fresh powder scent—it was the best smell in the world. Out of nowhere, the prick of tears at her eyes warned her that she hadn't fully shut down the emotions from her conversation with Clare and Violet last night.

If this meeting went as intended, this might be her last

interaction with Kyle. And the babies. They were so precious and the thought of only seeing them again in passing shot through her heart.

"I'm here to see Kyle," she told Hadley as she passed the babies back reluctantly. She had a job to do, and it wasn't anyone's fault except hers that she didn't have a baby of her own.

"He's at the barn. Expect that will be the case from now on." Hadley shook her head in wonder. "I have to say, Kyle is nothing like I remember. He had no interest in the ranch before. Right? You remember that, too, don't you?"

Greedily, Grace latched on to the subject change and told herself it was strictly because she wanted additional validation that she was doing the right thing in trusting Kyle with his daughters. "I do recall that. But he's taking over the cattle side, or so I understand."

"That's right. Liam's about to come out of his skin, he's so excited about the prospect of focusing solely on his quarter horses. He didn't think Kyle was going to step up. But Liam has admitted to me, privately of course, that he might have been wrong about his brother."

Liam saw it, too. Kyle had changed.

That was very interesting food for thought.

"Do you think Kyle would mind if I visited him down at the barn? I need to talk to him about the report I'm filing."

Grace was already on her feet before she'd finished speaking, but Hadley just nodded with a smile. "Sure. Bring Kyle back with you and stay for lunch."

"Oh. Um…" Grace stared at Hadley gently rocking both babies in her arms and realized that her recommendations were going to affect Hadley and Liam, too. And not in a good way. She hated the fact that she was going to upset them after they'd spent so much love and effort in caring for Kyle's babies in his stead. There was a long conversation full of disappointment in Liam and Hadley's future.

All at once, she didn't want this job any longer. She should have figured out a way to pass the case off the moment she'd heard Kyle's name over the phone when Liam called. But she hadn't been able to, and people's lives were at stake here. She'd have to figure out how to handle it.

"Thanks for the lunch invite, but I have to be getting back to the office. Maybe next time," she said brightly, and escaped before Hadley could insist.

The cattle barn was a half mile down a chipped rock path to the west of Wade House, and faster than she would have liked, Grace pulled into the small clearing where a couple of other big trucks sat parked. She wandered into the barn, hoping Kyle would be inside.

He was.

The full force of his masculine beauty swept through her as she caught sight of him through the glass wall that partitioned the cattle office from the rest of the large barn. He was leaning against the frame of an open door, presumably talking to someone inside, hip cocked out in a way that should seem arrogant, but was just a testament to his incredible confidence.

Working man's jeans hugged his lean hips and yeah, he still had a prime butt that she didn't mind checking out in the slightest. There might be drool in her future.

And then Kyle backed out of the doorway and turned, catching her in the act of checking out his butt. *Shoot.* Too late, she spun around but not before witnessing the slow smile spreading across his face. How in the world was she going to brazen this out? Heat swirled through her cheeks.

Kyle exited the office area with a clatter. His eyes burned into her back and she had the distinct impression his gaze had dipped below her belt in a turnabout-is-fair-play-kind of checkout.

"Hey, Grace," he said pleasantly.

She couldn't very well ignore his greeting, so she sighed and faced him, smug smile and all. "Hi."

"See anything you like?"

How was she supposed to answer that? *Men*. They all had egos the size of Texas and she certainly wasn't going to cater to inflating his further. He was lucky she didn't smack him in his cocky mouth. "Nothing I haven't seen before."

Except she really shouldn't have been all high-and-mighty, when she was the one who'd been ogling his butt. It was her own darn fault she'd gotten caught.

"Really?" His eyebrows shot up and amusement played at his mouth. Not that she was staring at it or anything, or remembering how dark, hard and fierce that kiss had been. "You've been shopping for cattle before?"

"Cattle?" She made the mistake of meeting his glittery green eyes, vibrant even in the low light of the barn, and he sucked her in, mesmerizing her for a moment. "I...don't think... I'm not here to buy cattle."

Her fingers tingled all at once as they flexed in memory of clutching his shoulders the other night during their kiss. And then the rest of her body got in on that action, putting her somewhere in the vicinity of hot and bothered. A long liquid pull at her core distracted her entirely from whatever it was they were talking about.

"Are you sure? That's what we do here at Wade Ranch. Sell cattle. Figured you were in the market since you came all this way."

"Oh. No. No cattle." Geez, was there something wrong with her brain? Simple concepts like English and speaking didn't seem to be happening.

Kittens. Daffodils. She had to get her mind off that kiss with something that wasn't the slightest bit manly. But then Kyle shifted closer and she caught a whiff of something so wholly masculine and earthy and the slightest bit piney, it nearly made her weep with want.

"Well, then," he murmured. "Why are you here if it's not to peruse the goods?"

Oh, she was *so* here to peruse the goods. Except she wasn't and she couldn't keep falling down on the job. "I wanted to talk to you."

"Amazing coincidence. I wanted to talk to you, too."

"So I'm not bothering you?"

"Oh, yeah. Make no mistake, Grace. You bother me." His low, sexy voice skittered across her nerves, standing them on end. "At night, when I'm thinking about kissing you again. In the shower, when I'm *really* thinking about kissing you again. In the saddle, when I think kissing you again is the only thing that's going to make that particular position bearable."

A stupid rush of heat sprang up in her face as she pictured him riding a horse and caught his meaning.

It was uncomfortable for Kyle to sit in a saddle. Because he was turned on. By her.

It was embarrassing. And somehow empowering. The thrill of it sang through her veins. Being in love with Kyle she remembered. Being a source of discomfort, she didn't. Sex had been so new, so huge and so special the first time around. They hadn't really explored their physical relationship very thoroughly before everything had fallen apart due to Kyle's strange moods and inability to express his feelings for her.

She suddenly wondered what physical parts they'd left unexplored. And whether the superhot kiss—which had been vastly more affecting than the ones ten years ago—meant that he'd learned a few new tricks over the years.

"You've been thinking about our kiss, too?" she asked before she thought better of it.

"Too?" He picked up on that slip way too fast, his expression turning molten instantly as he zeroed in on her. "As in *also*? You've been thinking about it?"

He was aiming so much heat in her direction she thought she might melt from it.

"Um…" Well, it was too late to back out now. "Maybe once or twice. It was a nice kiss."

His slow smile set off warning bells. "*Nice*. I must be rusty if that's the best word you can come up with to describe it. Let me try again and I can guarantee *nice* won't be anywhere in your vocabulary afterward."

Before he could get started on that promise, she slapped a hand on his chest, and Lord have mercy, it was like concrete under her fingers, begging to be explored just to see if all of him was that hard.

"Not so fast," she muttered before she lost her mind completely. "I'm here in an official capacity."

"Well, why didn't you say so?"

"You were too busy trying to sell me a side of beef, if I recall," she responded primly, and his rich laugh nearly finished the job of melting her into a big puddle. She shouldn't let him affect her like that. Quickly, she snatched her hand back.

"Touché, Ms. Haines." He crossed his arms over his powerful chest and contemplated her, sobering slightly. "Is this about my girls?"

She nodded. "I've provided my recommendations in a report to my supervisor. But essentially, I have no objections to you having sole custody of your daughters."

Kyle let out a whoop and swept her up in his arms, spinning her around effortlessly. Laughing at his enthusiasm, she whacked him on the arm with token protests sputtering from her lips. This was not the appropriate way to thank his caseworker.

And then he let her slide to the floor again, much more

slowly than he should have, especially when it became clear that there was very little of him that wasn't hard.

She cleared her throat and stepped away.

"Thanks, Grace. This means a lot to me." Sincerity shone in his gaze and she couldn't look away. "So it's over? No more site visits?"

"Well…" She couldn't say it all at once. Her excuse to continue seeing him would evaporate if she said yes. "Maybe a few more. I still plan to keep an eye on you."

The vibe between them heated up again in a hurry as he leaned into her space. "But if you're not my daughters' caseworker any longer, then there's no reason I can't kiss you again."

True. But she couldn't have it both ways. Either she needed an excuse to keep coming by, even though that excuse would prevent anything from happening between them, or she could flat out admit she was still enormously attracted to him and let the chips fall where they may.

One option put butterflies in her stomach. And the other put caterpillars in it. The only problem was she couldn't figure out which was which.

"I'm not closing the case yet," she heard herself say before she'd fully planned to say it. "So I'll come by a couple more times, just to file additional support for the recommendation. It could still go the other way if anything changes."

"All right." He cocked his head. "But if you've already filed the report, there's no issue with your objectivity. Right?"

And maybe she should just call a spade a spade and settle things once and for all.

"Right. But—" she threw up a hand as a smile split his face "—that's not the only thing going on here, Kyle, and you know it. We haven't been a couple for a long time, and

I'm not sure picking up where we left off is the best idea. Not saying never. Just give me space for now."

So she could think. So she could figure out if she was willing to trust him again. So she could understand why everything between them felt so different this time, so much more dangerous and thrilling.

He nodded once, but the smile still plastered across his face said he wasn't convinced by her speech. Maybe because she hadn't convinced herself of it, either.

"You know where to find me. If you'll excuse me, I have some cattle to tend to."

She watched him walk off because she couldn't help herself apparently. And she had a feeling that was going to become a theme very shortly when interacting with Kyle Wade.

Six

Kyle didn't see Grace for a full week, and by the seventh day, he was starting to go a little bonkers. He couldn't stop thinking about her, about picking up that kiss again. Especially now that the conflict of interest had vanished.

But then she'd thrown up another wall—the dreaded *give me space*. He hated space. Unless he was the one creating it.

So instead of calling up Grace and asking her on a date the way he wanted to, he filled his days with things such as learning how to worm cattle alongside Doc Glade and his nights learning which of his daughters liked to be held a certain way.

It was fulfilling in a way he'd have never guessed.

And exhausting. Far more than going for days at a stretch with no sleep as he and his boys cleared a bayside warehouse of nasty snipers so American supply ships could dock without fear of being shot at.

Kyle would have sworn up and down that being a SEAL

had prepared him for any challenge, but he'd been able to perform that job with a sense of detachment. Oh, he'd cared, or he would never have put himself in the line of fire. But you had to march into a war knowing you might not come out. Knowing that you might cause someone else to not come out. There was no room for emotion in the middle of that.

Being a father? It was 100 percent raw emotion, 24-7. Fear that he was doing it wrong. Joy in simply holding another human being that was a part of him, who shared his DNA. Worry that he'd screw up his kids as his parents had done to him. A slight tickle in the back of his throat that it could all change tomorrow if Grace suddenly decided that she'd made a mistake in awarding him custody.

But above all else was the sense that he shouldn't be doing it by himself. Kids needed a mother. Hadley was nurturing and clearly cared about the babies, but she was Liam's wife, not Kyle's. Now that the news had come out about Grace's recommendations, it didn't seem fair to keep asking Hadley to be the nanny, not when she'd hoped to adopt the babies herself.

It was another tangle he didn't know how to unsnarl, so he left it alone until he could figure it out. Besides, no one was chomping at the bit to change the current living situation and for now, Kyle, Liam and Hadley shared Wade House with Maggie and Maddie. Which meant that it would be ridiculous to tell Hadley not to pick up one of his daughters when she cried. So he didn't.

Plus, he was deep in the middle of growing the cattle business. Calving season was upon them, which meant days and days of backbreaking work to make sure the babies survived, or the ranch lost money instantly. He couldn't spend ten or twelve hours a day at the cattle barn *and* take care of babies. That was his rationale anyway, and he repeated it to himself often. Some days it rang more true than others.

A week after Grace had told him he'd earned custody of his daughters, Kyle spent thirty horrific minutes in his office going through email and other stuff Ivy, Wade Ranch's bookkeeper and office manager, had dumped on his desk with way too cheery a smile. The woman was sadistic. Death by paper cuts might as well be Ivy's mantra.

God, he hated paperwork. He'd rather be hip-deep in manure than scanning vet reports and sales figures and bills and who knew what all.

A knock at his door saved him. He glanced up to see a smiling Emma Jane and he nearly wept in relief. Emma Jane had the best title in the whole world—sales manager—which meant he didn't have to talk to people who wanted to buy Wade Angus. She handled everything and he blessed her for it daily.

"Hey, boss," she drawled. "Got a minute?"

She always called him "boss" with a throaty undertone that made him vaguely uncomfortable, as if any second now, she might declare a preference for being dominated and fall at his feet, prostrate.

"For you, always." He kicked back from the desk and crossed his arms as the sales manager came into his office. "What's up?"

With a toss of her long blond hair, Emma Jane sashayed over to his desk and perched one hip on the edge, careful to arrange her short skirt so it revealed plenty of leg. Kyle hid a grin, mostly because he didn't want to encourage her. God love her, but Emma Jane had the subtlety of a Black Hawk helicopter coming in for landing.

"I was thinking," she murmured with a coy smile. "We've mostly been selling cattle here locally, but we should look to expand. There's a big market in Fort Worth."

Obviously she was going somewhere with this, so Kyle

just nodded and made a noncommittal sound as he waited for the punch line.

"Wade Ranch needs to make some contacts there," she continued, and rearranged her hair with a practiced twirl. "We should go together. Like a business trip, but stay overnight and take in the sights. Maybe hit a bar in Sundance Square?"

First half of that? Great plan. Spot-on. Second half was so not a good idea, Kyle couldn't even begin to count the ways it wasn't a good idea. But he had to tread carefully. Wade Ranch couldn't afford for Kyle to antagonize another employee into quitting. Liam still hadn't replaced Danny Spencer, and Kyle was starting to worry his brother was going to announce that he'd decided *Kyle* should be the ranch manager.

"I like the way you think," he allowed. "You're clearly the brains of this operation."

She batted her lashes with a practiced laugh, leaning forward to increase the gap at her cleavage. "You're such a flatterer. Go on."

Since it didn't feel appropriate for the boss to be staring down the front of his employee's blouse, no matter how obvious she was making it that she expected him to, Kyle glanced over Emma Jane's shoulder to the window. And spied the exact person he'd been hoping to see. *Grace.* Finally.

He'd been starting to wonder if she was planning to avoid him for the next ten years. From the corner of his eye, he watched her park her green Toyota in the small clearing outside the barn and walk the short path to the door. His peripheral vision was sharp enough to see a sniper in a bell tower at the edge of a village—or one social worker with hair the color of summer wheat at sunset, who had recently asked Kyle to give her space.

"No, really," he insisted as he focused on Emma Jane

again. Grace had just entered the barn, judging by the sound of the footsteps coming toward his office, which he easily recognized as hers. "You've been handling cattle sales for what, almost a year now? Your numbers are impressive. Clearly you know your stuff."

Or she knew how to stick her breasts in a prospective buyer's face. Honestly, there was no law against it, and he didn't care how she sold cattle as long as she did her job. Just as there was no law against letting Grace think there was more going on here in his office than there actually was.

She wanted space, didn't she? Couldn't give a woman any more space than to pretend he'd moved on to another one. If he timed it right, Grace would get an eyeful of exactly how much *space* he was giving her. He treated Emma Jane to a wide smile and put an elbow on the desk, right by her knee.

Emma Jane lit up, just as Grace appeared in the open doorway of his office.

"Thanks, sweetie." Emma Jane smiled and ran one hand up his arm provocatively. He didn't remove it. "That's the nicest compliment anyone's ever given me."

Grace halted as if she'd been slapped. That's when he turned his head to meet her gaze, acknowledging her presence, just in case she'd gotten it into her head to flee. She was right where he wanted her.

"Am I interrupting?" Grace asked drily, and Emma Jane jerked back guiltily as she figured out they weren't alone anymore.

Yes, thank God. He'd have to deal with Emma Jane at some point, but he couldn't lie—he'd much rather have Grace sitting on his desk and leaning over strategically any day of the week and twice on Sunday.

"Not at all." Kyle stood with a dismissive nod at Emma Jane, whose usefulness had just come to an end. "We were just talking about how to increase our contact list in the Fort Worth area. We can pick it up later."

"We sure can," Emma Jane purred, and then shot Grace a dirty look as she flounced from the room.

"That was cozy," Grace commented once the sales manager was out of earshot. Her face was blank, but her tone had an undercurrent in it that he found very interesting.

"You think so?" Kyle crossed his arms and cocked a hip, pretending to contemplate. "We were just talking. I'm not sure what you mean."

Grace rolled her eyes. "Really, Kyle? She was practically draped over your desk like a bearskin throw rug, begging you to wrap her around you."

Yeah. She pretty much had been. He bit back a grin at Grace's colorful description. "I didn't notice."

"Of course you didn't." Her eyebrows snapped together over brown eyes that—dare he hope—had a hint of jealousy glittering in them. "You were too busy being blinded by her cleavage."

That got a laugh out of him, which didn't sit well with Grace, judging by the fierce scowl on her face. But he couldn't help it. This was too much fun. "She is a nice-looking woman, I do agree."

"I didn't say that. She's far too obvious to be considered 'nice-looking.'" Grace accompanied this with little squiggly motions of her forefingers. "She might as well write her phone number on her forehead with eyeliner. She clearly buys it in bulk and layers it on even at ten o'clock in the morning, so what's a little more?"

The more Grace talked, the more agitated she became, drawing in the air with her whole hand instead of just her fingers.

"So she's a little heavy-handed with her makeup." He waved it off. "She's a great girl who sells cattle for Wade Ranch. I have no complaints with her."

Grace made a little noise of disgust. "Except for the way she was shamelessly flirting with you, you mean? I can't believe you let her talk to you like that."

"Like what?" He shrugged, well aware he was pouring gasoline on Grace's fire, but so very curious what would happen when she exploded. "We were just talking."

"Yeah, you're still just as clueless as you always were."

There was that word again. *Clueless*. She'd thrown it at him one too many times to let it go. There was something more here to understand. He could sense it.

Before he could demand an explanation, Johnny blew into the office, his chest heaving and mud caked on his jeans and boots from the knee down. "Kyle. We got a problem. One of the pregnant cows is stuck in the ravine at the creek and she went into labor."

Instantly, Kyle shouldered past a wide-eyed Grace with an apologetic glance. He hated to leave her behind but this was his job.

"Take me there."

Liam had put Kyle in charge of the cattle side of Wade Ranch. This was his first real test and the gravity of it settled across his shoulders with weight he wasn't expecting.

He followed Johnny to the paddock where they kept their horses and mounted up, ignoring the twinge deep in his leg bone, or what was left of it. He could sit in his office like a wimp and complain about paperwork or ride. There was no room for a busted leg in ranching.

Kyle heeled Lightning Rod into a gallop and tore after Johnny as the ranch hand led him across the pasture where the pregnant herd had been quartered—to prevent the very problem Johnny had described. The expectant cows shouldn't have been anywhere near the creek that ran along the north side of Wade Ranch.

Kyle hadn't been there in years but he remembered it. He and Liam had played there as boys, splashing through the shallow water and gigging for frogs at dusk as the fat reptiles croaked out their location to the two bloodthirsty boys. Calvin had made them clean and dress the frogs when he found out, and they had frog legs for dinner that night. It was a lesson Kyle never forgot—eat what you kill.

They arrived at the edge of the pasture in a couple of minutes. A fence was down. That explained it.

"What happened?" Kyle asked as he swung out of the saddle to inspect the downed barbed wire and wooden stake.

"Not sure. Slim and I were running the fence and found this. Then he went to the creek to check it out. Sure 'nuff, one of the cows had wandered off. Still don't know how she got down there. Slim stayed with her while I came and got you."

"Good man. Hustle back to the barn and grab some of the guys to get this repaired," Kyle instructed, his mind already blurring with a plan. He just had to check out the situation to make sure the extraction process currently mapping itself out in his head was viable.

Johnny nodded and galloped off.

Kyle let Lightning Rod pick his way along the line of the creek until he saw Slim down in the ravine, hovering over the cow. She was still standing, which was good. As soon as a cow lay down, that meant they had less than an hour until she'd start delivering. They'd have to work fast or she'd be having her baby on that thin strip of ground between the steeply sloped walls and the creek. If the calf was in the wrong position, it would be too hard to assist with the birth, and besides, all the equipment was back at the barn.

Somehow, he had to figure out how to get her out. Immediately. Clearly, Slim had no idea how to do it or he wouldn't have sent Johnny after the boss. This was Kyle's battle to lose. So he wouldn't lose.

Kyle galloped another hundred feet to check out the slope of the creek bed walls, but they were just as steep all the way down the culvert as they were at the site where the cow had gone down. As steep as they'd been when he was a boy. He and Liam had slid down the slope on their butts, ruining more than one pair of pants in the process because it was too steep to walk down. But that had been in August when it was dry. In March, after a cold winter and wet spring, the slope was nothing but mud. Which probably explained how the cow had ended up at the bottom—she'd slipped.

Kyle planned to use that slick consistency to his advantage.

"Slim," he called down. "You okay for another few minutes? I have to run back to the barn to get a couple of things, and then we're gonna haul her out."

Slim eyed Kyle and then the cow. "*Haul* her out? That's a dumb idea. And not what Danny Spencer would have done."

Too bad. Wade Ranch was stuck with Kyle, not the former ranch manager. "Yep."

Not much else to say. It wasn't as if he planned to blubber all over Slim and ask for a chance to prove he could be as good as Spencer. He firmed his mouth and kept the rest inside. Like always.

The ranch hand nodded, but his expression had that I'll-believe-it-when-I-see-it vibe.

Kyle galloped back to the barn and found exactly what he was looking for—the pair of hundred-foot fire hoses Calvin had always kept on hand in case of emergency. They'd been retrofitted with a mechanism that screwed into the water reservoir standing next to the barn. The stock was too valuable to wait on the city fire brigade in the event of a barn fire, so a smart rancher developed his own firefighting strategy.

Today, the hoses were going to lift a cow out of a creek bed.

Kyle jumped into the Wade Ranch Chevy parked near the barn and drove across the pasture, dodging cows and the stretches of grass that served as their grazing ground as best he could. Fortunately, Johnny and the other hands hadn't fixed the fence yet, so Kyle drove right through the break to the edge of the creek.

By the time he skidded to a halt, the hands had gathered around to watch the show. There was no time to have a conversation about this idea, nor did Kyle need anyone else's approval, so if they didn't like it, they could keep it to themselves. Grimly, Kyle pulled the hoses from the truck bed and motioned to Johnny.

"I'm going to tie these to the trailer hitch and then throw them down to Slim. I'll rappel down and back up again once we have the hoses secured around the cow. You drive while I watch the operation. We'll haul her out with good old-fashioned brute strength."

Johnny and the other hands looked dubious but Kyle ignored them and got to work on tying the hoses, looping one end around the trailer hitch into a figure-eight follow-through knot. It was the best knot to avoid slipping and his go-to, but he'd never used it on a fire hose. Hopefully it would hold, especially given that he was the one who would be doing the rappelling without a safety harness.

When the hoses were as secure as a former SEAL could get them, Kyle tossed the ends down to Slim and repeated the plan. Slim, thankfully, just nodded and didn't bother to express his opinion about the chances of success, likely because he figured it was obvious.

Kyle waited for Slim to drop the hoses, and then grabbed on to one. His work gloves gripped better than he was expecting, a plus, given the width of the line. Definitely not the kind of rappelling he was used to, but he probably had more experience at this kind of rescue than anyone there.

He'd lost count of the number of times he'd led an extraction in hostile conditions with few materials at his disposal. And usually he was doing it with a loaded pack and weapons strapped to his back. Going down into a ravine after a cow was a piece of cake in comparison.

Until his boot slipped.

His bad leg slammed into the ground and he bit back a curse as a white-hot blade of pain arced through his leg. *Idiot.* He should have counterbalanced differently to compensate for his cowboy boots, which were great for riding, but not so much for slick mud.

Sweat streamed down his back and beaded up on his forehead, instantly draining down into his eyes, blinding him. Now his hell was complete. And he was only halfway down.

Muttering the lyrics to a Taylor Swift song that had always been his battle cry, he focused on the words instead of the pain. The happy tune reminded him there was still good in the world, reminded him of the innocent teenagers sitting at home in their bright, colorful rooms listening to the same song. They depended on men like Kyle to keep them safe. He'd vowed with his very life that he would. And he'd carried that promise into the darkest places on the planet while singing that song.

Finally, he reached the bottom and took a quarter of a second to catch his breath as he surveyed the area. Cow still standing. Hoses still holding. He nodded to Slim and they got to work leading the cow as close to the slope as possible, which wasn't easy, considering she was in labor, scared and had the brain of a—well, a cow.

The next few minutes blurred as Kyle worked alongside Slim, but eventually they got the makeshift harness in place. Kyle hefted the heavy hoses over his shoulder and climbed back up the way he'd come. The men had shuffled to the edge of the ravine to watch, backing up the closer Kyle got to the top. He hit the dirt at the edge and rolled onto the hoses to keep them from sliding back to the bottom.

He was not making that climb again.

Johnny grabbed hold of the hoses so Kyle could stand, and then made short work of tying them to the trailer hitch next to the other ends. He waved at Johnny to get in the truck. It was do-or-die time.

Johnny gunned the engine.

"Slow," Kyle barked.

The truck inched forward, pulling up all the slack in the hoses. And then the tires bit into the ground as the truck strained against the load. The cow balked but the hoses held her in place. So far so good.

The hoses gradually pulled the cow onto her side and inched her up the slope as the truck revved forward a bit more. It was working. The mud helped her slide, though she mooed something fierce the whole time.

Miraculously, after ten nail-biting minutes, the cow stood on solid ground at the top of the ravine. Kyle's arms ached and his gloves had rubbed raw places on his fingers, but it was done.

Johnny jumped from the truck and rushed over to clap him on the back, breaking the invisible barrier around Kyle. The other ranch hands swarmed around as well, smiling and giving their own version of a verbal high-five. Even Slim offered a somewhat solemn, "Good job."

Kyle took it all with good humor and few words because what was he supposed to say? *Told you so? That's okay, boys. I'm the boss for a reason?*

The ranch hands wandered off, presumably to finish the job of fixing the fence. Eventually, Kyle stood there, alone. Which was par for the course.

Was it so bad to have hoped this would become his new team?

No. The bad part was that if a successful bovine extraction couldn't solidify his place, he suspected nothing would. Because everyone was still waiting around for him to either fail or leave. Except Kyle.

Even Grace didn't fully believe in him yet, or she wouldn't have qualified her recommendations with a "We'll see," and the threat that she wasn't closing the case.

What more did he have to do to prove that honor, integrity and loyalty were in his very fiber?

Grace stood at the wide double door of the barn and watched horses spill into the yard as the hands returned from the cow emergency. They dismounted and loudly recounted the rescue with their own versions of the story. Seems as if Kyle had used fire hoses to drag the animal out of the ravine, which the hands alternately thought was ingenious or crazy depending on who was doing the talking.

Apparently it had worked, since one of the ranch hands had the cow in question on a short lead.

She should have left. She'd told Kyle what she'd come to say, witnessed an exchange between Kyle and another woman that she hadn't been meant to see, and now she was done. But you could have cut the tension in the barn with a chain saw, and she'd been a little bit worried about Kyle. Sure, he'd grown up on the ranch, but that didn't automatically make him accident-proof.

No one mentioned anything about Kyle, so he must be okay. But she wanted to see him for herself. Once she'd assured herself of it—strictly in her capacity as his daughters' caseworker, of course, no other reason—then she'd leave.

Finally, the truck he'd taken off in rolled into the yard and he swung out of the cab, muddy and looking so worn, she almost flew to his side. Except the little blonde bearskin rug beat her to it. Emma Jane. Or as Grace privately liked to call her—The Tart.

Like a hummingbird auditioning for the part of the town harlot, Emma Jane fluttered over to Kyle, expertly sashaying across the uneven ground in her high-heeled boots, which drew the attention of nearly every male still milling around the yard, except the one she was after.

Kyle pulled long lines of flat, muddy hoses out of the bed of the truck, dragged them to the spigot on the water tower beside the barn and attached one, using it to hose off the other.

Which was also pretty ingenious in her opinion.

Emma Jane crowded Kyle at the water tower, smiling and gesturing. Grace was too far away to hear what she was saying, but she probably didn't need to hear it to know it was along the lines of *Oh, Kyle, you're a hero* or the even more inane *Oh, Kyle, you're so strong and brave!*

Please. Well, yes, he was all of those things, no question, but Grace didn't see the point in shoving half-exposed breasts in a man's face when you said them.

The strong and brave hero in question glanced up at Emma Jane as he performed his task. And smiled. It was his slow, slightly naughty smile that he'd flashed Grace right after kissing her senseless, the one that had nearly enticed her back into his arms because it was so sexy.

It was a smile that told a woman he liked what he saw, that he had a few thoughts about what he planned to do with her. And there he was, aiming it at another woman!

That…*dog.*

Breathe, Grace. He was just smiling.

She crossed her arms, leaning forward involuntarily though there was no way she would be able to pick up the conversation from this distance, not with the clatter going on in the yard, all the hands still chattering and watering their horses at the trough running between the water tower and the barn.

Then Emma Jane placed her talons on Kyle's arm and he leaned into it. Something hot bloomed in Grace's chest as she imagined him kissing Emma Jane the way he'd kissed her. He said something to Emma Jane over his shoulder and she laughed. Grace didn't have to hear what was being said. He was enjoying Emma Jane's attention, obviously.

Or he was just washing a hose and having a conversation with his employee, which was none of her business, she reminded herself. She didn't own Kyle, and he'd certainly had female companions over the years who weren't Grace, or he wouldn't currently have two daughters.

She'd just never had that shoved in her face so blatantly before.

Now would be a great time to leave. Except as she started back to her car, Kyle stood and walked straight toward her, calling to one of the hands to lay the hoses out to dry before putting them away. Emma Jane trailed him, still chattering.

He was coming to talk to Grace. With Emma Jane in tow.

Or Kyle could be walking toward the barn. Grace *was* standing in the doorway.

But then his gaze met hers and the rest of the activity in the yard fell away as something wholly encompassing washed through her.

Seven

"Ms. Haines." Kyle nodded.

And then walked right past her!

Had she just been dismissed? Grace scowled and pivoted to view the interior of the barn. Kyle squeezed Emma Jane's shoulder at the door of the office and The Tart disappeared beyond the glass, presumably to go sharpen her claws.

Then he strolled across the wide center of the barn and disappeared around a corner.

Without a single ounce of forethought, Grace charged after him. She'd waited around, half-crazy with worry to assure herself he was okay, and he couldn't bother to stop and talk to her? How dare he? Emma Jane had certainly gotten more than a perfunctory nod and a platitude.

She skidded around the corner, an admonishment already forming in her mouth.

It vanished as she rounded the corner into a small, enclosed area. Kyle stood at a long washbasin. *Wet. Shirtless. Oh, my.*

Obviously she should have thought this through a little better.

Speechless, she stared unashamedly at his bare, rippling torso as he dumped another cupful of water down it. Water streamed along the cut muscles, running in rivulets through the channels to disappear into the fabric of his jeans.

Some of it splashed on her. She was too close. And way too far.

Every ounce of saliva fled from her mouth, and she couldn't have torn her gaze from his gorgeous body for a million dollars. She'd have *paid* a million dollars, if she'd had it, to stand in this spot for an eternity.

"Something else you wanted, Ms. Haines?"

She blinked and glanced up into his diamond-hard green eyes, which were currently fastened on her as he glanced over his shoulder. Busted. Again. There was no way to spin this into anything other than it was. "I didn't know you were washing up. Sorry."

Casually, he turned and leaned back against the long sink, arms at his side, which left that delicious panorama of naked chest right there on display. "That really didn't answer my question, now, did it?"

He was turning her brain mushy again, because she surely would have remembered if there had been talking. "Did you ask me a question?"

His soft laugh crawled under her skin. "Well, I'm trying to figure out what it is that you're after, Grace. Maybe I should ask a different way. Are you here to watch, or join in? Because either is fine with me."

Her ire rushed back all at once, melding uncomfortably with the heat curling through her midsection at the suggestion. "That's a fine way to talk after flirting with Ms. Cattle Queen."

Kyle just raised an eyebrow. "Careful, or a man might start to think you cared whether he flirted with another woman. That's not the case. Right?"

She crossed her arms, but those diamond-hard eyes drilled through her anyway. "Oh, you're right. I don't care." Loftily, she waved off his question. "It just seems disingenuous to make time with one woman mere minutes before inviting another one to *wash up*."

All at once, she had a very clear image of him dumping a cup of water over her chest and licking it off. The heat in her core snaked outward, engulfing her whole body. And that just made her even madder. Kyle was a big flirt who could get Grace hot with merely a glance. It wasn't fair.

She didn't remember him affecting her that way before. And she would have. This was all new and exciting and frustrating and scary.

"Maybe." That slow smile spilled onto his face. "But you're the one standing here. I'm not offering to *wash up* with Emma Jane."

"Yeah. Only because she didn't have the foresight to follow you."

"You did." He watched her without blinking and spread his arms. "Here I am. Whatever are you going to do with me?"

That tripped off a whole chain reaction inside as she thought long and hard about the answer to that question. But she hadn't followed him for *that*. Not that she knew for sure he even meant *that*. But regardless, he had a lot of nerve.

Hands firmly on her hips—just in case they developed a mind of their own and started wandering along the ridges and valleys of that twelve-pack of abs, which she was ashamed to admit she'd counted four times—she glared at him. "This is not you, Kyle. Liam? Yeah. He's a playboy and a half, but you've never been like that, just looking for the next notch in your bedpost."

There. That was the point she was trying to make.

He laughed with genuine mirth. "Is that what you think this is? Kyle Wade, playboy in training. It has a nice ring. But that ain't what's going on."

"Then by all means. Tell me what's going on," she allowed primly.

"Emma Jane is my employee. That's it." He sliced the air with his hand. "You, on the other hand, are something else."

"Oh, yeah? What?"

He swept her with a once-over that should not have been so affecting, but goodness, even the bottoms of her feet heated up. "A woman I'd like to kiss. A lot."

As in he wanted to kiss her several times or he just wanted to really badly?

She shook her head. Didn't matter.

"Well, be that as it may." She tossed her head, scrambling to come up with a response, and poked him in the chest for emphasis. He glanced down at her finger and back up at her, his eyelids shuttered slightly. "You wanted to kiss Emma Jane a minute ago. Pardon me for not getting in line."

"Grace." Her name came out so garbled, she hardly recognized it. "I do not want to kiss Emma Jane."

"Could have fooled me. And her. She definitely had the impression you were into her. Maybe because you were telling her jokes and letting her put her hands all over you."

"And maybe I let her because I knew you were watching."

"I— What?" All the air vanished from her lungs instantly. And then she found it again. "It was on purpose? Flirting with Emma Jane. You did that on *purpose*?" She was screeching. Dang near high enough to call dogs from another county. "Oh, that's…"

She couldn't think of a filthy enough word to describe it. *He'd been playing her.* Kyle Wade had picked her up and played her like a violin. Of course he had. She might as well have Bad Judge of Character tattooed on her forehead so people could get busy right away with pulling one over on her. And she'd waltzed to his tune with nary a peep.

And speaking of no peeps, Kyle was standing there watching her without saying a word, the big jerk.

"It was all a lie?" she asked rhetorically, because he'd just said it was, though why he'd done it, she couldn't fathom. "What were you trying to accomplish, anyway?"

His grin slipped as he pinned her in place with nothing more than his gaze. He swayed forward, just a bit, but his heat reached out and slid along her skin as if he'd actually brushed her torso with his.

She couldn't move. Didn't want to move. The play of expression across his face fascinated her. The heat called to her.

"No lies. See this," he murmured and wagged a finger between them, drawing her eye as he nearly touched her but didn't. "Just what you ordered. Space. Anytime you feel inclined to make it disappear, I'll be the one over here minding my own business."

Oh! Of all the sneaky, underhanded, completely accurate things to say.

Mute, she stared at him and he stared right back. He'd been giving her exactly what she asked for. Never mind that she'd rather drink paint thinner than admit he might have a point. And the solution was rather well spelled out, too.

She didn't want him to flirt with other women? Then close the gap.

There was no more running, no more hiding. This was it, right here. He wanted her. But he wasn't going to act on it.

They shared a fierce attraction and the past was in the past. She'd held him at bay in order to get her feet under her, to make sure he wasn't going to hurt her again. It was the same tactic she employed with her cases. If she wanted to be sure she wasn't letting her emotions get the best of her, wanted to be sure she was making an unbiased decision, she stepped back. Assessed from afar with impersonal attention.

This wasn't one of her cases. This was Kyle. As personal as it got. And the only way she could fully assess what they could have now was to dive into that pool. Wading in an inch at a time wasn't working.

Rock solid, not moving a muscle, he watched her. This was her show and he was subtly telling her he'd let her run it. Except he was also saying she couldn't keep talking out of both sides of her mouth.

Either she could act like a full-grown woman and do something about the man she wanted or keep letting their interaction devolve into an amateurish high school game.

She picked doing something.

Going on instinct alone, she reached out with both hands and pressed them to Kyle's bare chest, her gaze on his as she did it, gauging his reaction. His eyes darkened as her fingers spread and she flattened both palms across his pectoral muscles. Damp. Hot. Hard.

One muscle flexed under her touch and she almost yanked her hands back. But she didn't. He hadn't felt like this before. He was all man and it was a serious turn-on, especially because it was still Kyle underneath. When he was looking at her the way he was right then, as if the center of the universe had been deposited in his palm, it was easy to remember why she'd fallen for him. All the emotion of being in love with this man rushed back.

"There you go," she said breathlessly. "No more space."

"Grace," he growled, and she felt the vibrations under her fingers. "You better mean it. I'm only human."

Her touch was affecting him. *She* was affecting *him*. It was something she hadn't fully contemplated, but she did get that it wasn't fair to lead him on and keep dancing back and forth between yes and no.

"I mean it. If you want to kiss me, it's fine."

"*Fine.*" There came that slow smile. "That's almost as bad a word as *nice*. I think it's time to fix your vocabulary."

All at once, Kyle's arms snaked around her, yanking her tight against his hard body. But before she could fully register the contact, his mouth claimed hers.

The crash of lips startled her. And then she couldn't think at all as his hands slid down her back, touching her, trailing heat along her spine, sliding oh, so slowly against her bottom to finally grip her hips and hold them firmly, pulling her taut against his body.

His very aroused body. The length of him pressed into her soft flesh as he kissed her. It was a whole-body experience, and nothing like the front porch kiss that she'd thought was so memorable that she couldn't shake it. That kiss had been wonderful, but tame.

This was a grown-up kiss.

The difference was unfathomable.

This kiss was hungry, questing, begging for more even as he took it.

Kyle changed the angle, diving deeper into her mouth, thrilling her with the intensity. His tongue swirled out, and instinctively, she met him with her own. He groaned and she felt it to her toes.

Kyle. She'd missed the feel of him in her arms. Missed the scent of him in her nose.

Except this Kyle wasn't like the warm coat she'd envisioned sliding into, wholly familiar and so comforting.

No, this Kyle was like opening a book expecting a nice story with an interesting plot and instead falling into an immersive world full of dark secrets and darker passions.

His hands were everywhere, along her sides, thumbs circling and sliding higher until he found her breasts beneath her clothes. The contact shot through her as he touched her, and then he shoved a leg between hers, tilting his hips to rub against her intimately.

This was not a kiss—it was a seduction.

And she had just enough functioning brain cells to be aware that they were not only in a barn, but she hadn't fully figured out what was supposed to come next. She didn't know what had changed that might mean things would work between them this time. She didn't fully trust that he was here for good, and even if he was, that he was going to meet her standards any better today than he had ten years ago.

Oh, he was certainly earning a ten in the Sweeping Her Off Her Feet category. But Happily Ever After carried just as much weight as Expressing His Feelings. And neither of those were on the board yet.

Breaking off the kiss—and nearly kicking herself at the same time—she pushed back and mumbled, "Wait."

His torso shuddered as he dragged in a ragged breath. "Because?"

"You know why." Her Professional Single Girl status was in jeopardy and she had to make sure he was worth the price of relinquishing it. Sure, he was hot and a really great kisser, but she didn't sleep around. An interlude in the barn didn't change that.

"I did not develop ESP at any point in the last ten years," he rasped, his expression going blank as he stared at her.

"Because of what happened before, Kyle." Exasperated, she stared at the wall over his head so his delicious chest wasn't right in her field of vision. "There's a lot of leftover emotion and scrambled-up stuff to sort out. I have to take it slow this time."

"Then you should leave," he said curtly. "Because I'm definitely not in the mood for slow right now."

She took his advice and fled. It wasn't until she'd reached her car and slid into the driver's seat that she realized leaving was the one surefire way to *never* figure out what they could have together.

Maybe slow wasn't any better an idea than space.

And at this moment, the only *s* word she seemed capable of thinking about ended in *ex*, which was the crux of the problem. She and Kyle had a former relationship and it muddied everything, especially her feelings.

Kyle stabbed his hands through his shirt, nearly ripping the sleeve off in the process.

Grace wanted to take it *slow* because of what had happened before.

Furiously, he fingered the buttons through the holes haphazardly, none too happy about having to spend the rest of the workday with a hard-on he couldn't get rid of, no matter what he thought of to kill his arousal—slugs, the Cowboys losing the Super Bowl, his mother. Nothing worked because the feel of Grace in his arms was way too fresh, and had been cut way too short.

Because of what had happened *before*. She meant when she'd fallen for Liam and he'd thrown her over. While Kyle appreciated that she wanted to figure out her own mind before taking things further with him, he wasn't about to stand by and let what happened in the past with his brother ruin the present.

Liam was married now and Grace should be completely over all of that. Bygones included forgetting about *everything* that happened in the past.

He didn't have any choice but to let it go for the time being. He had a job to do and men to manage.

By the time the sun set, the entire Wade Ranch staff was giving Kyle a wide berth. So the cow extraction hadn't earned him any points. Figured. His surly mood didn't help and he finally just called it a day.

When he got back to the main house, Liam met him in the mudroom off the back.

"Hey," Liam called as Kyle sat on the long bench seat to remove his boots, which were a far sight cleaner than they'd been earlier, but still weren't fit to walk the floors inside.

Kyle jerked his chin, not trusting himself to actually speak to anyone civilly. Though if anyone deserved the brunt of his temper, it was Liam.

"Hadley and I are flying to Vail this weekend. Just wanted to give you a heads-up." Liam's mouth tightened. "You'll be okay handling the babies for a couple of days by yourself, right?"

"Yep."

Liam hesitated, clearly expecting more of a conversation or maybe even an argument about it, but what else was there to say? Kyle couldn't force the couple to stay, and Maddie and Maggie were his kids. He'd figure it out. Somehow. The little pang in his stomach must be left over from Grace. Probably.

"Okay. We're leaving in an hour or so."

Kyle let the first boot hit the floor with a resounding *thunk* and nodded. Liam kept talking.

"I'm flying my Cessna, so it's no problem to delay for a bit if you need to talk to Hadley about anything."

The other boot hit the floor. Hadley had already imparted as much baby knowledge as she possibly could. Another hour of blathering wasn't going to make a difference. "Not necessary."

Liam still didn't leave. "You have my cell phone number. It's okay if you want to call and ask questions."

"Yep."

Geez. Was his brother really that much of an ass? Liam had taken care of the babies before Kyle had gotten there without anyone standing over him waiting for his first mistake. Did Liam really think babysitting was something only he could do and that Kyle was hopelessly inept? Seemed so. Which only set Kyle's resolve.

He wouldn't call. Obviously Liam and Hadley had plans that didn't include taking care of Kyle's children. Who was he to stand in the way of that? Never mind that Kyle had never even stayed alone in the house with the babies. Hadley had always just been there, ready to pick up the slack.

This was the part where Kyle wished he had someone like Hadley. His kids needed a mother. Problem was, he could only picture Grace's face when thinking of a likely candidate. And she was too skittish about *everything*. Mentioning motherhood would likely send her over the edge.

Finally, Liam shuffled off to finish packing or whatever, leaving Kyle to his morose thoughts. It was fine, really. So he'd envisioned asking Grace if she'd like to drive into Odessa for dinner and a movie. Get out of Royal, where there were no prying eyes. Maybe he would have even talked her into spending the night in a swanky motel. He had scads of money he never spent and he couldn't think of anyone he'd rather spend it on than Grace.

Guess that wasn't happening. A grown-up field trip didn't sound too much like Grace's definition of *slow* anyway, so it hardly mattered that his half-formed plan wasn't going to work out.

No matter. He'd spend the weekend with his daughters and it would be great. They'd bond and his love for them would grow. Maybe this was actually a good step toward relieving Hadley permanently of her baby duties. He could keep telling himself that she loved them and didn't mind taking care of his daughters all he wanted, but at the end of the day, it was just an excuse.

He'd decided to stay in Royal, taking a job managing the cattle side of Wade Ranch, and it was time for him to man up and start building the family life his daughters needed.

Liam and Hadley left in a flurry of instructions and worried backward glances until finally Kyle was alone with Maddie and Maggie. That little pang in his stomach was back and he pushed on it with his thumb. The feeling didn't go away and started resembling panic more than anything else.

God Almighty. Maddie and Maggie were babies, for crying out loud. Kyle had faced down a high-ranking, card-carrying member of the Taliban with less sweat.

He wandered into the nursery and thought about covering his eyes to shield them from all the pink. But there his girls were. Two of 'em. Staring up at him with the slightly unfocused, slightly bemused expression his daughters seemed to favor. The babies were kind of sweet when they weren't crying.

They couldn't lie around in their room all night.

"Let's hang out," he announced to his kids. It had a nice ring.

He gathered up Maggie from her crib and carried her downstairs to the family room, where a conglomeration of baby paraphernalia sat in the corner. He dragged one of the baby seats away from the wall with one bare foot and placed Maggie in it the way Hadley always did. There were some straps, similar to a parachute harness, and he grabbed one of Maggie's waving fists to thread it through the arm hole.

She promptly clocked him with the other one, which earned a laugh even as his cheek started smarting. "That's what I get for taking my eye off the ball, right?"

The noise she made didn't sound too much like agreement, but he nodded anyway, as if they were having a conversation. That was one of the things Hadley said all the time. The babies were people, not aliens. He could talk to them normally and it helped increase their vocabulary later on if everyone got out of the habit of using baby talk around them.

Which was fine by Kyle. Baby talk was dumb anyway.

Once Maggie was secured, he fetched Maddie and repeated the process. That was the thing about twins. You were never done. One of them always needed something, and then the other one needed the same thing or something different or both.

But here they were, having family time. In the family room. Couldn't get more domestic than that. He sat on the couch and looked at his daughters squirming in their bouncy seats. Now what?

"You ladies want to watch some TV?"

Since neither one of them started wailing at the suggestion, he took it as a yes.

The flat-screen television mounted to the wall blinked on with a flick of the remote. Kyle tuned to one of the kids' channels, where a group of grown men in bright colors were singing a song about a dog named Wags. The song was almost horrifying in its simplicity and in the dancing that would probably lace his nightmares later that night, assuming he actually slept while continually reliving that aborted kiss with Grace from earlier.

The babies both turned their little faces to the TV and for all intents and purposes looked as though they were watching it. Hadley had said they couldn't really make out stuff really well yet, because their eyes weren't developed enough to know what they were looking at, but they could still enjoy the colors and lights.

And that's when Maddie started fussing. Loudly.

Kyle pulled her out of her baby seat, cursing his burning hands, which were still raw from his climb out of the ravine. Liam's timing sucked. "Shh, little one. That's no way to talk to your daddy."

She cried harder. It was only a matter of time before Maggie got jealous of the attention and set about getting some of her own with a few well-placed sobs. Hadley could usually ignore it but Kyle didn't have her stamina.

Plan A wasn't working. Kyle rocked his daughter faster but she only cried harder. And there was no one to help analyze the symptoms in order to arrive at a potential solution. This was a solo operation. So he'd run it to completion.

Bottle. That was always Plan B, after rocking. It was close to dinnertime. Kyle secured Maddie in the chair again, forced to let her wail while he fixed her bottle. It seemed cruel, but he needed both hands.

He'd seen some guys wear a baby sling. But he couldn't quite bring himself to go that far, and he'd never seen Liam do it, either, so there was justification for holding on to his dude card, albeit slight.

Maddie sucked the bottle dry quicker than a baby calf who'd lost its mama. Kyle burped her and resettled her in her bouncy seat, intending to move on to Maggie, who was likely wondering where her bottle was.

Maddie was having none of that and let loose with another round of wails.

In desperation, he sang his go-to Taylor Swift song, which surprisingly worked well enough to ease his pounding headache. He sang the verse over again and slid into the chorus with gusto. The moment he stopped, she set off again, louder. He sang. She quieted. He stopped. She cried.

"Maddie," he groaned. "Tim McGraw should have been your daddy if this is how you're going to be. I can't sing 24-7."

More crying. With more mercy than he probably deserved, Maggie had been sitting quietly in her seat the whole time, but things surely wouldn't stay so peaceful on her end.

Feeling like the world's biggest idiot, he sneaked off to the kitchen to call Hadley. There was no way on God's green earth he'd call Liam, but Hadley was another story.

She answered on the first ring. "Is everything okay?"

"Fine, fine," he assured her, visualizing Liam throwing their overnight bags into the cockpit of the Cessna and flying off toward home without even pausing to shut the door. "Well, except Maddie won't stop crying. I've tried everything, bottle, rocking, and it's a bust. Any ideas?"

"Did you burp her?"

"Of course." He hadn't changed her diaper, but his sense of smell was pretty good and he didn't think that was the problem.

"Temperature?"

He dashed back into the family room, cringing at the decibel level of Maddie's cries, and put a hand on her forehead. Which was moronic when he'd been holding her for thirty minutes. "She doesn't feel hot."

"Is that Maddie crying like that?" Now Hadley sounded worried, which was not what Kyle had intended. "Take her temperature anyway, just to be sure. Then try the gas drops. Call me back in an hour and let me know how it's going."

"Won't I be interrupting?" He so did not want to know the answer to that, but it was pretty crappy of him to call once, let alone twice.

"Yes," Liam growled in the background. "Stop coddling him, Hadley."

Kyle muttered an expletive aimed at Liam, but his wife was the one who heard it. "Excuse my French, Hadley.

Never mind. I got this. You and Liam go back to whatever you were doing, which I do *not* need details about."

"We should come home," Hadley interjected. This was accompanied by a very vehement "No!" from Liam, and some muffled conversation. "Okay, we're not coming home. You'll be fine," Hadley said into the phone in her soothing voice that she normally reserved for the girls, but whether it was directed at Liam or Kyle, he couldn't say. "Call Clare if you need to. She won't mind."

"Clare?" Liam's incredulity came through loud and clear despite his mouth being nowhere near the phone. "She's already got plenty of babies that Royal Memorial pays her to take care of. Call Grace if you're going to call anyone."

Grace. He could get Grace over here under the guise of helping with the twins and get to see her tonight after all. Now that was a stellar idea if Kyle had ever heard one. Not that he was about to let Liam get all cocky about it. "Sorry I bothered you. Good night."

Kyle eyed the still-screaming baby. Fatherhood wasn't a job for the fainthearted, that was for sure. Nor was it a job for the clueless, and thankfully, Ms. Haines already had him cast in her head as such. She thought he was clueless? Great.

Time to use that to his advantage.

Eight

When the phone rang, Grace almost didn't answer it.

The oven had freaked out. Worse than last time. It turned on and heated up fine, but halfway through the cooking cycle, the element shut off. Cold. Which described the state of her dinner, too. The roast was still raw inside and she could have used the potatoes to pound nails.

But there was no saving it now. The oven wouldn't start again no matter how much she cursed at it. She'd checked the power cord but it was plugged in with no visible frays or anything. Last time, she'd been able to turn it off and turn it back on, but that didn't work this time.

So why not answer the phone?

Except it was Kyle. His name flashed at her from the screen and she stared at it for a moment as the *wow* from earlier flooded all her full-grown woman parts. So this was taking it slow? Calling her mere hours after she'd broken off a kiss with more willpower than it should have taken—for the second time?

"This better be important," she said instead of hello, and then winced. Her mama had raised her better than that.

"It is." Something that sounded like a tornado siren wailed in the distance. "Something's wrong with Maddie."

That was *Maddie* doing the siren impression? *Relapse.* Her heart rate sped up. Those harrowing hours when they didn't know what was wrong with Maddie came back in a rush. Heart problems were no joke, and Maddie'd had several surgeries to correct the abnormalities.

"What's wrong? Where's Hadley?" She might be hyperventilating. Was that what it was called when you couldn't breathe?

"She and Liam went to Vail. I didn't want to bother them."

Vail? Suspicion ruffled the edges of Grace's consciousness. The couple had just gone to Vail a couple of months ago. Was this some kind of covert attempt to get Kyle to take his fatherhood responsibilities more seriously? Or an elaborate setup from the mind of Kyle Wade to get his way with Grace?

"Okay," she said slowly, feeling her way through the land mines. "Did you try—"

"Yep. I tried everything. She's been crying like this for an hour and it's upsetting Maggie. I wouldn't have called you otherwise." He was trying hard to keep the panic from his voice, but she could tell he was at the end of his rope. Her heart melted a little, sweeping aside all her suspicion.

It didn't matter why Liam and Hadley had gone to Vail. Maddie—and Kyle—needed help, and she couldn't ignore that for anything.

"Do you need me to come by?" She shouldn't, for all the reasons she hadn't stayed with him in the barn earlier that day.

Plus, and this was the kicker, he hadn't asked her to come over. Maybe it was supposed to be implied, but this was typical with Kyle. He had a huge problem just coming out and saying what he thought. That might be the number one reason she hadn't stayed in his arms, both back in high school and today.

Nothing had changed.

"That's a great idea," he said enthusiastically, and she didn't miss that he was acting as though it was all hers, and not what he'd been after the whole time. "I'll cook you dinner as a thank-you. Unless you've got other plans?"

Ha. If she couldn't hear Maddie's cries for herself, she'd think he'd set all this up. Grace glanced at her oven and half-cooked dinner, then at the lonely dining room table where she'd eaten a lot of meals by herself, especially in the past three years upon becoming a Professional Single Girl.

The timing was oh, so convenient. But even Kyle couldn't magically make her oven stop working at precisely the moment he'd asked her to come over for dinner. Thus far she'd avoided having any meals with him and his family because that would be too hard. Too much of a reminder that a husband and children was what she wanted more than anything—and that there was nothing on the horizon to indicate she'd ever get either one.

But this was an emergency. Or at least that was what she was going to keep telling herself.

"I'll be right there," she promised, and dumped the roast in the trash. If she freshened up her makeup and put on a different dress, no one had to know.

She drove to Wade Ranch at four miles per hour over the speed limit.

Kyle opened the door before she knocked. "Hey, Grace. Thanks."

His pure physical beauty swept out and slapped her. Mute, she stared at his face, memorizing it, which was silly when she already had a handy image of him, shirtless, emblazoned across her brain. She'd just seen him a few hours ago. Why did she have to have a reaction by simply standing near him?

"Where's Maddie?" she asked brusquely to cover the catch in her throat.

"Right this way, Ms. Haines."

Grace followed Kyle through the formal parlor and across the hardwood floor into the hall connecting to the back of the house. Why did it feel like the blind leading the blind? She didn't have any special baby knowledge. Most kids in the system were older by the time their cases landed on her desk, which brought back her earlier reservations about the real reason he'd called her. It wouldn't be the first time today that he'd manufactured a scenario to get a reaction from her.

In the family room, two babies sat in low seats, wide-eyed as they stared at the TV, both silent as the grave.

Grace pointed out the obvious. "Um. Maddie's not crying."

"I gave her Tylenol while you were on your way over here." He shrugged. "Must have worked."

"Why didn't you call me?"

"She didn't stop crying until a few minutes before you got here," he replied defensively, which was only fair. She'd heard Maddie crying over the phone. It wasn't as if he'd shoved Liam and Hadley out the door, and then faked an emergency to get her into his clutches.

She sighed. "I'm sorry. I'm being rude. It's just... I was convinced this was all just an elaborate plot to get me to have dinner with you."

Kyle blinked. "Why on earth would I do that?"

"Well, you know." Discomfort prickled the back of her neck as he stared at her in pure confusion. "Because you faked all that stuff with Emma Jane earlier today. Seemed like it might be a trend."

He cocked his head and gave her a small smile. "I called

you because it was the best of both worlds. I needed help with Maddie and I wanted to see you, too. Is that so terrible?"

Not when he put it that way. Chagrined, she shook her head. "No. But it just seems like I'm a little extraneous at this point. I should probably go. Maddie's fine."

"Don't be silly." His smile faltered just a touch. "She might go off again at any moment and Maggie could decide to join in. What will I do then? Please stay. Besides, I promised you dinner. Let me do something nice for you for coming all this way."

The panicky undercurrent had climbed back into his voice, bless his heart. She couldn't help but smile in hopes of bolstering his confidence. "It wasn't that far. But okay. I'll stay."

"Great. It's settled then." He held out his hand as if he wanted to shake on it but when she placed her hand in his, he yanked on it, pulling her toward the bouncy seats. "Come on, grab a baby and you can watch me cook."

Laughing, she did as commanded, though he insisted on taking Maddie himself. She gathered up Maggie, bouncy seat and all, and followed him to the kitchen, mirroring his moves as he situated the seat near one of the two islands in the center of the room, presumably so the girls didn't feel left out.

She kissed Maggie on the head, unable to resist her sweet face. This baby was special for lots of reasons, but mostly because of who her daddy was.

Wow. Where had that come from? She needed to reel it back, pronto.

"We'll let them hang out for a little while," Kyle said conversationally. "And then we'll put them to bed. Hadley has them on a strict schedule."

"Sure. I'd be glad to help."

It sounded great, actually. The children she helped always either had families already, or were waiting on her to find them the best one. Grace never got to keep any of the children on whose behalf she worked, which was a little heartbreaking in a way.

But here she was, right in the middle of Maddie and Maggie's permanent home, spending time with them and their father outside of work. The smell of baby powder clung to her hands where she'd picked up Maggie, and all at once, soft jazz music floated through the kitchen as Kyle clicked up an internet radio station at the kitchen's entertainment center. It was a bit magical and her throat tightened.

This was not her life. She didn't trust Kyle enough to consider where this could lead. But all at once, she couldn't remember why that was so important. All she had to do right this minute was enjoy this.

"Can I do something to help with dinner?" she asked, since the babies were occupied with staring at their fists.

Kyle grinned and pulled a stool from behind the island, pointing to it. "Sit. Your job is to keep me company."

Charmed, she watched as instructed. It wasn't a hardship. He moved fluidly, as comfortable sliding a bottle from the built-in wine refrigerator as he was handling the reins of his mount earlier that day.

The cork gave way with a *pop* and he poured her a glass of pale yellow wine, handing it to her with one finger in the universal "one minute" gesture. He grabbed his own glass and clinked it against hers. "To bygones."

She raised a brow. That was an interesting thing to toast to. But appropriate. She was determined not to let the past interfere with her family moment, and the future was too murky. "To bygones."

They both drank from their glasses, staring at each other over the rims, and she had the distinct impression he was evaluating her just as much as she was him.

The fruity tang of the wine raced across her tongue, cool and delicious. And unexpected. "I wouldn't have pegged you as a Chardonnay kind of guy," she commented.

"I'm full of surprises." With that cryptic comment, he set his wineglass on the counter and began pulling items from the double-doored stainless steel refrigerator. "I'm making something simple. Chicken salad. I hope that's okay. The ladies didn't give me a lot of time to prep."

She hid a smile at his description of the babies. "Sounds great."

Kyle bustled around the kitchen chopping lettuce and a cooked chicken breast, leaving her to alternate watching him and the twins. Though he drew her eye far more than she would have expected, given that she was here to help with the babies.

"I don't remember you being much of a connoisseur in the kitchen," she said as he began mixing the ingredients for homemade dressing.

They'd been so young the first time, though. Not even out of their teens, yet their twenties were practically in the rearview mirror now. Of course they'd grown and changed. It would be more shocking if they hadn't.

"In a place like Afghanistan, if you don't learn to cook, you starve," he returned.

It was rare for him to mention his military stint, and it occurred to her that she typically shied away from the subject because it held so many negative associations. For her, at least. He might feel differently about the thing that had taken him away from her, and she was suddenly curious about it.

"Did you enjoy being in the military?"

He glanced up, his expression shuttered all at once. "It was a part of me. And now it's not."

Okay, message received. He didn't want to talk about that. Which was fine. Neither did she.

"I'm at a stopping point," he said, his tone a little lighter. "Let's put the girls to bed."

Though she suspected it was merely a diversion, she nodded and followed him through the mysterious ritual of bedtime. It was over before she'd fully immersed herself in the moment. They changed the girls' diapers, changed their outfits, put them down on their backs and left the room.

"That was it?" she whispered as she and Kyle took the back stairs to the kitchen.

"Yep. Sometimes Hadley rocks them if they don't go to sleep right away, but she says not to do that too much, or they'll get used to it, and we'll be doing it until they go to college." He waved the mobile video monitor in his hand. "I watch and listen using this and if they fuss, I come running. Not much more to it."

They emerged into the kitchen, where the tangy scent of the salad dressing greeted them. Kyle set the monitor on the counter on his way to the area where he'd been preparing dinner.

He'd clearly been asking Hadley questions and soaking up her baby knowledge. Much more so than Grace would have given him credit for. "You're taking fatherhood very seriously."

He halted and whirled so fast that she smacked into his chest. But he didn't step back. "What's it going to take to convince you that I'm in this for the long haul?"

Blinking, she stared up into his green eyes as they cut through her. Condemning her. Uncertain all of a sudden, she tried to take a step back, but he didn't let her. His hands shot out to grip her elbows, hauling her back into place. Into his space. A hairbreadth from the cut torso she'd felt under her fingers earlier today.

"What will it take, Grace?" he murmured. "You say something like that and it makes me think you're surprised that I'm ready, willing and able to take care of my daughters. *Still* surprised, after all I've done and learned. After I've become gainfully employed. After I've shown you my commitment in site visits like you asked. This isn't about me anymore. It's about you. Why is this all so hard for you to believe?"

"Because, Kyle!" she burst out. "You've been gone. You didn't come home when Liam called you about the babies. Is it so difficult to fathom that I might have questions about your intentions? You just said the military was a part of you. What if you wake up one day and want to join up again? Those girls will suffer."

I'd suffer.

Where had that come from? She tried to shake it off, but as they stood there in the kitchen of Wade House with his masculinity pouring over her like a hot wind from the south, the emotions welled up again and she cursed herself. Cursed the truth.

Sometime between his coming home and now, she'd opened her heart again. Just a little. She'd tried to stop, tried asking for space, but the honest truth was that she'd never gotten over him because she still had feelings for him. And it had only taken one kiss to awaken them again, no matter how much she'd tried to lie to herself about it. Otherwise, that scene with Emma Jane would have rolled right off like water from a duck's back.

And she didn't trust him not to hurt her again. It was a terrible place to be stuck.

"Grace," he murmured. "I'm here. For good. I didn't get Liam's messages, or I would have been back earlier. You've got me cast in your head as someone with my sights set on the horizon, but that's not true. I want to live my life in Royal, at least until my daughters are grown."

He wasn't aiming to leave the moment he changed his mind. He was telling the truth; she could see it in his eyes.

Maybe she wasn't such a bad judge of character after all. Maybe she could let her guard down. Just a little.

The tightness in her throat relaxed and she took the first easy breath since smacking into him. "Okay. I'll shut up about it."

"Just to make sure, let me help you shut up."

He hauled her up and kissed her. His mouth took hers at a hard, desperate angle that she instantly responded to. Maybe she didn't have to resist if he wasn't going to leave again. Maybe she didn't have to pretend she didn't want more. Because he was right here, giving it to her. All she had to do was take it.

His hands were still on her elbows, raising her up on her tiptoes as he devoured her with his unique whole-body kiss. Need unfolded inside, seeking relief, seeking Kyle.

Yes. The darkness she sometimes sensed in him lifted as he dropped her elbows to encompass her in his arms, holding her tight. He backed her up against the counter to press his hard body to hers, thrusting his hips to increase the contact.

A moan bloomed in her chest, and her tongue vibrated against his as he took the kiss deeper, sliding a hand down her back, to her waist, to her bottom, molding it to fit in his palm. His touch thrilled her even as she pressed into it, willing him to spread the wealth. And then he did.

His hand went lower, gripping the back of her thigh, lifting it so that her knee came up flush with his thigh, which hiked her dress up, and *oh, my*. She was open to him under her skirt, flimsy panties the only barrier between her damp center and his very hard body.

He thrust his hips again, igniting her instantly as the rough fabric of his jeans pleasured her through the scrap of fabric at her core. Strung tight, she let the dense heat wash through her, mindless with it as she sought more. His mouth lifted from hers for a moment and she nearly wept, following him involuntarily with her lips in hopes of reclaiming the drugging kiss.

"Grace," he murmured, and dragged his lips across her throat to the hollow near her ear, which was so nice, she forgot about kissing and let her head tip back to give him better access.

He spent a long moment exploring the area, and finally nipped her ear lightly, whispering, "You know, when I said I wanted to live my life in Royal, I didn't picture myself alone."

"I hope not," she murmured. "You have two daughters."

He laughed softly, as she'd intended, and hefted her a little deeper into his arms as he lifted his head to meet her gaze. "You know that's not what I meant."

Of course she did. But was it so difficult to spell out what was going on his head? So difficult to say how he felt about her? She wanted to hear the words. This time, she wasn't settling for less than everything. "Tell me what you're picturing, Kyle."

"Me. You." He slid light fingertips down the sweetheart neckline of her dress until he reached the spot right between her breasts and hooked the fabric. "This dress on the floor."

Shuddering in spite of herself at the heated desire in his expression, she smiled. "Let's pretend for argument's sake I'm in favor of this dress on the floor. What would you say to me while you're peeling it off?"

The glint in his eye set off another shower of sparks in her midsection. "Well, my darling. Why don't we just find out?"

Slowly, he pulled down the shoulders of the dress, baring her bra straps, which he promptly gathered up, as well. She heartily blessed the impulse that had caused her to pick this semibackless dress that didn't require unzipping to get out of. Which might not have been an accident.

"Beautiful." He kissed a shoulder, suckling on it lightly, then following her neckline with the little nibbling kisses until she thought she'd come apart from the torture.

When she'd asked him to talk about what was on his mind, she'd been expecting a declaration of his feelings. This was so much better. For now.

All at once, the dress and bra popped down to her waist in a big bunch of fabric, baring her breasts to his hot-eyed viewing pleasure. And look he did, shamelessly, as if he'd uncovered a diamond he couldn't quite believe was real.

"Grace," he rasped. "Exactly like I remembered in my dreams. But so much more."

That pleased her enormously for some reason. It was much more romantic than what she recalled him saying when they were together ten years ago. He'd seen her naked before, but always in semidarkness, and usually in his truck. Bench seats were not the height of romance.

With a reverent curse, he brushed one nipple with his thumb, and her breath whooshed from her lungs as everything went tight inside. And outside.

"Kyle," she said, and nearly strangled on the word as he lifted her up onto the counter, spreading her legs and stepping between them. Then his mouth closed over a breast and she forgot how to speak as he sucked, flicking her nipple with his tongue simultaneously.

She forgot everything except the exquisite feel of this man's mouth on her body.

Her head fell back as he pushed a hand against the small of her back to arch her toward his mouth, drawing her breast deeper into it. She moaned, writhing with pleasure as the heat swept over her entire body, swirling at her core. Where she needed him most.

As if he'd read her mind, his other hand toyed with her panties until she felt his fingers touching her intimately. It was cataclysmic, perfect. Until he placed his thumb on her nub, expertly rubbing as he pleasured her, and that was even more perfect. Heat at her core, suction at her breast, and it all coalesced in one bright, hot pinnacle. With a cry, she crested in a long orgasm of epic proportions.

She'd just had an *orgasm* on the *kitchen counter*. She should probably be more embarrassed about that…

Before she'd fully recovered, Kyle picked her up from the counter and let her slide to the floor, then hustled her up the stairs to a bedroom. Heavy, masculine furnishings dominated the room, marking it as his, but a few leftover items from his youth still decorated the walls. He dimmed the light and advanced on her with his slow, lazy walk.

"Oh, there's more?" she teased.

"So much more," he growled. "It's been far too long since I've felt you under me. I want you naked. Now."

That sounded like a plan. The warm-up in the kitchen had only gotten her good and primed for what came next.

Breathless, she stood still as he peeled her dress the rest of the way from her body and let it fall to the carpet. She promptly forgot to worry about the extra pounds she'd gained in her hips and thighs since the last time he'd seen her.

He stripped off his shirt, exposing that beautiful torso she'd barely had time to explore earlier.

When his jeans hit the floor, she realized his chest was only part of the package, and the rest—*oh, my*. He turned slightly, holding one leg behind him at an odd angle, almost as if he was posing for her. Well, okay then. Greedily, she looked her fill, returning the favor from earlier when he'd gorged on the sight of her bare breasts.

In the low light, he was quite simply gorgeous, with muscles bulging in his thighs and a jutting erection that spoke of his passion more effectively than anything he could have said. The power of it coursed through her. She was a woman in the company of a finely built man who was here with the sole intent of pleasuring her with that cut, solid body. And she got to do the same to him.

Why had she waited so long for this?

"Grace."

She glanced up into his eyes, which were so hot, she felt the burn across her uncovered skin, heightening her desire to *get started* already. He was going to feel amazing.

"You have to stop looking at me like that," he rasped.

"Because why?"

He chuckled weakly. "Because this is going to be all over in about two seconds if you don't. I want to take my time with you. Savor you."

"Maybe you can do that the second time," she suggested, a little shocked at her boldness, but not sorry. "I'm okay with you going fast the first time if I get to look at you however much I want. Oh, and there's going to be touching, too."

To prove the point, she reached out to trace the line of his pectoral muscles, because how could she not? He groaned under her fingertips and that was so nice, she flattened her palms against his chest. "More," she commanded.

He raised his eyebrows. "When did you get so bossy?"

"Five minutes ago." When she'd realized she was a woman with desires. And she wanted this man. Why shouldn't she get to call a few shots?

With a small push at his torso, she shoved him toward the bed. And to his credit, he let her, because there was no way she'd have moved him otherwise. He fell backward onto the bed and she climbed on to kneel next to him, a little uncertain where to start. But determined to figure it out.

"Just be still," she told him as he stared up at her with question marks in his gaze. Then she got busy exploring.

What would he taste like? There was only one way to find out. She leaned down and ran her tongue across his nipple, and it was as delicious as she'd expected. He hissed as the underlying muscle jerked.

"Staying still is easier said than done when you're doing that," he muttered, his voice cracking as she ran her tongue lower, down his abs and to his thigh.

She eyed his erection and, curious, reached out to touch it. Hard and soft at the same time, it pulsed against her palm.

He cursed. "Playtime's over."

Instantly, he rolled her under him in one fierce move, taking her mouth in a searing kiss that rendered her boneless. She melted into the comforter as he shoved a leg between hers, rubbing at her core until she was in flames.

He paused only for a moment to sheathe himself with a condom, and then nudged her legs open to ease into her slowly.

Gasping as he filled her, she clung to his shoulders, reveling in the feel of him. This was so different than she remembered. The experience was so much stronger and bigger. The leftover emotion that she'd carried with her for the past ten years exploded into something she barely recognized. Before, Kyle had been in a compartment in her mind, in her heart. Something she could take out and remember, then put back when she got sad.

There was no putting this back in a box.

The essence of Kyle swept through her, filling every nook and cranny of her body and soul. No, he hadn't bubbled over with lots of pretty words about being in love with her. But that would come, in time. She had to believe that.

And then he buried himself completely with a groan. They were so intimately joined, Grace could feel his heartbeat throughout her whole body. They moved in tandem, mutually seeking to increase the pleasure, spiraling higher toward the heavens, and she lost all track of time and place as they lost themselves in each other.

The rhythms were familiar, like dancing to the same song so often you memorized the moves. But the familiarity only heightened the experience because she didn't have to wonder what would happen next.

Just as he'd done when they'd been together before, he stared into her eyes as he loved her, refusing to let her look away. Opening his soul to her as they joined again and again. The romance of it swept through her and she held him close.

This was why she'd fallen in love with him. Why she'd never had even the slightest desire to do this with any other man. He made her feel that she completed him without saying a word. Sure, she wanted the words. But times like this made them unnecessary.

Before she was fully ready for it to end, his urgency increased, sending her into an oblivion of sensation until she climaxed, and then he followed her into the light, holding her tight against him as they soared.

She lay there engulfed in his arms, wishing she never had to move from this spot.

Kyle must have been reading her mind, because he murmured in her ear, "Stay. All weekend."

"I don't have any of my stuff," she said lamely as reality nosed its way into the perfect moment.

"Go get a bag and come back."

It was a reasonable suggestion. But then what? Were they jumping back into their relationship as if nothing had happened and ten years hadn't passed? As if they'd dealt with the hurt and separation?

That was too much reality. She sat up and his arms fell away to rest on the comforter.

"I see the wheels turning," he commented mildly as he pulled a sheet over his lower half in a strange bout of modesty. "This is a beginning, Grace. Let's see where it takes us. Don't throw up any more walls."

She shut her eyes. Romance was great, but there was so much more that she wanted in a relationship. There'd been no declarations of undying love. No marriage proposal. Why did he get a pass that no other man got? She was caught between her inescapable feelings for Kyle and her standards.

And the intense hope that things might be different this time.

How would she ever find out if she left?

"Okay." She nodded and ignored the hammering of her pulse. "Let's see where it goes."

Nine

Kyle waited on Grace to come back by pretending to watch TV.

His body had cooled—on the outside—but the inside was still pretty keyed up. He wasn't really interested in much of anything other than getting Grace back in his bed, but this time for the whole night.

When the crunch of gravel sounded outside, breath he hadn't realized he'd been holding whooshed out. She'd come back.

He met Grace at the door, opening it wide as she climbed the front porch steps, her hair still mussed from their thorough lovemaking of less than an hour ago. Her face shone in the porch light, so beautiful and fresh, and his chest hitched as he soaked in the sight of her.

"Hey, Grace," he said, pretty dang happy his voice still worked.

He'd wondered if she might back out, call and say she'd changed her mind. She was still so skittish. She might have let him into her body but he didn't fool himself for a second that she'd let him into her head, or her heart. It wasn't the way it had been, when he'd been her hero, her everything. There was distance now that hadn't been there before and he didn't like it.

Of course, some of that was his fault. Not much. But a little. He didn't fully trust her, and while he'd sworn in theory to forget about the past, it was proving more difficult to do in practice than he'd thought it would be, so he didn't press the issue of the yawning chasm between them.

"Hey." She had a bag slung over her shoulder and a shy smile on her face.

Shy? After the temptress she'd been? It caught him up short. Maybe some of the distance was due to sheer unfamiliarity between them. As comfortable as *he* felt around Grace, that didn't mean she was totally in the groove yet. Plus, they didn't know each other as well as they used to. Ten years didn't vanish just because two people slept together.

"We never had dinner," he commented. "Come sit with me and we'll eat. For real this time."

She nodded and let him take her bag, following him to the table where he laid out silverware and refilled their wineglasses. They ate the chicken salad and polished off the bottle of wine, chatting long after clearing their plates. Grace told cute stories about the children on her case docket, and Kyle reciprocated with some carefully selected anecdotes about the guys he'd trained with in Coronado during BUD/S. Carefully selected because that period had been among the toughest of his life as his training honed him into an elite warrior—*while* he was fighting his own internal battle against the hurt this woman had caused. But he'd survived and wasn't dwelling on that.

Couldn't dwell on it. Liam wasn't a factor and he wanted

to do things with Grace differently this time. And by the time Kyle was done with her, she'd be asking, "Liam who?"

A wail over the monitor drew their attention away from their conversation and Grace gladly helped him get the girls settled again. It was nearing midnight; hopefully it would be the only time the babies woke up for the night.

Kyle didn't mind rolling out of bed at any hour to take care of his daughters, but he selfishly wanted to spend the rest of the night with Grace, and Grace alone. He got his wish. They fell asleep wrapped in each other's arms, and Kyle slept like the dead until dawn.

His eyes snapped open and he took a half second to orient. Not a SEAL. Not in Afghanistan. But with *Grace*. A blessing to count, among many.

Until he tried to snuggle her closer. White-hot pokers of pain shot through his busted leg as he rolled. He bit back the curse and breathed through it.

The pain hadn't been so bad last night, but of course, he'd been pretty distracted. Plus, he normally soaked his leg before going to bed but hadn't had a chance last night. Apparently, he was going to pay for it today.

All the commotion woke Grace.

"Good morning," she murmured sleepily, and slid a leg along his, which was simultaneously arousing and excruciating.

"Wait," he said hoarsely.

"Don't wanna." She stretched provocatively, rubbing her bare breasts against his chest, which distracted him enough that he didn't realize she'd hooked her knee around his leg. She fairly purred with sexy little sounds that meant she was turned on. And probably about to do something about it.

"Grace." He grabbed her shoulders and squared them so he could be sure he had her attention. "Stop."

Her expression went from hot and sleepy to confused

and guarded. Her whole body stiffened, pulling away from his. "Okay. Sorry."

"No, don't be sorry." Kyle swore. *Moron*. He was mucking this up and all he wanted to do was pull her back against him. Dive in, distract himself. But he couldn't. "Listen."

He took a deep breath, fighting the pain, fighting his instinct to clam up again.

He hadn't told anyone about what had happened to him in Afghanistan and didn't want to start with the woman who still had the power to declare him an unfit parent if he admitted to having a busted leg. But as he stared into her troubled brown eyes, his heart lurched and he had to come clean. This was part of closing that distance between them. Part of learning to trust her again.

She'd said she was going to let him keep his girls. He had to believe her. Believe *in* her, or this was never going to work, not now, not in a hundred years.

"I didn't tell you to stop because I wanted you to."

Her gaze softened along with her body. "Then what's going on, Kyle?"

"I got wounded," he muttered. Which made him sound as much like a wuss as he felt. "Overseas."

"Oh, I didn't know!" She gasped and drew back to glance down the length of his body, her expression darkening gorgeously as she took in his semiaroused state. "You don't *look* wounded. Everything I see is quite nice."

And now it was a fully aroused state. Fantastic. This was so not a conversation he wanted to have in the first place, let alone with a hard-on. "My leg. The bone was shattered. I had a lot of surgeries and they put most of it back together. But it still hurts, especially in the morning when I haven't stretched it."

Sympathy poured from her gaze as she sat up and pulled the sheet back, gathering it up in her hand as she sought the scar. When she found it along the far side of his calf, she touched the skin just above it lightly with her fingers. "You hid this last night. With the low light and striking that weird pose. Why didn't you tell me?"

"It's…"

How to explain the horror of being wounded in the line of duty? It wasn't just the pain and the fact that he wasn't ever going to be the same again, but he'd been unable to protect the rest of his team. He'd been unable to *do his job* because his leg didn't work all at once. A SEAL got back up when he was knocked down. *Every time.* Only Kyle hadn't.

Maybe he'd fail at being a parent, too, because of it. That was his worst fear.

"I don't like being weak," he finally said, which was true, if not the whole truth. "I don't like giving you ammunition to take away Maddie and Maggie. Like I might not be a good daddy because my leg doesn't work right."

"Oh, Kyle." She laid her lips on the scar for a moment, and the light touch seared his heart. "I would never take away your daughters because of an injury. That's ridiculous."

He shrugged, unable to meet her gaze. "You were going to take them away because I didn't come home for two months. But I was in the hospital."

"Well, you could have said that!" Exasperation spurted out with the phrase and she shook her head. "For crying out loud. Am I supposed to be a mind reader?"

Yes. Then he wouldn't have to figure out how to say things that were too hard.

"Now you know," he mumbled instead. "That's why I had to stop earlier. Not because I wasn't on board. I just needed a minute."

"Okay." But then she smiled and ran a hand up his thigh,

dangerously close to his erection. "It's been a minute. How about we try this instead, now that I know?"

The protest got caught in his throat as she rolled him onto his back and crawled over him, careful not to touch his leg, but deliberately letting her breasts and long curls brush his skin from thigh to chest. She captured his wrists and encircled them with her fingers, drawing his arms above his head, holding them in place as her hips undulated.

"What are you doing?" His voice scraped the lower register as she ignited his flesh with her sexy movements.

She arched a brow. "Really? I should hope it would be fairly obvious. Since it's not, shut up and I'll make it clearer for you."

He did as advised because his tongue was stuck to the roof of his mouth anyway. And then she leaned forward, still holding his wrists hostage, and kissed him. Hot. Openmouthed. The kind of kiss laden with dark promise and he eagerly lapped it up. He could break free of her finger shackles easily, but why the hell would he do that?

She had him right where she wanted him, apparently, and since he could find no complaint with it, he let her have the floor. She experimented with different angles of her head as she kissed him, looking for something unknown and he went along for the ride, groaning with the effort it took to hold back.

Then she trailed her mouth down his throat, nipped at his earlobe and writhed against his erection all at once, slicing a long, hot knife of need through his groin. His hips strained toward hers, rocking involuntarily as he sought relief, and he started to pull his arms loose so he could roll her under him to get this show on the road. But she shook her head and tightened her grip on his wrists.

"No, sir," she admonished with a wicked smile. "You're not permitted to do anything but lie there."

This was going to kill him. Flat out stop his heart.

He got what she was doing. She wanted him to keep his leg still, while she did all the dirty work. Something tender hooked his heart as he stared up at her, poised over him with an all-business look on her face that was somehow endearing.

But he wasn't an invalid.

"I hate to break it to you, darling, but that's not happening." He flexed his hips again, sliding his erection against her bare, damp sex, watching as her eyes unfocused with pleasure. "I suggest you think about how you're going to get a condom on me with your hands occupied because I'm going to be inside you in about point two seconds."

"Don't ruin this for me." She mock-pouted and promptly crossed his wrists, one over the other, and held on with one hand as she wiggled the fingers of her free hand in a cheery wave. "I always dreamed of being a rodeo star. This is my chance."

He had to laugh, which downright ached. All over. "That's what's on your mind right now? Rodeo?"

"Oh, yeah." She leaned against his abs, holding on with her thighs as she fished around in the nightstand drawer and pulled out a condom, which she held up triumphantly. "I'm going for a ten in the bucking bronco event."

"I'll be the judge of that," he quipped, and then raised a brow at the condom. "Go ahead. I'm waiting."

In the end, she had to let go of his arms to rip open the foil package. But he obediently held his wrists above his head as she had so sweetly asked. Then there was no more talking as she eased over him, taking him gently in her hands to pleasure him as she rolled on the condom.

He groaned as need broke over him in a wave, and then she slowly guided him into her damp heat. He slid all the way in as she pushed downward and it was unbelievable. They joined and it was better than it had been last night.

Deeper. More amazing, because there were no more secrets between them.

She knew about his injury and hadn't run screaming for her report to revise it. She hadn't been repulsed by his weaknesses. Instead, she'd somehow twisted it around so they could make love without hurting his leg. It was sweet and wonderful.

And then she got busy on her promise to turn him into a bucking bronco, sliding up and down, rolling her hips and generally driving him mad with want. He obliged her by letting his body go with the sensation, meeting her thrusts and driving them both higher until she came with a little cry and he followed her.

Clutching her to his chest, he breathed in tandem with her, still joined and not anxious to change that. He held her hot body to his because he didn't think he could let go.

"You're amazing," he murmured into her hair, and she turned her head to lay her cheek on his shoulder, a pleased smile on her face.

"I wouldn't say no to thank-you flowers."

He made a mental note to send her a hundred roses the moment his bones returned and he could actually move. "Where'd you get that sexy little hip roll from?"

She shrugged. "I don't know. I've never done it before. It just felt right."

All at once, his good mood vanished as he wondered what moves she *had* done before with other men that she hadn't opted to try out on him. Like Liam. Was he better in bed than his brother? Worse? About the same? And yeah, he recognized that the burn in his gut was pure jealousy.

Totally unable to help himself, he smiled without humor and rolled her off him casually, as if it were no big deal, but he didn't really want her close to him right then. "It was great. Perfect. Like you'd practiced it a lot."

What an ass he was being. But the thought of Grace

with another man, some guy's mitts on her, touching her, put him over the edge. Especially since one of those Neanderthals had been his brother.

She quirked a brow. "Really? You're not just humoring me?"

The pleased note in her voice didn't improve his mood. What, it was a compliment to be well-practiced in bed?

"Oh, no," he said silkily. "You've got the moves, sweetheart. The men must line up into the next county to get in on that."

Not only was he jealous, he was acting as if he'd been a choirboy for the past ten years when there was nothing further from the truth. He'd been the king of one-night stands because that was all he could do. It wasn't what he'd wanted or what he'd envisioned for himself, but the reason he wasn't able to move on and find someone to settle down with was sitting in his bed smiling at him as if this was all a big joke.

But as always, he wasn't going to say what was really on his mind. That was how you got hurt, by exposing your unguarded soft places.

And then she laughed. "Oh, yeah. They line up, all right. As long as we're having confession time, I have one of my own."

He needed a drink first. A row of shots would be preferable. But it was—he scowled at the clock—barely 6:00 a.m., and the babies were going to wake up any second, demanding their breakfast. "We don't have to do this, Grace."

"No, I want to," she insisted. "You told me about your leg, which was clearly hard for you. I think this is just as important for you to know. I'm not practiced. At all. It's kind of funny you'd say that actually, since you're the last man I slept with."

Shyly, she peeked at him from under lowered lashes as she let that register.

He sat up so fast, his head cracked against the headboard. "You...what?"

She hadn't been with anyone since *him*? Since ten years ago? *At all?*

Grace nodded. "I guess you could say you ruined me for other men. But that's not the only reason. I just never found one I thought measured up."

To him. She'd never found another man she'd thought was good enough. Had he been working himself up for no reason?

Grace had never been with another man. She'd been a virgin when they met. Kyle Wade was Grace's only lover. The thought choked him up in a wholly unexpected way.

And then his brain latched on to the idea of Grace refusing suitors over the years and shoved it under the lens of what he knew to be the truth. His mood turned dangerously sharp and ugly again. "Well, now. That's a high compliment. If it's true."

Confusion crept across her expression. "Why would I lie?"

"Good question. One I'd like the answer to, as well." He crossed his arms over his thundering heart. "Maybe you could explain how it's possible that you've never been with another man, yet I practically caught you in the act with one. Liam."

Just spitting his name out cost Kyle. His throat tightened and threatened to close off entirely, which would be great because then he couldn't throw up.

"Oh, Kyle." She actually *smiled* as she tenderly cupped his face. "You've certainly taken your time circling around back to that. Nothing happened with Liam. I didn't think you'd even noticed."

"You didn't..." He couldn't even finish that sentence and jerked away from her touch. "His hands were all over you. Don't tell me nothing happened."

"First of all, we were broken up at the time," she reminded him. "Secondly, it was a setup, honey. I wanted to get your attention, and honestly, I was pretty devastated it didn't work. Liam was a good sport about it, though. I've always appreciated that he was willing to help."

Kyle's vision went black and then red, and he squeezed his eyes shut as he came perilously close to passing out for the first time in his life. *Breathe. And again.* Ruthlessly, he got himself back under control.

"A setup," he repeated softly.

She nodded. "We set it up for you to catch us. It was dumb, I realize. Blame it on the fact that I was young and naive. I was expecting you to confront me. For us to have it out so I could explain how much you meant to me. How upset I was that we weren't together anymore. It was supposed to end differently. But you left and I figured out that I wasn't all that important to you."

A setup. To force a confrontation. And instead, she'd decided his silence meant she wasn't important to him, when in fact, the opposite was true.

"Why?" He nearly choked on the question. "Why would you do something like that? With *Liam* of all people?"

His brother. There was a sacred line between brothers that you didn't cross, and she'd not only crossed it, she'd been the instigator. Liam had put his hands on the woman Kyle loved as a *favor*. Somehow, and he wouldn't have thought this possible, that was worse than when Kyle had thought his brother was just adding another name to his growing list of conquests. The betrayal was actually twice as deep because it had all been a *setup*.

The reckoning was going to be brutal.

"Because, Kyle." She caught his gaze and tears brimmed in her eyes. "I loved you. So much and so intensely. But you were so distant. Already seeking that horizon, even then. We'd stopped connecting. Breaking up with you didn't faze you. I figured it would take something bold to shake you up."

Yeah, it had shaken him up all right. "But *that*?"

He couldn't wrap his head around what she was telling him. He'd enlisted because of a lie. Because he'd felt as though he couldn't breathe in Royal ever again. Because he'd sought a place where people stood by their word and their honor, would take a bullet for you. Where he could be part of a team alongside people who valued him. And *found* that place.

Which wasn't here.

"Yeah. Like you used Emma Jane to make me jealous." She shrugged. "Same idea. Funny how similar our tactics are."

The roaring sound in his head drowned out her words. Similar. She thought the idea of Kyle flirting with a woman out in the open in broad daylight was the same as walking by Liam's bedroom and hearing Grace's laugh. The same as peeking through the crack at the door to see the woman he'd given his soul to entwined with his brother *on his brother's bed*.

"Go." He shoved out of the bed, ignored his aching leg and dressed as fast as he could. "I can't be around you right now."

"Are you upset, Kyle?" She still sounded confused, as though it wasn't abundantly clear that none of this was okay. And then her face crumpled as understanding slowly leached into her posture.

He couldn't respond. There was nothing to say anyway.

It wasn't the same. He'd started to trust her again—no, he'd *forced* himself to forget the past despite the amount of pain he still carried around—only to find that her capacity for lies was far broader than he'd ever have imagined.

He slammed out of the room and went to make the babies' bottles because he couldn't leave as he wanted to. As he should. Grace would twist that around, too, and somehow find a way to rip his heart out again by taking his daughters away.

But he wouldn't give Grace Haines any more power in his life.

Since he couldn't leave, Kyle stewed. When Liam and Hadley returned from Vail the next afternoon, Kyle wasn't fit company.

Which made it the perfect time for a confrontation.

"Liam," Kyle fairly growled as he cornered his brother in the kitchen after Hadley went to the nursery to see the babies.

"What's up?" Liam chugged some water from the bottle in his hand.

"Grace fessed up." Crossing his arms so he wouldn't get started on the beating portion of the reckoning too soon, he shifted the weight off his bad leg and glared at the betrayer who dared stand there scowling as though he didn't know what Kyle was talking about. "Back before I went into the navy. You and Grace. It was a lie."

"Oh, that." Liam shook his head. "Yeah, you're a little slow on the uptake. That's ancient history."

"It's recent to me because I just found out about it."

With a smirk, Liam punched him on the arm. "Maybe if you'd stuck around instead of flying off to the navy, you'd have known then. That was the whole purpose of it, according to Grace, to get you to confront her. I was just window dressing."

"I went into the navy because of window dressing," Kyle said through clenched teeth, though how his brain was still functioning enough to spit out thoughts was beyond him. "Glad to know this is all a big game to everyone. I've been missing out. Where's Hadley? I'm looking forward to getting in on some of this fun. Would you like to watch while I feel up your wife or would you rather walk in on us?"

"Shut your filthy mouth."

Kyle was ready for his brother this time and blocked Liam's crappy right hook easily, pushing back on his twin's torso before the man charged him. "Not so fun when you're on the other side of it, huh?"

Chest heaving and eyes wild with fury, Liam strained against Kyle's immovable blockade. "What do you care? You ignored Grace to the point where she cried so much over your sorry hide, I thought she was going to dry up like an old withered flower."

"Aren't you the poet?" He sneered to cover the catch in his heart to hear that Grace had cried over him. And how did Liam know that anyway? It probably wasn't even true. This was all an elaborate bunch of hooey designed to throw Kyle off the scent of who was really to blame here. "I cared, you idiot. You're the one who didn't care about the big fat line you crossed when you put your hands on my woman."

"*Your* woman? I got a feeling Grace would disagree." Liam snorted and stepped back, mercifully, allowing Kyle to drop his hand from his brother's chest. Another few minutes of holding him back would have strained his leg something fierce. "What line did I cross? You broke up. You weren't even together when that happened, remember?"

"*She* broke up. I didn't," Kyle countered viciously. "I was trying to figure out how to get her back. Not so easy when a woman tells you she's through and then makes out with another guy. Who happens to be my brother. Which never would have happened if you'd told her no. *That's* the line, Liam. I would never have done that to you."

Something dawned in Liam's gaze. "Holy cow. You were in love with her."

"What the hell do you think I've been talking about?"

Disgusted with the circles and lies and betrayals, Kyle slumped against the counter, seriously thinking about starting on a bottle of Irish whiskey. It was five o'clock 24-7 when you found out your twin brother was a complete moron.

"You were in love with her," Liam repeated with surprise, as if saying it again was going to make it more real. "Still are."

Well, *duh*. Of course he was! Why did Liam think Kyle was so pissed?

Wait. No, that wasn't— Kyle shut his eyes for a beat, but the truth didn't magically become something else. Of course he was still in love with Grace. That's why her betrayal hurt so much.

"That's not the point." Nor was that up for discussion. It didn't matter anyway. He and Grace were through, for real this time.

"No, the point is that this is all news to me. Probably news to Grace as well, assuming you actually got around to telling her." More comprehension dawned in Liam's expression. "You haven't. You're still just as much of a jackass now as you were then."

Kyle was getting really tired of being so transparent. "Some things shouldn't have to be said."

Liam laughed so hard, Kyle thought he was going to bust something, and the longer it went on, the more Kyle wanted to be the one doing the busting. Like a couple of teeth in his brother's mouth.

Finally, Liam wiped his eyes. "Get your checkbook because you need to buy a clue, my brother. No woman is going to let you get away with being such a clam, so keep on being the strong, silent type and sleep alone. See if I care."

"Yeah, you're the fount of wisdom when it comes to women, Mr. Revolving Door. Do you even know how many women you've slept with over the years?" Cheap shot. And Kyle knew it the moment it left his mouth, but Liam had him good and riled. He started to apologize but Liam waved it off.

"That doesn't matter when you find the right one." Liam glanced up the back stairs fondly, his mind clearly on his wife, who was still upstairs with the babies. "But guess what? You don't get a woman like Hadley without knowing a few things about how to treat a woman. And keeping your thoughts to yourself ain't it. Look what it's cost you so far. You willing to spend the next ten years without the woman you love because of your man-of-few-words shtick?"

Yeah, he didn't blather on about the stuff that was inside. So what? It was personal and he didn't like to share it.

Keeping quiet was a defense mechanism he'd adopted when he was little to shelter him from constantly being in a place he didn't fit into, lest anyone figure out his real feelings. Some wounds weren't obvious but they went deep.

The old-fashioned clock on the wall ticked out the seconds as it had done since Kyle was old enough to know how to tell time. Back then, he'd marked each one on his heart, counting the ticks in hopes that when he reached a thousand, his mother would come back. When he reached ten thousand, she'd *surely* walk through the door. A hundred thousand. And then he'd lose count and start over.

She had never come back to rescue him from the ranch he didn't like, didn't comprehend. Nothing had ever fit right until Grace. She was still the only woman who ever had.

And maybe he'd messed up a little by not telling her what she meant to him. Okay, maybe he'd messed up a lot. If he'd told her, she probably wouldn't have cooked up that scheme with Liam. Too little, too late.

"We good?" Liam asked, his gaze a lot more understanding than it should have been.

"Yeah." Kyle sighed. "It was a long time ago."

"For what it's worth, I'm sorry."

Liam stuck his hand out and Kyle didn't hesitate. They shook on it and did an awkward one-armed brotherly hug that probably looked more like two squirrels fighting over a walnut than anything. But it was enough to bury the hatchet, and not in Liam's back, the way Kyle had planned when he'd stormed into the kitchen earlier.

"Listen." Liam cleared his throat. "If we're all done crying about your girlfriend, I've got something to tell you that's been rubbing me the wrong way."

"You need me to go underwear shopping with you so we can get you the right size?" When Liam elbowed him, Kyle knew they were on the way back to being brothers again instead of strangers. "Because you have a wife for that now."

"Shut up. This is for serious. There's an outfit called Samson Oil making noises around Royal and I don't like it. They're buying up properties. Even offered me a pretty penny for Wade Ranch. Wanted to make sure you're on the same—"

"You said no, right?" Kyle shot back instantly. This was his home now. The place he planned to raise his daughters. No amount of money could compensate for a stable home life for his family.

"Well, I wanted to talk to you first. But yeah. The right answer is no."

Relief squeezed his chest. And wasn't that something? Kyle had never thought he'd consider the ranch home. But there you go. The threat of losing it—well, he didn't have to worry about that, obviously.

"So it's a no. What's the big deal then?"

Liam shrugged. "I dunno. It just doesn't sit well. The

guy from Sampson, he didn't even look around. Just handed me some paperwork with an offer that was fifteen million above fair market value. How's that for a big deal?"

It ruffled the back of Kyle's neck, too. "There's no oil around here. What little there is has a pump on it already."

"Yeah, so now you're where I'm at. It's weird, right?"

Kyle nodded because his throat was tight again. It was nice to be consulted. As if he really was half owner of the ranch, and he and Liam were going to do this thing called family. He hadn't left this time and it might have made a huge difference.

It gave Kyle hope he might actually become the father his girls deserved. Grace, however, was a whole other story with an ending he couldn't quite figure out.

Ten

Grace kicked the oven. It didn't magically turn on. It hadn't the first time she'd hauled off and whacked it a minute ago, either.

But kicking something felt good. Her foot throbbed, which was better than the numbness she'd felt since climbing from Kyle's bed, well loved and then brokenhearted in the space of an hour. The physical pain was a far sight better than the mental pain.

Because she didn't understand what had happened. She'd opened her heart to Kyle again, only to be destroyed more thoroughly the second time than she had been the first time. This was a grown woman's pain. And the difference was breathtaking. Literally, as in she couldn't make her lungs expand enough to get a good, solid full breath.

Determined to fix something, Grace spent twenty minutes unscrewing every bolt she could budge on the oven, hoping something would jump out at her as the culprit. Which failed miserably because she didn't know what it was supposed to look like—how would she know if something was out of place? The oven was just broken. No matter. She wasn't hungry anyway.

She wandered around her small house two blocks off the main street of Royal. She'd bought the house three years ago when she'd claimed her Professional Single Girl status, and set about finding a way to be happy with the idea of building a life with herself and herself only in it. She had, to a degree. No one argued with her if she wanted to change the drapes four times a year, and she never had to share the bathroom.

The empty rooms hadn't seemed so empty until now. Spending the weekend with Kyle had stomped her fantasy of being single and happy to pieces. She wanted a husband to fill the space in her bed, in her heart. Children who laughed around the kitchen table. A dog the kids named something silly, like Princess Spaghetti.

A fierce knock sounded at the door, echoing through the whole house. She almost didn't answer it because who else would knock like that except a man who had a lot of built-up anger? At her, apparently. After ten years of turning over every aspect of her relationship with Kyle, analyzing it to death while looking for the slightest nuance of where it had all gone wrong, never once had she turned that inspection back on herself.

But she'd made mistakes, that much was apparent. Then and now. Somehow.

Only she didn't quite buy that what happened ten years ago was all her fault.

And all at once, she wanted that reckoning. Wanted to ask a few pointed questions of Kyle Wade that she hadn't gotten to ask before being thrown out of his bed two long and miserable days ago.

She yanked open the door and the mad she'd worked up faltered.

Kyle stood there on her doorstep in crisp jeans, boots and a work shirt, dressed like every other man in Royal and probably a hundred other towns dotting the Texas prairie. But he wasn't anything close to any other man the world over, because he was Kyle. Her stupid heart would probably never get the message that they were doomed as a couple.

He was holding a bouquet of beautiful flowers, so full it spilled over his hand in a riot of colors and shapes. Her vision blurred as she focused on the flowers and the solemn expression on Kyle's face.

"Hey, Grace."

No. He wasn't allowed to be here all apologetic and carrying conciliatory flowers. It wasn't fair. She couldn't let him into her head again, and she certainly wasn't offering up her heart again to be flattened. He didn't have to know she'd given up on getting over him.

"What do you want, Kyle?" She didn't even wince at her own rudeness. She got a pass after being shown the door while still undressed and warm from the man's arms.

"I brought you these," he said simply without blinking at her harsh tone. He held out the bouquet. "Thank-you flowers. Because I owed you."

Wasn't *that* romantic? She didn't take the bouquet. "You *owed* me? You definitely owe me, but not flowers. An explanation would be better."

Kyle dropped the bouquet, his expression hardening. "May I come in then? Your next-door neighbor is out on the porch with popcorn, watching the show."

"Mrs. Putter is seventy-two." Grace crossed her arms and propped a hip against the doorjamb. "This is all the fun she gets for the year."

"Fine." Kyle sighed. "I came to apologize. I shot first and asked questions later. It's the way I do things, mostly because people are usually shooting at me, too."

Not an auspicious start, other than the apology part. "And yet I still haven't heard any questions."

"Grace." Kyle caught her gaze, and something warm spilled from his green eyes that she couldn't look away from. "You meant something to me. Back then. You have to understand that I had a lot of stuff going on in my head that I didn't want to deal with, so I didn't. I shut down instead. That wasn't fair to you. But you were the best thing in my life, and then you were gone. I was a wreck. Seeing you with Liam was the last straw, so I left Royal because I couldn't stand it, assuming that you'd found the Wade brother you preferred. There was never a point when I would have confronted you about it."

Openmouthed, she stared at him. That was the longest speech she'd ever heard him give and it loosened her tongue in kind. "I get that I messed up with Liam. I was young and stupid. I should have been more up-front about my feelings, too."

Kyle nodded. "Goes for both of us. But I still owe you a thank-you. I joined the military because I wanted to be gone. I figured, what better way to forget Royal and the girl there than to go to the other side of the world in defense of my country? But instead of just a place to nurse my shattered ego, I found something I didn't expect. Something great. Being a SEAL changed me."

Yes, she'd seen that. He'd grown up, into a responsible, solid man who cared about his daughters. "You seem to have flourished."

"I did," he agreed enthusiastically. "It was the team I'd been looking for. I never fit in at the ranch. That's part of what was weighing me down back then. The stuff inside. I was contemplating my future and not seeing a clear picture of what I should do going forward. If you hadn't staged that ploy with Liam, I might never have found my unit. Those guys were my family."

The sheer emotion on his face as he talked about his fellow team members—it was overwhelming. He'd clearly loved being in the military. It had shaped him, and he'd soaked it up.

Her heart twisted anew. If he didn't fit in at the ranch, why had he taken over the cattle side? During one of her site visits, he'd told her that was his job now—he hoped to create a stable home for his daughters. He planned to stick around this time. Was that all a lie? Or was he just doing it because she'd forced him into it, despite hating that life?

"I don't understand," she whispered. "If you liked being in the military so much, why did you come home?"

"My leg." His expression caved in on itself, and it might have been the most vulnerable she'd ever seen him. She almost reached out to comfort him, was almost physically unable to prevent her heart from crying in sympathy at what he'd lost. He was hurting, and that was so hard for her to take.

But she didn't reach out. "You came home because you were injured," she recounted flatly.

That was the only reason. Not because he missed Grace and regretted splitting up. Not because he wanted his daughters, or the simple life on a ranch with his family. He'd been forced to.

And what would he do when he got tired of an ill-fitting career? What would happen when the allure of the great wide open called to him again?

He'd leave. Just as he'd done the first time, only he'd take his babies with him—there was no law that said he had to stay in Royal to retain custody. He'd go and crush her anew, once she'd fallen in love with three people instead of just one.

He hadn't confronted her about Liam ten years ago because he hadn't wanted to stay in the first place. Not for her, not for anything. If he had, he'd have fought for their love; she had no doubt.

Kyle could pretend all he wanted that he'd enlisted because he'd caught her with Liam, but that had been—by his own admission—the last straw. Not the first.

"Yeah." He jerked his head in acknowledgment. "I was honorably discharged due to my busted leg. I didn't have anyplace else to go. But when I saw Maddie and Maggie for the first time…and then you came back into my life… Well, things are different now. I want to do things different. Starting with you."

"No." Her heart nearly split in two as she shook her head. "We've already had one too many do-overs. You shot first and asked questions too late."

She'd begun to trust him again, only to have the carpet ripped out from under her feet. She couldn't do that again. She could be single and happy. It was a choice; she just had to make it.

"Don't say that, Grace." Kyle threw the bouquet on the wicker chair closest to the door and captured her hand, squeezing it tight so she couldn't pull away. His green eyes beseeched her to reconsider, hollowing her out inside. "I lie awake at night and think about how great it would be if you were there. I think about what it's going to be like for the girls growing up without a mom. It's not a picture I like. We need someone to keep us sane."

This was delivered with a lopsided smile that she ached to return. If only he'd mentioned the condition of his heart in that speech and how it was breaking to be away from her. How he couldn't consider his life complete without her. Anything other than a string of sentences which sounded suspiciously like an invitation to make sure Maddie and Maggie had a mother figure.

And she wanted a family so badly she could picture easily falling into the role of Mama to those precious babies. At what cost, though?

"You have Hadley for that," she said woodenly. "I'm unnecessary."

"You're not listening to what I'm saying." He held her hand against his chest, and she wanted to uncurl her palm so she could feel his heartbeat. "Hadley is Liam's wife. I want one of my own."

It was the closest thing to a proposal she'd ever gotten. She was certifiably insane for not saying yes. Except he hadn't actually asked her. As always, he couldn't just come right out and say what he meant. That's what had led to the Liam fiasco in the first place, and nothing had changed.

None of this was what she'd envisioned. Kyle was nothing like her father. What about her standards? Her grand romance and fairy-tale life? How in the world would their relationship ever stand the test of time with staged jealousy-inducing ploys and the inability to just talk to each other as their starting point?

"I can't do this, Kyle. I can't—" Her voice broke but she made herself finish. "I thought we were starting something and the moment things get a little rough, you bail. Just like before."

"That's an excuse, Grace." He firmed his mouth, and then pointed out, "I'm here now, aren't I?"

"It's too late," she retorted, desperate to get this horrific conversation over with. "We have too many trust issues. We don't even want the same things."

His green eyes sharpened as he absorbed her words. "How can you say that? I want to be together. That's the same."

"Except that's not what I want," she whispered, and forced herself to watch as his beautiful face blanked, becoming as desolate as a West Texas ravine in a drought. "Goodbye, Kyle."

And before she took it all back in a moment of weakness, she shut the door, dry-eyed. The tears would come later.

Now that Johnny and Slim had a grudging respect for Kyle as the boss, they got on okay.

Which was fortunate, because Kyle drove them all relentlessly. Himself included, and probably the hardest. Spring calving season was in full swing and eighteen-hour days fit with Kyle's determination to never think, never lie awake at night and never miss Grace.

At this point, he'd take two out of three, but the hole where Grace was supposed to be ached too badly to be ignored, which in turn guaranteed he wouldn't sleep. And as he lay there not sleeping, his brain did nothing but think, turning over her words again and again, forcing him to relive them because he deserved to be unhappy. He couldn't be with Grace because she didn't want to be with him. Because she didn't trust him.

All the work he'd done to get over his trust issues, and she'd blindsided him with her own. Because he'd left when life got too difficult. When all he'd wanted was to find his place in the world. And when that place spat him back out, he came back. To forge a new place, put down roots. It had been hard, one of the toughest challenges of his life, and yeah, when it got rough, he dreamed of leaving. But he hadn't. Only to have that thrown back in his face.

If it didn't hurt so bad he'd laugh at the irony.

A week after Operation: Grace had gone down in flames, Liam invited him to the Texas Cattlemen's Club for an afternoon of "getting away from it all" as Liam put it. Curious about the club his grandfather had belonged to, and now Liam, too, apparently, Kyle agreed, with the caveat that they'd only stay a couple of hours tops. The cattle weren't going to tend themselves, after all.

The moment Kyle walked into the formerly men-only club, the outside world ceased to exist. Dark hardwood floors stretched from wall to wall, reflecting the pale gold wallpaper that warmed the place. It was welcoming and hushed, as if the room was waiting for something important to happen. The sense of anticipation was compelling.

Kyle followed Liam to the bar, where some other men sat nursing beers. Kyle recognized Mac McCallum, who'd been Liam's buddy for a long time, and Case Baxter.

"Case is the president of the Texas Cattlemen's Club," Liam said as he introduced everyone around. "And this is Nolan Dane."

"Right." Kyle shook the man's hand. "Haven't seen you in ages."

"I'm back in town, practicing family law now," Nolan explained with a glance at Liam. "Your brother's a client."

Kyle nodded as his lungs hitched. Liam had a legal retainer who practiced family law? Didn't take a rocket scientist to do that math. When Liam had talked about papers and warned Kyle he'd need a lawyer, it hadn't been an idle threat. They hadn't talked about it again, and Kyle had hoped the idea of adoption had been dropped.

Obviously it hadn't.

But why stick it in Kyle's face like this? It was a crappy thing to do after all the hoops Kyle'd been forced to jump through to prove his worth as a father. *Especially* after they'd had their Come To Jesus discussion and Liam had apologized for the Grace thing.

Wasn't that indicative of Kyle's Royal welcome thus far? That's why he shot first. When he didn't, he invariably took a bullet straight into his gut.

Mouth firmly shut as he processed everything, Kyle took a seat as far away from Liam as he could. When the conversation turned to Samson Oil, it piqued his interest sufficiently to pull his head out of his rear long enough to participate. Especially when Nolan Dane excused himself with a pained look on his face.

"More offers for land coming in," Liam affirmed. "Wade Ranch included. I think we've got a problem on our hands."

The other men seemed to share his brother's concern. Kyle leaned in. "What does Samson Oil want? They have to know the oil prospects are slim to none around here. People been drilling for over a hundred years. There's no way Samson will find a new well."

Case Baxter shook his head. "No one knows for sure what they're up to. Fracking, maybe. But the Cline Shale property is mostly bought up already in this area."

"If you've got concerns, I've got concerns," Kyle said as his senses tingled again. "I know a guy in the CIA. Owes me a favor. I'll have him poke around, see what Samson Oil is up to."

The offer was out of his mouth before he'd thought better of it. He didn't owe these people anything. It wasn't as if they'd rolled out the red carpet for the returning war veteran. Or acknowledged that Kyle Wade owned half a *cattle ranch* and wasn't even a member of the Texas Cattleman's Club.

Royal clearly wasn't where Kyle fit, any more than he had ten years ago.

"I knew you'd come in handy." Liam fairly beamed.

"That would be great," Mac threw in. "The more information we have, the better. The last thing we need is to find out they're looking for a site to house a new strip mall after it's too late."

The expectant faces of the men surrounding him settled Kyle's resolve. He couldn't take it back now. And for better or worse, this was his home, and he had a responsibility to it. He shrugged.

"Consider it done." Kyle sat back and let the members

of the club do their thing, which didn't include him. If he kept his mouth shut, maybe everyone would forget about him. It wasn't as if he wanted to be a member of their exclusive club anyway.

But then Liam's phone beeped, and he glanced at it, frowning. When his grave and troubled gaze met Kyle's, every nerve in Kyle's body stood on end.

"We have to go," Liam announced. "Sorry."

Liam hustled Kyle out of the club and into his truck, ignoring Kyle's rapid-fire questions about the nature of the emergency. Because of course there was one. Liam's face only looked like that when something bad happened to one of his prized horses.

Liam started the truck and tore out of the lot before finally finding his voice. "It's Maddie."

All the blood drained from Kyle's head and his chest squeezed so tight, it was a wonder his heart didn't push through two ribs. "What? What do you mean, it's Maddie? What happened?"

Not a horse. His daughter. Maddie.

"Hadley's not sure," Liam hedged. Kyle gripped his forearm, growling. "Driving here. Causing me to have a wreck won't get you the information any faster. I'm taking you to Royal Memorial. Hadley said Maddie wouldn't wake up and had a really high fever. With Maddie's heart problems, that's a really bad sign because she might have an infection. Hadley called an ambulance and left Maggie in Candace's capable hands. We're meeting them there."

The drive couldn't have taken more than five minutes. But it took five years off Kyle's life to be trapped in the cab of Liam's truck when his poor defenseless Maddie was suffering. The baby was fragile, and while she'd been growing steadily, obviously her insides weren't as strong as they should be. His mind leaped ahead to all the ugly possibilities, and he wished his heart *had* fallen out earlier, because the thought of losing one of his daughters—it was far worse than losing Grace. Worse than losing his place on his SEAL team.

Liam screeched into the lot, but Kyle had the door open before he'd fully rolled to a stop, hitting the pavement at a run. It was a much different technique from jumping out of a plane, and his leg hadn't been busted on his last HALO mission.

Pain knifed up his knee and clear into his chest cavity, which didn't need any more stress. The leg nearly crumpled underneath him, but he ignored it and stormed into the emergency room, looking for a doctor to unleash his anxiety on.

The waiting room receptionist met him halfway across the room. "Mr. Wade. Hadley requested that you be brought to the pediatric ICU immediately. Follow me."

ICU? Shades of the tiny room in Germany where Kyle had lain in a stupor for months filtered back through his consciousness, and his stomach rolled involuntarily, threatening to expel the beer he'd been happily drinking while his daughter was being subjected to any number of frightening people and procedures. The elevator dinged but he barely registered it above the numbness. Liam and the receptionist flanked him, both poor wingmen in a dire situation. But all he had.

Finally, they emerged onto the second floor and set off down the hall. Hadley rushed into Liam's arms, tears streaming down her face. They murmured to each other, but Kyle skirted them, seeking his little pink bundle, to assure himself she was okay and Maggie wouldn't have to grow up without her sister. The girls had already been through so much, so many hits that Kyle had already missed.

But he was here now. Ready to fight back against whatever was threatening his family. And that included his brother. The adoption business needed to be put to rest. Immediately.

"Who's in charge around here?" Kyle growled at the receptionist, who must have been used to people in crisis because she just smiled.

"I'll find the nurse to speak to you. Dr. Reese is in with your daughter now."

The receptionist disappeared into the maze of hospital rooms and corridors.

Hadley and Liam came up on either side of Kyle, and Hadley placed a comforting hand on his arm. "Dr. Reese is the best. He's been caring for Maddie since she was born. He'll know what to do."

That was far from comforting. If only he could see her, he'd feel a lot better.

A woman in scrubs with balloon decals all over them emerged from a room and walked straight to Kyle. "Hi, Mr. Wade, I'm Clare Connolly, if you don't remember me. We've got Maddie on an IV and a ventilator. She's stable and that's the important thing."

"What happened? What's wrong with her?" Kyle demanded.

"Dr. Reese is concerned about the effects of her high fever on her heart," Clare said frankly, which Kyle appreciated. "He's trying to bring the fever down and running some tests to see what's happening. The last surgery should have fixed all the problems, but nothing is guaranteed. We knew that going in and, well, we're going to keep fighting. We all want to win this thing once and for all."

This woman genuinely cared about Maddie. He could see it in the worried set of her mouth. Nurses were never emotional about their patients, or at least the German ones weren't.

"Thanks. For everything you're doing. May I talk to the doctor?"

"Of course. He'll want to talk to you, too. We all want to see Maddie running alongside her sister and blowing out candles on her birthday cakes for a long time to come. When Dr. Reese is free, he'll be out," Clare promised, and extended her hand toward the waiting room outside the pediatric unit. "Why don't you have a seat until then."

Clare bustled back into the room she'd materialized from, and Kyle nearly followed her because the waiting room was for people who had the capacity to wait, and that did not describe Kyle.

But Hadley's hand on his arm stopped him. "Let the doctor do his thing, Kyle. You'll only be in the way."

Long minutes stretched as Kyle hovered outside his daughter's room. What was taking so long? Pacing didn't help. It hurt. Everything inside hurt. Finally, another nurse dared approach him, explaining that the hall needed to be clear in case of emergency. Wouldn't he please take a seat?

He did, for no other reason than it would be a relief to get off his leg. Now if only he could find something to do with his hands.

People began filtering into the waiting room. Mac McCallum came to sit with Liam and Hadley, who promptly excused herself to fill out paperwork for Maddie, which she'd offered to do in Kyle's stead so he could be available the moment the doctor came out with news. Hadley's friend Kori came in and took a seat next to Liam.

They all had smiles and words of encouragement for Kyle. Some had stories of how Maddie was a fighter and how many people had sat with her through the night when she was known as Baby Janey. This community had embraced his daughter before they'd even known whom she belonged to. And now that they did, nothing had changed. They still cared. They were all here to provide support during a crisis, which is what the very best of neighbors did.

And then the air shifted, prickling Kyle's skin. He looked up.

Grace.

She rushed into the room, brown curls flying, and knelt by his chair, bringing the scent of spring and innocence and everything good in the world along with her. As he soaked up her presence, he took his first easy breath since Hadley's message to Liam had upended his insides.

"I came as soon as Hadley called me," she said, her brown eyes huge and distressed as her gaze flitted over him.

The muffled hospital noises and people and everything around them faded as they focused on each other. Greedily, he searched her beautiful face for some hint as to her thoughts. Was she getting any sleep? Did she miss him?

She slid her hand into his and held on. "I'm sorry about Maddie. How are you doing?"

"Okay," he said gruffly.

Better now. Much better. How was it possible that the woman who continually ripped his heart out could repair it instantly just by walking into a room?

It was a paradox he didn't understand.

She climbed into the next chair, her grip on his hand never lessening. Her skin warmed his, and it was only then that he realized how cold he'd been.

"What did Dr. Reese say?" she asked.

Did everyone in town know the name of his daughter's pediatrician? "He hasn't been out yet. The nurse, Ms. Connelly, said her fever might be causing problems with her heart, but we don't know anything for sure."

His voice broke then, as sheer overwhelming helplessness swamped him, weighing down his arms and legs when all he wanted to do was explode from this chair and go pound on someone until they fixed his precious little bundle of pink.

"Oh, no." Grace's free hand flew to her mouth in anguish. "That's the one thing we were hoping wouldn't happen."

He nodded, swallowing rapidly so he could speak.

"Thanks," he said. "For coming."

He wouldn't have called her. But now that she was here Grace was exactly what he'd needed, and he never would have taken steps to make it happen. What if she'd said no? But she hadn't, and he didn't care about anything other than sitting here waiting on news about his daughter with the woman he loved. Still. In spite of everything.

If only it made a difference.

Eleven

Grace normally loved being at Royal Memorial because 99 percent of the time, she was there because someone was giving birth. That was a joyous event worthy of celebration. Waiting on news about the health and well-being of Kyle's baby was hands down one of the most stressful things she'd ever done.

At the same time, it was turning into a community event, the kind that strengthened ties and bonded people together. And she hadn't let go of Kyle's hand once. People seemed unsurprised to see them together. Not that they were "together." But they were easy with each other in a way that probably looked natural to others.

Inside, she was a bit of a mess.

How many times had she replayed that last conversation with Kyle in her head, wondering if she'd been too harsh, too unforgiving? If her standards were too high? She'd finally had to shut it down, telling herself ten times a day that she'd stood up for what she wanted for a reason. Kyle wasn't a safe bet for her heart. He'd proven that over and over.

But being here with him in his time of need brought all the questions back in a rush. Because it didn't feel as if they were through. It felt as if they were exactly where they were supposed to be—together.

It was all very confusing. She just hoped that supporting him during this crisis didn't give him the wrong idea—that she might be willing to forget her standards. Forget that he'd stomped on her heart again the moment she'd let her guard down.

Grace had lost track of the hour and only glanced at the clock when Kyle's stomach grumbled. Just as she was about to offer to get him something to eat, Dr. Reese appeared at the entrance to the waiting room, looking worn but smiling.

The entire room ceased to talk. Move. Breathe.

She and Kyle both tightened their grip on each other's hands simultaneously. When he rose, she followed him to the edge of the waiting room, where Dr. Reese was waiting to talk to Kyle privately. She stepped closer to Kyle in silent support, just in case the news wasn't as good as the expression on Dr. Reese's face might indicate.

"I'm Dr. Reese." Parker held out his hand for Kyle to shake. "Your daughter is stable. I was able to bring the fever down, which is a good sign, but I don't know if it adversely affected her heart yet. I need to keep her overnight for observation and run some more tests in the morning after we've both had some sleep. She's a fighter, and I have high hopes that this is only a minor setback with no long-term effects. But I'll know more in the morning."

"Call me Kyle. Formality is for strangers," Kyle said, and his relieved exhale mirrored Grace's. "And any man who saved Maddie's life is a friend of mine. Can I see her?"

Parker nodded instantly. "Sure, of course. She's asleep

right now, but there's no reason you can't stay with her, if you want—"

"Yes," Kyle broke in fiercely. "I'll be there until you kick me out."

That meant Grace wasn't going anywhere, either. If there were rules about that sort of thing, someone could complain to the hospital board, the mayor and Sheriff Battle. Tomorrow. No one was going to stand between her and the man who needed her.

Unless Kyle didn't want her there.

Would be weird to spend the night in the hospital with a man she'd told to get lost?

But then he turned to her, his expression flickering between cautious optimism and fatigue. "I'm glad you're here."

And that decided it. It still might be weird for her to stay, but he needed her, and she could no sooner ignore that than she could magically fix Maddie's frightening health problems.

They gave the others a rundown of the situation and implored them to spend the night in comfort at their homes with a promise to call or text everyone with more news in the morning. With hugs and more murmured encouragement, one by one, the full waiting room emptied out. Kyle smiled, shaking hands and accepting hugs from the women, while Grace watched him out of the corner of her eye to ensure he was doing okay.

What she saw surprised her. His small smile for each person was genuine and he returned hugs easily. For someone who hadn't wanted to come home, he'd meshed into the community well enough. Did he realize it?

Hadley stayed where she was.

"Liam and I will wait with you," she insisted, stubbornly crossing her arms.

Liam quickly hustled Hadley to her feet with a hushed

word in her ear. Whatever he said made her uncross her arms but didn't get her moving out of the waiting room any faster.

"I appreciate that," Kyle said. "But it's not necessary. You've done enough. Besides, I need someone I trust at home with Maggie, so Candace can get back to her housekeeping. That's the most important thing you can do for me."

Grace's heart twisted as she got more confirmation that she'd made the right decision in leaving Maddie and Maggie with Kyle—he clearly had both his daughters' interests in the forefront of his mind.

"Candace is trustworthy," Hadley countered. "She's watched Maggie plenty of times."

Liam captured his wife's hand and pulled on it, his exaggerated expression almost comical. "Sweetie, *Grace* is staying with Kyle."

Comprehension slowly leached into her gaze as Hadley finally caught her husband's drift. She started shuffling toward the exit. "Well, if you're sure. We'll be a phone call away."

And then they were gone, leaving Grace alone with Kyle. There was still tension between them but for now, the focus was on Maddie. This was the part where they'd be adults about their issues, just as they should have been all along, and get through the night.

"Guess they thought they'd leave us to our romantic evening," Kyle commented wryly as he nodded after Hadley and Liam. "I'm pretty sure that's why they went to Vail. To give me the house to myself for the weekend in hopes that I'd call you."

Not to get him to step up for his girls. That wasn't even necessary, probably hadn't been from the beginning. Liam and Hadley had gone to Vail for *her* benefit. Hers and Kyle's. And it would have been perfect if she and Kyle had only hashed out their issues before getting involved again, instead of hiding behind their defense mechanisms.

That's why she couldn't give him the slightest false hope that she was here because she wanted to try again. The problem was that she might have given *herself* that false hope.

For all her conviction that she'd made the right decision to walk away from him, something inside kept whispering that maybe it wasn't too late to take a step toward talking about their issues.

"Will you go with me to see Maddie?" Kyle's eyes blinked closed for a moment. "I'm not sure I can go in there by myself."

He'd been stalling. How had she missed that? Because she was busy worrying about what was going on with the state of their relationship instead of worrying about the reason they were here: Maddie. Some support system she was.

Grace smiled as she took his hand again, holding tight. "I'm here. For as long as you need me."

When his eyes opened, he caught her up in that diamond-hard green gaze of his. "Grace," he murmured, "come sit with me."

Meekly, she complied, following him into the hospital room where Maddie lay asleep in a bed with a railing. It looked so much like her crib at home, but so vastly wrong. Machines surrounded her, hooked to wires and tubes that were attached to her tender skin. Grace almost couldn't stand to internalize it.

Clare was checking something on one of the machines and smiled as they came in. "She's doing okay. Worn out from the tests. That couch against the window lies flat, like a futon, if you plan to stay. I have to check on some other patients but we've got Maddie on top-notch monitors, and I'll be back in a couple of hours. Press this button if you notice any change or need anything."

She held up a plastic wand with a red button at the end. Kyle nodded. "Thanks. We'll be fine."

Then Clare bustled out of the room, leaving them alone with Maddie.

"I would trade places with her in a New York minute," Kyle said softly, his gaze on his daughter. "I would *pay* if someone would let me trade places. She's so fragile and tiny. How is her body holding up under all of those things poked into her? It's not right."

Grace nodded, her throat so raw from holding back tears, she wasn't sure she could speak.

All at once, he spun toward her, catching her up in his desperate embrace, burying his head in her hair. She clung to him as his chest shuddered against hers while they both struggled to get their anguish under control.

"I'm sorry," she whispered, forcing the words out.

"Thank you for staying with me. My life was so empty, Grace," he murmured. "For so long, I was a part of something, and then I wasn't."

"I know." She nodded. "You told me how much the military meant to you."

"*No*. Not that. *You*." Fiercely, he clasped her face in both palms and lifted her head and spoke directly to her soul. "Grace. Please. We have to find a way to make it work this time because I can't do this without you. I need you. I love you. I always have."

And then he was kissing her, pouring a hundred different meanings into it. Longing. Distress. Passion. Fear.

She kissed him back, because *yes*, she felt those things, too. He was telling her what she meant to him, first verbally and then through their kiss, and she was finally listening. But this was how it was with them. She got her hopes up and he dashed them.

What could possibly be different this time? She took

the kiss down a notch, and then pulled back. "Sit down with me and let's talk. For once."

That was *not* what she'd meant to say. She should have said no. Told him flat out that they were not happening again. But the eagerness on his face at her suggestion—maybe talking was that start toward something different than what she'd been looking for.

"We're not so good at the talking, are we?" he asked rhetorically, and let her lead him to the couch. They settled in together and held hands as they watched the monitors beep and shush for a moment. "I'm sorry about Emma Jane."

That was so out of the blue, she glanced at him sideways. "I've already forgotten that."

"I haven't. It was low. And totally unfair to both of you. I apologized to her, too." He stared at Maddie, his gaze uneasy. "I wish I had a better excuse for why I did it. I have a hard time just coming out and saying what's going on with me."

She bit her tongue—hard—to keep from blurting out, *Hallelujah and amen*. She didn't say a word. Barely.

"It doesn't come naturally," he continued, his voice strained, and her heart ached a little as he struggled to form his thoughts. "I'm used to being stomped on by people I trust, and I guess I have a tendency to keep my mouth shut. My rationale is that if I don't tell people what I'm feeling, I don't get hurt."

The tears that had been threatening spilled over then, sliding down her face as she heard the agony in his words. He fell silent for a moment, and she started to give him a pass on whatever else he was about to say, but he glanced at her and used his thumb to wipe the trail of tears from her cheek.

His lips lifted in a wry smile. "Guess what? It doesn't work."

Vehemently, she shook her head, more tears flying. "No,

it doesn't. If I'd just told you how I was feeling ten years ago instead of breaking up with you and then pulling that ridiculous stunt with Liam, we'd be at a different place. Instead, I hurt both of us for no reason."

All of that had been born out of her own inability to tell him what was going on with *her*. They were so alike, it was frightening. How had she never realized that?

"I've already forgotten that," he said, and this time, his smile was genuine and full.

"I haven't," she shot back sarcastically in a parody of their earlier conversation. "I spent ten years trying to forget you, and guess what? It doesn't work."

"For the record, I forgave you way before I ever showed up at your door with those poor flowers."

Chagrin heated her cheeks. That was mercy she didn't deserve. Actually, none of this was what she deserved—which would be for Kyle to walk out of this room with his daughter and never speak to her again.

Instead, it looked as though they were on the verge of a real second chance. *Please, God. Let that be true.*

"I'm sorry about the flowers. I was just so hurt and mad. It never even occurred to me that part of the problem was that I wasn't opening my mouth any more than you were. I don't even have a good excuse. So I'm trying to do things differently this time. Starting now." She covered their joined hands with her other one, aching to touch him, to increase the contact just a bit. "I have a hard time with separating what I think something should look like from reality. I wanted you to be dashing and romantic. Sweep me off my feet with over-the-top gestures and babble on with pretty poetry about how I was your sun and moon. Silly stuff."

Saying it out loud solidified that fact as she took in Kyle's still closely shorn hair that the military had shaped. He'd traveled to the other side of the world in defense of his country, seeing and doing things she could only imagine. What could be more dashing and romantic than *that*?

"I'm sorry I don't do more of that," he said gruffly. "You deserve a guy who can tell you those things. I can try to be better, but I'm—"

"No," she broke in, even as her voice shattered. She wasn't trying to make him into someone different. He was perfect the way he was, and she'd finally opened her eyes to it. "You do something wonderful like bring me flowers, and I don't even take them. I'm just as much to blame for our problems as you are. Probably more. You'd never have left if I had just told you every day what you meant to me."

Kyle was never going to be like her dad, who left notes all over the house for her mother to find and surprised her with diamond earrings to mark the anniversary of their first date. She doubted Kyle even *knew* the anniversary of their first date.

The way Grace felt right now, none of that stuff mattered. She had a man who demonstrated his love for her in a hundred subtle ways if she'd just pay attention.

He tipped her chin up with a gentle forefinger and lightly laid his lips on hers. When he finally pulled back, he said, "But I'm not sorry I left. I gained so much from that. Foremost, the ability to come back to Royal and be a father. I was lost and being a SEAL is how I found myself. I might never have had the courage to enlist if things hadn't shaken out like they did. I'd never have had Maggie and Maddie. There was a higher power at work, and I, for one, am very grateful."

She nodded because her heart was spilling over into her throat, and she wasn't sure her voice would actually work.

Her "standards" had been a shield she'd thrown up to keep other men away, when all along her heart had belonged to this man. And then she'd kept right on using her standards as an excuse to avoid facing her own failures.

There was so much more to say, so she forced herself to open her mouth and spill all her angst about the possibility of Kyle leaving again, which had also been an excuse. It was clear he was here for good—what more proof did she need? But that didn't magically make her fears go away, much as being in love didn't magically make everything work out okay.

He let her talk, holding her hand the whole time, and then he talked. They both talked until Clare came back into the room to check on Maddie, then they talked until Maddie woke up howling for a bottle. When she fell back into an exhausted sleep, they talked some more.

When dawn peeked through the window, they hadn't slept and hadn't stopped talking. Grace had learned more about the man she loved in those few hours than in the entire span of their relationship. Even though Kyle hadn't said *I love you* again—which honestly, she could never hear often enough—and in spite of the fact that he would never be a chatterbox about his feelings, it was hands down the most romantic night of Grace's life.

If only Maddie had miraculously gotten better, it would have been a perfect start to their second chance.

When Clare Connelly came into Maddie's room shortly after dawn, Kyle had to stand up and stretch his leg. With an apologetic glance at Grace, he stood and paced around the hospital crib where his daughter lay.

He didn't want to lose that precious contact with Grace, but she didn't seem to be in a hurry to go anywhere. That could change at a moment's notice. He wished he could express how much it meant to him that she'd stayed last night. His inability to share such feelings was one of the many things that had kept them apart.

"Dr. Reese will be in shortly," Clare told them. "Why

don't you go get some breakfast while I change Maddie. You need to get some air."

Kyle nodded and grabbed Grace's hand to drag her with him, because he wasn't letting her out of his sight. Last night had been a turning point. They were in a good place. Almost. Grace deserved a guy who could spout poetry and be all the things she wanted. But she was stuck with him. If she wanted him. Nothing had been decided, and along with the concern about Maddie, everything weighed on him. He was exhausted and emotional and needed *something* in his life to be settled.

They grabbed a bite to eat and about a gallon of coffee. When they returned to Maddie's hospital room, Liam and Hadley were waiting for them. Perfect.

"Any news?" Hadley asked anxiously. "I hardly slept. I was sure we'd get a text at any moment and have to rush back to the hospital."

"Nothing yet. The doctor will be here soon. I guess we'll know more then," Kyle said.

As if Kyle had summoned him, Dr. Reese strode down the hall and nodded briefly. "I'm going to start some more tests. I'll be out to give you the results in a bit."

The four of them watched him disappear into Maddie's room. What was Kyle supposed to do now? Wait some more to find out what was happening with his daughter?

Liam cleared his throat. "Hadley and I talked, by the way. We ripped up all the adoption paperwork. We're formally withdrawing our bid for custody of your daughters. It's pretty obvious you're the best father they could hope for, and we want you to know we're here for you."

Somehow he managed to blurt out, "That's great."

Grace nodded, slipping her hand into his. "He's an amazing man and an amazing father. I wouldn't have recommended that he retain custody otherwise."

Their overwhelming support nearly did him in. He'd

left Royal to find a new team, a place where he could fit in and finally feel like a part of something, only to learn that there really was no place like home.

"Just like that?" he finally asked Liam and Hadley. "You were going to adopt Maddie and Maggie. It can't be easy to live in the same house and realize what you've missed out on."

He wouldn't take to that arrangement too well, that was for sure. If they'd somehow gotten custody, there was no way he'd have stayed. And he'd have ruined his second chance with Grace in the process. Leaving was still his go-to method for coping. But if things went the way he hoped, he had a reason to stay. Forever.

Hadley shook her head. "It's not easy. It was one of the hardest conversations we've had as a couple, but it was the easiest decision. We both love them, so much, and want the absolute best for them. Which means *you*. They're your daughters. We're incredibly fortunate for the time we've had together, and besides, you're not going anywhere, right?"

"No." Kyle tightened his grip on Grace's hand. "I'm not. Royal is where I belong."

The words spilled from his heart easily, despite never dreaming such a thing would be true.

"Then it will be fine," Liam said. "We're still their aunt and uncle, and we expect to babysit a lot in the future."

"That's a deal." Kyle shook his brother's hand and held it for a beat longer, just to solidify the brotherly bond that they were forging.

Hadley and Liam waited with Kyle and Grace, chatting about the ranch and telling stories about Hadley's cat, Waldo. Finally, the doctor emerged, and Kyle tried to read the man's face, but it was impossible to tell his daughter's prognosis from that alone.

Quickly, he stood.

"She's going to make a full recovery," Dr. Reese proclaimed. "The tests were all negative. The fever didn't cause any more damage to her heart."

Everyone started talking at once, expressing relief and giving the doctor their thanks. Numbly, Kyle shook the doctor's hand and stumbled toward Maddie's room, determined to see her for himself to confirm that she was indeed fine.

After a few minutes, Grace forced him to go home with her so he could get some sleep, but he couldn't sleep. Now that he could stop worrying about Maddie so much, he couldn't get Grace's comments about being swept off her feet out of his mind.

They'd talked, and things were looking up, but no one had made any promises. Of course, it hadn't been the time or place. They'd been in a hospital room while his daughter fought for her life.

But he owed Grace so much. And now he had to step up. This was his opportunity to give her everything her heart desired.

When Hadley called Grace to invite her to a horse show Friday night, Grace actually pulled the phone away from her ear to check and make sure it was really Hadley's name on the screen.

"I'm sorry. Did you say a horse show?" Grace repeated. "There's no horse show scheduled this time of year. Everyone is busy with calving season."

In a town like Royal, everyone lived and died by the ranch schedule whether they worked on one or not. And Kyle had been conspicuously absent for the better part of a week as he pulled calves, worked with the vet and fell into bed exhausted each night.

He always texted her a good-night message, though, no matter how late it was. She might have saved them all, even though not one had mentioned talking about the future. It had been almost a week since the hospital, and she and Kyle had had precious few moments alone together since then.

That's what happened when you fell in love with a rancher.

She'd hoped he might be the one calling her for a last-minute Friday night date so they could talk. It wasn't looking too promising since it was already six o'clock.

"Don't be difficult," Hadley scolded. "Liam is busy helping Kyle and I need some me time. Girls' night out. Come on."

Laughing, Grace said yes. Only Hadley would consider a horse show a girls' night out activity. "Your middle name should be Horse Crazy."

"It is," Hadley insisted pertly. "Says so on my birth certificate. I already asked Candace to watch the girls, so I'll pick you up in thirty minutes. Wear something nice."

Hadley was still acting in her capacity as the nanny, though often, Grace dropped by to spend time with the babies. She and Hadley had grown close as a result. Close enough that Grace felt totally comfortable calling Hadley out when she said something ridiculous.

"To a horse show?"

"Yes, ma'am. I will be dragging you out for a drink afterward, if you must know. Be there soon."

Grace chuckled as she hung up. As instructed, she donned a pink knee-length dress that hugged her curves and made her look like a knockout, if she did say so herself. Of course, she wasn't in the market to pick up an admirer, but it didn't hurt to let the male population of Royal eat their hearts out, did it?

The only arena in Royal large enough for a horse show was on the west end of downtown, and Grace was a bit surprised to see a full parking lot, given the timing.

"How come I haven't heard anything about this horse show before now?" Grace asked, her suspicions rising a notch as even more trucks poured into the lot behind them. This arena was normally the venue of choice for the county rodeo that took place during late May, and it held a good number of people.

"Because it was last-minute," Hadley said vaguely with an airy wave. "Liam has some horses in the show, and that's how I found out about it."

"Oh." There wasn't much else to do at that point but follow Hadley into the arena to a seat near the front row. "These are great seats."

"Helps to have a husband on the inside," Hadley acknowledged with a wink.

The grandstand was already half-full. Grace waved at the continual stream of people she knew, and hugged a few, like Violet McCallum, who was looking a lot better since the last time they'd seen each other. Raina Patterson and Nolan Dane strolled by, Raina's little boy in tow, as always, followed by Cade Baxter and his wife, Mellie. The foursome stopped to chat for a minute, then found seats not far away.

The lights dimmed and the show started. Sheriff Battle played the part of announcer, hamming it up with a deep voice that was so far removed from his normal tenor that Grace had to laugh. And then with a drumroll, horses galloped into the arena, crisscrossing past each other in a dizzying weave. It was a wonder they didn't hit each other, which was a testament to the stellar handling skills of the riders.

Spotlights danced over the horses as they began to fall into a formation. One by one, the horses galloped to a spot in line, nose to tail, displaying signs affixed to their sides with three-foot high letters painted on them. *G-R-A-C—*

Grace blinked. The horses were spelling her name. They

couldn't be. And then the *E* skidded into place. The line kept going. *W-I-L-L*.

Something fluttered in her heart as she started to get an inkling of what the rest of the message might possibly spell out. No. It couldn't be. "Hadley, what is all of this?"

"A surprise," Hadley announced unnecessarily, glee coating her voice. "Good thing you took my advice and wore a pretty dress."

Y-O-U. The last horse snorted as he pranced into place. And then came the next one. *M—*

Holy cow. That definitely was the right letter to start the word she fervently hoped the horses were about to spell. All at once, a commotion to her right distracted her from the horses. The spotlight slid into the stands and highlighted a lone man making his way toward her. A man who was supposed to be in a barn at Wade Ranch. But wasn't, because he was here.

The last horse hit his mark and the sign was complete. *Grace, will you marry me?* It was the most beautiful thing in the whole world, except for the man she loved.

Her breath caught as Kyle arrived at her seat, wearing a devastating dark suit that he looked almost as delicious in as when he was wearing nothing.

She didn't dare look away as he knelt beside her and took her hand. "Hey, Grace."

Tears spilled from her suddenly full eyes, though why Kyle's standard greeting did it when nothing else thus far had was a mystery to her. "Hey, Kyle. Fancy meeting you here."

"Heard there was a horse show. It so happens I own a couple of horses. So here I am." He held up a small square box with a hinged lid. "Okay, I admit I set all this up because I wanted to do this right. I love you, Grace. So much. I want nothing more than to put this ring on your finger right now, in front of all these good people."

Yes, yes, yes. A thousand times yes. There was never a possibility of anything other than becoming Mrs. Kyle Wade. She'd never expected a romantic proposal. She'd have been happy with a quiet evening at home, but this... this took the cake. It was a story for the ages, one she'd recount to Maddie and Maggie until they were sick of hearing it. Because she was going to get to be their mother.

"I'd be okay with that," she said through the lump in her throat.

"Not yet." To her grave disappointment, he snapped the box closed and pocketed it. "You asked to be swept off your feet."

And then he did exactly that. As he stood, he gathered her up in his arms and lifted her from her seat, holding her against his chest as if he meant to never let go.

She'd be okay with that, too.

The crowd cheered. She noted Hadley clapping out of the corner of her eye as Kyle began climbing the stairs toward the exit, carrying Grace in his strong arms.

Kyle spoke into her ear. "I hope you won't be disappointed, but you're missing the rest of the show."

She shook her head, clinging to Kyle's amazingly solid shoulders. "I'm not missing anything. This is the best show in town, right here."

Looked as if she was an excellent judge of character after all.

Once he had her outside, he set her down and pulled her into his embrace for a kiss that was both tender and fierce all at the same time.

When he let go, she saw that a long black stretch limousine had rolled to a stop near them. "What is this?"

"Part of sweeping you off your feet," Kyle acknowledged. "Now that Maddie has fully recovered, I'm whisking you away on a romantic weekend, just you and me, to celebrate our engagement. But I want to make it official."

Then he pulled the box from his pocket and slid the huge emerald-cut diamond ring onto her finger. It winked in the moonlight and was the most beautiful thing she'd ever seen. Except for the man she loved. "Tell me this is forever, Kyle."

He nodded. "Forever. I'm not going anywhere. I'm a part of something valuable. I'm a cattle rancher now with orders pouring in for the calves I've helped deliver. The Texas Cattlemen's Club voted me in as a member earlier today. My daughters are thriving, and I'm going to get the best woman in the world as a wife. Why would I want to leave?"

"Good answer," she said as the tears flowed again. "But if you did decide you wanted to leave for whatever reason, I'd follow you."

"You would?" This seemed like news to him for some odd reason.

"Of course. I love you. I know now I could never be happy without you, so…" She shrugged. "Where you go, I go. We're a team now. Team Wade, four strong. And maybe more after we get the first round out of diapers."

He laughed softly. "I like the sound of that. Keep talking."

* * * * *

COMING SOON!

We really hope you enjoyed reading this book
If you're looking for more romance
be sure to head to the shops when
new books are available on

Thursday 25th September

To see which titles are coming soon, please visit
millsandboon.co.uk/nextmonth

MILLS & BOON

MILLS & BOON TRUE LOVE IS HAVING A MAKEOVER!

Introducing

Love Always

Swoon-worthy romances, where love takes center stage. Same heartwarming stories, stylish new look!

Look out for our brand new look
COMING SEPTEMBER 2025

MILLS & BOON

FOUR BRAND NEW BOOKS FROM
MILLS & BOON MODERN

Indulge in desire, drama, and breathtaking romance – where passion knows no bounds!

OUT NOW

Eight Modern stories published every month, find them all at:

millsandboon.co.uk

OUT NOW!

THE TYCOON'S AFFAIR COLLECTION

CRAVING HIS LOVE

USA TODAY BESTSELLING AUTHOR
SHARON KENDRICK

Available at
millsandboon.co.uk

MILLS & BOON

afterglow BOOKS

Afterglow Books is a trend-led, trope-filled list of books with diverse, authentic and relatable characters, a wide array of voices and representations, plus real world trials and tribulations. Featuring all the tropes you could possibly want (think small-town settings, fake relationships, grumpy vs sunshine, enemies to lovers) and all with a generous dose of spice in every story.

- @millsandboonuk
- @millsandboonuk
- afterglowbooks.co.uk
- #AfterglowBooks

For all the latest book news, exclusive content and giveaways scan the QR code below to sign up to the Afterglow newsletter:

afterglow BOOKS

Let's Give 'Em Pumpkin to Talk About
She's grumpy. He's sunshine. Will love grow?
ISABELLE POPP

- ☀️ Grumpy/sunshine
- 🏠 Small-town romance
- 🌶 Spicy

The Secret Crush Book Club
Could this be the start of a new chapter?
KARMEN LEE

- 🌈 LGBTQ+
- 🏠 Small-town romance
- 🌶 Spicy

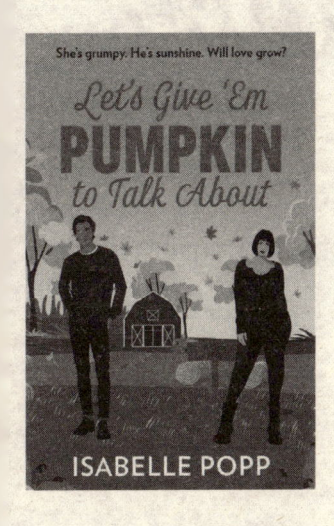

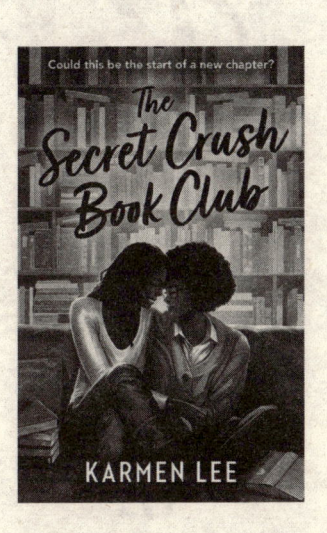

OUT NOW

Two stories published every month. Discover more at:
Afterglowbooks.co.uk

LET'S TALK
Romance

For exclusive extracts, competitions and special offers, find us online:

- **f** MillsandBoon
- **X** @MillsandBoon
- **◉** @MillsandBoonUK
- **♪** @MillsandBoonUK

Get in touch on 01413 063 232

For all the latest titles coming soon, visit
millsandboon.co.uk/nextmonth